MW00627816

GREETINGS FROM VENTNOR CITY

Also by Jane Kelly

GREETINGS FROM VENTNOR CITY

Jane Kelly

Plexus Publishing, Inc.

Medford, New Jersey

First printing, 2020

Copyright © 2020 by Jane Kelly

Published by:
Plexus Publishing, Inc.
143 Old Marlton Pike
Medford, NJ 08055

This is a work of fiction. Names, characters, places, and incidents either are the product of the author's imagination or are used fictitiously. Any resemblance to actual persons, living or dead, is entirely coincidental.

Printed in the United States of America.

Library of Congress Cataloging-in-Publication Data

Names: Kelly, Jane, 1949- author.
Title: Greetings from Ventnor City : a novel / by Jane Kelly.
Description: Medford, New Jersey : Plexus Publishing, Inc., [2019]
Identifiers: LCCN 2019019045 | ISBN 9781940091068 (pbk. : alk. paper)
Classification: LCC PS3561.E39424 G74 2019 | DDC 813/.54--dc23
LC record available at https://lccn.loc.gov/2019019045

President and CEO: Thomas H. Hogan, Sr.
Production Manager: Tiffany Chamenko
Book Designer: Jackie Crawford
Cover Designer: Erica Pannella *(photo taken in Ventnor by Erica Pannella)*
Marketing Coordinator: Rob Colding

To J. Waldron Fisher, Uncle Fisher,
a truly extraordinary gentleman,
who introduced the Kelly
family to Ventnor City.

Acknowledgments

As always, thank you to faithful friends and regular readers, Marilynn Benz, Linda Geiger, Denise Marconi Leitch, Anne Tanner, Carole Turk, and Debbie Wernert.

To my Sisters in Crime from the Delaware Valley chapter who took time from writing to read my Ventnor story: Kathleen Barrett, Sandra Carey Cody, Matty Dalrymple, Jane Gorman and Lisa Regan. Thanks not only for your time but your comments. To another Sister-in-Crime, and honorary cousin Jo-Ann Lamon Reccoppa for her keen eye. To Rabbi Ilene Schneider who loves to make others laugh and flatters me by finding humor in my characters.

To Marycatherine McGarvey, MLIS, of the Free Library of Springfield Township in Montgomery County, PA, lover of mysteries, thanks for your support of local authors

More thank yous. To one of a kind, our Uncle Fisher, J. Waldron Fisher, who, many, many years ago, introduced my family to a wonderful boarding house in Ventnor and to Miss Frances—or was it Miss Francis or Mrs. Francis? Whether it was her first or last name, she provided a wonderful summer experience with her helper, Mary. To Betty and John Woods, who became more than just summer friends. And, of course, to Mary and Dick Kelly, the parents who drove me there.

Thanks go out to Carolyn Anderson and Lisa Dudek for sharing their memories of Absecon Island and the Atlantic City Boardwalk in 1968. To Rick Kelly, for his recollections of visits to the Jersey Shore as a kid and of a career in hotels. To my niece, Kelly Henderson Sakowski, her husband John, and their friend, Leon Worrell, for sharing the memories they are currently building in Ventnor.

I need to send thanks to those who helped me with locations outside New Jersey. To Bridget McMahon for tips about Baltimore parks and highways. To Mary Corcoran and Bill Klear for driving me around Haight-Ashbury looking for a home for Faye Padilla.

A special thank you to Joseph, Robert, and Matthew Cerniglia for entering (and winning) a Name That Character Auction benefiting my favorite charity, For Pete's Sake, and for providing the name of their grandfather, Peter Bossow, for a most delightful character.

And last but hardly least, thanks to Tom Hogan, Rob Colding, Deb Kranz, Brandi Scardilli, and Tiffany Chamenko at Plexus Publishing, Inc. for providing support that often amazes me. And, to John Bryans, who guided Meg through earlier adventures.

Chapter 1

"Bahama babe."

I checked for a familiar face but didn't find one.

"Intrepid concierge."

The words came from the mouth of a long, lean stranger who moved close enough to cast shade on my book. Assuming I was the only concierge from a Bahamian hotel in the beach bar, I forced a tight smile, issued a civil hello and turned back to my reading, but the man kept talking.

"Why are you *not* looking at me that way? It's me—Xander."

"Xander?" My tone offered no glimmer of recognition.

"Xander Frost." He forced the words through pursed lips to avoid detection by any lip-readers drinking at nearby tables.

The man with the flat American accent wasn't even a good Xander Frost impersonator. "Yeah, right." I'd met Xander Frost, but you didn't have to know him personally to recognize that this guy with skinny white legs sticking out of wide Bermuda shorts was not one of the hottest rock stars to come out of England in the last fifteen years. The only thing on the guy that appeared at all cool were the tattoos, although their impact was lost on arms dangling from a white short-sleeved polyester shirt of a variety sold sometime in the 1950s—and, even then, to elderly men trying to appear more mature.

"No, it's me. Really." He plucked a chair from the next table, plunked it beside mine and planted himself in it.

I stared at what I could see of his face which wasn't much. He wore a cap pulled low to meet oversized sunglasses. His nose struck me as unremarkable, but now that his lips had relaxed, they matched the plastic molds sold at Xander Frost concerts. I let my book fall closed. Xander could have tucked his signature wild brown hair into the Yankees cap. I scrutinized his sunglasses and felt fairly certain they came with a rock-star price tag. I eyed the tattoos.

"See." He pointed to a peculiarly-shaped bouquet of roses on his forearm.

I recognized the spot. On one of Xander Frost's trips to the Artistical property in the Bahamas, I'd arranged to have the name of his former soulmate converted into that floral display. "Xander?"

"In the flesh."

"I didn't recognize you." Even his most rabid fan might have missed the famous rocker. "Where's Del?" Xander never made a move without his driver/bodyguard.

He leaned close and traded a flat American twang for his familiar British accent. "He's keeping a low profile, Del is."

I did not ask how a six-foot-six, three-hundred-pound stack of muscle whose style included bleached blond dreadlocks and colorful clothes from his native Polynesia, kept a low profile.

Xander resumed an American accent. "I am not Xander Frost at the moment. I am an ordinary visitor to the seashore. Happy to be away from my cubicle, I am, because I am an ordinary working bloke—not a bloke, a guy—on a nice ordinary vacation—notice vacation, not holiday—at the Jersey Shore. Just a regular American working man, getting away from the office, I am, to enjoy all Atlantic City has to offer including this lovely lounge with its view of one of the best things in life, the Atlantic Ocean. Getting back to basics, I am. No fancy hairdo. No sexy wardrobe. No VIP tables. I've taken one of the smaller suites."

How ordinary.

"Understand?"

I nodded although I didn't. "Where are the Xanadoes?" His entourage, Xander's tornadoes, enabled the star to do whatever he wanted no matter how many others in the vicinity might object. I perused the area but spotted no one from the group whose needs I administered to at the Bahama hotel—and there were a lot of them. Needs *and* group members.

"My posse isn't into real life." He and his chair sidled up to mine. His face screwed into an expression indicating he was about to be very, very sincere. My experience of Xander was that he could be petulant, arrogant and self-centered, but always sincerely petulant, arrogant and self-centered. "I am here to experience what it is like to be an ordinary American. Are you on a similar quest, escaping your life to find meaning amongst the verisimilitude that is Atlantic City?"

One thing always differentiated Xander from the other stars I dealt with: his ability to form interrogative sentences. Declarations, sure. Demands, absolutely. Celebs were good at those. But questions? Not so much. At least Xander asked about me, even if the question smacked of self-interest, which I discovered his did when he continued without waiting for my response.

"I'm due in the Bahamas in a few weeks. You'd better get back down there to take care of me, although I realize I am not particularly high maintenance."

Xander didn't comprehend the generally accepted definition of *high maintenance*. I ignored his statement and provided him with the basics of my situation. "I've been exiled to this property while the Bahamian Artistical resort gets buffeted by Hurricane Frieda."

"Great." Not the usual response to an impending disaster, but I realized, when he clarified, a typical Xander reaction. "You won't get home for a while, so you'll have time to show me what ordinary people do in this land we call New Jersey. Wait, you can't address me as Xander. Someone will hear. Call me Rex like Del does. Rex, the ordinary dude. Get it?"

"Rex means king." To my mind, not ordinary.

"I never heard of a King Rex."

"That would be like King King," I suggested.

He didn't bother to figure out what I meant. He liked the name Rex. "Simple. Plain. Ordinary." He pushed his sunglasses higher on his nose and adjusted his cap to refresh his disguise.

"Why are you spending your ordinary vacation here?" I asked. *Here* was the Artistical Hotel and Casino in Atlantic City, New Jersey.

"Well, the last time I worked the Artistical in the Bahamas, your

3

most charming and generous boss, Mr. Bing, offered me a complimentary suite at this lovely location anytime I so desired."

"I don't work at this property, you realize." I blurted out the words to clarify that catering to his every whim in New Jersey was not my job as it had been in the Bahamas.

"I wouldn't dream of asking you to respond to my needs. I have to become more self-sufficient. The way I've been living is not real. I don't get up in the morning and ride the train to work."

He didn't get up in the morning, full stop.

"I am not out there. Part of the bustling crowd."

"I've been there." I shook my head. "Overall, it's overrated."

"I wouldn't know, would I?" Then, with a dramatic flair, he checked out the tables and the bar. "Where is the love of your life?"

"Andy?"

"Who else? Andy, the dandy eye candy. I assume he is responsible for that ring on your finger."

I smiled at the sunlight shimmering on the diamond on my left hand as I explained. "He's in the Bahamas taking care of Hurricane Frieda issues. And, yes, we got engaged."

"I'd be happy to sing at your wedding." He responded as if asked to perform. "I believe I could add to the festivities and would love to bless the union of two such appealing people. I am sure your guests would find my presence an exciting surprise. A wedding to remember."

Xander viewed my major life event in terms of his participation. No shocker there.

"We have no plans to get married at the moment, but now I can call Andy my fiancé, not my boyfriend. I always felt like a thirteen-year-old girl when I said boyfriend."

"Nothing wrong with the youthful exuberance of thirteen-year-old girls. They attend my concerts and buy my music. They are full of brightness and light. The way I once was and can be again." He sighed theatrically.

"I know who you are."

I didn't even glance up. After all, who else at our table for two would the voice be addressing other than Xander Frost, rock star and aspiring actor?

Xander didn't deny his true identity. "I'm sorry. I don't have anything to write with." He patted his shirt to prove he had no pockets to hold a pen.

Surprised by the ensuing silence, I squinted into the sun and saw an overly-tanned, gray-haired woman staring at Xander with genuine confusion.

He explained, "For my autograph. You want my autograph. Probably for your daughter or granddaughter. I understand." Hard to tell behind his sunglasses but I suspected he winked at me. He knew many grandmothers found him as adorable as his younger fans, the DeFrosters, did.

"No, I'm sorry. I didn't mean you. I meant your companion." She turned to me. "I know who *you* are."

"Me? Who am I?"

"You're the woman who knows all about the sixties."

I caught Xander counting on his fingers. "No," I explained to him, "I am not old enough to remember them."

"But she solves cases from the sixties." The woman spoke to Xander.

"One. I solved one. One case from the 1960s." I made a combo gesture of shrug and bowed head. "Other current cases, yes, but not old ones."

"I saw the story in the newspaper, but my friend over there," she pointed to a woman watching from a nearby table, "she has a business colleague who knows someone acquainted with the family, and she told me you were the one responsible for finding the truth about that woman. Meg something. You. Not her."

"Daniels, Meg Daniels," I confirmed.

"Yes, that's it. Well, Meg, I am certain you can help me. My sister ran away in the sixties. Nineteen-sixty-eight to be precise."

A very different 1960s than the 1964 case I investigated.

"You find people from the sixties?" Xander asked me.

"Not really." I repeated, "One, I discovered what happened to one."

"You can help me. I'm sure of it." The woman pulled another chair from the next table and settled at my left, across from Xander.

The shocked rocker recoiled. Had his Xanadoes been in attendance they would have had the woman in a headlock and out of the bar by now,

5

despite her age which I reckoned to be old enough to remember the sixties. I offered a more polite response. "I believe you are mistaken."

"Nope. My friend pointed you out, told me what you did to help the family of that waitress at the convention."

"I did some research, that's all. I'm not an investigator."

"So maybe you can do some research for me?"

"My fiancé might be able to help you."

She didn't control her look of shock when she glanced at Xander.

"No, not him. My fiancé has been called back to the Artistical's Bahama location but he will be back in a week, maybe two. You could talk to him then." I had no idea if Andy wanted this job or any job, in New Jersey or anywhere, but that would be his decision. "Give me your number and I can have him contact you. He's a professional investigator."

"But you are the one who helped that other family. I didn't hear a word about him."

Xander nodded in support, as if he knew.

"I got lucky. I asked the right questions and solved an old mystery," I explained to both of them.

"I can pay you." The woman patted her purse as if she had the money on her person.

"No, you can't. I am not a licensed investigator."

She turned to Xander. "Maybe not, but she solved a fifty-year-old case. Fifty years. More, actually. That's why I am positive she can find my sister."

"What happened to her?" Xander, in his new persona of Rex, albeit Rex who forgot to hide his British accent, seemed truly interested.

"She left home in 1968. Home was Ventnor." She pointed south as if he would be able to see the town through the dunes. "At nineteen she got into all that sixties stuff and just left."

"But she left voluntarily?" Xander asked.

"It appears that way, but what kept her from returning home for fifty years?" Emotion rose in the woman's voice.

"That's quite a long time ago that she left now, isn't it?"

"Are you English?" The woman responded to his accent.

"I live in the UK now. Accent simply stuck."

Largely because he had worked so hard to develop it. He probably didn't remember the drunken night in the Bahamas when he confessed the unfiltered version of his life story—including the truth of his birth in Akron.

The woman still focused on his accent. "It's lovely."

"Thank you, but I was making a point here, love. Your sister left many, many years ago. If she wanted to return home, she would have done so by now, wouldn't she?"

"Exactly." The woman confused me. "I can't believe she didn't want to come back. She was a rebel at the time but she'd be getting on towards seventy now. Why didn't she come home?" She turned to me. "You could find out."

I doubted it. "I'm sorry . . . I didn't get your name."

"Marianne. Marianne Dulles."

"Marianne, your sister could be anywhere in the world," I pointed out.

"Yes, but she should be here, with us, in Ventnor City."

Chapter 2

Rex, the ordinary guy, and I leaned back in our chairs and sipped frothy drinks from embarrassingly large glasses with umbrellas sticking out—something Xander Frost would never be caught dead doing. We soaked up the sun and listened to the story of Marianne's older sister—leading up to the day Sally Johnson, after protesting at the Miss America Pageant in September 1968, left her home in Ventnor and was never heard from again. From what I knew of the late sixties, the part of the decade everyone viewed as *the sixties*, hers wasn't an unusual tale. Sheltered Catholic school girl goes away to college, discovers sex, drugs, and rock and roll—in her case all three in the person of one Lou Blair— outrages and clashes with conservative parents, leaves home in search of peace, love, and truth. However, unlike many women of her day, Sally never returned to reconcile with the family she'd deserted.

"She was due back at Wallmann College in Pennsylvania—but she never showed up. We have no idea where she went. Somebody said maybe California, but that's a big state. We never heard a word from her." After five decades Marianne still sounded amazed.

I heard myself decline her request to check out Sally's disappearance, but Marianne wasn't catching my meaning. And, Xander wasn't helping me deliver my message. He insisted she record all her information on a napkin. He checked that her writing was legible and passed her note to me. "Make sure you give the lady your card." He held out his hand so he could guarantee I complied.

"I'll get back to you with more information about my sister. It's fate, isn't it? Running into you. Right now. While the pageant is going on."

She stretched out her T-shirt adorned with a vintage photo of early Miss America contestants and pointed to the words *Miss America Pageant*. "When I'm here to watch the parade. It's God's will." She slipped my card into her handbag.

"Absolutely. Whoever that might be." Xander gave the woman a reassuring hug before he guided her back to her friend.

"It is incredible she found us." Xander sounded truly amazed as he settled into his chair.

Us?

"Especially now when the pageant is on." He repeated her sentiment before asking, "What is this pageant?"

"The Miss America Pageant?" I asked. Had Xander been so involved in his own personal transformation that he failed to note the women wearing banners and tiaras in the hotel lobby? Overlooking the presence of attractive females was not typical Xander behavior. "The Miss America Pageant. The event Sally protested."

"Like Miss Universe but covering a smaller geographic area? Excludes Venusians and Martians?" He chuckled at his own witticism.

I smiled. "A beauty pageant, but not the same."

"Girls aren't pretty?"

"Of course they are pretty, but maybe not the same type as the Miss Universe contestants. More wholesome."

"All-American?"

"I guess that's the image. A few are staying at the Artistical. If you haven't seen women wearing crowns, you must have seen the welcome signs."

He hadn't. "And they have a parade? That woman's going. Can we go? I can see for myself."

What was this *we*? "Anyone can go. The parade kicks off at five or six. It's all about shoes."

"I suppose all parades are, aren't they. I mean no shoes, no marching. There must be barefoot parades somewhere, I imagine. Do you have them, perhaps, in the tropics? You live in the islands. Do you ever encounter barefoot processions?"

I did, in fact, but wasn't up for a discussion of parade footwear. "No, in this cavalcade of convertibles the contestants wear fancy shoes they probably can't walk in."

"I don't understand."

"The shoes depict events or themes related to their home state."

He stared at me. He wasn't getting it, and I wasn't about to waste my time selling him on the idea. Not a parade fan, I didn't relish the idea of standing on the Boardwalk while bands, drill teams, color guards, miscellaneous former beauty queens, and contestants from fifty states, Puerto Rico, and the District of Columbia rode by at five miles an hour. Xander lifted his glasses and let his deep brown eyes beg.

I had no plans for the evening except waiting for updates on Hurricane Frieda from Andy. "Okay, *Rex*, going to a local event is an extremely ordinary thing to do. I will show you the parade."

"It will give us something in common with the woman we are helping." He leaned back and released a long satisfied sigh. "What a wonderful opportunity she is offering us."

What did he mean *us*? My expression must have asked him to explain.

"The chance to help another human being. Hands on, I mean. I have a foundation, you know. Well, you probably don't know. I'm not one to brag about giving. My manager gives money and helps people. Kids. He likes to help kids. I mean *I* like to help kids. Sometimes I make a visit and talk to them and that's lovely. Those kids are amazing. Most of them." His face told me he was thinking about the minority that were not. I expected a downbeat story, but his excitement resurfaced. "Anyone can give money and make visits. Assisting this woman in her quest involves me in the hands-on, up-close, dirty work of helping someone. A project. 'Think globally. Act locally.'" He quoted a bumper sticker I hadn't seen recently. "A search for a missing person could be fun and rewarding to do."

Xander remained more positive about the prospect than I did.

"If I weren't on this sabbatical, I could simply go on TV and mention the story in an interview, or ask at every concert, or tweet. But I am not doing those things right now. So we'll have to proceed as any ordinary bloke—I mean bloke and gal—would." His next statement broke the spell and reminded me that Xander lurked close beneath the surface of ordinary guy, Rex. "Finding Sally Johnson is the way for me to create a new image. You know, give my life the appearance of meaning."

"Or simply *meaning*?" I asked.

"That's what I said. I can see the spread in *People* magazine now. 'Rock Star Reunites Family after Fifty Years.' Not 'Rock Star Uses Fame to Reunite Family.' No, 'Rock Star Works to Reunite Family.' There we'd be. Me. Her."

"Marianne." I filled in the name.

"And her long-lost sister."

"Sally." Again, I provided the name.

"And you, of course."

Of course. At least he included me, if only as an afterthought.

He leaned forward and met my stare with eyes that radiated hope and excitement. "We can do this."

"How in the name of God am I supposed to find a woman who could be anywhere in the world? For one thing, she might be dead."

"And she might not be." He had a quick answer.

"What if she doesn't want to be found?" I was just as quick with another question.

"Good point." One he hadn't previously considered. "It might be good that I am on a break. What if she is in your Yankee Witness Protection Program? What if she is hiding from a crazed ex-lover? We need your expertise to find her, you know, discreetly. Privately."

"I don't have those skills."

"Marianne believes you do."

"Marianne, your new best friend?"

"I'm simply saying that you are stuck here for a few days while your boyfriend, excuse me, fiancé, battles his fierce meteorological foe, Frieda, in the Caribbean. You've got nothing but time. You have, here, the opportunity to do something worthwhile. I mean, your beau, Andy, is doing his part. Saving lives and helping people. Wouldn't it be brilliant if you could tell him you've also done a good deed in his absence?"

His enthusiasm, paired with his rapid-fire delivery, was wearing me down.

"You can help me as well. I am sure you view me as a fortunate person who is not in need of help, but I am here on a mission, seeking a different way of life. Playing private investigator would certainly let me see how the other half lives."

I couldn't take offense. In Xander's eyes I had always been part of the other half, actually more like the other ninety-nine percent, one of the others who served the rock stars and his fellow celebrities.

"This would be something real to get my hands on, to get my heart into. I have a heart that needs to help." He released his inner poet. To express his true feelings or to manipulate me? I couldn't know. "She needs us."

Again with the *us*? When did Xander and I become *us*?

"She's such a meek little thing."

"You really think so?" I found her a little pushy.

"Let's do it. Please." He paused as if searching for my name. Carlos, the member of Xander's entourage assigned the task of remembering names, was nowhere in sight.

"Meg."

"Beg? You want me to beg?"

"No, I said Meg. My name. My name is Meg Daniels."

"Of course, I knew that. Even if you hadn't just told Marianne, I remembered." He paused. "No, I didn't. You said it and I forgot. That's something I will have to learn. Ordinary people remember names." Out of his pants pocket, he pulled a small notebook and turned to a page near the back. With a pencil he appeared to have appropriated from a miniature golf course, he printed my name in block letters. He held the book aloft and riffled through the pages. "See, I keep a list of things ordinary people do." The orange book, with *Acting Notes* written across the front cover in a florid scrawl and *Ordinary* printed less than neatly on the back, was tattered and the pages, filled with bold handwriting, were dog-eared. Apparently, he'd been working on his project for a while.

"I have another one. Write this down. It should be number one. Ready?"

He held his pencil aloft to indicate he was.

"Number 1. Ordinary people don't carry lists so they can appear ordinary."

He didn't make a note but kept his pencil poised above the paper. "What's number 2?"

Chapter 3

Xander and I didn't actually go to the *Show Me Your Shoes Parade*. It came to us. We lingered at the beach bar, sipping frothy cocktails, and watching the surf. I had no problem keeping an eye on my phone for word from Andy while Xander waxed poetic about the power of the Atlantic Ocean, his desire to have a serious acting career, and the existential dilemma of being an outrageously wealthy man, albeit one who let me sign the tab.

Xander tired of telling his story, and we found a place to watch the festivities over the heads of viewers who had arrived early to find a prime spot for their beach chairs. Xander frowned as pedestrians passing behind us jostled him. "I thought if I came in September, after your Labor Day holiday, the crowds would have thinned a bit."

"Hence the Miss America Pageant," I explained. "Almost a hundred years ago, the town management created the event to entice people to stay at the beach for an extra week."

"But that Sally girl, Marianne's sister, she lived here. I guess she wasn't due back at college yet."

"I guess."

"Sally may have spent one of her last nights at this parade," Xander marveled.

That I doubted, but she had spent her final days as a resident of the area embroiled in the controversy that enveloped the Miss America pageant in September 1968. "I'm not sure this parade existed back then. But if it did? I think Sally would have attended only if she came as a protestor."

"I don't understand what Sally had against this event." Xander sounded genuinely flummoxed.

"What she might have found offensive about the pageant as a whole was the objectification of women. I am sure she found it true of all beauty pageants, but probably a little more so of this one because of its perceived support for squeaky-clean, traditional views of women and, I would guess, Sally rebelled against those stereotypical roles."

"Oh. I see," he said, but I doubted he did.

The color guards, drill teams, local officials, and marching bands did not entertain Xander. "I'm not into marching bands. I will be able to endure the performance as long as they don't play *Hopeless Aspirations*." One of his early hits that paired a decidedly upbeat rhythm with an oddly downbeat message made an unusual but frequent selection of marching bands nationwide. "Just because I am currently taking a hiatus from my life as a musician, doesn't mean I can tolerate musical atrocities."

"Well, you can't stop being a music lover."

"No, but I am trying to take a break from my career. No writing. No playing. I don't even hum."

"But how can you do that? Why would you? I would think hiding from music would be like draining the blood from your veins."

"Exactly. I want to become an empty vessel to refill." Looking a bit embarrassed, he changed the subject back to the parade. "This is boring. I thought there were going to be beautiful women." Xander introduced a Russian accent as part of his disguise. I didn't ask why.

"They're coming," I assured him.

Not fast enough for Xander. He suggested abandoning the effort, and a sympathetic security guard let us cross the Boardwalk during a break in the parade, but then last year's Miss America came into view showing off her red, white, and blue impossibly high heels.

"She doesn't look so wholesome," he observed.

"Tell me what about her doesn't look wholesome," I mumbled in return, but got no response.

The reigning Miss America wore a glamourous, yet modest, dress. She waved and offered a sweet smile to our section of the crowd without responding to Xander's Russian-inflected chant of "Bootiful, bootiful, bootiful."

He had better luck with the beauties that followed. The Boardwalk, wide for strolling but narrow for a parade, made for an intimate event, and Xander drew each contestant's attention to himself with loud clapping and shouts of encouragement in a heavy Russian accent. To me, he added, "Is not right. In my country, all are equal. Here in America, you make queen."

"Trust me. If we were at the Miss Universe pageant, you'd find one woman had been singled out and made queen for Mother Russia."

I was waiting for him to argue, to continue fighting the inequity of beauty pageants, but the egalitarian expressed concern, not that there were beauty queens, but that those representing states lower in the alphabet would be slighted. "These states. They come by alphabet. What if crowd thins before car number fifty-two passes? I tell you who not equal. What state come last?" He persisted in playing a Russian.

"Miss Wyoming."

"This woman. She gets, how you say, a raw deal. We walk." He pointed up the Boardwalk. "We find end. We offer support to person you call Miss Wyoming."

With nothing more exciting on tap, I strolled the Boardwalk with Xander in search of the end of the parade. We were passing New York Avenue when, through the space between Miss Massachusetts's pilgrim hat and her raised button boot with five-inch heels, I caught sight of Marianne Dulles at the edge of a group of women clustered on beach chairs watching the action. She was folding up her chair and heading out early. I could understand why her friends might seem more enthusiastic than she did. In her mind, the Miss America Pageant and her sister's disappearance were forever intertwined, and the afternoon's conversation with Xander and me had probably called those sad memories to the surface.

"Do you find the event offensive?" Xander dropped the Russian accent in favor of an American twang.

"It isn't what I would choose to do, but then again, being a beauty queen was never an option for me. I'm not possessed of a body able to stand the scrutiny of millions of eyes when paraded across the stage in a bikini."

He, familiar with women who fit that description, didn't argue.

So, I continued, "I would never criticize someone because they thought they could use pageants to better themselves, and today women are picking the pageant route as one of the many options available to them. Back in Sally's day, beauty pageants like these were one of the few opportunities for women—a competition judging them only on their appearance. Sally and her friends were protesting that women are more than pieces of meat, that they have brains and personalities that should be taken into account."

"They should have had interviews and other competitions, like talent," he suggested.

"They did."

He used an elaborate contortion of his facial features to communicate his confusion.

"To its credit, the Miss America pageant included talent and interviews a long time ago. Now the swimsuit competition has fallen out of favor, but in those days people watching on national television saw women parading in swimsuits and ball gowns along with demonstrations of a talent not always perceived as ..." I fought for a word and came up with *talent*. "Even if they awarded scholarships, people never mistook the pageant for a rocket scientist competition, although, for all I know, there were lots of rocket scientists behind those sweet facades."

"I don't fully comprehend the issues. I would call this good clean fun. Wholesome."

"To understand Sally, view the event in the context of her time and women's rights in that era. There were no comparable activities for men. They were never asked to parade across a stage on national television wearing bathing suits so they could win a college scholarship."

He reverted to his own English accent. "I parade across the stage in minimal clothing and don't find it demeaning. I find my ability to use my sexuality empowering."

"It's not the same."

"Why?"

"Because you are not being judged, and by that I mean literally.

Someone is not grading you on your body."

"But success is not actually about a perfect body, is it?"

Maybe not for men. "I don't know, Xander. The Miss America pageant only came on my radar three hours ago. Can I get back to you?"

Chapter 4

Back in my room I resumed my major activity: waiting to return to the Bahamas. My anxiety had rendered me incapable of multitasking. I saw my job as watching *The Weather Channel* for news of an *all clear* signal. I felt disloyal changing the channel, but even I had to admit that watching Hurricane Frieda spin around the Atlantic Ocean could get boring. I also had to admit that I could get boring. If I were twenty-two and had gotten engaged after a whirlwind courtship, I might have run around visiting friends in Pennsylvania and New Jersey to show off the ring Andy had presented to me—along with the information that he wanted to quit his job—two days before he flew off to the Caribbean to defend the Artistical Resort against Frieda. But Andy was old news— we'd been together for six years—and, having no idea what we would do next, I had nothing to report about our future. His pending unemployment would not be greeted with excitement by many of my friends—the ones who found my way of life with Andy a bit sketchy to begin with. I could predict their best reactions. *At least he's not a PI anymore. Ah, unemployed is interesting.* And the worst, *really?* I'd wait until Andy and I had time to make a plan before I mentioned my engagement.

To distract me from the mini-bar treats, I did a quick online check—just to confirm Marianne Dulles was an upstanding citizen. Discovering she was not would put the kibosh on the whole idea of helping her. I learned nothing online about her except that a Marianne Dulles existed and lived in Ventnor with others bearing the Dulles surname. Nothing disqualifying.

Since that didn't take much time, I moved on to see if I could discover anything about Sally Johnson, a woman with one of the most common names in the USA. I like to start with obituaries, just to guarantee I don't waste time. If the person is dead, I'll find all the information in one spot. Pages of Sarah "Sally" Johnsons had died. None appeared to be the one I was seeking. The number of hits on the dead Sarahs paled in comparison to the count of articles on the living ones.

I kept one eye on the Weather Channel and one on my laptop while I consumed several minibar items from both the sugar and salt food groups. I tried a variety of terms before *Sarah Johnson and Wallmann College* uncovered a hit, not for Sally at Wallmann, but on a reunion site for the class of 1967 from St. Cecelia's Academy, a private Catholic girls' high school which was, according to Google maps, within striking distance of Ventnor. Listed among the missing graduates was Sarah Anne Johnson of Ventnor. Last known year of contact, 1968. Last known place of residence, Wallmann College.

This had to be Marianne's sister. She appeared on a list of graduates the organizers wanted to contact, but the site offered no further information, no clue as to where she had gone, or why. As I scrolled through the reunion website, I found a link to *The Cecelian*, the school's yearbook. A 1967 graduate named Anastasia Silver had been kind enough to scan the entire volume and had done a good job of it. I browsed through the pages, which offered a gateway to a very different era—an innocent time, based on the style of high school seniors with fresh-scrubbed faces and clothes their thirty-five-year-old mothers might have worn.

The pages featuring honor students were near the front, so it didn't take me long to find a photo of Sarah Anne Johnson. The honors listed under her picture included a scholarship to Wallmann College. This had to be my girl. Gazing over her left shoulder into a future of unlimited possibilities, she looked just as pretty as Marianne had described. I felt satisfaction but all I had proven was Sally Johnson existed, or had in the sixties. I moved through the file to the back of the book where each senior had an entry. Sarah Anne Johnson's confirmed she was known as "Sally" and an over-achiever. She'd had first honors through all four years, so her admission to the National Honor Society was a given. But she wasn't all about studying. She had found time to captain the field hockey team and join the cheerleading squad for basketball season, all the while managing to serve as a class officer. In her final year, she was elected class president. Her goal, to see the world, I took to mean that I would have to expand my search to include the entire globe. I found her favorite phrase haunting: Over my dead body. Her nickname was Frick, which to me said there had to be a Frack and there was. I found her back in the Gs. Gina Garth, a similarly impressive graduate, was known as Frack.

If it weren't for Sally, Gina might well have been the class beauty. With dark hair, dark complexion, and dark eyes, she made a perfect foil for the fair-haired Johnson girl.

I browsed through the book and found shots of the two girls, often together, engaged in one of their many activities. For students who were not on the yearbook staff, they managed to get their photo on a lot of pages—and I doubt I spotted every shot.

I found Marianne in the sophomore class photo, but not by sight. I went through the listing of names under the picture. Even after I counted to the third from left in the back row, I still didn't recognize her. Time had not been kind to Marianne, which was especially cruel because nature had not been generous to her in the first place. She was, at best, plain, with hair cut into waves more suitable for a grandmother. I felt my first kind feelings towards her. Life could not have been easy for the gawky younger sister of the cutest girl in school. I didn't see Sally pictured with Marianne in any shots, but I wasn't surprised. The class two years behind might as well have been attending classes in Siberia.

Reviewing the 1967 *Cecelian* might not have made for an exciting Saturday night, but it did make for a restful one. I was out cold by 10:00. When the room phone woke me, I could see the sun was up. So was Xander. Very up and sounding painfully cheerful at the other end of the line. I never should have told him my name.

"You sound disappointed to hear from me."

"Surprised. It's early. What are you doing up? Or haven't you gone to bed yet?" A valid question for Xander.

"How many times do I have to tell you? I am a new person. Del and

20

I had dinner in my suite, watched a movie, and took a nighttime stroll on the Boardwalk. Then, I came back to my own bedroom, read a book, and fell asleep."

"What book?" I tried to sound interested, but Xander was onto me.

"You don't believe me." He didn't sound offended but offered the name of a volume at the intersection of self-help and philosophy. "What will it take to convince you that I am not the same old Xander?"

"Rising before noon is a good start." I checked the clock. 7AM. Whoa. Way before noon.

"I've already done my workout. When do you work out?"

"Alternating Tuesdays in months with the letter z in them during leap year."

"I don't…Oh, wait, good one."

"What's up?" I suspected Xander had an agenda, and he did.

Turns out he had been thinking about our encounter with Marianne at the beach bar and wanted to make a case for visiting the Dulles home. "Just a simple gesture. She is a woman with a problem. I want to meet people with problems. Ordinary people have ordinary problems."

"Her problem might not be unheard of, but it is not ordinary. Besides, you met her yesterday."

"Well, you're being a bit disingenuous, aren't you? Or should I say snide. I want to *really* meet her, to engage her. I have been quite clear about wanting to help you solve her problem. We won't make any promises. We will simply drop by for a visit. You can tell her you are transcribing the info so you can brief your fiancé…."

"Andy," I interrupted.

"Right, then. You can fill Andy in, and then, if you and I cannot produce any results, you can do just that, brief your fiancé as promised."

"We can talk about it tomorrow." I wasn't ready to focus on Marianne's sad story. I had my own worries.

"Why tomorrow? Is your diary, sorry calendar, completely full for today? Why not today?"

"It's Sunday."

"So?"

"The Dulleses probably go to church." Better to use Marianne as an excuse rather than my own desire for a day of rest. After all, what was I resting from?

"All day? I doubt that. We can go in the afternoon. You must realize Marianne has prayed for her sister's safe return every Sunday for half a century, and now, today, finally, her prayers are being answered. You and I are heaven-sent, the answer to all those pleas that received no response."

"She's been waiting fifty years, she can wait until Monday." I didn't mean to sound callous, but I missed the mark.

"But why should she have to?"

The conversation went back and forth, and back and forth, and back and forth, with Xander winning based on pure word count. If I could say something in three words, Xander could express his position in thirty, and more quickly than I did. I blamed the blinding sun bouncing off the Atlantic and Xander's machine-gun delivery for wearing me down. I relented but rolled back into bed with my back to the window. I waited until noon to give Marianne Dulles a call. No answer. At noon. At 1PM. At 2PM. At 3PM. And on every half-hour in-between.

I called Xander in his room. "I think we'll have to wait until tomorrow."

"Doesn't she have a mobile?" He was frustrated.

"I am calling her cell phone. Obviously, she is somewhere she doesn't want to be disturbed."

"I am not inclined to give up."

I didn't know much about the rock star, but that much I knew.

Chapter 5

I consider myself a master of deceit—at least with myself. Others see through my motivations a lot more quickly than I do. I actually believed the story I told the woman in the mirror. I just needed a breath of fresh air. Thanks to The Weather Channel—not even a network devoted to meteorological news could devote every moment of air-time to the threats of a stalled storm—I learned the weather was beautiful in Atlantic City. One of those irresistible September days with bright sun and crisp air, the kind that teased autumn lovers into thinking their time had come. The kind of day one needed to get out of the hotel to experience. I forced myself out the door.

The heat wave that had oppressed the region for weeks had broken, so a leisurely stroll was not out of the question, but why not take a walk on a different, unfamiliar beach? Say, for example, Brigantine. Perhaps the town just north of Atlantic City popped into my mind because, over my morning Coke, I had gone back to St. Cecelia's 1967 Reunion website and discovered that Gina Harris, nee Garth, aka Frack, was organizing the reunion from her home in Brigantine, at an address I found online. It occurred to me that I might have time to drop by. It wasn't as if I put her house number in the rental car GPS—at least not until I crossed the tall bridge and found myself in the town. I speculated I could find time to stop on my way home from my walk. Then, realizing I'd gotten a late start, I concluded I'd better go to the Harris house first.

I rehearsed an explanation for Xander about why I started without him. I knew that was how he would view my visit to Brigantine. *Before I got involved, I wanted to check out Marianne Dulles, a person I know nothing*

about, by talking to Gina Garth Harris, another person I know nothing about.
Not a particularly persuasive argument. Better: *You are a celebrity, Xander, and therefore vulnerable. I didn't want to put you in a situation where we were dealing with unscrupulous people. I did due diligence for you.* Yes. That was the Xander-centric type of argument the rock star would fall for. I had to protect him. What if the Dulles family was well-known in South Jersey for providing people with cement overshoes and taking them out to sea on one-way boat rides? That information I could not uncover on the Internet.

When my GPS guided me down the street where Gina Garth Harris, aka Frack, lived, I couldn't help wondering if she was living the life Sally had fled. Attractive house on an attractive street, easily stereotyped as part of the suburban myth. The woman who answered my knock fit into the myth.

"May I help you?" She spoke through the screen door.

"Excuse me. I am sorry I couldn't call, but I couldn't find a number." I didn't mention that I didn't try.

"No problem," she said, when I might have asked *who are you* and *why are you on my front steps?*

"Are you Gina Harris who is organizing the fiftieth reunion for St. Cecelia's Academy?"

"Why yes. Are you interested in attending?"

I was a little hurt she didn't notice our thirty-year age difference, but I think her question was just a knee-jerk reaction. "I wasn't in your class."

"Oh, no. Of course not. How silly of me. You don't look sixty-eight. You don't look fifty-eight, or forty-eight, or thirty-eight." She stopped.

That was fine with me. I let the topic of age die. "I hate to bother you at home, but I couldn't figure out what else to do. Since I was going to be in Brigantine . . ." I let the unfinished sentence hang in the air hoping she wouldn't ask why. She didn't. "My name is Meg Daniels. I was asked by the family of one of your classmates to see if anyone involved in the reunion had talked to her. Sally Johnson."

"Oh my God. Sally was my best friend."

I didn't let on I knew.

"They used to call us Frick and Frack."

"Really? That close! Do you keep in touch with her?"

"Sally is on our list of people we are trying to find. We have a lot of *missing* classmates. We are already behind. We'll be lucky to get this reunion together for our sixtieth anniversary. Do you have any idea where Sally is?" She opened the door and stepped onto the brick landing.

I moved back to make room for her. "I was hoping you would."

"No. We sent a letter to her old address, but I imagine her parents are long dead. It came back marked *Not at this Address*. Not surprising after fifty years in an area that has changed so much, but we give all the original high school addresses a try. You said her family asked you to inquire. Who is left? I heard her father died and I believe her mother did too."

"I only met her sister, Marianne."

"Of course, Marianne would be alive. Is she still in the area?"

"Yes."

Her smile was shaded by nostalgia. "She used to follow Sally and me around. She and her boyfriend, kind of a nerdy couple, but Sally was always nice to them. Although Jimmy, the boyfriend, his last name was Dulles, so we used to call him Jimmy Dullest. Sad to say, but the name fit. He and Marianne were a perfect match."

"You spent a lot of time with them?"

"Not intentionally. We didn't have a lot in common. They were a couple of years younger and in high school years, that is a monumental difference, but I'm not sure things would have been different if Marianne had been in our class."

I sensed she had more to say, but I wasn't sure she wanted to. After a brief pause, she went on. "If I was straight compared to Sally—and I mean straight in a general lifestyle sense not a sexual sense—then those two were super straight. Times were changing and Sally kept up on all the trends. I wasn't so free."

"And Marianne?"

"She didn't notice things were changing when I knew her. When, or if, she finally figured the sixties out, I am sure she didn't approve. Is she doing okay?"

"I only just met her. She seems fine except that she hasn't heard from Sally in fifty years."

Gina took in the information but didn't seem shocked by it. "That's sad. Marianne sent Jimmy to see me, in 1968, right after Sally left, to find out if I knew anything, but I hadn't seen Sally in months, and I had only talked to her a few times in the past year. She went away to college. I went to work." She gripped the wrought iron railing with both hands. "What a gorgeous day!"

I wasn't going to let her distract me with talk of the weather. "So you couldn't give Marianne and Jimmy any information that would help?"

She surveyed the bright blue sky as if searching for a cloud. The effort was fruitless. The day was flawless. I was wondering if I had lost her attention to the beauty of the day, when she spoke again. "Back then, I'm not sure I would have given them any info even if I could have. Sally wanted to get away. Marianne knew that. She just wouldn't admit it. She was convinced she didn't hear from Sally because something horrible had happened to her. I gathered Marianne wanted us all out searching the sides of highways for her, for her body really."

"Was there something wrong in the Johnson household that compelled her to leave? I assumed theirs was a typical American family. Respectable." I hoped I was offering her the opportunity to warn me off if the family had connections to organized crime, drug trafficking or pyramid marketing schemes seeking recruits.

She turned to face me. "Nothing that wasn't wrong in houses all across the US. A big generation gap. Depression and World War II parents trying to raise Vietnam-age kids they didn't understand. Now that I am older, and a parent, I feel a lot of sympathy for them, all those parents. I didn't create many problems for mine, but as we got older Sally did for hers. Nothing horrible. She just wanted to be out having fun, tasting the counterculture. She worked hard. She wanted to play hard. Her father was of the opinion that all work and no play made Sally exactly the kind of daughter he wanted."

"So you never worried that something bad happened to her? It is odd she didn't leave a note."

"She might have. I'm not sure. Jimmy told me that Sally thought the world was changing and she wanted to be part of it. Something like that.

Teenage angst of some sort."

"Weren't you worried when she didn't come back?"

"I never expected her to get in touch back then or show up at any reunions. We'd grown apart. I had a family. I didn't think about Sally very often. I was surprised, and worried, when I ran into Marianne at St. Cecelia's years later. She had a girl there, a freshman when mine was a senior. She asked if I had ever heard from Sally. I was shocked she hadn't. That was the only time I felt a pang of concern, but not a serious fear about what might have happened to her. I figured she was off somewhere living the life she wanted. If you find her, please tell her about the reunion. Everyone would love to see her."

I promised I would and moved fast to ask my next question before she could send me away. "Before she disappeared, did Sally have a boyfriend anyone suspected of *malfeasance*?"

When she smiled a wistful expression crossed her face. "Certainly not in my eyes." She looked to me for a reaction, but I had no idea what response she wanted. "I married Sally's ex."

My first response was "Oh." My second was, "When?" Because in the seconds between my two responses, I'd managed to construct a scenario where one member of the couple, or possibly both working together, had killed Sally and disposed of the body so they could be together.

"I married Bobby in 1970. He—Bobby Aniston—was despondent when Sally dumped him. She told him now that she was at college, she didn't want to be tied down. He was devastated at first, but when she visited and he saw how she had changed, he realized she wasn't the girl for him. Bobby and I got together shortly after Sally arrived home for her first summer after college. I guess her only summer after college. I'd been consoling him since Thanksgiving, but all that changed when he saw her for what she was."

"Which was?"

"A hippie. A free spirit. A rebel. The kind of girl he wouldn't be interested in. As I said, everything in our relationship changed. We got married a couple years later. Had four wonderful children. We shared a great life for almost thirty years. And then, cancer. Out of the blue. No warning.

Three months and he was gone."

"I am so sorry."

"It was a lot of years ago now—1998. I've remarried. Made a decent life, but he was the father of my children, the love of my life."

"And neither of you ever heard from Sally?"

"Not from *Sally*. For a few years after Sally left, Bobby noticed he kept running into Marianne *by accident*." She used air quotes. "She never voiced a direct accusation, but she made it clear she thought Bobby had done something to Sally. All we could figure was she judged him guilty by virtue of *if I can't have you no one can*. Pretty insulting to me really. The harassment went on for a couple of years, but just died down. Neither of us mentioned the incidents when I ran into her at St. Cecelia's. She had been so upset and grasping at straws there for a while, I let it go."

"Do you remember the last time you saw Sally?"

"Very clearly. July 4th, 1968."

She addressed the shock on my face.

"Thirty years to the day before Bobby died. He and I went to Cape May. It wasn't as fixed up or trendy back then, but the town was still beautiful. No pedestrian mall yet. Obviously the Victorian houses were there, maybe not looking so fancy. But we were kids. Our friends didn't bother driving forty miles to Cape May. We never expected to see anyone we knew. It wasn't a good beach day as I recall. Bobby and I weren't old enough to drink. I am pretty sure we had fake IDs if we needed them, but we weren't looking to get drunk. We just needed a place to hang out, get something to eat, be by ourselves. We thought no one we knew would be in The Ugly Mug but we ran into Sally and her new boyfriend. His name was Lou. I think I have that right. It stuck because she used it all the time, like a pre-teen girl with a crush. She might just as well have ended every sentence with 'Lou is the most wonderful man in the universe.'"

"Did you think he was?"

"I did think he might be about be the cutest." She laughed. "When I think of Sally, I don't remember her the way she was that day. She'd changed so much. She wanted us to buy her act that she was unconventional, but she was a stereotypical hippie, spouting all the usual garbage."

Gina caught herself sounding harsh. "I am sure she and Lou had some good ideas, but they didn't present them convincingly. I think they were both stoned. She was still sweet and sincere, but I could tell Lou was mocking us. We were not cool, and we didn't care. We didn't like him. By the time we left the restaurant, I don't think we liked her much either. Such a shame what she did to that nice family of hers."

Bingo. *Nice family.* That was the information I needed. I had nothing to fear from Sally's family.

"Bobby once told me he never appreciated me more than at that moment."

"You never saw her again?"

"No. She was gone a couple months later. It was funny, Bobby and I didn't talk about her very often, and never after a year or two, but in the last month my husband was alive—I guess he was reviewing his entire life—he said her name a few times. He was out of it. I wasn't jealous."

Which, of course, convinced me she was.

Chapter 6

My first attempt to grab my cell phone knocked it to the floor. I groped under the bed until I found it and, since I couldn't get my eyes open, answered without checking the screen. I wasn't sure if the call was coming in on Sunday night or Monday morning.

"I am so sorry. You called yesterday. I didn't recognize your number. Not even your area code. And Jimmy—that is my husband, Jimmy—he said, 'Don't answer it. God only knows what kind of scammer it might be on the other end,' but then last night when I was going to sleep and thinking about the day and those funny calls, I remembered that we had met. I climbed right out of bed and found your card in my purse and sure enough, there it was. Your number. But I thought it was too late to call, so I waited until morning."

"Mrs. Dulles?" I couldn't think who else the woman on the other end of the line could be.

"Marianne. Please, call me Marianne."

"Sure, Marianne. What time is it?"

"7:05. I didn't want to call too early."

"No, of course not." I got my eyes open, but the light of the sun, not far above the horizon, forced them shut.

"You said you'd like to stop by. Please do. Come at noon. We can have lunch."

"No, that won't be necessary." I pulled myself into a sitting position. "We, Rex and I, just wanted to ask you a couple of questions."

"Is Rex your fiancé?"

"No, he's the fellow I was with when we met." I forced my eyes open.

"Rex Lampier." I hoped she didn't notice my hesitation on his last name.

"Oh yes. The English fellow. He's rather unusual but seemed nice. Please do bring him along."

I went back to sleep with my mobile in my hand. The room phone rang at 7:22. I checked as I answered.

"Did you call her?" The voice belonged to Xander.

"We're going there at noon."

"Why so late?"

"She picked the time."

"Too bad. I'd rather get an early start on the day." That had to be Rex talking. No such words ever came out of Xander's mouth.

Apparently, I am capable of communicating annoyance through silence. When Xander spoke again, he sounded apologetic.

"Of course, you take the lead. You're the one with all the experience." Then, he laid out his plans for the conversation with Marianne. "And, of course, we can find out a little more about that hippie guy she mentioned and talk to him. We need to determine if he was aware of any untoward events surrounding the fate of young Sally Johnson."

"Anything else?"

He missed the sarcasm in my tone. "I suppose you saw that our girl, Miss Wyoming, did not make it into the final group."

I waited for him to tell me he suspected a conspiracy against Miss America contestants at the end of the alphabet, but evidently he had made the best of the situation. "I was going to change the channel, but I did find the girl from South Carolina rather fetching. And California. I quite liked the winner, but I figured she would be busy. But I thought the ones that didn't win might have extra time. Of course, that was only a fun fantasy. I am on a voyage of self-discovery and should not allow myself to get sidetracked."

"Of course."

"Did you realize these contestants have chaperones?"

I suspected his question indicated the real reason Xander did not veer from his path to personal development. I said, "They have teams, each member probably willing to act as a chaperone." I did not add that few of those chaperones would approve of Xander Frost as an escort for one of their girls, as he called them. In the world at large, it might be true that there is no such thing as bad publicity, but in Miss America's world? I suspected Xander Frost was the personification of undesirable press exposure.

"Did you watch?"

"The Weather Channel didn't carry it." I didn't admit to changing channels to catch the tape of Bert Parks serenading the winner, a sweet-looking blond who had promised to end the scourge of world hunger. Yes, I knew the whole coronation was corny—and that Sally Johnson would despise and disdain me for watching—but I loved seeing people happy. I tried not to think about the fifty-one losers on the stage behind the new Miss America or to judge whether being crowned with rhinestones and sent down a runway to be serenaded for beauty and femininity was a valid reason to be happy. Sally would have called the Miss America Pageant a crime, and had I argued a victimless crime, she would have countered with an argument that every little girl in every state—not to mention the District of Columbia and Puerto Rico—was a victim of its outdated ideal of the female role.

Xander not only watched, he wrote a theme song for our investigation. "Or at least, I would have if I weren't on a break from music. All I did was take the Miss America theme and change it to 'There she isn't...' Get it? Because Sally isn't here."

"I get it."

"Well, I know it wasn't the best joke ever. It's Rex. He's just not that witty. Lucky you are working with Xander. I cannot allow you to waste your time sitting in front of the TV in your room watching a storm crawl across the ocean. In this day and age, you can be out and about and still watch a storm crawl across the ocean. I am so glad we are calling on Marianne this afternoon. We should get together earlier to prepare."

"I don't think I can." I didn't need to cook up an excuse. A loud ringing provided one. "I have another call coming through on my cell phone. See you later."

I was happy to hear Andy's voice. "Sorry to call so early."

"This is one of the reasons I love you, Andy. You and I define early the same way. Are you being careful?" Not careful enough for my taste, which would have required getting himself out of the Bahamas. He had gone back to the islands to quit his job, not give his life for it. I knew from the news, however, any opportunity to evacuate had passed.

"I am so sorry I didn't call last night. By 10pm, I'd fallen asleep on the couch in my office—with the phone in my hands. I hope you didn't worry."

"Sorry, but I worry."

"Don't. You understand weathermen like dire predictions. We might not even take a direct hit. You've seen how it goes. Frieda could turn north or just peter out. No matter what happens, we are prepared. I will take care of myself the best I can."

All he could do was batten down the hatches and wait. He couldn't talk long but in the few minutes we spoke he recited a long to-do list including moving the Artistical's impressive art collection to a safer locale.

"Maybe you should hide with the Cezanne."

"I sent that to the mainland as soon as I got back, but would you feel better if I stuck with the Picasso drawings?"

I would have felt better if he had left with the Cezanne.

He said he would be careful, but the excitement in his voice convinced me he had no interest in evacuating—even if his job allowed.

"You sound so energized." I tried not to add an accusatory intonation to my statement.

"There is so much to do and so little time. I'll call when I can. Don't worry if you don't hear from me. Communications might be a problem. If I don't have time to call, that does not mean I am in trouble. I'll try to text, but please, promise me you won't worry."

I promised, but I was lying.

"Anything big to report from Atlantic City?"

"Just worrying about you." I am sure if Andy hadn't had so much to report about Hurricane Frieda and her assault on the island, I might have mentioned seeing Xander Frost, but I wasn't about to waste valuable phone time talking about the rock star.

Chapter 7

At 11:30, I found Xander in his Rex, the ordinary dude, disguise bouncing up and down in front of the Rothko in the lobby.

"I get the 'art' in Artistical but what's with the 'istical'?" he asked.

"Magical and mystical, although now that I think of it, magical is underrepresented in the name."

"Magical and mystical. I like that." He stared at the abstract painting. "And I like the feeling you get from the way this entrance is set next to the painting." He moved left to examine the doorway where carpet, paint and lights mimicked the shapes and shades of the artwork. "Brilliant. You feel as if you are walking into the painting."

"But, you end up in *Squares*. It's a dance club. I guess that's the *magical* part."

"Eh, I get it, but not for squares, right?" He chuckled.

"I guess so." I had limited familiarity with the New Jersey Artistical location.

"You didn't catch my little quip. That was an example of ordinary people's humor. Don't you agree that Rex makes corny jokes?"

"I am sure he does. You know what else ordinary people do? They wear clothes that are remotely tasteful. You could maintain the subterfuge with jeans and a shirt from this century."

"You don't think I look cool like this?" He held his bermudas away from his legs like a young girl approaching a curtsy.

"I had no idea you were trying to look cool. The fake glasses are a nice touch, but I can't tell if they are meant to be nerdy or hip. Is your outfit meant to be ironic?"

"I do not have the time or energy for irony. Appearances are no longer important to me, Meg." He sounded inspired. "I am ready to embark on our project."

"Marianne is expecting us, me and Rex Lampier."

He scowled. "What kind of name is Lampier? Where did you get that?"

"I was sitting next to a lamp and I glanced out the window and noticed Steel Pier in the distance. You didn't tell me your full alias."

"You saw Steel Pier. Why not Rex Steel? That has character."

"That could *be* a character. You want real. Rex Lampier sounds real."

"Maybe so, but I probably need another alias for detective work."

"I don't think Marianne would accept that your name has changed since we spoke this morning. Sorry, you are Rex Lampier."

"Rex Lampier." He mumbled under his breath. "What kind of ordinary guy is called Lampier? Smith or Jones, I can see, but Lampier. I never met a Lampier."

"Well, for today's visit, you are going to be Rex Lampier." I had a feeling I was going to regret our activities, but I had nothing else on for the day, the week, actually, until Frieda blew by and I could return to the Bahamas. I started for the garage but Xander didn't follow. He was on his phone.

"Are you coming?" I asked.

"Texting Del to bring the car around."

"No. Del is welcome to follow us if you want security, but you and I are taking my rental car. It is a modest model of the sort ordinary people, the ones you are so curious about, drive."

Xander dropped his phone in his pants pocket and headed toward the hotel's front door.

"No. I don't valet park. We have to retrieve the car from the lot. It's the ordinary thing to do."

He issued a long, meaningful groan that I ignored. The combination of long halls, elevators, and parking lot ramps did nothing to improve his mood. "I would make an observation that ordinary people waste a lot of time walking to their cars. It's much more efficient to have your vehicle brought to you."

"I'm sure you're right, but we have arrived." I stopped at my parking space.

"This is it?"

"It's a rental."

"You are aware that there are decent cars available to rent?" Xander took in the horror of an ordinary car.

"Not in my price range. Hop in."

Xander made a great show of trying to get comfortable in the passenger seat of the compact model. "Good thing I didn't invite Del along. The spatial inadequacies of this vehicle would have required strapping a larger gentleman, such as Del, to the roof."

"Xander, you were not born a rock star. Don't tell me you can't remember life without all the perks before your first hit song." I knew he was only thirteen when his first record reached number one, but still. I remembered being twelve.

"My only memories are of Xander. That is why I have so much to learn."

"Right. Well today's lesson is in Ventnor, a town just south of here."

"Ventnor." He repeated the town name as if learning a new language, and I guess in a way he was.

"I did a little due diligence to confirm Marianne Dulles was who she claimed to be." I downplayed my Sunday activities. "I did some basic checking for her sister. Nothing about her online. No social media accounts that I could find."

"Well, that's what *we're here* to do, isn't it?" Xander didn't question my methods.

36

Chapter 8

"Everything in Atlantic City is not as fancy as the inside of the Artistical, is it?" Xander sounded sad as well as curious as we drove towards Ventnor.

"Hardly. This city has had some rough times. The casinos were supposed to cure all its ills, but it didn't turn out that way. On the way back to the hotel, I'll show you around."

In the meantime, Xander was full of questions. I felt as if I was failing a quiz for the entire ride. He was as excited by the *Welcome to Ventnor City* sign, as Hannibal must have been when told he'd actually crossed the Alps. I was relieved we didn't have far to go to the address Marianne Dulles had given me. We, and his questions, stopped when the Boardwalk, the beach and the ocean beyond blocked our way.

"Here." I tossed a small notebook at Xander and handed him a pen. "I stopped in the gift shop and got two notebooks. One for you. One for me. Investigators take notes. Now let's do this."

Xander appeared as delighted with his five-dollar gift as a kid with a baseball autographed by his favorite Hall-of-Famer. He touched it with affection and respect. "Tradition. Still working on paper."

"Less intimidating. Let's go put our low technology to good use."

The Dulles family lived in a large, shingle structure sitting on the lot closest to the beach. I couldn't identify the style, but I could guess whoever built it had done so around 1900 and had needed a lot of money to complete it. And to maintain it. The house boasted loving details like window boxes and potted bushes, but the siding was weathered, the shutters were faded and the awnings at the upstairs windows were frayed. The building needed care, although its position, overlooking the Boardwalk to the Atlantic Ocean, made it easy to forgive its flaws. Ten steps led to a wide porch that wrapped around the home in both directions.

"Well, these ordinary people live rather nicely." Xander stopped at the foot of the stairway with his hands on his hips and took a deep breath of sea air. "This is a lovely spot."

"This is not an ordinary house. Perhaps the Dulles family is not so ordinary after all."

"Whatever the story, I love it. A porch. Old timey. With rockers. I like it. Very...."

"Not ordinary." I cut him off.

"I was going to say classic." He sounded more hurt than miffed. "I quite like this look and the setting, although I am not certain I like the idea of people walking down that Boardwalk right outside my window."

"That part is not negotiable. Come on."

He climbed up the stairs behind me. "And look at this," he said like an excited child on Christmas morning. "Double screen doors. Like in olden days, I bet. These are probably original. What a lovely, ordinary life people must have lived here. Sitting on their porch, greeting their neighbors. How lovely, how...."

"Not ordinary." I interrupted him. "Ordinary at the turn of the twentieth century would have been more like sitting on a fire escape in a city trying to catch a breeze on your one day off from your dull job at the hosiery factory. Didn't you ever take history?"

"I didn't have ordinary schooling. I focused on my music."

"Of course." I knocked hard on the rim of the screen door. The reverberation against its frame made more noise than my hand on the wooden surface.

A voice in the distance responded. "I'm coming. One moment, please."

When she appeared at the end of the long hall, I realized the voice belonged to Marianne Dulles. With motions I viewed as timid, repressed, and somehow archaic, she scurried to the door and greeted us with a big smile. "Come in. Please. Come in."

We stepped into 1900 or so. I couldn't pinpoint the year. I wasn't an expert but the structure was full of elaborate detailed woodwork that I judged to be from the turn of the twentieth century. Along with the overwrought décor, the house was a precise mismatch for its owner's simplicity.

Marianne Dulles had revealed not an ounce of style at our first meeting, and that day she projected the same image: neat, clean, and, unlike every detail of her home, unwilling to draw attention, just like the girl in the sophomore class photo at St. Cecelia's. I had no idea where or when she'd bought her cropped pants with the tiny print, but I knew the store was not Saks and the time was not yesterday. Her sweatshirt advertised Atlantic City.

Unlike her home, Marianne's husband Jimmy Dulles appeared to be a perfect match for her, and not just because he was wearing an identical sweatshirt. Pleasant but shy and deferential, he apologized for interrupting when he returned home to find us in the hall with Marianne. "Back from the post office." He displayed a tall pile of mail. "All of this from today. Must get on it." He apologized again, this time for abandoning us.

Marianne led us into a small sitting room, and Jimmy continued into the adjoining dining room. He sat down at a table facing a row of windows and ignored the view across the porch and Boardwalk to the sea beyond. Whatever was in the mail absorbed him. He seemed to forget that the Atlantic Ocean was nearby. I could not. I was mesmerized by the spectacular scene outside the row of windows lining the front wall.

Marianne perched on the edge of a wicker love seat. Xander took the seat next to her. I settled into a matching chair on the opposite side of the coffee table, where a few folders lay in the center.

"I was so pleased you called. I pulled out information I collected about Sally's disappearance. There is not much. The police considered her a runaway and didn't investigate. The story got no press coverage except for an article I managed to get into the newspaper by begging a guy from the *Atlantic City Press*." She glanced at her husband to see if he had a reaction, but I didn't see one. "I do have a few pictures of Sally for you. I'm not an idiot. I understand she won't look the same, but I thought you'd want to know what she was like. Here is one with me, and one with our entire family. This is her high school graduation portrait, but by the time she left she didn't look like that anymore."

I couldn't read much into the photo of the two sisters together. Yes, Sally was definitely the more attractive, but if the older sister's beauty created animosity between the two, it didn't show in either of their facial expressions or their body language. They stood with arms wrapped around each other and big smiles that were as evident in their eyes as in their wide display of teeth.

On the other hand, the family photo suggested someone had picked four random strangers on the Boardwalk and asked them to pose with the Johnson home behind them. Mr. Johnson was large and what I thought of as burly. Without a shred of evidence, I attributed a personality to him to match that description. The expression on his face said he felt proud of his family but he kept a physical distance from all of them. He had planted a hand on each of Sally's shoulders, but he held her at arm's length as if holding her in place. There was air between his wife on one side and his younger daughter on the other. I might have assigned the blame for the position of the subjects in the photo to the wrong party. Maybe the women had distanced themselves from the man of the house.

Sally's graduation portrait, the same one I'd seen online, offered the clearest shot of the missing girl. If gifts were divided between the sisters, she had gotten more than her share of the beauty allocation. I saw nothing plain about Sally. Could her eyes have possibly been the bright blue the colorized portrait showed? Without makeup or a good haircut, she radiated the appeal of a fresh-scrubbed sixties girl. Her long blonde hair, straight and parted in the middle, disappeared behind her shoulders. Despite her attire, a demure white blouse buttoned up to a wide collar, I found it easy to envision her shucking that outfit and heading off barefoot in cutoffs and peasant blouse to Woodstock.

"Wow, she was quite hot for her era, wasn't she?" Xander blurted out. Something in my glance prompted him to reconsider his wording. Embellishments were never an effort for Xander. "I don't mean that in a sexual way. In fact, her image is rather wholesome, virginal actually, but most assuredly attractive. Extremely attractive. Lovely eyes. Big. Innocent. Alluring. I mean as a young man, a teen, I am still a young man, but as a youth, I am sure I would have found her quite appealing."

I didn't think he would ever pause for a breath but he did and Marianne took up the slack. "She was the pretty one. They used to say I got the brains in the family and she got the looks, but in truth she got both."

"Oh come now." Xander patted her hand. "I am sure you were very smart."

I grimaced but Marianne didn't flinch. "She was so nice to me, I never felt jealous. She was kind of special and no one expected me to live up to her. Certainly, not in the looks department. She was popular with girls and boys. She always had dates. But like I said, I wasn't jealous. I only needed one boy."

She smiled towards her husband. "We started dating in high school and have been together ever since." Her expression indicated she remained perfectly happy with the arrangement as if she had won the prize. I had no idea what Jimmy thought. Although he could easily hear our conversation, he kept his eyes on his paperwork and gave no indication he wanted to participate.

"The trouble with being pretty, like Sally, is that all kinds of men get attracted to you. Not always the right kind."

"Do you mind if I take notes?" Xander interrupted.

"Of course. Please do." Marianne beamed.

Xander pulled out his new notebook with a flourish and held his pen above the empty page. "You were saying she met the wrong type of men."

"Boys. Even in high school. I didn't like this guy she went out with. Bobby Aniston. He was kind of upset when they broke up. For a while I did suspect him."

"You stalked him."

Xander and I both jumped when Jimmy's voice came from the dining room.

"I admitted my initial reaction involved some suspicions, but then Jimmy convinced me I was being ridiculous. Bobby moved on, married Sally's best friend."

"And her name would be?" Xander asked.

"Gina Aniston, but no need to talk to her. I heard Bobby died years ago. Like I said, I didn't approve of him, but compared to what followed, he was an angel. Sally had bad taste in men, especially after she changed her image. She became kind of a hippie. Always barefoot, in cutoffs and peasant tops, or those long granny dresses they used to wear. Here is the only shot I could find of her from 1968."

She handed us a discolored photo of a young woman in a bikini wrapped in the arms of a blond hippie in cutoff jeans. Despite their dated style, the two made an undeniably attractive couple.

"Sally kept that on her mirror for a while. After she left home, I found it in her drawer. I tried cutting him out, but I couldn't get rid of him without damaging part of her."

"And he is?" Xander tried to be all business.

"Her boyfriend from college, from the last spring before she left. Lou Blair."

"Do you know what happened to him?" I asked.

"Not a clue. He used to call the house after she left. I wondered if all his calls were a ruse, but he claimed he had no idea where she went. He gave up after a few months."

"You don't have more pictures?" Xander's tone was disapproving.

"Not the way she looked when she left. She showed up in the background of a picture in the newspaper." She pointed to Sally, the revised, hippie Sally, the only woman in the photo who appeared anti-establishment. The outfits on the other women suggested limited overlap between the hippie community and that segment of the women's movement.

"Say, what's going on there, in that photo?" Xander interrupted.

"Miss America Pageant. September 1968. The protest I mentioned. A big furor. Made the national news. Horrible, really. Sally got friendly with a few of those women's lib types and went with them to protest on the Boardwalk. Those demonstrations were a travesty. That pageant had been part of Atlantic City's history for forty years, and those women wanted to disrupt things, to protest that women weren't meat. Of course, they weren't. Those contestants were nice girls seeking a good start in life. Disgraceful protestors. But Sally thought the entire pageant was disgraceful."

"Yes, my partner explained to me how some women do not appreciate beauty pageants." Xander shot a brief glance in my direction and returned his focus to Marianne with an expression that said, but *we know better, don't we?*

"Those girls are lovely." Marianne's tone went beyond defensive to anger.

"Did you and Sally argue about that?" I asked.

"You didn't argue with Sally. At least I didn't. As the younger sister, I just listened to her go on and on about what she found wrong about our country. Vietnam. Racial Discrimination. Miss America. Really." Marianne paused to let out a huff of disapproval. "By 1968, she didn't like any of America. I blame the way she changed on her boyfriend, Lou, the one in the picture. She had always been a normal girl, but then she began dressing like a hippie when she met him. And, it wasn't only her clothes that changed. Once, before she came home that summer—1968—in the spring, I visited her. That trip proved to be quite a shock for a nice girl like me."

I wondered how Sally would have told the same story, but we could only hear Marianne's version.

Marianne Dulles
Bucks County Pennsylvania
April 1968

She couldn't believe her sister lived in a place like this. Sally had fooled her mother and father into believing she was still resident in her dorm, but Marianne knew better. Sure, her sister probably spent an occasional night on campus, so she could make a collect call home to assure her parents she was safe and happy and studying hard, but Marianne understood Sally saw this rundown farmhouse surrounded by abandoned, overgrown fields as her home. And not just at school. The center of Sally's world had shifted to this scruffy property. For now. She accepted that playing the hippie was a phase in her sister's life. She prayed that playing the hippie was a phase in her sister's life.

The land was pretty, and the house might have been, if someone bothered to apply a little paint or even a little elbow grease, but Sally didn't mind. She never stopped smiling, kind of a goofy expression that suggested she had died and gone to heaven. Marianne had never been to heaven, but she had a fairly good idea when she got there—and she was certain she would—it would be nothing like this old farm in Bucks County.

Of course, it wasn't only her housing that made Sally smile. It was that guy, Lou. Marianne didn't like him. Well, she hadn't met him yet, but she didn't like what she heard. When Sally came home for Christmas, she couldn't stop talking about him. Marianne knew the type. The kind of hippie boy all the girls wanted, at least the girls who were interested in rebel types. Marianne wasn't. She knew this hippie-thing was just a trend that would end as quickly as it began. And then what kind of men would these women find themselves stuck with?

"So, what do you think?" Sally asked. "This place is really groovy, isn't it?"

Marianne figured the place represented the definition of groovy, but she wasn't sold on the whole groovy concept. People were roaming around in old clothes, funny clothes, and, in most cases, not enough of them. Not only the girls. The guys too. Although the day was bright and sunny, the spring weather was far from hot. Nonetheless, the boys were wearing shorts but no shirts. Most of their ill-fitting pants sat so far down on their hips that she feared they would continue their slide south—and she didn't see any sign of underwear. Shoes were out of the question. She hadn't spotted a single pair aside from some sandals kicked off in a corner inside the front door.

"How many people live here?" She tried not to sound appalled as she asked.

"Oh, it depends. There are twelve of us who are here all the time, but friends come and go. Kids on the road, passing through town. We never know who we'll find in the living room to rap with. It's exciting."

Marianne thought it sounded awful and her face said so even if she didn't want to disagree with her sister.

"Marianne don't be so uptight. This is what life should be like. No stupid rules. No pretenses. Everyone acting the way they really feel, not the way they believe they should."

"Do you have your own room?" she asked although she was afraid of the answer. Her hands tightened around the handle of her American Tourister train case.

"Lou and I crash upstairs." Sally smirked at the hard-sided suitcase in Marianne's hands. "Bring your bag up. Our room has a great view of the farm.

44

Let me show you.”

Our room. *Marianne understood what that meant, but she didn't want to dwell on her sister's relationship with Lou. She focused on her physical environment. Marianne figured the farmhouse had once been lovely. She could imagine how bright the rooms had been in their heyday when the owners had taken care. Now, the wallpaper was stained and faded and she expected the stairs to give way under her weight. Sally flew up them without worry. “We crash up here. Come and see.”*

“What is there to see?” Marianne asked when Sally led her into a sun-filled room with gorgeous views but no furniture. Marianne didn't consider the lone item, a mattress thrown on the floor, furniture. She knew she sounded critical, even unkind, but Sally was being so foolish. Books and magazines Marianne had never heard of were piled in every corner of the room and scattered across the floor. The only décor on the walls was a sloppy display of newspaper clippings held up by scotch tape. The items of clothing hanging from nails, for a male as well as a female, cleared up any doubts she had about the living arrangements. “There's nothing but a mattress on the floor and some nails on the walls for clothes.”

“That's how it should be, Marianne. Why should we be encumbered by material possessions?”

“Are they Lou's clothes?” Marianne felt embarrassed to ask.

“Don't look so shocked, Marianne. Sex is beautiful. Mom and Dad wanted to keep us away from it, but that is an old way of thinking. Everyone should experience pleasure as often as they can.”

“But is he going to marry you?”

Sally burst out laughing. “Marriage has nothing to do with it. Right now we want each other, we enjoy each other. We might even love each other, but we don't need a piece of paper to formalize what we feel. Marianne, the world is changing. Don't let Mom and Dad control you. You could come and stay here. I am sure everyone would welcome you.”

Marianne didn't want to hurt Sally's feelings, but she would never want to live under that roof. She couldn't imagine how she was going to last one night. God only knew what creatures, human and otherwise, came out after dark. She would get through her thirty-six-hour visit and never come again.

She wandered to the window, mainly to avoid making eye contact with her sister. At the bottom of a neglected lawn, a group of what she would call hippies sat in a circle. Two guys played guitars and, when they weren't passing a marijuana joint, the rest sang a familiar tune. Peter, Paul and Mary. At least she could feel comfortable with one aspect of life on the farm. Not that she would have felt comfortable joining the impromptu singing group. Whether or not she could overcome her discomfort didn't matter. They would have spotted her as a super-straight, uptight virgin, and they wouldn't have been wrong.

"Sunshine. Introduce me to your little sister."

She turned towards the voice. So, this must be Lou. The wonderful Lou. His charm was not apparent to Marianne. She supposed he was cute, but barely distinguishable from the other boys she'd seen scattered across the lawn. Skinny with straggly blond hair hanging like a girl's almost to his shoulders. His entire outfit consisted of cut-off jeans and a silver ring on the middle finger of his right hand. His feet were filthy with a crust of dirt that suggested they hadn't been washed for some time. Sally had turned her life upside down for this person? Marianne could not understand the attraction, but his power over her sister was clear.

He wrapped an arm around Sally and slid his other hand under her blouse to caress her in a way that embarrassed Marianne. Sally was so busy kissing Lou she forgot she had company. Marianne didn't know what to do, so she did nothing. She waited.

Sally's eyes were glistening when Lou pulled away from the kiss but still held Sally in place. He turned his attention to her. "So, what is your name?" He made it clear the sight of her standing there in her neat cotton shift amused him.

"Marianne."

"That won't do. Marianne." He made it clear he was judging her name and her—and finding both wanting. "From now on you are Merry. Merry and Sunshine. The Holiday sisters."

"Our name isn't Holiday," she protested.

He began to laugh—no to giggle. Not like the cool guy he wanted to be but like a little boy. He fell onto the bed and rolled back and forth, laughing for such a long time that Marianne again found herself in an uncomfortable position. She had no idea what behavior was expected of her. She looked to

Sally, who smiled at the sight of a grown-up acting like a two-year-old. When he finally composed himself, he reached up and pulled Sally onto the mattress with him. "Sunshine. Your sister is a hoot. We've got to teach her the facts of life. Real life. Not that bogus life she's been living at home with your parents."

Sally laughed and kissed him and didn't seem to mind at all that there were no sheets on what was clearly a dreadfully old mattress—well-worn and stained, probably by people they didn't even know.

"Merry Holiday. Come here." He patted the bed beside him.

"I am fine where I am."

"Are you afraid to muss that little Tricia Nixon dress you're wearing?" He turned to Sunshine. "Is your sister a closet Republican?"

"I'm not old enough to vote," Marianne answered.

"That doesn't matter. You have got to get involved, Merry, or little Tricia is going to move into the White House. Our country, our world, is in a crisis, Merry. Get involved. Help us change the world."

*****

Fifty years later, Marianne's face still registered disapproval. "Lou fancied himself a radical, but from what I could tell, he passed his time sitting around, smoking marijuana, and repeating political platitudes he heard around campus. I only spent a couple of hours with him, but even then, I could recognize a phony. Jimmy saw through him too, but Sally claimed she loved him."

"Your husband met Lou?" I glanced into the dining room. No reaction from the diligent worker.

"Not that Jimmy was happy about it. Jimmy drove me to the farm and dropped me off. I had a brand-new license, but no way my father would let me drive myself to another state. Jimmy was supposed to come back on Sunday night, but he sized up the situation. He came back after an hour, just in case I didn't want to stay. And I didn't. He was the one who insisted we make nice and accept their invitation for lunch, or whatever they called the big communal pile of incompatible edible items they spread out on this long table in the kitchen. I don't remember what the food was, but it wasn't like any meal I'd ever eaten." She lowered her voice as if her husband wouldn't be able to hear, but he clearly still could. "Jimmy knew what to expect at that farm. He tried to warn me. He suspected I would be upset at what I found. And I was. He worried Sally and I might quarrel. We never did, but I could tell she was disappointed at how I felt. I was so agitated I drove off without my suitcase. We went back for it and Jimmy ran inside while I sat in the car. I remember the expression on Sally's face when she came to the door with him. She understood I didn't approve. I never said a word, but she knew."

I had no doubt Sally realized her uptight, traditional sister would never condone any unconventional behavior.

"So, she ran away with Lou?" Xander asked.

"No. She was finished with him by the time she left, or at least she was rethinking their relationship. I guess that's why she tossed the picture in the drawer. She didn't put it in the trash, but I believe she was done with him."

"Didn't it occur to you that he might have hurt her?" Xander asked.

"Lou? He called the house a bunch of times. I didn't think he knew anything. Sally wanted to get away from him. Jimmy thought of driving up to see him, but the police told us to back off, that they had checked around, talked to him as part of their 'investigation.'" Sarcasm dripped from the word. "Besides, by the time she disappeared, she had this new group of friends. Women. The protestors I told you about, at the pageant."

Xander picked up the newspaper clipping. "These women?"

"Maybe not those specific women but people from that group. She was always forming instant friendships. Too easily influenced, that girl. She thought I was naïve, but now I see she was no better. I couldn't see that at the time. I viewed her as such a sophisticate. But really?" Her face registered distaste for her sister's new friends. "I never would have talked to one local lady she got close to."

"Can we see her here?" Xander passed the photo to Marianne.

"I don't see her. I only met her twice—the first, when I went on the Boardwalk with Sally early that day. Just to see what was going on. But I got embarrassed. I didn't want to be there and become associated with those people. Good thing I left. There were photographers there, from newspapers, and television people. I didn't want anyone to assume I participated in those protests. Sally and I went with the local woman into a bar. I didn't want to go. I wasn't old enough. Neither of us were, but I wasn't the type to get a fake ID. Besides, I didn't drink. But it turned out we didn't go there to drink. We went there to talk. At least that woman talked. Talked! She lectured, like she was on a soap box. She'd been married and had a kid but I wondered if she liked men at all, if you get my drift. I wondered the same thing about all of them back in 1968."

Her language wasn't direct, but she didn't appear disapproving.

"Her name was Suzania Martini. Or Mancini. Definitely an *ini* or maybe *iti* ending. One of those lyrical Italian names. A lot of those women came from New York, but she lived down here, at the shore. Jimmy and I went to see her after Sally left. She had an apartment at the north end of Ventnor. She and some other women. She told us Sally had to be herself, do what she wanted, go where she belonged. She could no longer be stifled by life in her hometown, our life. Jimmy had to comfort me and make me understand her viewpoint. They both concluded Sally was a runaway, like so many young people in those years—which was the police's conclusion. Sally kept going through so many changes I thought one of those changes would bring her back to where she started."

"In all the years since she left, have you ever had any sightings?" I asked.

"Never a real one. Not even any false alarms in many, many years. Although a friend of mine saw someone she thought might be Sally a few years ago in Baltimore."

"Pittsburgh." Jimmy came to life. "She saw the woman in Pittsburgh."

"Did she talk to her?" Xander asked.

"No, no. I wish she had. She said the woman had come and gone before she thought to get up and chase her. I was excited because years earlier there had been another sighting in Baltimore."

"I don't recall that one, but the last one happened in Pittsburgh, so I don't think the earlier one would have mattered," Jimmy called from the dining room. "Don't go sending them off on a wild goose chase."

Marianne seemed to shrink in her chair. "Sorry. I certainly wouldn't want to do that. I certainly wouldn't."

"I understand Sally didn't offer any indication of where she was going, but did she leave a note about why she was leaving?" I asked.

Marianne shook her head. "Not that I saw."

"Did your parents mention one?" Xander followed up.

"Never."

"Can you tell me about the last time you saw your sister?" I imagined that instant would be seared into her memory.

She pulled a tissue out of her pocket, as if anticipating tears. "Here is the horrible thing. I don't know. I can't remember the moment I last saw her. She came home that night, and I was in the living room, right over there." She pointed across the hallway. "And she came in that door and went upstairs. I remember she asked if Mother and Dad were home, and I said no. They were playing bridge at a friend's house. That I remember, but I don't remember if she came downstairs again. She probably didn't because my parents came home not long after she did. So, the last time I recall laying eyes on her? When I barely glanced away from the television. Want to hear the ironic part?"

Both Xander and I did.

"I was watching the Miss America pageant, and she came home near the end. I didn't want to argue with her and miss anything, so I barely spoke to her. The last opportunity I had to talk to my sister, and I ignored her."

"I see the irony." Xander's response was subdued.

"When did your parents realize she was gone?"

"In the morning, they asked if I had seen her. They assumed she sneaked out. They were angry. Still mad when she didn't come home for dinner. She was supposed to go back to school the next day. My mother went through her room and figured out she had taken her clothes with her. I remember my father's reaction. 'She'd better show up at school.' That was his big concern."

"It was important to him that she finish college." I stated an assumption.

"He didn't care at all. He wondered if he had time to stop payment on the tuition check if she didn't show. She didn't."

What kind of father could be so unconcerned?

Xander was more practical. "Did he get his money back?"

"You'd better believe he did. It wasn't easy, but he knew how to squeeze a nickel as they used to say." Marianne didn't seem perplexed, let alone horrified, by her father's priorities. "I have to admit, I inherited that gene."

"Ask her about the awnings." Jimmy called from the next room.

"My husband thinks we need new awnings."

I thought so too but didn't jump into the argument. I smiled politely. "Wasn't your father worried?"

"Not so much worried as angry. Sally knew how to make him mad." Then as if embarrassed by the revelation and eager to change the subject, she pulled a photo from an end table. "These are my children. James Jr., Andrew and Mary Josephine Dulles, now Carson."

Sadly, none of the young Dulleses resembled Sally. Other than sharing their mother's coloring, the two boys didn't resemble either parent. The girl, however, was the spitting image of her father.

Chapter 9

"The Dulleses have a nice house, but the Boardwalk is a problem. I saw people checking us out. One old broad stopped and pretended to lean against the railing to rest so she could look in the window." Xander was disgruntled as we climbed back into the car.

"What made you think the *older woman* was pretending?"

"Well, there are benches up and down the Boardwalk, and even if you do not want to walk to them, why rest with your back to the ocean?"

"Because it's a more comfortable position?" I asked.

"That gives you a clear view of the Dulles sunroom." He was emphatic.

"How long did she stand there?"

"Too long. Maybe three minutes."

"Xander, you are used to being stared at. No one is interested in most of us. Maybe while resting, she did check out the room and the furniture. I've done that. If she wanted to stalk us, she wouldn't have walked away after three minutes. You might think I know nothing about stalkers, but I've had to chase rabid fans away from the Artistical. They don't walk away after three minutes."

"My DeFrosters?" He sounded excited at the mention of his admirers.

"Probably. On occasion. But can we move on? Literally and figuratively. Put on your seat belt." I pulled away from the Dulles house. "Did anything strike you odd about the Dulles kids?"

"Aside from the unfortunate fact that none of them had inherited whatever genes had accounted for Sally's good looks? No. With any luck, those looks might skip a generation and the grandkids might be more fortunate. Why? Did something strike you as unusual?"

"If you loved and missed your sister, don't you think you might want to name your daughter after her?"

"Not if I didn't like the name."

"Sarah is a good solid name," I protested.

"Maybe Jimmy didn't like it. Besides, if they believed something bad happened to Sally, Sarah, whatever, maybe they thought giving their daughter that name would curse her."

That explanation I could buy.

"No matter what she thought of the name back then, it is clear Marianne Johnson Dulles wants her sister back now. Marianne was a bit of a stick in the mud back in the day, wasn't she?" Xander asked.

I defended her although I suspected his assessment was accurate—in 1968 and currently. "I'd like to believe she was a nonconformist who didn't succumb to peer pressure."

"But?" He asked. "You'd like to think that, but what do you actually believe?"

"My impression is she feared change and possessed a will of iron to oppose it."

"Me too. I can see why a girl like Sally, who appeared to be quite cool, or at least on the road to being quite cool, would want to leave her hometown. The question is why she never wanted to come back. Even if familial affection didn't bring her home, wouldn't curiosity require taking a quick check to see what happened to everyone?" His tone turned defensive. "Why are we stopping here?"

Here was a recreational area only a few blocks away from the Dulles house.

"You can watch ordinary people doing ordinary things—kiddies playing in the playground, adults playing on the tennis courts. I need to look for something."

"In your phone?"

"Frieda hasn't moved."

"Ah, checking the weather. I'm shocked." Not shocked enough to stop his one-sided discourse. "I am not convinced Marianne should have dismissed Sally's high school friends out of hand. Her boyfriend did marry her best friend," Xander protested.

I looked up from my phone to hold his gaze. "Marianne didn't see that as a road we should go down." There was my opportunity to fess up about my visit to Gina Garth Harris, but I let the moment pass. I needed time to think. "Right now, let's focus on Sally's life immediately before she left town. If we hit a dead end, we'll dig back further, but at this point I don't see doing any more with old friends she hadn't seen since high school graduation."

"We don't know that, now do we?" Xander objected.

"I wasn't being literal." I changed the subject. "I believe I have found Sally's feminist friend on Facebook, assuming she is now Suzania Martini Alton." My alleged Suzania Martini lived in Longport, was in the right age group, and was the only Suzania who popped up—in the online phone directory or on Facebook.

"Let's go." I shifted the car into drive.

"Should we call first?" Xander asked.

I explained that, as a general rule, calling ahead opened the possibility of outright rejection. I did not mention to him that in this case we had a secret weapon to get us in the door: his celebrity. I saw on Suzania's Facebook page that she had an abundance of grandchildren, many of them females between the ages of ten and thirty. If Suzania rejected us, we could confide Xander's true identity and hope his fame paved the way to an interview. "Let's just drop by." I didn't add *and hope someone recognizes you.*

Xander was okay with the part of the plan I revealed to him. "I get to see more ordinary American homes, and maybe get inside another one."

"Now here is something interesting." I pointed to the neighborhood on our right. "Did you ever play *Monopoly?*"

His face said he had no idea what I was talking about.

"A board game."

Still no glimmer of recognition.

"Well, you wouldn't care then."

"I care. I want to learn everything I can. Tell me." He turned in his seat to get a good look at the houses we passed.

"In my day, people still played board games and *Monopoly* was about the biggest board game going. An American tradition."

"Did you play it?"

"I hated it. A game went on forever, but you can't go by me."

He switched positions and stared at me. "What does a board game have to do with the houses I am looking at?"

I explained how Monopoly worked. "So you buy all these properties and one of them was Marven Gardens. And, that is Marven Gardens. Right on the border of Ventnor and Margate. Marven Gardens. Get it?"

"Ah. Ventnor. We put the *ven* in Marven Gardens."

"Not on the *Monopoly* board. The gamemakers misspelled it. They put M-A-R-V-*I*-N Gardens."

As we drove south, Xander enthused about the ordinary housing, much of which was in no way ordinary and some of which was downright magnificent. I made a turn up to Atlantic Avenue. I said so we could ride closer to the ocean, but I really hoped to change Xander's conversation about ordinary housing.

"Excuse me, Meg. Did you see a giant elephant? Just now. Off to our left." He sounded genuinely concerned. Not surprised, simply apprehensive.

"Big, gray and wooden?"

"Yes."

"Maybe five stories high?"

"Yes."

"That would be Lucy. She is a local landmark. We're in Margate. Lucy has lived here for as long as I can remember."

"Oh good." He released a long stream of breath. "I've seen elephants like that before, but generally the people with me didn't."

Totally believable.

Xander went back to his enthusiastic review of ordinary American architecture until we reached Longport and he saw the Martini homestead. "This mansion could be in Bel Air." His tone broadcast disappointment.

But unlike the homes in Bel Air, this one did not have a hedge to hide it. We could see right in, right through it, actually, to the water behind it. So we knew someone, possibly Suzania was home. Seeing that an entertainment news show covered one of the largest screens I had ever seen outside of a sports arena, I concluded that unmasking Xander might be a good ploy at this address. "You take the lead this time."

"Really?" He grew excited. "I feel confident I am ready to assume that role. I had a guest shot on *Law & Order* once and, of course, my movie, *Hidden Mystery*." His eyes were bright as he climbed out of the car and up the wide staircase.

When a woman answered the doorbell, he didn't give her a chance to resist his well-honed charisma. "Hello, so sorry to bother you." Xander led with his charming English accent, in a tone so polite it could be termed unctuous.

The woman fell for it the way most women did. "No bother, I'm sure. What can I do for you?"

"My name is Rex Lampier."

She stared hard at him. "Really?" She hadn't turned her attention towards me since she laid eyes on Xander.

"Why do you ask?"

"You look familiar. Have we met?"

"I don't think so. I'm from Britain."

"Okay." She nodded slowly while I watched her reconcile the information and the figure standing before her.

"Are you Suzania Martini?"

"Yes." She answered not so much with reluctance, as skepticism. I was pretty sure Xander's cover was blown. "I mean I was. My name is Alton now."

"How lovely to meet you. May I call you Suzania?"

"Please." The single word did not so much give permission as beg. *Yes, call me anything.* And this woman was old enough to be his grandmother. I did not get it.

"This is my friend and associate…."

I didn't yet trust Xander to get my name right.

"Meg Daniels." I reached forward to shake Suzania's limp hand.

"And, again, you are…?" Her attention returned to Xander. Whom am I kidding? Her attention never left Xander.

"I told you. My name is Rex Lampier." He held up his palm as if to block any comments. "I know. It's an unusual name." He glanced at me. "One might even say stupid. I can imagine what you're thinking. What do a lamp and a pier have in common?"

"Perhaps Mrs. Alton, Suzania, would like to hear why we are here." I spoke before Xander's whine could turn into a rant.

He changed his approach and, somewhere in the middle of the sentence, his tone, as he switched from frustrated to charming. "Meg and I are trying to find an old friend of yours. Sally Johnson."

Suzania utilized elaborate facial expressions to communicate that, despite her best efforts, she did not remember Sally.

"We thought you might have met her at a protest on the Boardwalk in 1968."

"Nineteen sixty eight? I have trouble remembering last month." What might have been a chuckle devolved into a giggle under Xander's gaze.

I handed her the newspaper photo Marianne had given us. "She's right here."

She squinted at the blurry image. "The Miss America pageant? Wow, that was a long time ago." She pulled a pair of reading glasses out of her pocket. "The picture's not especially clear." She made her excuse to Xander as she frowned at the photo. "Of course, I recognize *her*. I can't believe I didn't recognize her name. Sally, you say?" She made a great show of thinking for a moment before recognition spread across her face. "No. I didn't know her as Sally. You mean Sarah. I knew her as Sarah. Although when I was introduced to her she was using one of those silly hippie names. Rain. Rainbow. Sky. Sunshine. That's it. Sunshine. During that weekend, she went back to using her given name. Sarah. You said her last name was Johnson? I didn't remember that, although I must have at the time. Now that I think about it, I recall a sister, or maybe her husband, contacted me at some point looking for Sally, but he would have had a different last name. He asked if I had any idea where she had gone. All I could figure was she'd run away. At least, that's my recollection."

"How wonderful that you recall her," Xander enthused.

Eager to please her charming visitor, not me, Suzania went on. "I do remember her. She was a beautiful girl. And so ready to learn, to change.

Wow, it's all coming back to me. She brought a little drama along with her. She became friendly with one of the women from out of town. I thought they might have become an item." She chuckled. "So did Sarah's boyfriend, or ex-boyfriend. I remember he showed up and made a big stink."

"We would love to hear about that, if you have a moment." Xander opened his wide eyes and stared into Suzania's. She said nothing, but she realized she was not staring at Rex Lampier. She was getting lost in the eyes of Xander Frost. "Why don't you come in?" She paused and then added with a sardonic tone, "Rex."

No one invited me, but I followed along into the huge living room that the enthralled Suzania led us to. She muted the TV and sat with her back to the video. She directed Xander to a seat beside hers. I found a spot on the sectional on the other side of the wide coffee table.

Xander pulled out his notebook. "We would love to hear what you remember of any encounters you had with Sarah." Xander's smile was bright, seductive, and inappropriate for the topic.

Thrilled to confide a secret in the superstar pretending to be Rex Lampier, Suzania was not at all reluctant to share.

Suzania Martini Alton
Atlantic City Boardwalk
September 7, 1968

At first, she was annoyed by the women from New York, acting as if they were the only ones who ever thought of mounting a protest. Suzania knew she wasn't the sole woman in the area with an interest in taking action at the Miss America Pageant, but she found it hard to make a stand against an institution that had brought pleasure to many local people and money to the local economy for almost half a century. She never would have initiated a protest. She hated to admit she found it easier to be a follower, to support the out-of-towners and blend in with them when the protest went public.

The women didn't look like radicals. They looked the way she did. They dressed the way she did. But, most importantly, they thought the way she did.

They'd not only read The Feminine Mystique, *they'd given her lists of other books they'd read. These women weren't going to live their mothers' lives any more than she was going to repeat hers. She found being with them refreshing, even exciting, and always intellectually stimulating. She felt envious of the young girls, the ones who figured things out before they made their first big mistake. Not that her son was a mistake. No, he was the best thing in her life, but the marriage that produced him had certainly been a major misstep. And now, as a young, single mother, she was finding it hard to get her life back on track, trying to build a career when the men who hired her were more interested in her body than her mind. She was convinced traditions like beauty pageants supported the males' chauvinist attitudes.*

She admired the older women and envied the younger. She was jealous of the hippie-type from Ventnor, the one who called herself Sunshine when she arrived at the first meeting but had already begun evolving into Sarah. Suzania liked hanging around her. She reminded her of the girl she had once been. Only a few years younger, Sarah retained the youthful optimism that had deserted Suzania before she left her teens.

"This has been a great day, hasn't it?" She joined Sarah who was leaning on the railing across the JFK Plaza, back to the beach, watching the action in front of the convention center. "Even if people don't understand, we got their attention."

"The world is so much more complex than I was led to believe." The hippie girl sounded excited, not disappointed, by the realization.

"Our parents don't want us to know too much. They want us easy to control." Suzania was proud to dispense advice based on her life experiences, not her age.

"I realize my parents love me in the only way they know, but they want to hold me back." Sarah turned to gaze into Suzania's eyes. "I want to experience life."

"We can help you with that." Feigning exhaustion, Faye, one of the out-of-towners, a San Francisco resident who happened to be visiting New York, plopped against the railing on Sarah's other side and dropped her head on the girl's shoulder. "This has been an exhausting day. Exhilarating but exhausting." She grabbed Sarah's hand and squeezed. "Thank you so much for your

help. It's nice to have someone from the area involved."

Suzania kept her laugh inside. I'm from the area. *But she didn't expect any recognition from the activist. She understood what was going on here. The youthful innocence Suzania admired in Sarah kept the younger girl from catching on to the true nature of Faye's interest. Suzania thought it had been love at first sight on Faye's part. She'd studied the way the woman dealt with Sarah, giving her advice, guiding her to a name change within hours. Her interest was real, total.*

Sarah was oblivious to the sexual overtones in Faye's actions. She recited stories about the day's experiences as the older woman stroked her hair.

"Well, what have we here?" The voice came from the mouth of a full-fledged hippie from the headband tied around his long hair to the dirty feet sticking out of his flip-flops.

Sarah opened her mouth but, before she could speak, the man, a boy really, leaned in for a kiss.

Faye's eyes were a combo of sadness, rage, and fear as she came to attention, but she said nothing. She lifted her head and let go of Sally's hand, but she did not move away to make room for the hippie on the rail next to his girlfriend. Neither did Suzania, but he didn't notice her.

"Hey, Sunshine, why aren't you marching? I thought you came here to march?" His voice was loud, and his tone was mocking. Suzania wondered if he'd been drinking or doing whatever hippies did to achieve that glassy-eyed effect.

"I'm taking a break, to rest, to watch, to talk about my day with my new friends. I loved meeting these women."

"And I can tell they loved you." He ignored Suzania and focused on Faye with one of those hard stares that cause the weak to look away. Faye didn't flinch but responded with a matching glare. If Suzania had any doubts about Faye's intentions, they vanished as she watched the two wannabe lovers—one fearing rejection and one awaiting encouragement—posture over Sarah who seemed perplexed by the hostility so easily understood by others.

"Come on, Sunshine. Let's go. I drove all the way down here to see you. You've spent enough time with . . ."

Careful kid, she thought.

"*…your new friends.*"

"*We're not done here. We're talking.*" Sarah *answered with extreme politeness but no warmth.*

"*You're done.*" *As he reached for her arm, he nudged Faye away.*

"*Hey.*" *Faye was not one to be nudged. With what looked like a genuine karate chop, she broke his grip on Sarah.*

Sarah extended an arm to separate the two. "*It's okay.*" *She assumed the role of peacemaker.*

"*No, it is not okay.*" *Faye positioned herself between Sarah and her visitor.* "*Look kid, I don't know who you are or what your relationship is to Sarah, but she's busy right now. When she's done here, I am sure she'll be happy to talk to you, although I can't imagine why.*"

"*I am her boyfriend. And I have a name. Lou. Not that I want you to use it. I want you to get lost.*" *He pushed Faye back against the railing and yanked Sarah towards him.* "*You're coming with me.*"

"*No, I am not.*" *Sarah freed herself and knocked Lou off balance with two hands to his chest.* "*I am staying here with my friends. If you'd like to talk later, I will meet you on the Boardwalk in front of my parents' house. If you want to wait. I'm not sure what time I'll be finished here.*"

Suzania watched Lou's hands curl into fists, but he made no move to touch Sarah.

"*I won't wait forever,*" *he threatened.*

"*That's up to you. Now, if you would leave me with my friends.*"

*****

"That girl was tough." Even fifty years later Suzania had a look of admiration on her face.

"Did he leave?" I asked the first question.

"Yeah, but with a lot of bravado if you get what I mean. He backed away, staring and snarling, but he left. Had a swagger." Suzania moved her upper body to imitate Lou's arrogant posture.

"How did Sarah react?" Xander regained her attention.

"If she found his behavior unforgivable, she didn't let on. Maybe she was used to being treated that way. But she wasn't worried about him. She was mesmerized by Faye." Suzania had more to say but was reluctant to say it. "I don't mean to criticize because from what you say, she disappeared right after the pageant, but she was kind of naïve. She was so sweet, I sometimes wondered if her whole persona was an act. Looking back, I don't believe it was. That demeanor combined with her beauty...." She mouthed the word *wow*. "My boyfriend came to pick me up from a meeting we locals put together with a couple of out-of-towners the night before the pageant. I could tell he had the hots for her. I resented her. The irony. Protesting but still feeling the need to compete over some worthless piece of male meat."

"You dumped that jerk, I guess." Xander's voice was jovial.

"Oh no. I married him."

Chapter 10

Xander was exhilarated. "Well, investigating doesn't seem too hard now, does it?"

Not for an international superstar with sex appeal that, while inexplicable to me, removed all obstacles. I didn't answer, but Xander's question didn't require a response. He described the techniques he had utilized to elicit information without once mentioning the two fundamentals: flirting and fame. The way Suzania said good-bye to Rex, she made it clear she understood she was in on the joke.

"You shouldn't have given her your number. I am sure she realizes you're a celebrity. She might put your private information out there. I bet she at least gives it to a granddaughter, and I can only imagine what she'll do."

"I didn't give her my number. Are you insane? I gave her yours at the hotel." Without considering the ramifications of that move, he changed the subject. "So, what next? Let's find our two suspects." His eyes opened wide but his mouth barely moved. He whispered. "Let's review the story and figure out who we should tail. I used the term on *Law & Order*, although I was the one who was being tailed. My line was 'You tailing me?' I think tailing is the answer."

"The crime happened fifty years ago. Surveillance might not be the key." I stated what I thought was the obvious.

"Well, we should wait here a few moments, now shouldn't we? To see if she runs out to a pay phone. That happens all the time on the telly."

"In movies from the sixties. Where do you expect her to find a pay phone?"

Xander spoke with confidence. "Criminals know."

"Yes. Criminals. Suzania is a kindly grandmother whose life probably revolves around those grandchildren whose pictures are all over the living room. If she runs out of the house, it's because she was so enthralled with you—and the possibility she had a rock star in her living room— that she forgot to pick someone up at soccer practice."

"What if she and her accomplice try to move the body? They thought they were home free, but when people started nosing around, they got scared. That's how I got my guy in *Hidden Mystery*."

"There would not be much left to move—if there is a body. We have no reason to believe there was foul play."

"Marianne feels there was."

"She has to. Otherwise, she can't explain her sister's rejection."

"Marianne idolizes that sister of hers, doesn't she? In a similar situation, I would have hated her. She was prettier, smarter and got all the blokes. I bet she killed her sister and hired you to pin the crime on someone else." Xander's voice reeked of confidence.

"Number one, we have no evidence a crime was committed. But if she did kill her sister, that crime has long since been forgotten. That's number two. And, number three, why on earth would she hire someone to investigate a murder she committed that was long ago forgotten?"

"Well…."

I'd never known Xander to be at a loss for words before. I waited but none were forthcoming. "You made a good point about all the guys in her life." I tried to cheer him up.

"We have to find out what men, boys, had crushes on Sally. Who gave her trouble? It figured in the plot of *Hidden Mystery*."

I had no idea; I hadn't seen the movie. Not many had.

"So, we find more people who knew her." I drove three blocks, pulled over and focused on my phone. It took under five minutes searching the Internet to discover that Faye who was involved in the demonstration on the Boardwalk was Faye Padilla, a feminist scholar who wrote both for scholarly journals and popular magazines.

"Okay. Let's go talk to her." Xander was psyched.

"The last Suzania knew, she lived in San Francisco. And that matches the last biographical information I see here."

"Okay. Let's get going."

My stare was my only response.

"You don't have anything holding you in Atlantic City right now, do you? All you do is check the newsfeed on your phone to see how storm Frieda is progressing. The same phone, I might mention, on which you can call your fiancé from anywhere in the country and on which he can reach you anywhere you go."

"Andy."

"I remember his name. Now. You do understand that you could actually place a call *to* Andy. This is the twenty-first century now, isn't it? Women call men, especially if they are engaged to them."

"Let me explain why I don't call or text him. He is busy. He's involved in dangerous work down there. Okay, maybe not dangerous, but tricky given the weather conditions. I don't know *what* he is doing *when*. Picture him on a ladder in hurricane-force winds."

"Why would he be on a ladder in hurricane-force winds? That seems rather reckless, don't you think?"

My stare silenced him.

"A shutter has broken loose. The winds threaten to tear it off the building making it a lethal weapon."

"Yes, but if everyone stays inside."

Again, my stare silenced him.

"That's not actually your point, is it? Continue."

"He's on the ladder. The phone rings or beeps. Whatever. The notification startles him. He falls off the ladder to the stone patio below."

"Really? You believe a ringing phone, or a simple beep, would rattle him that much?"

"Or worse. Suppose he decides he can respond. He reaches for the phone. In the rain, it slips from his hand. He stretches to catch it and loses his balance."

"I get it. And, falls to his death on the stone patio below." Xander frowned at me. "You are obviously a glass-half-empty type, aren't you?" He shook his head to indicate his disapproval but hadn't finished with his arguments. "If I agree that you are right not to call him, it remains that he can reach you anywhere. Anywhere."

I felt a little bit of the Xander charm working on me, but mostly his logic. I couldn't help Andy. All I could do was keep busy. I did, however, have other concerns. "I can't imagine how much a ticket to San Francisco will cost last minute."

"You're adorable sometimes. I don't fly commercial. You'll enjoy the trip in a private plane, won't you? When was the last time you flew to San Francisco in a corporate jet?"

I tried to recall the last occasion Business took me there, let alone Coach.

"I'll make a call. We can leave the car at the airport. I suspect it will be safe."

"We have to pack."

"Again, you're adorable. We should be able to make it back and forth in twenty-four hours, but if we don't, we can have our hotel room stocked. You, of all people, should understand that."

"Rooms." I emphasized the s. "But I'm hard to fit." I reacted not to the extravagance of the gesture, but the practicality. "Besides, we can't arrive at Faye Padilla's door without doing our homework."

Xander shuddered. "I hate homework."

"Let's call it background then. We have to make a trip to the library and learn as much as we can, so we can approach Faye with relevant questions to ask."

"Why do we have to go to the library?"

"To read what she has written."

"You can't do that on your phone?" he asked.

"Library."

Something in my tone made him give in. "Okay."

"And I want to learn about that Miss America Pageant and what kids like Sally were doing in 1968."

"Why?"

"So we can ask informed questions."

"We can check all that online while we're in the air."

"We can do that too," I explained and went on to extol the virtue of newspapers and their ability to give you the full picture.

"Won't someone at the library bring them to you?"

"You don't have to come with me, but it is what . . . ."

"I know, *ordinary people do*. Well then, going to the library makes sense, doesn't it?"

I kept selling past the close. "I like to see research as an adventure, like a trip to 1968."

"I always wanted to time travel." He opened those big eyes wide. "And 1968! What a year to be a rock star."

I couldn't think of a bad year to be a rock star.

"I'd love to go to 1968."

Sold. "Well, now is your chance."

I set off for the Atlantic City Library with Xander, I mean Rex, beside me. His phone buzzed but he didn't make a move towards whatever pocket he'd stashed it in.

"Trying to quit?" I asked.

"Told friends and relatives, I'd be out of touch for a spell. Part of the plan to be ordinary."

"Ordinary people stare at their phones constantly."

"But they have ordinary people on the other end. I don't know any ordinary people. Anyone I know isn't ordinary because they know me, and I give them extraordinary experiences. Do you see my point?" As usual, Xander didn't expect an answer. He stared out the window as I drove us through the Atlantic City that was not all about gambling and good-times, the part of town that couldn't hide its economic woes. I was surprised he actually absorbed the scene. "There must be a lot of people who work nights in this town."

"If they are lucky enough to have jobs." I followed his gaze and saw a lot of people who looked as if they didn't have much to do. Like work.

"I've heard things can be rough for ordinary people." Xander's expression turned thoughtful, even sad.

"Atlantic City suffers not only from the vagaries of the world economy, but from the fate of the gambling industry in New Jersey. This city has had more than its share of ups and downs," I explained.

"Times change." Xander grew pensive.

"Let me show you around before we hit the library."

I drove him to the Inlet at the north end of Absecon Island, so he could see how times had changed in Atlantic City.

"Such hope gone wrong." He eyed the flattened lots and lone buildings standing on full city blocks. "I assume the plan was to build on all this open space."

"My assumption too. The city thought casinos would bring about more change. Positive change."

When we got to the library, I explained my suspicion that the wide variety of people searching on the computers, and there were a lot of them, was an indication of tough times.

"Job seekers?" He asked.

I couldn't be certain but wouldn't have been surprised. No one was reading old newspaper articles. I encountered no competition for the microfilm reader. I tried to impart my enthusiasm for old newspapers to the rocker, without success. His eyes kept wandering to the computer terminals.

"You don't have to stay with me. You might want to tour around. I'll be here for a while," I explained to Xander.

"I'm going to take a walk-about, check things out, observe."

"You might want to put on your fake glasses, but if not, try to avoid your wide-eyed expression. Pursing your lips wouldn't hurt either," I whispered. "People might recognize you. Even in your disguise."

I watched Xander meander through the library, glancing over shoulders, seeing what people were up to. No one looked twice at the guy in the ill-fitting Bermuda shorts, oversized shirt and baseball cap. I shuddered to think what pandemonium would ensue if he doffed that cap and let his hair explode into its signature tangled mass of curls. I knew Xander wouldn't make that mistake, but there were dozens of other ways he could betray his true identity. Hoping he didn't, I left Xander in the twenty-first century and headed for 1968.

My preference was to check out original newspapers—okay, original newspapers on microfilm—not only for coverage of the event but to drink in the world the victim lived in. What were people watching on television? Seeing at the movies? What were the hot topics on their lips? It would all be there in copies of the *Atlantic City Press* from 1968. At least, I am sure it would have been. I'd printed out one story about the protests when I heard the commotion.

Chapter 11

"I warned you to control that wide-eyed look. It's a dead giveaway." Xander protested. "I couldn't help myself. Some of the stories I heard were shocking, appalling actually."

We had taken refuge in the glass-walled office housing the Heston Collection where an exceedingly kind librarian had offered us shelter, creating a zoo of sorts where we were on display for interested patrons. And, there were a couple dozen or more. Two security guards stayed close in case a need arose to keep the crowd in check, but couldn't stop people from staring.

"How are we going to get out of here?" I sounded frustrated because I was.

"Don't blame me. You're the one who insisted we come here. I was simply honoring your wishes, now, wasn't I? I can't be blamed for this ruckus. I was in disguise, mingling, getting acquainted with ordinary people and maybe letting my eyes get a little round at some of the stories I was hearing when I met this guy. He kept saying I looked like Xander Frost but he knew I couldn't be because Xander Frost would never come into a library. Because a rock star didn't have to know anything. Because he could just go through life as an idiot. And Xander Frost was obviously an idiot. That's when I told him. I had no choice really. I had to convince him that I was not an idiot, now didn't I? So, I confessed who I was and asked him to keep my secret. And he did. For a bit. I was talking to people, ordinary people, and their lives are so difficult. I couldn't help myself. My eyes were opening wider and wider because some of the stories I heard were heartbreaking. And then I hear the guy who said he wouldn't tell a soul, telling all the souls within hearing distance. 'That's Xander Frost you're telling your story to.' The crowd just grew and grew."

That crowd was now milling around outside the office. "We have to get out of here. We are disrupting things." I was sure we were trying the librarian's patience.

"I don't understand all the fuss. Lots of celebs come to Atlantic City."

"But I don't think a lot of them sit around the library having long conversations which, although pleasant, tends to attract the patrons' attention and disrupt library operations."

"Again, not my fault." He waved a finger in my direction. "The problem got worse when school let out. I couldn't expect that word I was in the building would spread amongst my fan base, now could I? Certainly that was not my fault. I guess we should go back to the hotel."

"We can't go right back to the hotel or they will follow, and we'll have groupies hanging around in the lobby."

"No, no." He protested. "I can put my sunglasses on. See. No eyes at all."

I shook my head. "Too late. We need another plan."

But we didn't, because several policemen came to guide us to our car. They formed a cordon around us as we made our way out of the library and across the parking lot. By the time we got close to the inconspicuous rented vehicle, a small crowd had closed in again.

One kind cop, C. Smythe according to the patch on his chest took my arm and guided me past the bland rental. "No one would ever suspect a rock star had arrived in *that*. Keep walking." He made a call on the radio before he continued. "You won't be able to drive away from here. Don't let on that is your car. Leave it for now and come with us." And with that a police cruiser pulled to a halt in front of us and Officer Smythe helped Xander and me into the back seat.

"Guess you two never found yourselves in the back of a police car before, right?" In the front seat, Smythe laughed. Neither Xander nor I answered, if you didn't count our weak smiles. I'd been in a few but Xander had probably been in more cop cars than the officer had.

"So, where to?" The driver turned and smiled. "I'd love to invite you to ride along on our shift but my boss wouldn't like that. My daughter will be so disappointed. She is a huge fan. Huge. I recognized you from the poster in her room. I cannot wait to tell her I met you. Now, where can we take you?"

Xander suggested it might not be against the rules if he rode along at least to the policeman's house where he could surprise his daughter.

Del met us there in a long, white limo and dropped me three blocks from the library so no one would connect me with the flashy vehicle. I walked back to the library, but my zeal for research was gone—especially on a good beach day. I was considering my options for the rest of the afternoon as I pulled into the Artistical lot. But as I climbed out of the car, I found the limo was back. Xander threw the door open. "I found Lou Blair."

I climbed in next to him. "Our Lou Blair?"

He answered with an exaggerated nod. "I expect so."

"How?"

"Research." He beamed.

"Yes, but how did you find him so quickly? I only left you half an hour ago." I glanced at my phone. "Not even."

He made a sheepish, shrug-like action and turned his back to the window.

"How?"

"I admire your detailed approach to research, but you, yourself, said you were not a professional with access to professional sources, so I made a few calls."

I wasn't mad. I wasn't surprised. My only reaction was curiosity. Where was Lou Blair?

"Have you eaten?" He didn't wait for me to answer. "I haven't had a thing since breakfast. We can pick up some lunch and then head down to Cape May."

"Lou Blair is in Cape May?"

Before I could ask more questions, my phone rang. I answered with an anxious hello.

The voice on the other end was equally anxious. "Can you hear me?"

72

"Andy. Yes. Talk. Tell me how you are. Quick before I lose you."

"Still waiting for Frieda. We're as ready as we can be. It doesn't sound like she is going to veer off course and sideswipe us. We're going to take a hit."

I felt my stomach do a flip. "Where will you hide?"

"We'll all go into the safe room when it hits. That's the big conference room. Internal with buffer internal rooms on every side. We've got food and water. We'll be fine. "

"And that's a safe place?"

"Sure." He fumbled the one word. We both knew there were no safe places in a storm like the one Frieda had become.

"Want to go to Facetime?" I asked.

"I need to save my battery but just for a quick kiss." Looking rugged and windblown and excited by his situation, Andy appeared on my screen and threw a kiss. I threw one back. A quick one. I wanted him to have every ounce of power he needed. I didn't want to waste battery time on a long fake kiss and certainly not on Xander who stuck his head into the shot to go cheek-to-cheek with me. "Hope you are weathering the storm but, even better, keeping that evil storm at sea."

"I'm sorry. I don't recognize…." Andy's tone was not as apologetic as his words.

"It's me. Xander. I guess Meg told you she and I spent yesterday together."

"Another phenomenon of being an ordinary person." I spoke to Xander. "Mentioning I ran into you was not my top priority." I turned my attention to Andy. "I ran into Xander Frost. He is researching what it is like to be an ordinary person. Like me. Or you. I'm advising him."

Xander pulled the phone close. "I remember you. You wouldn't let my pusher into the hotel elevator in the Bahamas last year."

"Yeah, well…." Andy fought to find polite words, but Xander didn't wait.

"Not to worry. Best thing that ever happened to me that was. I enjoyed being straight that weekend—aside from the headaches and the nausea. Never would have thought to try it, but now I've been clean and sober, well clean, for seven months. I owe you. That's why I am happy I didn't sleep with your woman."

"I didn't offer." I nudged Xander out of the picture.

"Meg and I are working on a case," Xander yelled.

"A case?"

Andy appeared more worried about the possibility that I was sharing my investigative skills than my romantic talents. I was mumbling something like "not a real case" but Andy probably could not hear me over Xander's roar.

"Don't sound so shocked. I can help with a case. I played a detective in *Hidden Mystery*. Did you see it?"

Andy dodged the question. "Real detective work isn't that interesting, Xander."

"I found that out today, I did. So far we've talked to two older ladies and gone to the library. But we are just getting started."

"Well, good luck. Can I speak to Meg, privately?"

"I understand. A little love talk, eh? I'll just put on my earphones, I will. Lovely getting to say hello." He slid on oversized headphones and lost himself in whatever he was listening to now that he had sworn off music.

"Meg, Maggie, sweetie. What is he talking about?"

"Nothing. We had a conversation with a woman who had seen me on television and she asked me to see if I could find any news about her sister."

He ignored the case and addressed the topic of Xander. "Does he understand that you're engaged?"

"Trust me. That is not a concern. No interest."

"On your part or his?"

"I would say the lack of feeling is mutual. To Xander, a woman in her thirties might as well be his grandmother."

"I hope so. I can't get away to challenge him to a duel."

"Trust me. Not needed."

"Good. I've got to get back to work." But he didn't hang up. "I don't trust that guy."

"He's morphing into a new person before my eyes."

"Right. He's still self-centered enough to use our limited phone time.

74

Explain to Xander why his assistance is not required."

"I will. You take care."

Andy promised and I knew he would be careful, in his way. His way, solving every problem that popped up, did not make me feel particularly comfortable.

"So, are we ready to go?" Xander pulled off his headphones the second my finger terminated the call.

"I'm not sure I feel comfortable approaching a man who might be the wrong Lou Blair."

"He's not the wrong Lou Blair. Trust me. Trust my source."

"And your source is…?"

"Confidential." He held up a hand to forestall any questions. "Del, take us to the White House." He turned to me. "My source tells me they make the best hoagies in town."

"I knew that." And, that I sounded like a three-year-old.

Chapter 12

"So was Andy jealous I was here?" Xander asked as we headed down the Garden State Parkway in search of Lou Blair. He had finished off his sandwich before we left Absecon Island. I was still working on mine twenty-five miles later as we passed Exit 13. Xander had to wait for my answer while I chewed.

"Why would Andy be jealous?" Expecting more grilling, I took a tiny bite.

"Well, I am rather well-known for my sexual prowess. No bragging here. It's a fact, now isn't it? Almost a joke in the press, which can be quite painful sometimes. I am so much more than an impressive sexual partner." He paused. "Maybe that is how Sally felt about the Miss America Pageant. Women are so much more than their sex appeal. I've always seen that." Luckily, he didn't expect me to comment on what I perceived to be a blatant lie, or maybe an incredible lack of self-perception. "Your man probably thought you'd be interested. I wasn't sure about the rules of your relationship."

"Rex." The way I spoke the name Rex, it sounded more like "Xa-Rex," but I'd get used to it. "Rex, that is none of your business. It's none of Xander's either." Nor of Del's. I wasn't convinced he couldn't hear the chatter in the back of the limo despite the glass partition.

"How many men have you slept with?"

I frowned.

"I don't mean to pry. I want to learn what ordinary people do. For example, how many men have you slept with so far this year?"

"All you need to know is that I have had one boyfriend for six years now." I quickly took another bite to end the conversation.

Xander missed the cue. "So?" He asked, his expression pure innocence.

"So, for most, admittedly not all, ordinary people, there is a correlation between the term boyfriend and the number of lovers. How many women have you slept with?"

"I have no idea." He grew uncomfortable, almost shy, an emotion I never detected in Xander. "Just to be sure, I have to ask. Did we ever?" He completed the thought with a descriptive gesture.

"Xander. Look at me. Do you honestly believe *we* ever?" I returned the descriptive gesture.

"I mean you're lovely, of course, but you're not exactly what I would call my type, now are you? I admire this kind of *I don't give a damn look* you've got going, but I usually go for more hair, more makeup…less age. Except for…." He named a well-known movie star.

I knew it! They had denied it, but a concierge sees all. I didn't react.

"Still, my tastes are quite catholic so I can never be sure."

"I realize this is probably puzzling to you, Xander, but, trust me, you can be absolutely sure."

"We never had even one night of love?" He sounded doubtful.

"No."

"Daytime? I'd like that. Were we in the sea? On the beach?"

"We were nowhere." I had blotted out the memory of the moment he did make a sort of half-hearted offer, or at least provide an opening for me to pursue him. Given his condition that night, I didn't worry he would remember. "It never happened."

"Really?" In the one word, he revealed he was both perplexed and reflective. He gave the news careful consideration.

"If you want to be an ordinary guy, believe it. A lot of women say *no* to ordinary guys."

He sat with his lips pursed, lost in thought. "That would be different, wouldn't it? Right now, I am kind of everyone's type. I mean not the way I am dressed today, but in my normal attire." Normal for him meant tight faux leather pants barely hanging onto his hips and flowing silk shirts open to the waist. Offstage. Onstage he preferred spandex. Both styles sent a clear message that most women he encountered understood. "I mean you've probably seen photos of me—I'm in all the newspapers, online, on telly, all the time—with lovely young girls. Very often more than one."

I didn't tell him that because housekeeping had once misinformed me, saying his suite was empty and ready for inspection, I could testify to his ability to handle multiple partners based on personal observation. He hadn't noticed my accidental intrusion then, and I wasn't going to confess now.

Xander grew thoughtful, briefly. "A woman might have rejected me once or twice, because she was too high or feeling sick, but that didn't matter because I always found another one right beside her or at least waiting in the wings. I suspect you assume I behave badly, but I never do. Believe me, my manager and my lawyer have reviewed the rules of engagement with me more times than I care to remember."

Okay, not the highest of motives but at least he knew and adhered to the rules.

"You must have experienced some form of rejection in life. You weren't born a superstar."

"I was a child star in Akron. Local but famous and then we moved to the UK. I hit right away. So, I can barely remember a time before I was a superstar. I only remember being the phenomenon I am today."

I doubted any man who referred to himself as a phenomenon was going to take to life as an ordinary person, but I didn't challenge him. I took a bigger bite of my hoagie.

For the rest of the ride he maintained the appearance of contemplating the scenery, but I suspected he was contemplating his future and reconsidering his desire to be an ordinary guy. I was reconsidering if I could finish the oversized sandwich.

"Ordinary houses are lovely," Xander proclaimed when we pulled up in front of a beautifully maintained Victorian on a tree-lined Cape May street.

"I swear to you this is not an ordinary house, or an ordinary town. We are in a historic district. What you are looking at is called a painted lady. Notice how all the different colors highlight the detailed work."

"Oh yes. My source told me we would find beautiful Victorian architecture in Cape May. The street looks very All American to me. Ordinary."

I didn't argue the merits of the building itself. "Check out the view when we get to the front door. I would be surprised if Lou can't see the Atlantic Ocean from his porch."

Xander did as I suggested but protested that only a sliver of the ocean was visible and only through the trees.

"Cape May's beauty is enhanced by the Atlantic Ocean. It doesn't need a waterfront to maintain its status on any top ten list of prettiest towns. Having its ocean view obstructed by trees does not make this home ordinary."

Xander surveyed the area but didn't indicate any agreement. "I've seen towns like this in old movies."

"Yes. Movies. Sets. Idyllic locations. Not ordinary. Are you going to be Rex or Xander?" I asked as I raised my hand to knock. "Xander works well for this purpose. I'm not worried you will draw a crowd in Lou's living room. Besides I suspect the limo is pretty much a dead giveaway."

Or would have been if anyone had been around.

"Maybe they went out to dinner. It is about that time. Although he does run a store and his website says it's open tonight." I peeked through a window into a comfortably decorated living room and saw no signs of life.

"Probably at work. Let's go." Xander headed down the stairs.

"No. We don't want to catch him while he is distracted unless we're forced to. Let's wait and try catching him here before we go to his shop, where he would feel obligated to defer to customers." And where his customers, if they recognized Xander, could jeopardize our entire operation.

"Well, sitting on this porch won't help our investigation." Xander was right.

"Maybe we can gather information from another source. Would Rex or Xander like to meet some of my friends?"

"We both would."

Chapter 13

I directed Del through historic Cape May to the Parsonage Bed and Breakfast, where he insisted on waiting with the car.

Xander and I headed to the front door of the large Victorian painted in the bright colors of the era. "This is not even a private home. It's a B&B. So don't go calling it ordinary."

When we knocked, the door was answered immediately by a man whose excitement indicated he had been standing in the hallway for the last few years waiting for my return.

"She's here, Claude," George called. "She's here."

It wasn't easy to rouse Claude from his comfortable chair, but he arrived in the hallway with atypical speed, iPad still in hand, perhaps anticipating the unexpected resurrection of Princess Diana of Wales. George released me from a tight hug only so Claude could offer a light one.

"Claude. George. This is my friend who wants to be known as ordinary guy, Rex, Xander Frost."

Claude didn't recognize Xander, but George provided him with a reasonable explanation about his celebrity. Xander appeared annoyed by both the need for an explanation and the insufficiently laudatory description, but George did hit all the high points. I trusted eventually the couple's charm would win Xander over.

"So, what brings you two to Cape May?" George asked but by the time he'd finished the question, he didn't care if he got an answer. He had spotted my ring. "Oh my God, oh my God!" he screeched. "Did Andy pick that?" His tone added *I didn't think Andy was capable of picking something so appropriate.*

"All by himself."

"Well, come sit in the drawing room and tell us all about it." George led the way.

I felt certain Xander was a bit surprised to find he'd lost his position as the center of attention so quickly. He trailed us into the Victorian wonderland. He found a seat in a deep chair with a high back while George and I sat together on the couch. Claude, of course, returned to the easy chair where, as far as I knew, he spent ninety percent of his waking hours.

"Wait. Not that I am not dying to hear your story, *but* we must have a toast. Do not say a word until I return." George vanished into the hallway, but seconds later stuck his head back around the corner. "You can discuss the world situation or such but nothing about Andy and your wedding."

Claude and Xander engaged in what I considered typical get-to-know-you chit-chat that threw Xander. I imagined it had been a long time since someone had asked Xander what he did for a living. George's return ended a discussion of tour logistics when he burst in with a silver tray topped with a bottle of champagne and four glasses.

I told George the basics of our engagement and he was off and running. "We will do the wedding. We'll do it here. In the garden."

"You should have known better than to break the news to George before every detail was planned." Claude offered no sympathy.

"I'm doing the music." Xander leaned forward in his seat and jockeyed for position in the conversation and the wedding ceremony.

"All three of you are getting ahead of Andy and me. We haven't talked about a wedding."

George stared at me as if I'd said something outrageous.

"We didn't have much time. We had two days together and then he had to go back to the Bahamas because of Hurricane Frieda. They evacuated most of the guests, so no one needed me there. I am on an extended vacation."

"Giving you time for wedding planning." George's tone implied tsk-tsk. "What have you been thinking?"

"I haven't been actually."

"Girl, what is wrong with you? We are going dress shopping. I don't see you in a mermaid, but maybe a fit and flare. No. Wait. Grecian draping. Something sophisticated. What do you think, Claude?"

Clearly, Claude did not think about wedding gowns.

"At least, *you* came by to tell us." George chided Andy in absentia.

"Andy wanted us to visit together so we could make the announcement. I hope he isn't annoyed I came alone."

Beside me, Xander cleared his throat, but I ignored him.

"We will plan a celebratory dinner when Andy can be here. I didn't want to wait because I actually have a favor to ask. We are searching for information for the project Xander and I are working on."

"And what does this project involve?" George's disappointment was replaced by anticipation. He turned to Xander. "Adventure is Meg's middle name."

Xander didn't have to utter a word to indicate his skepticism. His sneer did.

"Nothing exciting. We're simply trying to locate someone." I downplayed the excitement potential.

Xander jumped back into the conversation with a synopsis of Marianne Dulles's problem.

I handled the explanation for our visit to Cape May. "We suspect the Lou Blair who runs The Wild Potter once knew the woman we are trying to locate. A long time ago. *Knew* her a long time ago. Are you familiar with him?"

George glanced at Claude.

"He's become quite respectable. He has nothing to hide. No need to rehash old issues. Why do you want to know?" Claude asked.

"We're just trying to locate his old girlfriend." I tried to minimize the intrigue—unsuccessfully.

The two exchanged another look.

George spoke as if there were no free will at his disposal. "We have to tell. He has been a perfect citizen for decades now, but he was involved in a little controversy a few years back."

I felt a surge of excitement that matched the look on Xander's face.

"Fifteen, maybe twenty years." Claude clarified. "One of his girlfriends disappeared, but it turned out she had simply left him."

"Or so the police say." George's distorted features said he wasn't buying their story.

Claude had a special exasperated face for responding to George's more exotic claims. He used it now. "Why would they lie?"

George gave a big theatrical shrug designed to ask why not, before turning to me. "She had to sneak away because she was afraid. He used to drink and get a little violent." George accompanied the information with drinking and punching mime.

"We haven't heard a bad word about him in years," Claude countered.

But Xander and I weren't interested in recent history. We were interested in what Lou Blair was like years ago. And *what he was like* wasn't good.

"How did you find out all this?" Xander asked.

"The poor girl would be seen around town with bruises occasionally. She tried to hide them and we tried not to notice, but those contusions weren't her real problem. She was horrified at what he did, of course, but she was more frightened of what he might do. So she just up and disappeared. Never came back."

"That is hearsay," Claude interrupted.

"I've never seen her since. But I did see the bruises back then. That part is not hearsay." George countered.

"So how do you know she actually left town?" I asked, expecting the worst.

"She finally got in touch with the police, but she left old Lou swinging in the breeze there for a while. Everyone in town figured he murdered her. Some people, those who haven't seen her with their own eyes, still do." Claude tilted his head towards George.

Chapter 14

"Well, that was easy. Clearly, Lou did it." Xander relaxed into the plush limo seat.

"We cannot reasonably conclude that." Although agreeing with Xander's conclusion was tempting. And, I reminded him, "We are not even certain there is an *it*."

"Oh, there's an *it*, all right, there is. I can feel it."

"Well, try not to be accusatory when we meet Lou. Innocent until proven guilty."

Xander managed only a harrumph in response.

We circled back to the Blair house and found no signs of life. "Looks like we'll have to stop by his shop." I wasn't happy but saw a store visit as our only choice. We'd spent enough time hoping he'd come home.

"Picturesque, not ordinary," I explained to Xander as we walked down the pedestrian mall that is the commercial heart of Cape May. Though not packed to July-weekend levels, the walkway hosted a jovial group of fall visitors.

"People gathering and mingling." Xander stated the obvious, then got lost in thought as if about to solve an equation that had stumped math geniuses for generations.

The Wild Potter occupied the first floor of one of the more nondescript buildings on the walkway. The decorative items in the window accounted for its charm. We'd hardly passed through the front door before Xander found himself entangled in a plant hanger dangling from the ceiling.

"What is this?" He pulled his arm free as if recoiling from a snake.

"Macramé. Big in the seventies."

Xander stepped back and launched a wind chime concert with his head. The sounds blended nicely with the New Age tones coming through the store's speakers. I, who had managed to get into the building unscathed, surveyed the business. Lou Blair stocked some small pieces for the tourist trade, but the bulk of his inventory was original paintings, hand-crafted wall-hangings and handmade pieces of pottery, a limited number with abstract patterns but most with sand or sea motifs.

We didn't find any customers, but we did find a twenty-something woman with a young child on her hip. If it weren't for the big rock on her ring finger, the woman could have been Sally Johnson wandered in from Woodstock. She wasn't the only thing that suggested Woodstock. The whole store could have been transported from 1969.

I explained we were looking for Lou Blair.

"You want my husband." She responded to our inquiry with a sweet smile.

"Lou." She called into the storage area behind beaded curtains. "You have visitors."

Based on the photo Marianne had provided and my own prejudices, I had a clear mental vision of an older Lou Blair. His appearance turned out to be exactly what I expected and a perfect match for the store he ran. With his hair still in a ponytail, but now gray and starting a lot farther back on his head, he wasn't unattractive and did not appear fatigued by the responsibilities of being a husband to a woman forty years his junior and a father to a young child. If I hadn't seen his picture showing how beautiful he was as a young man, it wouldn't have made me sad to consider the changes time had wrought. He remained a handsome man.

Based on the big smile he offered, Lou was happy to meet us. He had heard of Xander but wasn't familiar with his music. Classic rock and roll was his thing. Xander professed his love of classic bands, and I stood back and let their relationship get off to an auspicious start. I saw no sign that the connection weakened when Xander raised the topic of Sally Johnson.

"Man, that takes me way back. I know she left the area. Did she ever come back?"

Xander, ever the optimist about his own investigative talents, replied, "Not yet."

"I'm not surprised. That family. Man, they were the pits. I guess the parents must be dead. They were dead when they were alive. Or so I heard. I wasn't exactly welcome at their house. Not their type. I was not surprised Sally felt the need to get out of Dodge. That sister of hers raised quite a ruckus, but I didn't believe anything bad had happened to her. I just figured she split. She needed to escape from that Goldwater Republican family of hers."

"Were there problems at home?" Xander led the questioning.

"Not as long as she kept her mouth shut and that is what she did. She had the guts to live the way she wanted, but only out of the sight of the parental units. As far as her mother and father knew, the youth movement was just a fashion trend for their little Sally. They didn't like her new clothes but they thought they were lucky they had a daughter who didn't smoke pot and have sex out of wedlock."

"And they had one?" I asked.

"They did. One, but it wasn't Sally." He chuckled. "The other one."

"Marianne," I offered.

"If you say so. The younger one. She was a real drip. Liked things— the family, the world—the way they were. Didn't mind the government sending boys over to die in Southeast Asia."

"Very different from Sally." Xander spoke to himself more than Lou.

"Couldn't be more different. I heard a lot but only met her once. She and that dweeb boyfriend of hers came to visit Sally. Lasted about an hour on our commune. I realize I sound cruel, but . . ." A phrase frequently used by the judgmental. "I would be shocked if either of them have experienced one iota of change in the last fifty years."

I suspected he was right so I couldn't defend the Dulleses, but neither did I confirm his suspicions.

"Sally felt sad Marianne wouldn't break away from life in Ventnor. Sally hoped to experience all that life had to offer and she wanted the same for her little sister." He glanced at the front of the store where his wife was entertaining their baby by playing "Three Blind Mice" on the wind chimes that had entrapped Xander. He lowered his voice, almost imperceptibly. "That girl broke my heart. We called her Sunshine and the name fit, and not just because she was beautiful, although she was. She was a little ray of sunshine in everyone's day. She was special." His tone changed from sentimental to defensive. "But don't think my feelings for her were superficial. We went through a lot together. You aren't old enough to remember 1968, a horrible year. We lived through two assassinations within three months. Martin Luther King in April and Bobby Kennedy in June. When Bobby was shot, I drove through the night to be with her in Ventnor. I was there when he died. I did the same thing when things got crazy at the Democratic Convention in Chicago. We watched together. We shared all of that. I couldn't believe she could toss all that over for a beauty pageant protest."

Before I could speak up, Xander was in Lou's face. "Do you still not understand that the aim of the protest was much bigger than closing down a single beauty contest?"

I was surprised Xander understood.

"That protest marked a very significant moment in the history of feminism. Those protesting women felt that unrealistic standards of beauty oppressed women. Women did not need to be physically perfect to be valued. Women are real, multi-faceted human beings, not fantasy figures. Come on, mate. You know that now, but I bet you didn't back in the day. Someone needed to teach you. You should have seen that her involvement in the protest was not a rejection of what you taught her, but a reflection of what you two learned together. You wanted to be the teacher. And you were good. Look at how you expanded her world. She took what you taught her and applied all that sensitivity to the broader issues she felt the Miss America pageant represented. You should have let her teach you, man. You should have welcomed, taken pride, in the changes in her."

Lou seemed stunned by Xander's words. I know I was.

"Given the perspective of age, I can see why I resisted change in Sunshine." Lou stuttered through the first few words of his defense before his voice grew firm. "She was so soft and lovely like those sixties girls were.

By the end of our time together, however, she was turning into one of those seventies women. You know the stereotypical libber kind. Shrill. Strident. I wasn't what I would call enlightened back then, so our relationship wouldn't have survived even if the shot I took at changing her back had succeeded."

"Changing her back? From being shrill?" Xander asked.

"From playing for the other team. To tell you the truth, I wasn't convinced she was a lesbian. I felt she didn't understand what she was, who she was. Every movement, every trend, every style that came down the pike, she tried on for size. That's what she did with me. Tried the anti-war movement on. She was sincere but peace protests never turned her on the way the women's movement did—and I suspect that was because someone in the women's movement turned her on more than I did."

"She left you for a woman?" Xander asked.

"She never said that, but she fell under the spell of some feminist type who came down to protest with the New Yorkers, but she was from San Francisco. Got under Sunshine's skin in only one day. Crazy, yeah? I figured the attraction must have been sexual. Could have been intellectual. There were times I felt Sunshine was more interested in my brain than in my body. Even though you must find it hard to believe it seeing me now, that didn't happen much, back in the day."

Not hard for me who had marveled at his youthful beauty in an aging, discolored photo.

"I assume the police talked to you when she left," I asked.

"Called me on the phone at school. Chatted. Nothing heavy duty, even though I was the jilted lover. If they suspected foul play, I would have expected them to be more suspicious of me. They concluded she ran off. I told them I thought so too. And that was it. One of them asked me if I had hurt her. As if I would have said yes to a cop about anything in those days."

"Did you hurt her?" I tried to keep my tone non-confrontational.

"No way. Never. No. Not Sunshine. No."

Xander interrupted Lou's string of denials. "When was the last time you saw her? Do you remember?"

"Oh yeah, I remember that last day. I was a complete jerk. Thought I knew her better than she knew herself. Simply did not understand how she could give a guy like me up. I'm not sure if my arrogance or my stupidity was more marked." He was shaking his head as he started his story.

Lou Blair
Atlantic City Boardwalk
September 7, 1968

Lou couldn't believe Sunshine was hanging with these women. They were so straight, in hairdos and clothes they could have worn in high school, and some of them hadn't seen the inside of a school in decades. Not a cool-looking chick in the crowd. Only Sunshine with her long hair, blond and silky, glistening in the sun. If any of these libber types had good bodies, he couldn't see them under prim skirts and blouses.

Sunshine was walking with them, carrying a sign claiming Women Are Not Meat. *He didn't understand what that meant, but she wasn't the only one carrying that message. She waved her placard in the air in the way he had taught her, marching up and down, chanting angry slogans until a woman pulled her out of line and leaned in close to whisper in her ear. Sunshine listened intently. Lou saw the woman wrap an arm around her waist and wondered if she was a lesbian. His father said most of these women's lib types were. He couldn't tell. He just thought they looked like dorks. Sunshine was too naïve to watch out for that type. She knew homosexuals existed, but he doubted she saw them as predators. He was wise to this woman's tricks.*

He tried to make Sunshine feel his gaze. That had always worked before, but she'd grown immune to his powers. As soon as she moved back into line, he stepped up to walk beside her.

"Never met a protest I didn't like."

"We don't need your help, if that's what you're thinking."

"Ladies only?"

"Men aren't welcome here. Male protestors are not needed. We were told not to talk to male reporters."

"What's your gripe anyway? These girls angry that they didn't win Miss Podunk, that they'll never win Miss Podunk? And trust me, you're the only one here with a shot at a title."

"Go away, Lou. You just don't get it."

He searched for teasing in her words but heard only annoyance that she tried to hide but couldn't.

A shout from behind offered a similar sentiment. "We don't want you here. We don't need you here."

He figured he'd better cut his losses, at least for the time being. "Can we get together later?"

"I'm going to be busy here and probably into the night."

He knew when he was being blown off, and Sunshine was definitely blowing him off. She was just too kind to be blunt.

"Where are you staying?" she asked.

He stared at her.

"I can't take you to my parents, but I can find you a place. Meet me back here at 10PM. I'll be here. I promise."

*****

"Was she?" I asked when it became clear he was not going to continue.

"I didn't wait until ten, like she told me. That probably made her mad. She blew me off again. Told me to meet her on the Boardwalk in front of her parents' house. She'd be there when the pageant was over. I waited there and she showed up after midnight. She was in a hurry. She could only spare a minute, but she had actually found me a place to sleep. She was like that."

"But not with her?" Xander asked.

"She was totally unresponsive to my charms. At least, what she used to see as my charms. I wasn't sure if the rejection was personal or because I was male. No matter. She wasn't buying my act. She had something big to do, but she made time to dump me. In my memory, it was a beautiful night. Maybe a little chilly, the way summer nights at the shore used to be, but not as chilly as she was. She told me she had changed. She wasn't going to be Sunshine anymore. She was Sarah. She tried to let me down easy, but I wasn't going quietly."

"Did you touch her?" I asked.

"Not after she rejected my first moves. Like I said, I wasn't so sure the rejection was personal."

"I didn't mean affectionately." I tread lightly. "I mean did you try to be physically persuasive."

"Not then but I did earlier, back on the Boardwalk, I didn't hit her or anything. Never would have. I grabbed her arm, which back then I didn't see as a big deal. I found out how wrong I was when a flock of clucking feminist hens descended on me. Truthfully just one, but I knew the rest of the group would jump in and help her. At any rate, she told me to let Sunshine go. I did. I wasn't going to mess with those women, especially the one Sunshine seemed to like so much. She had her arm around my girlfriend and the way Sunshine was leaning into her, I was afraid she was in love. Excuse me, not Sunshine. Sarah. Sarah was in love."

"Do you know the woman's name?" Xander asked.

"She didn't shave her legs, so I called her Hairy Harriett. Not out loud, of course. I may not have been enlightened, but I learned fast not to bring the wrath of those women down on me." He smiled, kind of a rueful expression. "Funny. Now, I'd probably like that woman, support her goals, but back then I didn't want to compete with her for my girlfriend."

"And the last time you saw Sunshine was at her parents?" I took over the questioning.

"On the Boardwalk near their house."

"Did you go stay in the place she found for you?"

He laughed. "I didn't want a place if she wasn't in it. I drove back to the farm I lived on in Pennsylvania."

"Alone?"

"Unfortunately, yes. I had no idea where Sunshine went."

"Did you ever try to contact her?"

He seemed reluctant to answer. "I did. I tried calling the Dulles house back then, but all they said—her father, mother, sister, whoever answered—was she didn't live there anymore. I got the one call I told you about from the cops and that confirmed the family's story. After that, I gave up."

"Did any of her friends hear from her?"

"We lived with a bunch of kids, but no one heard from her. Word on campus was she moved out west, but no one knew where. I have no idea about the source of the rumor. Like I said, I moved on, met someone new. I was in college. I wasn't going to pine away over some chick, but I never forgot. After my last big break-up, before I got married, I tried again. I mean who doesn't reminisce about old loves at a time like that. We all do. So, I did the regular stuff. Checked out social media, but I didn't find any sign of her."

So, he went out and found a girl who could be her twin. He didn't say that. I did.

Chapter 15

"Why do we have to leave so early? I'd barely gotten to bed before my alarm went off," I protested as I climbed into the limo. It might have been Xander's car, but, I could tell by his outfit, Rex was in the backseat. He was upbeat and cheerful. I missed Xander, the night owl, who did nothing but grunt until well after noon.

As Rex, he was full of explanations, but I didn't hear his rationale because my phone rang. "Andy."

"You sound so wide awake."

"I am." I offered no explanation. "Tell me about the storm. I haven't seen the news yet this morning."

If Andy found it odd that I had abandoned my post in front of my TV, he didn't mention it. "Frieda is still heading right for us. Moving slowly. Building force. Ocean is rough but the sky is beautiful. I wish you could see it. The contrast is gorgeous."

"When can I come back?"

"We can't say until after the storm passes. Even after it leaves here, you'll still have to worry about traveling through it to get here. I don't want you to take any chances."

"I wouldn't do that."

"Tell lover boy I said hello," Xander called.

"And that is. . .?"

"Xander."

"Xander?" Andy did not sound amused. "Tell him you don't work at that property and are not required to cater to his needs, especially at the crack of dawn."

93

"It's okay." I didn't want to elaborate.

"Doesn't your sweetie want to say hello to me?" Xander asked.

"Andy says hello."

"No, I didn't. Tell him not to bother you. You're not getting paid. You don't need to waste personal time taking care of his bizarre requests."

With Xander listening, I didn't think the time was right to fill Andy in on Xander's miraculous transformation.

"Look, I'll check in later. I've got to go walk the property. Take care. And tell Xander to stop bugging you. Love you."

"Back at you," I said.

Andy hung up. I panicked. What if something catastrophic happened? Those would be the last words he heard from me. I typed a quick text. I LOVE YOU TOO. Andy, the romantic, sent a thumbs up emoji back.

My boss, the owner of all Artistical properties, sometimes shuttled his employees from one to another in one of the small jets we jokingly called Air Bingo. So, I knew my way around the Atlantic City airport. My knowledge wasn't required, however, because the limo stopped beside a Gulfstream model I recognized, not from personal travel experiences, but from meeting celebrity guests in Nassau.

"We'll be in and out of San Francisco by 5PM Pacific Time. We do our business, grab a bite to eat, and sleep on the way back. You won't even realize you went out of town."

I found it hard to see Xander as Rex when he was operating as the master of a private jet, chatting with the pilot, charming the flight attendant. "Not my own, but not bad, eh?" he asked when we reached our cruising altitude. "Thanks, babe." Xander, not Rex, took a drink from the flight attendant's hand and stretched out on a leather couch not only as if he owned the plane, but the world. "So, let's get to work. Faye Padilla lives above the Haight. Nice place." He not only knew the address, he knew the room count, the most recent selling price and that the countertops in the kitchen were granite.

"And you know this because?"

"My source."

"Does your source have a name?"

"Yes. Of course, he has a name, but I am not sure I should share it with you."

"Are we or are we not partners?"

"Of course, we are."

"So?"

"So what?"

"So, what is your source's name?"

He didn't want to say, but since we were in a small jet forty thousand feet up, he couldn't avoid me. "Peter. His name is Peter."

"Does he have a last name?"

"Of course."

"And that would be?"

"Bossow. Peter Bossow."

"I don't know him, but he did nice work for you. We'll be ready for Faye Padilla. No thanks to you and me. We didn't prepare well for this visit. I got a little information. I meant to do more when we got back from Cape May last night, but I was beat."

"And you had to catch up on your Weather Channel viewing," he teased.

I wouldn't acknowledge he was right. I stuck to business. "First encounters are important, and we only get one—if we get to see her. She might not be in town." I sounded like what my young self would have called an old fuddy-duddy but didn't seem able to shake the attitude.

"She's in town. I checked. At least my source did."

"You mean Peter Bossow checked."

"Yes." He glanced around the empty cabin as if someone might overhear.

"Do we have an appointment?"

"Not exactly. She is aware of us and our schedule. She plans to be in town."

"She could change her plans. People do."

"So, then we eat some fresh California produce, freshly-baked sourdough bread and top it all off with a nicely aged Napa Valley wine. What's the harm?"

Even the fuddy-duddy in me couldn't see any harm. I didn't have anything pressing to do. And cost was not a consideration. A plane to San Francisco in Xander's world was equal to a taxi to Ventnor in mine. Actually, more like a jitney from Atlantic City to Ventnor in mine.

Over freshly baked muffins, gourmet jam and my morning Coke, I filled him in on what I knew. "I bookmarked some of the articles she's published. I'll read them on the trip." I tried but I don't possess an academic's mind. One article and I fell asleep.

When the flight attendant woke me to tell me we were landing, Xander was peering out the window like a child searching for the Magic Kingdom on his first trip to Disneyland. "I was always so obsessed with what was going on around me, I never looked out the window before. At least after I turned thirteen. I always took the phrase *flyover states* literally. I spotted some intriguing things out this window while you were busy sleeping. The landscape was fascinating. So many geometric patterns. Now that I've seen the US from up here, I feel the need to experience what is down there. Maybe we should drive back."

"Xander, do you have any idea how many miles, how many hours, how many days, that would be?"

"I have all the time in the world."

"Then *you* drive back."

"You don't want to see the real America?"

"I have. Several times."

"Always changing, I'd wager. Don't you want to see the new USA?"

"I do, but I need to get back to Atlantic City."

"Why?"

I didn't have what I would have considered a good reason. Except one. "Because I want to."

96

Chapter 16

Faye Padilla lived in Haight Ashbury. Above it, actually. Away from the hustle and bustle of the intersection of the two famous streets, which, unless one noticed the corporate names, looked surprisingly similar to the scene shown in newsreels of its heyday in 1967. I cut Xander off before he could admire the lovely, ordinary house. "This would be a lovely townhouse in any location, but it is in one of the most expensive real estate markets in the country."

"I get it. Not ordinary."

"Hardly," I confirmed.

The driver Xander had retained agreed to circle until he found a parking space or we texted him, whichever came first. We climbed the wooden steps and knocked on the wood and glass door. I sneaked a look to my left through the bay window but gave no sign I saw the figure crossing the living room to greet us.

"Ms. Padilla. I am Meg Daniels." I took the lead. I didn't believe Xander's notoriety as a world class womanizer would help us here. I was wrong.

"And you are Xander Frost. I heard you would be in town and might be dropping by." Her eyes lit up. "Please come in."

Like Lou Blair in Cape May, Faye Padilla did not appear to have fully extricated herself from the sixties. Her clothes, all black, were sleek and modern, but her accessories suggested another time. What I could see of her furniture matched current standards, but the artwork on the tall walls, the books on the long shelves and the guitar leaning against the couch recalled earlier days when this living room might have served as headquarters for a variety of movements. I only knew about her role in women's rights, but her photos suggested she was no stranger to the anti-war and civil rights movements and the writers and musicians who supported them.

Photos of Faye with popular recording artists of the sixties and seventies suggested a fondness for the music world. I suspected that explained her focus on Xander. If not, I would have felt insulted that the feminist ignored the female investigator, which she did, making more than polite conversation with my musician companion.

"I met Sarah through the protests at the 1968 Miss America Pageant. I guess you weren't born then and with that accent, I suspect you are not familiar with the Miss America Pageant."

"Oddly enough, I just happened to be in Atlantic City for this year's pageant. A coincidence. I knew nothing of the whole Miss America phenomenon when I arrived in town, but the pageant was hard to miss. There is a big parade. We watched it." He nodded my way reminding Faye I was in the room. "But I realized there is a big inequity in that contest."

I knew where he was headed and tried to catch his eye to indicate ix-nay on what he viewed as the controversial alphabetical order issue.

Faye assumed he was headed in a different direction. "Inequality was just one of the issues we were protesting. The Miss Black America pageant was going on at the same time. We didn't steal their thunder on the race issue, but we still made it clear that we found it objectionable that no woman of color had ever worn, or even competed for, the crown, which was true in 1968. We had a lot of issues we cited, but our basic objection to Miss America was based on the organization's promotion of an unrealistic ideal American woman. I don't know about you, Ms. Daniels, but I have bulges, blemishes, and a belly that has taken on a life of its own."

The five-foot-seven woman, who must have weighed all of one hundred and ten pounds, was exaggerating her own flaws. I wasn't sure she was far off when it came to mine.

"The press tried to make light of us. Called us bra burners, although no bras were burned. Nothing was burned. We couldn't get a permit. We threw all sorts of items of female torture, I think we called them, into a Freedom Trash Can, but we couldn't light a fire on a wooden Boardwalk.

I understood that. We were exceedingly polite protestors—except for crowning a sheep. That was a bit theatrical, and I realize, now that I am wiser, probably upsetting to the sheep. For the most part, however, we walked in a circle, an oval really, and handed out our leaflets. The people heckling us were a lot louder than we were. I think the police were more worried about their behavior than ours."

"What exactly were items of female torture?" Xander asked.

"Anything related to the stereotype of the American woman. Girdles. High heels. Women's magazines. And household items. Detergent."

"With the exception of girdles, don't those things still torture women today? I mean, I go to award shows and I cannot imagine how those women walk in their shoes."

"You sound like you think our protest was a failure. We may not have gotten rid of high heels, but that protest marked a pivotal moment in the women's movement. We brought a lot of attention to our cause. We raised the consciousness of a lot people, not just women."

"And that was what happened to Sarah?" Xander handled the transition deftly.

"Yes. That is exactly what happened." She seemed happy to tell her story—to Xander.

Faye Padilla
Atlantic City Boardwalk
September 7, 1968

She perceived something otherworldly about the girl who called herself Sunshine. Faye could forgive the superficial hippie affectations, because she spotted nothing fake about the girl's sweetness. She radiated kindness. Faye concluded she was special as soon as she spotted her. She felt proud she was the one who convinced the girl to use her given name, Sarah. A strong name for a strong woman who demands to be taken seriously.

Faye saw the kid coming and enjoyed the expression on his face when he saw her holding his girlfriend's hand and stroking his girlfriend's hair. She was looking forward to his reaction. She expected a combination of macho posturing and childishness.

Sarah would never have a boyfriend like this jerk, but Sunshine certainly would. He was almost as beautiful as she was. Faye could have picked him out of a lineup without ever having seen them together. Long hair, silky and golden. Smug expression of a young stud who believed he could get any girl he wanted, but he only wanted the best. And Sarah was the best. Not that the kid understood why. He probably didn't realize how smart she was. He only saw long, lean limbs, perfectly-shaped features, and wide eyes that betrayed how eager she was to learn, to be manipulated. That was one thing she and the kid had in common. They both realized Sarah could be easily managed—at least if you had a new experience to offer.

She had sized him up earlier when he tried to horn in on the protest. This was a women's march. They didn't need male support. He had his issues to protest, issues they had in common. The war. Racism. Maybe they would welcome him over at Miss Black America, an event she admired for sticking it to the Miss America organization, even if it accomplished its goals through yet another archaic pageant based on beauty.

Faye could read the hippie, and she saw that he could read her. She pulled away from Sarah. Why cause her trouble? But when he nudged her aside as he grabbed Sarah, she reacted instinctively, breaking his grip with a hard blow to his arm. She wasn't surprised Sarah tried to play the peacemaker, but Faye wasn't so forgiving. The kid knew what he was doing when he bumped into her. She wasn't going to take that crap from a punk like him, and she wouldn't allow Sarah to either. She tried to place herself between the young woman and her boyfriend, but the kid pushed her back against the railing and pulled Sarah towards him. Faye was planning her next move but realized Sarah was taking care of the situation, of herself. Faye smiled. Golden boy was slinking away with his tail between his legs. She knew she had won.

*****

Judging by a facial expression resembling a cat's, one that had recently swallowed a canary, the thought still gave Faye pleasure.

"Were you and Sarah involved for a long time?" I asked.

"If you consider a couple of months a long time, and I suspect *you* might." She winked at Xander. When did activists take up winking? I never knew an activist who winked.

"I should have insisted she fly out with me, but she had an independent streak a mile wide. She came by bus. Bus! Insisted on paying her own way. Ridiculous. She was a mess when she got here but didn't want to talk about what had caused the change. She wasn't the cool, calm young girl I had met in Atlantic City. She wouldn't tell me what had happened, which doesn't exactly start a relationship off on the right foot. You know what else doesn't start a relationship off on a good foot?"

"Disease." Xander answered and then realized hers was a rhetorical question. Well, he realized after she explained that to him.

"Although disease was a good answer, the right one was pregnancy," Faye told him.

"Pregnancy?" This time I was the one with the inappropriate response. I yelped.

Faye seemed amused. "I take it no one on the home front knows. She would have done anything to keep the news from her father. She didn't want her sister to find out either, which was a shame because a sibling should have been the main source of support for her."

"We were not aware of this situation." Xander sounded calm and professional. "Did she ever share the identity of the father?"

"She wouldn't say. I assumed that Neanderthal boyfriend of hers. But people were fairly free in those days. It could have been anyone. I wasn't all that interested. I told her she couldn't mope around the house all day lamenting her fate. I gave her money and told her if she didn't use it to get rid of the baby by whatever means she saw fit, she couldn't come back." Neither of us said a word but Faye grew defensive. "Don't look at me that way. I had plans and they did not include parenthood. I'm not a monster. The choice was hers. I gave her enough cash to last her through a pregnancy if she chose. I believe if you have a child, its welfare should be your priority. Always. I didn't tell her what to do, just what I was not willing to do. Raising a child was not the way I wanted to spend my life."

"Do you know what choice she made?" I inserted myself into the conversation.

"No idea. Officially. She never showed up here again. Never called. Never wrote. If you asked me to place a bet, however, my money would be on motherhood. I can see her as the nurturing type."

"When did she leave?" Xander asked.

"Early 1969. She'd just begun to show. She packed up and walked out while I was at work. I never saw her again. I've lived in the same place since 1967, so if Sarah came back she would have found me."

"Where did she go?" I sounded concerned as if she had left about an hour before.

"I gave her the name of women I knew who were living in a commune near Boston. They were procreating like bunnies and all living together raising their kids. My guess is she went there and stayed, but I couldn't swear to that in court. I didn't keep in touch with any of those women."

"Don't young girls in that situation often go home to their parents?" Xander asked.

Faye released a loud, theatrical, totally unnatural guffaw. "Going back to Jersey is something that girl would never have done. That father of hers was a terror. Her mother was under his thumb. And her sister, well, she was a world-class weenie. I can't imagine Sarah would have gone home. She was afraid her father would kill her. Literally." My impression was she felt embarrassed to go on.

"And you never checked on her?" I asked, trying to hide that I found her behavior appalling.

"She had rejected me, chose motherhood over the life I could offer her. I had no further interest in her. If she had chosen to come back without a baby, she would have been more than welcome. I didn't want children. Certainly, not two. She was a child herself."

"Can you recall any of the other women's names?" Xander asked. "The ones in Boston."

"It was a long time ago. I remember first names." It took her thirty seconds to come up with a couple. "Diana. Elaine, or maybe Ellen. Other than that, I don't remember."

102

I gave her my card in case she did recall anything else.

"You're bringing up some sensitive memories for me. I was devastated at the time. I thought I might have something special with Sarah. Now, I understand my fascination with her was part of my unresolved issues. She was young, malleable. I viewed her as a giant lump of clay that I could mold. I've evolved quite a bit since those days."

I suspected we were in for a long description of Faye's personal development, so I brought her back to Sarah. "Was there something specific about Sarah that made you believe she would be easy to . . . influence?"

"Go ahead and say control. You might understand me better than I understood myself for decades." Faye sounded amused and ready to launch into her own issues.

I got my next question in quickly. "So you thought she could be controlled?"

"I *knew* she could be controlled. In the short time I knew her, I heard about it and I witnessed it. Her family had incredible control over her. I'm surprised they ever let her go away to college. Teachers at her high school had to shame her father into allowing it. He probably regretted that decision. In college, she discovered a whole other world. Worlds, actually. Mainly through the first men in her life. Men, not the dumb high school boyfriends." Faye's tone hinted at bitterness. "Her father kept her on a tight leash. He probably feared what would happen when he dropped her off at school. First, she became a wide-eyed academic-worshiping pawn for some idiot professor who took advantage of her. She was a virgin until she met him."

"Did she tell you his name?" Xander asked.

"No. The affair was over when I met her, and it had been rather short-lived. Couldn't survive Christmas break. She ended it, but only because she took up with someone else. Probably broke the professor's heart. I imagine he thought he could use her for the entire school year, until the new meat arrived in the fall."

"Do you know much about him?"

"I know he sounded like one of those posing, pompous academic wannabes. Big fish in a small pond. Married, of course. It's far too long ago to remember any details."

"I picture an aging academic in a tweed coat posturing at the front of an amphitheater full of worshiping girls. Kind of Indiana Jones without the adventure," I suggested.

Faye chuckled. "That's how I saw him too, although I didn't have Indiana Jones to compare him to in those days. But he was young, like Indiana in the first of the series. She fell for the authority of the position, not the age."

"You remember quite a lot now, don't you?" Not really a question from Xander, more of a statement.

"I've been honest with you. I was in love with her, and I believe she was in love with me, although I had no illusions about why, or about how long it would last. Sarah was in love with the professor, until the head of the campus anti-war movement wooed her. She was in love with him until she discovered feminism and me. God knows who she discovered when she left here."

I pictured Sally on a Greyhound bus headed back across the country. Given her pattern, Sally would have hooked up with the only authority figure on the bus, the driver. Or maybe the baby growing inside her changed her focus and she no longer looked elsewhere for inspiration. "Maybe she had found her true self," I suggested instead.

"I have no idea what the girl's true self was going to be, but I knew she wasn't going to abandon her search and I admired that."

If Sally/Sunshine/Sarah lived into the seventies I felt fairly sure she spent them roller-skating with the king of disco.

"Did you?" Xander finished with an obscene gesture.

"That might not be the appropriate gesture given the circumstances, but, yes, we did indulge in some preliminary displays of affection. She had much to learn and I had much to show her. I still regret missing that opportunity." She eyed Xander. "I am quite active in a number of charities. We do fundraisers. Perhaps we could call upon you." Faye's coy expression grew into a big smile directed at Xander.

"I am not sure what I'll be doing in the future." Xander dodged the invitation.

I caught his eye.

"But because of how kind you've been to us, I will absolutely make myself available to support any charity you support, assuming, of course, that you are not involved in any terrorist activities. Meg, give Faye your card. You can always reach me through Meg."

I gave her another card. "You can file this one under Xander's name."

On the way to the door, Xander stopped at the grand piano. "May I?"

She all but giggled. "Of course."

Xander sat down and hit a few keys. "Could use a tuning, but not bad. Do you mind? I've been on a sabbatical from my music, and the sight of a piano is more than I can resist."

Faye slipped onto the bench beside him as he launched into an unplugged version of one of his hits. I was not a Xander Frost fan and wasn't familiar with most of his music, but the one he played had blared on the radio and in the bars for a full summer. I'd heard it a thousand times, but I never realized how beautiful both the tune and lyrics were until I heard Xander play the song in that San Francisco living room. I was sorry when the impromptu concert ended.

I, who resisted coming to San Francisco, hated to leave California, actually California air. "Now that we are here, we should enjoy the city. Appreciate the views. Maybe we could eat somewhere by the Bay."

"There is food on the plane. We've got to find Sally's professor. What would you do first?"

"I would eat at a nice restaurant to keep my strength up."

"You wouldn't want to ruin your dinner, now would you?" Xander studied a loose thread on his shirt.

"Dinner? With the time change, we won't be back in Atlantic City in time for a nice dinner."

"I thought we'd make a quick stop in LA." The loose thread held his interest.

"LA. I can't stop in LA. I have to get back."

"Why?" He finally made eye contact.

"Because…." I couldn't produce a good reason, except that I wanted to sit alone by the television and watch the Weather Channel.

"Face it, Megarooney. You've got nothing going on. Your life is on that phone which you are currently clutching in your hand. If the storm miraculously clears, I can drop you in the Bahamas."

He knew how to defeat my argument.

"It isn't as if I am asking you to do something strenuous or stressful. I'd like to meet a couple of friends for a meal. My treat, obviously. Nothing fancy. We'll just grab a quick bite and head home." He made an abrupt topic change to signal the end of the discussion. "Do you believe the emerging wild-woman, Sally, would confide to her sister about an affair with a married professor?"

My gut told me no, but Sally wasn't quite a wild woman at that point. "If she believed she was truly in love and trusted the professor loved her in return, she might have. Her choice might have been daring, but traditional. *I am in love with my professor. We will get married and live happily after.* Do I think that is what happened? No. But I do think it's worth a shot. I do. I can believe the ever-proper Marianne would fail to mention that to us, even if her silence would jeopardize our investigation. She found it hard to admit Sally was having sex with her boyfriend. With her married professor? Maybe she found that impossible."

Xander seemed surprised to hear no more protests about a trip to LA. "Great. We will drop by the Dulles house tomorrow so we can watch her reaction. See, I am learning, using your techniques."

"I see that. Nice work. Even if Marianne doesn't have the entire story, she might have heard a name, or kept a college yearbook."

"If none of that pans out, what would you do?"

"It's a small school. I would go to their library and ask to see the old yearbooks. Then I would search the faculty for a young professor, handsome in the academic style Faye described."

"They let you do that?"

"We'll find out. It's not impossible. We have all day tomorrow."

"Right, because we can sleep on the plane. On the way home from LA. Now, I've got to change out of these clothes, don't I? We'll never get a good table at one of the finest eating establishments in the Los Angeles metropolitan area with me sporting this gear." He eyed my outfit.

"Had you provided some warning, I might have brought something along."

"You look lovely. Classic. Understated. My friend will love you just as you are."

Xander's friend turned out to be an internationally known movie star I always thought had more sense than to be Xander Frost's pal. He slipped into the eatery through the kitchen to avoid the paparazzi waiting at the front door, the entrance his equally famous wife used, alerting the bevy of photographers who snapped pictures of us eating dinner at a window table—in a restaurant we should have avoided if we wanted privacy.

I didn't bring that up. I worked on keeping my chin thrust out in case I, and my double chin, did not get cropped out of the photos.

Chapter 17

As I settled into the luxurious transportation Xander provided, I felt in awe of Sally's determination. I suspected that I complained more boarding a Gulfstream than she had climbing into a Greyhound bus. I dozed off envisioning worst-case scenarios of her cross-country trip from Atlantic City to San Francisco and woke up when I heard Xander's name on the TV at my seat. The morning shows were on, the hard news was over, and the anchors had turned the show over to the entertainment news reporters.

"Turns out Xander Frost has been doing more than working on a new album while he's been keeping out of sight. Take a gander at his date's left hand. It's hard to see, but I think that's a diamond."

I looked up to find a still photo of our dinner group with a pull-out focused on my left hand.

The unctuous young reporter frowned into the camera. "You would think hundreds-millionaire Xander Frost could have come up with a flashier ring for the fiancée he has kept hidden from the world."

But the coverage wasn't over. It took two people to report this breaking news story. The camera pulled back and a woman, who had chosen to wear a cocktail dress to work, continued. "Yes, Theo, this woman is a departure from the lifestyle we expect from Xander. Not to say she isn't attractive, but she appears to be somewhat older and rather conservative."

"Although she does have a great just-got-out-of-bed casual appeal." The male correspondent, I now knew as Theo, managed to sound lascivious and insulting at the same time. He looked into the camera much as a President does when speaking from the Oval Office. "A serious romance should not be a surprise for Xander. Rumors have been circulating that the rocker has been making some radical changes, including a new friendship with Evan Hollman, who, now that he is happily married and seen at more political gatherings than movie premieres, is allegedly mentoring Xander about adding meaning to his life. A real relationship might be the first step."

A third reporter, with more fake hair and cleavage than the first, chimed in. "No, Theo, I think the first step might have been buying that rather, shall I say, conservative ring."

"Small. I believe small is the word you're searching for." Theo stuck to his disapproval.

"I think it's sweet. If Xander wants to make a statement that proves he is serious about his love and a new life, that is it." The woman in the cocktail dress defended the engagement ring I loved. "Nothing frivolous about that piece of jewelry."

"Hey, look. You're on the telly. That's exciting now isn't it?" Across the aisle, Xander waved at the screen at his seat.

"No, Xander. It is not exciting."

"Why ever not? Everyone wants to be a celebrity."

"First of all, everyone does not want to be a celebrity. You claim even you don't want to be a celebrity."

"Hey, now wait a minute. I may want to make some changes, but I don't want to sacrifice all the perks. Our dinner experience was fun for you. Admit it. Anyone in America would have traded places with you. Not because of me necessarily, but you, my lady, dined with the hottest couple in Hollywood. It's a game for you. You only have to be on for one night."

"While they criticize my appearance and my age, and worst of all my engagement ring, which is, by the way, an absolutely fine engagement ring."

"Your phone is buzzing." To his relief.

Andy skipped over the amenities. The news he delivered shocked me.

"You are in a disaster area. How can you possibly know what is going on in *People* magazine?" I was afraid I was screeching.

"People.com? You never heard of Twitter?" he prodded.

"You are in a disaster zone and you have time to check Twitter?" I was amazed.

"Not only is the story trending online, it's on the morning news shows."

That was ridiculous. "How can you even see morning TV? There's a storm headed right for you. How do you have time to watch television?"

Xander could only hear my end of the conversation, but I was fairly sure he perceived how it was going based on my responses.

"No, I guess that isn't the point."

"I am so sorry, but one reporter said she thought it was, and I am quoting, 'a sweet ring.'"

"Technically, I didn't agree to go, but I don't fly the plane."

"We were in San Francisco on our case. My case. The case. Xander wanted to make a stop on the way back."

"Of course, they do, but I don't have the money to waste on a one-way ticket. That would be like $2500."

"I forgot about coach."

"We're on our way back now. In the air. Landing within the hour. Turns out Sarah, the missing girl, had someone waiting for her in San Francisco, but she only stayed there a short time and then, we suspect, moved on to Boston."

"For dinner. Xander had a business meeting."

"That doesn't make it a social occasion. Apparently, his wife often comes along on business meetings."

"We're almost back to Atlantic City. When can I come home?"

"Don't be ridiculous. Of course, I want to come home."

Across the aisle, Xander pretended to thumb through a magazine, but, no matter what his mentor said, he was not a great actor and could not disguise that he was listening. Listing all of his shortcomings to cure Andy's worries seemed unkind.

"I love it. I love you. I wish you were here."

I listened for a full minute, laughed and ended the call.

Xander threw the magazine down immediately. "I don't get you two."

"You don't have to."

"But indulge me. He's facing a storm that could kill him. You are in a private jet with a handsome rock star. You are arguing about a television news story that implied you and said rock star were in a serious relationship. And you laugh."

"That, Xander, is the way we roll."

"No. *That* makes no sense. I have seen you with him. You don't notice but I watch. Down in the Bahamas, I watch. I am an actor, you understand. Watching is part of the job. So I observe. You like, never touch each other."

"Not when you're there."

"No, I mean never. No little pinch on the bum. No little peck on the cheek. Not even a pat on the head."

"We're at work when you see us."

"But still, I never see you accidentally brush by each other, catch each other's hand as you pass."

"We are constantly touching. You can't see it. It's between us. An invisible touch."

"Don't go all Genesis on me." Xander held up a hand to silence me.

"When we are in the same room, I always sense where he is. He can make me turn around without saying a word. I hear his unspoken call. We can talk across the crowded room without saying a word."

"Nah. That's just creepy."

"Well, it's the way it is and everything else happens behind closed doors."

"Charlie Rich. I didn't realize you were a country fan. There's a lot I don't know about you." He sat silently for a moment. "Maybe there is an upside to this."

I didn't ask him what that might be; I just stared at him.

"Maybe he'll get you a bigger ring."

Chapter 18

The mystery of Sally Johnson, even the pregnant Sally Johnson, had not grabbed me the way earlier cases had. Maybe because I was pre-occupied with my concerns about Andy in the storm or maybe because I didn't disagree with Sally's decision to disappear. The investigation, how-ever, appeared to have given Xander a new zest for life. When we got to the Artistical, he suggested meeting back in the lobby in a half-hour.

"I need some downtime. If the doorman hadn't been there, I think I'd still be standing outside unable to open the door, waiting for someone to let me in."

"You slept on the plane." Xander offered little sympathy.

"In my seat. I feel the need to get horizontal for a while," I pleaded.

"Is that an offer?" Xander made a familiar gesture of the obscene kind. Before I could react, he apologized. "Sorry. Gut reaction. Old hab-its do die hard. My apologies. I understand you need a Weather Channel fix, but let's not waste the entire day."

I knocked on the door to Xander's suite an hour later. "You're here!" He memorialized my arrival with an exclamation worthy of MacArthur return-ing to the Philippines. "Wait until you see what Peter Bossow got for us!"

He clutched my elbow and dragged, more than guided, me into what might have been one of the smaller suites but still a huge living space with at least twenty feet of sixteen-foot-high windows overlooking the Atlantic Ocean. We descended three marble steps into the sunken living room full of sleek white leather furniture. A couple of chairs had been pushed aside to allow a white board to block fifty percent of the view. Sally Johnson's graduation picture appeared at top center. Below were color-coded columns of observations about each of the people we'd met, with a personal photo at the top. Xander observed his work with pride. "Just like we used in *Hidden Mystery*."

"Where did you get all these pictures?"

"Facebook. Getting the photos was the easy part."

"Printing them?"

He pointed to an office setup on the far wall of the room. "I didn't want to keep calling the Business Center all the time. And the staff isn't there twenty-four hours a day. Peter Bossow rented that for us. I had him pick up some supplies as well. We've got to get organized." He scolded me.

"Is Peter here? I'd like to meet him."

"No, he's off doing lifeguard training."

Of course. Our hero, saving lives.

"Now, let's review." Xander pointed to a couch he'd positioned to face the white board and I plopped on it.

"Sally. Sunshine. Sarah. Which one is our victim?" He pointed a laser at each Sally in turn. Since he didn't have a picture of Sarah, he had drawn a profile instead.

"Xander, we don't know if anything bad happened to her."

"Intuition, Meg. Intuition. I have it. Always have had. My mum told me that even as a baby I would know when someone was coming to our door before they knocked."

"Did you know who?"

"Well, I couldn't speak yet, now could I? So I really can't say. The point is I have talents that I can use to resolve Marianne's dilemma." He corrected himself. "That I can use to help you resolve Marianne's dilemma." His eyes were in full wild-man mode. "We are going to do this, if it's the last thing we do." He turned back to the board without waiting for my reaction. He used both hands to force his bushy hair flat against his head, exhaled and stared at his presentation. I knew when he released that hair, we would be off and running. We were.

"Over here I have our clients," he pointed to the edge of the board and photos of Marianne and Jimmy, labelled clients although neither was paying us.

"And, in the center, here, our suspects. I understand we may never uncover the culprit if we are dealing with a random crime."

"Or no crime," I interrupted.

He planted his hands on his hips and stared down at me. "Let's call whatever happened an incident. Allow me to reiterate. In the center, we have our suspects."

I didn't make the argument that not all, if any, of these people should be labeled suspects. I let him continue. I doubted I could have stopped him if I wanted to.

"Notice I restricted my investigation to personal issues. I do not believe that, even if the Miss America Organization wanted to take vindictive action against the protestors, they ever would have targeted a minor player like Sarah Johnson."

I agreed. "I feel confident stating that the Miss America organization was not involved in any skullduggery—unless it involved butt glue or duct tape. And I think in those cases, they would have been on the side of law and order."

"If I may proceed." He tossed his laser pointer aside in favor of an old-fashioned wooden version, which he slammed against the photo of Lou. "Lou Blair. Obvious choice. If he couldn't have her, no one could. And let's not forget how 1960s Lou would have felt about losing his lover to a woman. And now we have the added wrinkle. Did he know about her pregnancy? I maintain he is the most likely candidate for daddy."

Next, he slapped the image of Faye. "Jilted lover. Or was she? We only have her word that our victim left California. Enraged by the physical proof that her new lover had strayed, had she killed Sarah and disposed of her body in the cold, dark depths—and let me say they are exceptionally deep depths—of San Francisco Bay?"

He touched the photo of Suzania Alton with a lighter, kinder, touch. "Admittedly jealous of Sarah's youth and beauty. Motive for murder? Probably not, but I am not ready to discard the possibility. Had her future husband ever been alone with Sarah? He thought she was hot and Suzania knew it. She copped to being jealous, but the question is, how jealous?"

Next, he hit a piece of paper with Professor X printed on it in large black letters. "This is our next blank to fill in. Whoever this gent was, he had a lot to lose. Faye said the affair was over, but was it? Did he try to win Sally back? Did she threaten him, his marriage, his career? Today, we revisit Marianne to learn about this prime suspect." He turned to me with eyes more crazed than bright. "I feel good about this one. I can see how someone enraged or threatened by her pregnancy killed her."

"We have no proof she *was* killed. She could still be alive, maybe in hiding. You said that yourself. Remember we discussed why you wouldn't go online or on TV to ask for leads."

He stared at me and without uttering a single syllable told me he knew better. Something bad had happened to Sally, Sunshine, Sarah and he was going find out what.

"Let's make a list of the possibilities." He moved to an old-fashioned flip chart. "I, of course, believe something happened that prevented Sally Johnson from returning home, but I will admit the possibility exists that she simply left." He put two headings on the chart. *Voluntary Absence. Involuntary Absence.* "Can we agree on that?"

I agreed.

"Let's do Involuntary first, since I am quite sure that is what happened?"

"Xander, you cannot be . . ."

He held up a hand to silence me. "Intuition, Meg. Intuition." He wrote. "Dead is the obvious first entry. Probably murder. Possibly accident."

I asked him to cross out probably and possibly. His expression made it clear he was humoring me. "And you should include natural causes."

He did so, but reluctantly. He continued his list. *Kidnapped. Amnesia. Other mental illness. Witness protection program. Imprisonment.*

I couldn't argue that any of his suggestions were impossible and didn't want to waste my energy arguing they were improbable.

He moved on to voluntary reasons and scrawled: *Joined cult (commune). Hated family. Drugs. Controlling boyfriend/husband.*

"Can you suggest anything else?"

I struggled but couldn't come up with any other ideas. I felt useless. Xander was hijacking my case. I offered to do my part. "We don't have to surprise Marianne this time. I'll call and set something up."

"Done. She is expecting us at noon."

The feeling was unmistakable. I was jealous. Jealous that Xander was taking control of an investigation that was rightfully mine. Marianne Dulles didn't know Xander Frost existed when she approached me. "Great." I didn't let my resentment show. "But I don't feel we should tell her about the pregnancy. We can pump her to discover if she became aware, and, if she was, when did she find out."

"What did she know and when did she know it?" Xander's enthusiasm for the hunt was frightening.

"Exactly, but we need to tread lightly." I suggested we make a list of questions. Not because I felt we needed one. No, because I wanted to wrest management of the project out of Xander's surprisingly capable hands.

He turned to a new page on his flip chart with a flourish and, playing his new role perfectly, stood poised to write.

"Since we have to take the list with us, why don't we record it in one of our notebooks," I proposed.

"Right. Good idea. You have yours handy?"

Not what I had in mind, but he dictated to me. I felt less in charge and somewhat dejected when, list in hand, fifteen minutes later, we were ready to go.

Xander stopped me on the way to the door. "Would you mind wearing this?" He tossed a Tiffany's box at me.

I was already angry before I snapped it open. "What is this?"

"I simply thought we could forestall any talk about the size of your engagement ring, if you wore something a little more in accordance with my style."

"Xander, why on earth would I want to wear a ring more in accordance with *your* style?"

"I have an image to maintain."

"I am not part of your image." I snapped the box closed.

"But if you want to hang out with me…."

"Xander, I am not hanging out with you. You are hanging out with me. Well, not actually you. What happened to Rex, the ordinary guy?"

If Rex was in there, he didn't answer. "Just put it on if we see any press."

"No. I have a perfectly good ring that I happen to be extremely fond of, from a man about whom I feel exactly the same way. And you, and your paparazzi friends, may not realize this, but mine is a rather extravagant ring in the world of the other ninety-nine percent."

"Ninety-nine percent of what?" Xander did not appear to be kidding. He didn't understand.

"The world, Xander. The non-celeb, real world. The world Rex lives in, or would if you didn't keep reverting to your rock star ways."

"It's pretty." He pointed to the ring inside the box.

"This is pretty, and it means something." I gave him the finger, albeit the third finger of my left hand. "I love it. So take this ring, and shove it." I held the box out. "I would throw it at you, but I am sure it cost too much, and I hate it in movies when people toss extremely expensive jewelry around when the money could be used for so many other purposes. So here. Give the money to charity." I continued to hold it out, but he didn't take it. "Xander, do not make me throw it. It must be worth a fortune."

"Five hundred."

"Five hundred dollars? It's a fake. Man, that is a great copy."

"No." He snatched the box from me as if my lack of expertise with gems meant I did not have the right to hold it. "Five-hundred thousand."

"Five-hundred thousand dollars? How did you get it here so quickly?"

He turned towards the window, but he wasn't admiring the view. He was avoiding my gaze. "You can call from your plane, and they will open the store early so someone can rush an item to you. You know, they do that, for some people."

"You pulled all those strings, inconvenienced all those people and spent all that money so that wannabe-journalists who write about every little mistake made by anyone more successful than they are—which is by the way just about everyone—won't question that you gave someone a ring that cost less than you can afford. That is ludicrous. Rex would be embarrassed."

"Well, Rex doesn't have to read about every little misstep he makes in the newspaper, now, does he? Rex doesn't have to listen to people laughing about his clothes, or his behavior or how his latest album didn't live up to his last one. Or how he's getting older and some of the kids are running circles around him and don't respect him the way rockers his age respected those who went before. Rex doesn't have to worry about walking down the street and seeing his private life revealed for all to see in pictures plastered across the tabloids, does he? No, Rex does his little job, and no one judges him. He goes his little way and lives his little life with his little wife, and everything is hunky-dory all the time."

My tone was less angry than his, but firm. "Number one, nobody's life is hunky-dory all the time. We all have problems, but yours are significantly different. I am sorry if I don't understand, but I can tell you this. If you and I were in love and getting married, I would not need a big ring like that. I would want one so small the paparazzi couldn't see it. Because only then would it would be ours, not theirs. And some things in your life deserve to be private, Xander. They must be private if they're going to have any value."

Xander had a serious expression on his face, but what it meant I had no idea. He put the ring in his pocket. "Do you think Marianne still sees me as Rex Lampier?"

Chapter 19

We would have to wait, however, to find out if Marianne had learned Xander's true identity. In response to our knock at the Dulles house, Jimmy shuffled to the door and told us Marianne had gone to the store, but we were welcome to wait on the porch. He suggested we take two from the line of rocking chairs facing the ocean. The day was overcast but the gray skies didn't matter to me. I enjoyed the breeze and the view of the beach. I generally see no limit on the amount of time I can rock and stare at the ocean. Xander, however, could not only see a limit; he reached it in about two minutes. He tapped his feet and slammed his hands on the arm rests. He rocked fast. He rocked slow. "Let's go for a walk until she gets back."

"You go. I am perfectly comfortable."

He stared at me.

"Ordinary men take walks all the time. Keep your hat and glasses on. You don't want to draw a crowd."

"I am fully capable of taking a walk on my own," he protested, but his actions were so tentative when he headed for the Boardwalk and the beach beyond I believed the activity presented a challenge for him.

"Do you mind if I join you?"

I started, I didn't mind, but I was surprised to hear Jimmy's voice.

"This is a lovely spot, isn't it?" He synchronized his rocking motions with mine. "Marianne's great-grandfather built this house before the turn of the last century. The family's been in it ever since. You won't find many like these still standing on this Boardwalk. If the ocean didn't take them, the developers did."

"It's wonderful. Did you grow up around here?"

"Right next door." Without taking his eyes off the water, he pointed over his shoulder as if I could see through the walls. It didn't matter. He told me the old house had been replaced by a modern monstrosity. His term. "Our house was a lot like this one, except ours filled up with paying guests in the summer. We had a great place to grow up. We were always together. Sally. Me. Marianne. I don't ever remember not knowing Sally. Or Marianne for that matter." He added his wife's name like an afterthought. "I want to thank you for checking into the Sally thing for Marianne."

"Well, we haven't actually discovered anything." Anything we were ready to share.

"And I don't expect you will. I don't discourage Marianne. I helped her search when Sally first left, and then again when the Internet started, but without luck. Things aren't, weren't, as simple with Sally as Marianne makes it sound." Jimmy stared out over the ocean. "Sally wasn't a simple girl."

"How so?" I prompted when he didn't explain.

"Sally appeared to have everything. She was very beautiful, and she had this way about her. This sexiness, when we were too young to appreciate what sexy was."

His expression told me he had figured it out at some point.

"By the time Sally was a senior in high school, I knew she would leave town as soon as she could—even though she loved the beach and the ocean. I think she would have loved this house, but her parents were still in it. She didn't love her parents. Well, her father. I felt she was willing to hurt her mother because of the way she let the father control the girls. He didn't mean to be cruel. A lot of parents still went in for corporal punishment, and Mr. Johnson wasn't the worst I knew. Sally didn't run from the discipline, physical or otherwise, but from the control. The total control."

"He let her go away to college."

Jimmy laughed. "He regretted that. He only let her go because her teachers shamed him into it. One of them would not let him off the hook. Helped her get a scholarship. You didn't keep a girl with a brain like Sally's home. Ranked first in her class. Won lots of awards. The guidance counselor, whatever they called them back then, wasn't going to see her best student get a job clerking in a doctor's office."

But apparently keeping Marianne home was okay.

"You can bet he didn't make the same mistake with Marianne, but doing things his way never seemed to bother her. She did what he thought a good daughter should do. Graduated from high school, got a job, got married when I graduated from college, and kept working in the doctor's office until she got pregnant. Had babies. Stayed close. We lived in an apartment within walking distance, then we moved in here for her parents' last days. After they died, we stayed."

"Why stay in Marianne's childhood home?"

He thought for a moment. "Marianne would never have moved. She wanted to be here in case Sally came home. Still waiting. Look at all the new construction along this beach. Can you imagine the cash my wife is sitting on? If it were up to me this lot would have a high-rise condominium sitting on it, and I would be sitting in a luxury apartment on the top floor."

"Didn't the estate search for Sally?" I directed the conversation back to Sally's disappearance.

"Why? She was barely out of town before the old man disinherited her. I mean it. Sally left in September and didn't come home for Christmas. She was out of the will by New Year's Eve."

"Didn't they search for her at all?" I was amazed.

"The old man made a perfunctory request to the police, and Marianne got a friend on the newspaper to put something in some article about runaways, but Mr. Johnson believed she ran away. So many kids did back then. Marianne didn't want to believe her sister would cut off contact with her. She kept the search alive, but I did most of the leg work. I didn't come up with anything. Sally ran away. Plain and simple."

"Marianne said she didn't recall a note."

He scowled. "She would know. It's been so long. No way I can remember every detail. Simple truth is if Sally wanted to come back, she would have come back. We never moved. She knows where we are."

"Same phone number?" I asked.

He seemed startled by the question and then annoyed by his answer. "We had to change our number not long after Marianne's parents passed. We were getting prank calls. Hang-ups. Breathers. At first we thought people were calling to check if the house was empty. Never found out who or why, but we changed to an unpublished number. But we never moved. She could have written. We never heard a thing."

"Doesn't that say something bad might have happened to Sally?"

"A lot of things might have happened to Sally. In 1968 or yesterday. It doesn't change the fact that she chose not to come back."

"She would hurt Marianne that way?"

Jimmy didn't have a fast answer. "She may not have understood what a negative impact going away would have on her sister. She might have been so focused on herself that she didn't realize, or maybe she didn't care. I understood what she wanted to get away from: her father. She would have liked that her running away would upset him. Embarrass him. Wouldn't look good if his daughter ran off."

"That was his reaction?"

"On the one hand, Sally's disappearance destroyed her father. She was his favorite."

Yet another title Marianne did not manage to win.

"On the other hand, good riddance. He was a vengeful, bitter man. He enjoyed being vindictive. Taking her out of the will made him feel better."

"But not searching for his favorite daughter?" I couldn't imagine that, and my tone told him so.

"He knew he had blown his chance with her. Many chances. What I'm trying to tell you is that you are wasting your time. Sally ran away and made a better life for herself. She had the capability. Marianne can't accept that her sister didn't want to come home. I am sorry she has you wasting your time." He glanced down the street and spotted a black SUV. "Here she comes now. At least, your efforts are making her extremely happy," he said quickly and rose to greet her at the bottom of the steps, planting a light kiss on her cheek.

"Let me take those." Jimmy reached for Marianne's bags.

"Don't be ridiculous. I can carry my own groceries."

"I know but Miss Daniels is on the porch."

She glanced up and saw me. She handed over the grocery bag and let Jimmy empty the car.

"Wow. What have you got in here?" Jimmy followed his wife to the porch at half her speed. He rested the bags on a rocker.

"Men." Marianne mumbled as she greeted me. "Not all of them are muscle men." Her expression brightened as she explained she had heard all about my engagement on the news, not my actual engagement, but the one to Xander. "Congratulations. I recognized that mystery woman." She grasped me in a bear hug that lasted so long I thought the bear involved might have gone into hibernation with me in its clutches. "Where is your better half?"

She meant Xander. "He's not my better half, but Rex is on the beach."

"Isn't that cute? You still call him Rex. Is that a little pet name you have for him so you can be out in public without attracting attention?"

In a way she was right, so I didn't explain. I didn't have to. She saw Xander coming down the Boardwalk. "Rex," she rushed to the porch railing and called out making sarcasm drip from the one word. "You get up here so I can give you a big hug."

Xander still wore his cap and sunglasses but I felt fairly sure he was being tailed by fans—I assumed admiring ones. They didn't approach him, but trailed behind him, trying to appear casual but looking anything but. Three of them, a pair of teen-age girls and a lone woman conspicuous by the amount of clothing she wore to hide from the sun, found a good vantage point to watch the activity when Xander climbed onto the Dulles porch.

Marianne grabbed him and held on for a long time before holding him at arm's length. "You. A rock star. Who knew?"

Just about everyone except Marianne. But she knew now. "Jimmy, unzip your hoodie on three." She counted and on three, they both pulled down the zipper on their sweatshirts. Marianne, proudly. Jimmy, a bit reluctantly. Their actions revealed Xander's face plastered across their chests in loud colors. In the artwork, he wore an expression of such calm that I could hardly believe the image was his. "I had no idea you'd be here today when I set these out this morning. I ran out and bought them yesterday once I realized you had been a visitor in our home. I bought a couple, actually."

"Please, don't buy them. I will have some shipped to you," Xander offered.

Marianne demurred but managed to work in the information that they both wore XL into her protests. "We would love to wear your shirts. We feel as if we were in on the ground floor of your romance."

Ah, right. The romance. I hated to knock the cheerful expression off Marianne's face. She was beaming at the thought that she had helped our courtship along, but I insisted on telling her the truth. Finally, she pursed her lips and admitted the press gets a lot wrong. The press and the weathermen. She cursed them as she zipped up her hoodie. Jimmy closed the zipper on his sweatshirt as well, perhaps because he felt embarrassed facing the man whose image he wore on his chest.

Marianne surveyed the scene from her porch, but never noticed that our group was providing a backdrop for fan selfies. "They say this storm is coming up the coast, but I don't know what to believe. Last time they scared us all, and no bad weather materialized."

"And the time before, Sandy slammed New Jersey." Jimmy excused himself. "I have to move our storm supplies into the kitchen and then get back to work."

"I hope you can keep going through the storm. I mean I hope it hasn't stopped your search for Sally." Marianne pointed to the rockers. "You two sit down. I'll get you something to drink."

"That's not necessary. We just have a few questions."

Marianne obeyed an order from Xander to sit and selected a rocker beside his.

"Did Sally ever mention having a crush on a teacher at college?" Xander took the lead in identifying his favorite suspect.

"A teacher?" She seemed surprised by the suggestion.

"A professor."

"Of what?"

"We hoped you knew."

She barely shook her head. "If I ever knew what classes she took, I've forgotten. I do remember she majored in English, because she and my father argued about that. He called studying literature a huge waste of time. When she said she wanted to be a teacher, I remember he said, 'What? An English teacher? Teaching other people how to waste their time reading?' It wasn't easy to win an argument with my father. He was . . . quite something."

"Bastard." The voice came through the open window from the dining room. "Admit it, your father was a mean son of a bitch. Sally probably never would have run away if he hadn't threatened her. He wanted her to move home so she could live under his rules, like a, like a . . . ."

"Like me." Marianne sounded downtrodden, even fifty years later.

"You were a good girl, Marianne. You were a good daughter. You gave both of them much better than they deserved." Jimmy's words were all about love, but his tone conveyed a tinge of disapproval. The tone of a man who had sacrificed so his wife could be a perfect daughter?

I turned to talk to Jimmy through the window to the dining room where he had settled at his usual work spot. "Did you ever hear Sally talk about her college classmates? Did you have contact with any of them?"

"I barely talked to Sally after she left for college. I was a high school kid. She was a college kid. Never the twain shall meet."

"Now, sweetie, that's not true. You were always family to Sally. She never mentioned a name to me either." She turned to Xander. "We saw some of those college kids on that visit I told you about, but I never caught their names in the first place."

"And she never said a word about something specific that happened, that caused her to want to move away?" Xander asked.

"Like what?" Marianne appeared genuinely puzzled.

"Well, I don't know now, do I? If something bad happened here at home, if she felt she needed to be away, I wouldn't know what. Simply asking."

"No, nothing specific. She was just one of those rebel kids, but she's grown up now."

"She would be old." Jimmy called from the dining room.

"It's time to get this all resolved. That's all." Marianne persisted. "It's time."

Chapter 20

Given the demographics of his fan base, sneaking onto a college campus was not Xander's strong suit, but he insisted on accompanying me to the library at Wallmann College. He agreed to keep his wild hair hidden, his fake glasses on, and his thick lips pursed.

The campus where Sally Johnson spent her last year resembled a Hollywood set, cast with gorgeous actors playing enthusiastic students happy for the beginning of the new academic year. I felt old and completely out of it. Xander felt melancholy. "I missed all this."

"It would be hard to find a student on this campus who would not trade places with you." I tried to be positive, but I understood his youthful success had robbed him of the ordinary experiences he now craved. "Classes can be exceedingly boring."

"Not if I got to sit next to that one."

I checked out the woman walking towards us and pegged her as a professor. No matter what her profession, she was a mature woman in a sea of girls barely old enough to vote. I saw Xander's preference as a sign he was maturing. Like a ten-year-old with a crush, he asked her for directions to the library, and she pointed toward the end of a long quad at a modern intrusion among the classic stone buildings. Glass doors admitted us to a sleek space. Bright, spacious, and warm is not an easy combination, but this building nailed it. We found our way to a security desk where we signed in as guests, admittedly after I concocted a story about wanting to see my mother's yearbook. The sympathetic security guard pointed us to a friendly librarian, who in the first week of school didn't have a lot of time to listen to my story. She directed us to the yearbook collection. While I leafed through 1968, Xander searched the 1969 edition. "What a cool time!"

"Cool if you weren't an American male waiting to be drafted. Interesting is a better word."

"Were you alive then?"

I stared hard at Xander. "Did you ever take math?"

"I am simply reacting to your knowledge of the sixties."

"There is another course they give called history."

"You're mocking me."

He was right. I was. Given that he possessed, or had access to, every material thing a person could want, I felt I could tease him in a way I would never tease anyone else. "I am beginning to understand your need to be ordinary. I mean really understand it. Lots of people go back to college. You could at least take courses. I understand it wouldn't be the same as going at eighteen. You won't have the same social life." At least, I hoped he was mature enough that he wouldn't. "But you can have an academic experience."

"Maybe I'll study to be a PI." Xander didn't want to hear any more. He pointed at the yearbook in front to me.

I found the faculty pages and after discounting anyone who appeared to be over fifty or hopelessly straight-laced, I settled on a guy I guessed to be in his thirties and declared him to be Sally's lover. He was good-looking enough to attract women. His hair, cut to show deference to the growing counterculture, would have made him a likely choice for a girl eager to learn more about the world. No other faculty members pictured fit those characteristics.

I closed the book and passed it to Xander. "Now you pick."

He studied all the faculty pages closely before landing on the same picture. Charles Matheson, MA, PhD, Instructor, History Department. Not a full professor. Given the chance he took with a student, I wondered if he ever got tenure.

I went to a computer and felt no surprise that the teacher was no longer on the faculty. "Gone. Now we need to find out where he went."

"Heaven, I hope," Xander said.

"He wouldn't be that old. He could still be with us."

We made our way through the yearbooks, year by year. Matheson disappeared in 1979.

"But why?" Xander asked.

I went back to the more harried but still pleasant librarian to check if they kept copies of the campus newspaper. Of course, they did. The years we wanted were bound. Luckily the publication appeared only weekly. We checked 1978. No mention of Matheson leaving in the spring of 1978 or failing to return in the fall. No mention of him at all in the 1978-1979 papers.

"Is it typical for a professor to depart without a howdy-do?" Xander asked in his best American accent and worst American slang.

"I have no idea of the protocol."

"How do we find where he went next?"

"If not Google, I'll have to search for academic papers."

We moved to a workstation and found the answer immediately in the form of an obituary, albeit one that provided basic information only. One wife. One child. No siblings. No cause of death. No leads. Matheson left Wallmann in 1979 and died two years later. No word of how he occupied himself during those two years.

"Maybe he left teaching because he was sick. Maybe he knew he was dying. It would have been sad like *Good-bye Mister Chips* but tragic because he was a young man." Xander laid a hand on his heart.

"Then why no tribute in the school paper?"

"Check 1981 when he died."

"Wait, you've seen *Good-bye Mister Chips*?"

"I grew up in Britain. Just because I am not aware of every nuance of American life, does not mean I am a cultural illiterate. The movie is, after all, a British classic."

Touché.

"Check 1981."

I did, along with 1982, and found no mention of Matheson's passing.

"It's so long ago, no one will remember." Xander moaned.

"People who were here around that time could still be here." I pulled out the 1979 yearbook and compared it to the current year. "Two 1979 faculty members are still here. They might remember."

"If they remembered to come to work today."

"Ageism, Mr. Frost. Someday, fifty years from now, I want you to recall that comment, and feel deep regret for being so judgmental."

"I'll try, but...."

"Drop it, Xander," I interrupted. "I don't want to hear another word on the topic for fifty years."

Chapter 21

"Office hours are posted, and this isn't one of them." Professor Bowman had either graduated from a long line of elite schools with stodgy faculty or watched a lot of movies from the 1940s about elite schools with stodgy faculty. He had the tone and sneer down pat.

"No Mister Chips, eh?" Xander whispered in my ear.

"We're not students," I explained.

"So why should I talk to you at all?" Condescension dripped from every word, but most heavily from the word *you*.

Good question.

"I'm a historian." I pulled out an old excuse before I realized I had no way to make sense of that role to an actual historian. "Amateur."

I took a step onto the well-worn Oriental carpet. Based on the wear and tear on one spot only, I speculated that few people got much farther into the room full of shelves overflowing with fifty years' worth of books. "I'm trying to find someone who popped up in an old story, family story, not my family, or I'd be aware of the details, but a family that owned property that . . . . You probably don't want all these details but I thought you might have taught with the history professor called Matheson. Charles Matheson, PhD. Did you know him or teach with him?"

His face froze. I hoped he was pondering his next move. If not, we probably should have called 911.

An uncomfortable amount of time passed before he spoke. When he did, his tone was surprisingly light. "I guess there's no harm in discussing ancient history." He did not offer us a seat, but he did start talking. "Not that there is anything to discuss. You're not going to find any information about Charles Matheson here. Or anywhere. He's dead. Has been for twenty, thirty years. Maybe more." His last thought gave him pause. "Died after he left here. Happy to see him go. He had to, what with the scandal and all. Leave not die. Taking advantage of young girls the way he did. Disgraceful."

"He left because of the way he behaved with his students?" I asked.

Again, the man's features froze. I grew afraid he wasn't going to elaborate, but when he spoke he did so without any reticence. "He got away with untoward behavior for years. His actions were a disgrace, but everyone looked the other way. Until that young lady died. Then the college could not turn away. Not with a body lying dead on the roof of the dormitory."

Xander stepped by me to move closer to the professor at his desk. "He was involved with a student who died?" Given his excitement, he might as well have added *this is getting juicy* to his question.

As for Bowman, again with the blank expression. This time I didn't worry. This man wanted to dish. He had probably been waiting for years for someone to ask. He just needed a little time to collect his thoughts. "No one spoke of it. That is why I hesitated to talk to you."

He waved at two armchairs in front of his desk. Xander and I perched on the edge of the seats and leaned forward to encourage him to go on. "We all knew he was a womanizer. And we could recognize the next girl he'd choose, generally from the freshman class. A few of us would place bets. I guess our behavior was distasteful, but so was his. That's how we dealt with it. Not an enlightened time, in that respect at least. Looking back, I suspect we were all a little jealous. Matheson was handsome and young, and he wore a wedding band, so the young girls were forewarned. It didn't seem to matter. It was hardly the college's responsibility to protect those girls from their own loose morals. Each generation got freer and freer with their sexual favors. I remained far too upright to play those types of games." This time his face did not so much freeze as relax into a nostalgic expression. "Viewing the situation from the perspective of an old man, which I now am, I wonder if I wasted some golden opportunities."

"But Charles Matheson?" I called him back from his fantasy world.

"Ah, yes. Had he lived he would have had no regrets of that ilk. Although I must say he was monogamously bigamous, if I may coin a term. He held himself to one mistress from each class. Well, one at school from what we could tell."

"The girl on the roof? How did she die?"

"There is some uncertainty concerning the manner of her death, or rather the intent surrounding her death."

"Was she murdered?" Xander sounded almost gleeful.

"Nothing of the sort. The authorities could not determine if her death was accidental or if she intended to take her own life."

"Was she pregnant?" Xander asked.

"That's what I thought at the time, but apparently not. Unexpected paternity was a bullet he apparently dodged with all his ladies. That particular young woman had simply discovered what a lout he was, how he had a pattern. She realized there was nothing special about her at all. She took some alcohol and pills up to the roof and fell asleep staring at the stars. I believe the autopsy showed she froze to death. Quite an embarrassment for the school. They have security cameras there now."

"And Matheson was blamed?"

"The deceased student left a note listing the disappointments she suffered because of him, and, of course, her parents held him responsible. The administration didn't actually *blame* him—they identified the student as the problem—but he embarrassed the school and exposed it to a lawsuit. Most importantly if his behavior became well known it could affect enrollment and cost the school donations. He knew he had to go."

"So he never hurt the girls?"

He chuckled. "No. He wasn't the type, not that he was even physically capable. Kind of a weakling, physically as well as mentally. But one of his girls really gave it to him. Big shiner. I'll wager he had a hard time explaining that at home. He told us he caught the corner of his desk picking up an eraser. I guess it could have been true, but we didn't believe him."

"Did you by chance ever hear of a student called Sally, or Sarah, Johnson?" I asked.

"Doesn't sound familiar."

"Sally or Sunshine."

"Not ringing a bell."

"What year?"

"1967-68. An English major."

"Unlikely I would have encountered her, and it wasn't as if Charles brought his squeezes along to faculty events." He shook his head. "Although he was shameless. No doubt about that."

Professor Bowman had shifted back into his imperious persona when we said good-bye, but the trace of a smile on his lips told me he'd enjoyed his trip to the past.

Unlike Professor Bowman, Professor Jenkins of the English Department was a warm host and invited us into an office almost identical to Professor Bowman's. However, he had no new information to offer. He remembered Charles Matheson only because of the scandal involving the girl who froze to death on the roof. "Sally Johnson is such a common name. Nineteen sixty eight, you say. All those sixties girls looked alike. Long straight hair, a lot of it blond. Long limbs sticking out of those mini-skirts. Extremely tempting I am sure to a man like Charles Matheson. I heard he wasn't much of a scholar. Gossips said he only went into teaching to have access to young girls. A real dog, if you get my drift."

Xander and I did and had already heard about that angle, so we said our good-byes and headed for the door. I had my hand on the handle when the professor stopped us.

"Wait. I'm sorry I spoke so negatively about the man. I didn't know him well. I suppose everyone was a bit jealous of him. Many of us had struggled through graduate school, I mean financially. And then along comes a man like Matheson who has the life we all worked so hard for handed to him. I cannot judge if he lacked academic rigor or not, but conventional wisdom was his rich wife made his life possible. The old library bore her grandfather's name. I'm not saying that's how Matheson got his position, but many on campus had suspicions. I understand why his work would be under scrutiny and, perhaps, judged harshly by some envious associates. He might have been all right at some point, but he did self-destruct. His luck with the ladies did him in."

I didn't understand why Xander asked his next question.

"Do you accept more mature students?"

"Probably not in those days, but I don't believe Matheson would have bothered with one if we did."

"No, I was thinking of today. I actually never finished college."

He didn't mention that he had actually never started.

Professor Jenkins asked about his interests and the two had a conversation about how he could benefit from a liberal arts degree. We stepped out of his office with a shiny brochure and a link to the admissions website.

"So. What do you think? The wife? The wife did it," Xander said as soon as the door to Petrie Hall slammed behind us.

"We don't know that there is an *it*," I repeated for the umpteenth time, as my mother would say. "I didn't realize you wanted to go to college."

"I might. I'm exploring. Right now I'm exploring the world of Charles Matheson. So what do you think of the wife?"

"There were no rumors about a pregnancy, and Sally disappeared almost nine months after her affair with the professor ended—supposedly. Why would Matheson's wife care at that point? Sally had moved through Lou and onto Faye before she disappeared."

"Maybe." Xander's tone was coy. "But the wife didn't know that, now did she?" He spoke into his phone. "Peter. Could you see what you can find about a Charles Matheson, professor of history at Wallmann College. Died in 1981, we think. We need to find out what happened to his wife."

Xander listened intently. "Thanks, guy, you're the best." He smiled at me. "Pete's on it."

I felt my jealousy growing. Petty jealousy. Peter Bossow was good at what he did and, so far, it appeared he could do anything. No denying, I felt jealous. This was supposed to be my case using my expertise. Maybe I hadn't been overly enthusiastic about it, but Marianne Dulles had come to *me*. Now, not only was Xander involved, but he had Peter Bossow working as his assistant. Then again, I'm not sure I could have located the former Mrs. Charles Matheson, remarried but once again widowed, in under an hour. Peter Bossow could.

We were finishing our diner lunch when the tones of "Anything Goes" surprised me. "My ringtone for Peter Bossow," Xander apologized for having a song that defied his hipster image. "Really. Give it to me." Xander jotted something down in his notebook. "Brilliant." He wrote more. "Wonderful." He scrawled another note, a long one. "Fantastic, Pete. You're the best."

I couldn't protest. From all appearances, Peter Bossow actually was.

"Mrs. Matheson, now Mrs. Hillinger, widow of the late professor Harold Hillinger, still lives in the area." As it turned out in an imposing mansion overlooking the Delaware River and New Jersey beyond. We knew because Peter attached aerial and street-view photos.

Chapter 22

We drove up the long tree-lined driveway unannounced. I worried about how a woman in her eighties, living alone, according to Peter Bossow, on a twenty-acre estate, would greet visitors. I hoped it would not be with a gun. As it turned out, it was with a smile.

"Xander Frost, as I live and breathe," she gushed as soon as she opened the door. "What brings you to my front door?"

I was shocked, and not just because an eighty-year-old woman recognized a contemporary rocker, but because she recognized a contemporary rocker in disguise.

"Peter Bossow called and said you would be stopping by."

Of course. St. Peter, the man who could do it all.

"I had to look you up on the Internet, but I was rather impressed. You have made quite a career for yourself. So much music. Not my taste, as you might guess, but then again I don't suppose I am your key demographic."

"Well, my dear, I am pleased you approve."

Where he heard approval in her words, I didn't know.

"Maybe I can expand my fan base to include you and your friends. When I resume touring, I will make sure you have front row seats."

"I will see if I can convince my bridge club to spend the evening in a mosh pit. Is that what you call it?"

Mrs. Hillinger was a quick study.

"Right you are, Mrs. Hillinger."

"Oh please, call me Susan."

"Lovely, Susan. And you must call me Xander. My friend and I...," realizing I'd been excluded from his interaction with the woman, Xander gestured towards me. "Let me introduce my colleague, Meg Daniels."

"Lovely to meet you, Ms. Daniels. Mr. Bossow said Xander would be bringing his girl with him."

She extended her hand and I tried to wipe the scowl off my face as I took it.

"Please come in."

I expected the inside of the house to match the conservative, preppy clothing of its owner and the rooms we passed did. The room we settled in, however, was a surprise. The long glassed-in sunporch was decorated with mid-century classics, but not the kind that said *I bought this furniture in 1955 and have been using it ever since.* The space was a shrine to twentieth century design. Apparently, Susan Hillinger was more hip than her clothes suggested.

I slid back on a black Barcelona chair, and Xander perched on the edge of his. Mrs. Hillinger took the corner of a Corbusier sofa. "Now what can I do for you?"

Xander didn't even glance my way before he launched into an explanation. He handled the situation so carefully and politely that Susan cut him off.

"No need to be discreet, my dear. All of Charles's secrets came out. Not that they were ever really secrets. Charles was a lovely man in many ways. Handsome and charming, but by no means the sharpest knife in the drawer. He thought he was clever, but I knew what was going on. You know when I figured it out?"

She ignored me and gazed into Xander's eyes for an answer.

"I was crazy about Charles when we met. I was a senior in college, and he was a graduate student. I should have figured out that he recognized what I could do for him. I did have the same name as the Wallmann library. Nonetheless, I was young and stupid. I fell for his line when he professed to find me different from any other girl he ever met. I might have been unique because I was the best connected, but that was not the story he told. I was simply wonderful in every way."

I got the impression that she was imitating her husband's inflection, but having never met him, I couldn't testify to how good her performance was.

"I guess I should have asked him to be more specific. Ah, hindsight. He was exceptionally convincing, so when he said he loved me, I believed him. I was not only in love with him, I was in love with the life he proposed for us. He would be a professor, and I would be the perfect academic wife. It had worked for my parents, so why wouldn't it work for us? And it did—right through the wedding ceremony." She paused to let us digest the information.

Xander opened his mouth to react, thought better of it and waited for her to continue.

"It wasn't until we were in the receiving line that I noticed the way he was watching my maid of honor, Bitty Murdoch. The bridesmaids' dresses, a lovely shade of rose, had this cute little tulle apron. As we stood together holding the knife to cut the cake, I noticed Charles had a tiny, little piece of pinkish netting caught in his fly, and Bitty had a tiny, little rip in her apron. I told Charles he had an itty, bitty little piece of tulle stuck in his zipper. From that moment on, neither of us had any illusions. He ruined the reception for me. At least the ceremony was lovely."

"Why didn't you leave him?" I asked, thinking I might have found a better use for the knife.

Susan appeared surprised to see me and shocked to hear my voice. "That wasn't the way we did things back then. Besides, who had time to return all those presents?" She chuckled and gave Xander a slight slap on the knee. Her philandering husband was ancient history.

"So you knew he was seeing students?" Xander asked in a kind voice.

"Knew? I knew all right. I kept track of them." She leaned towards Xander with a flirtatious smile and crooked her little finger. "Follow me."

She led us into an office that could have been lifted from a 1940s film about the Ivy League, a neater version of the two campus offices we'd visited earlier. She took an armful of Wallmann College yearbooks from a bookshelf and laid them on the desk.

"Nineteen fifty-nine." She stood the book on its edge and let it fall open to a page of headshots, graduation pictures of fresh-faced women in crisp white blouses. One was framed by a heavy red circle. "Let's see. Henrietta 'Henny' Winston," she read. "I believe she was the first, the first that stuck, anyway. I don't think she knew about…" With a flourish she followed the same steps to reach an encircled picture in the 1960 yearbook. "Margaret 'Madge' Calhoun." She leaned in towards Xander and spoke in a conspiratorial tone. "We had a little trouble with her, because she did know about…." Another flourish, and we got to a face in the 1962 yearbook. "…Miss Alexandra Smith." She read the name. "I felt he took 1961 off. Possibly because our daughter arrived and he had to balance a career, our family and two girlfriends. Guess he needed to hold back a bit. As I said, he wasn't the brightest bulb on the Christmas tree."

Why did she keep these? Had she annotated these yearbooks when Charles Matheson was alive? Had he seen them? Had she made the markings as a surprise for him? Did she do it year by year or had she gone back after he died? I had a lot of questions and my protégé, Xander, asked them all. Susan relished telling us she had begun marking up the yearbooks in 1959 and wasn't aware, or concerned, if her husband had found them. She didn't ask and he didn't tell.

"Did you ever hear of a girl called Sally Johnson?"

"What year?" She asked without emotion.

"Academic year 1967-68. She didn't graduate," I explained.

"There were a few like that. Let me take a look." She grabbed the 1968 *Valiant* and it fell open to a page of graduate photos, one circled, but then she leafed through the book until she spotted another red circle. There, in a photo of a group of freshman women pretending to be engrossed in a lively discussion, was Sally Johnson, not the hippie Sunshine of the spring of 1968, but the fresh-faced, bright-eyed schoolgirl who had come to Wallmann seeking new experiences.

"I remember her. Of course. She dumped Charles shortly after Christmas. At least that was what I surmised. He was in a foul mood. He didn't get dumped often. I am sure he preferred the natural ending graduation provided. That year, he didn't come out of his depression until around Easter when, I recall, I spotted him with a new girl. I could always pick them out of the crowd at college events. They were no shrewder than he was. Now, where is that photo?" She flipped through the pages searching for her husband's next flame. "Must be in the next year's book."

"Did any of these girls ever come to your husband looking for help?"

Once again, Susan seemed surprised to hear me speak. "Do you mean did anyone ever come looking for child support?" She gave a firm shake of her head. "That was not a possibility. Our daughter was adopted. My husband was sterile."

Susan had yet to show any emotion when she walked us to the door and said goodbye to Xander—and as an afterthought, me.

Chapter 23

Xander waited until we got to the car to speak.

"That she was pregnant by some other man doesn't mean Matheson didn't kill Sally," Xander said as soon as the car door shut. "What are you doing?"

"Writing down the names of those women before I forget them. I didn't want to interrupt her concentration while she was talking. She was on a roll."

"So you believe she, not her hubby, did it?" Xander asked.

"She strikes me as a bit unhinged, don't you think? Calm appearance, but keeping a record to this day of the women her husband cheated with? Being able to differentiate and recall which one was which—after another marriage. Not ordinary."

"So you believe there is a possibility she did it?" Xander didn't. I could tell.

"We don't even know if there is an *it*, but if there is, I wouldn't be surprised." I snapped my notebook shut. "She never inquired as to why we were asking questions. Maybe she's been expecting a murder investigation for years."

"She moved on with her life, now didn't she? Married again," Xander argued.

"But she stayed with Matheson until he passed away. How did he die anyway?"

"Peter didn't send that information, and she didn't say. Although I have formulated a vision of his life after Wallmann. The disgraced professor, cut off from the work he loves...."

"Don't you mean, cut off from the sexual opportunities he loves?"

Xander made an adjustment. "Cut off from the work he enjoys and the women he exploits, the disgraced professor loses the will to live and drinks himself to death."

"Matheson suffered from guilt for putting Sally in a situation where his jealous wife killed her." I added an embellishment.

"Out of all the women he had seduced, including the maid of honor at his own wedding, Susan decides to eliminate Sally." Xander wasn't buying my story.

I had an explanation ready. "Of course, she couldn't kill them all. Wallmann is in a small town. People would notice if coeds start showing up dead." I reconsidered. "Or could she? She still has the record of her dead husband's infidelity. Even after a second marriage. Maybe she took her time working out her anger. Years. Decades. Revenge is best served cold."

"I should think someone would have noticed if all these women died or disappeared." Xander was not giving an inch.

"These women probably moved all over the country. No one would notice a disproportionate number of Wallmann grads from a twenty-year period disappearing or dying under suspicious circumstances."

"I should think the alumni office would." Xander had a retort ready.

"Not if she made every death appear like an accident, or, even better, natural causes."

"Susan does have quite a large greenhouse on the side of the building." Xander finally paid some respect to my theory. "God knows what she could be growing in there."

"Or maybe she saw something different in Sally. According to Susan, she was the only one who dumped him. Maybe he wasn't over her. Maybe Susan was willing to do anything to keep her husband."

"Or maybe Matheson finally realized *he* had to kill Sally. If he couldn't have her, no one could."

"Maybe." I redirected the speculation. "Or maybe Sally Johnson is rocking on a porch in Topeka, drinking an iced tea and minding her grandchildren."

"Should we go to Topeka?" Ever the zealot, Xander was ready to roll.
"Topeka was simply a placeholder. I'm not willing to say a crime was committed, but it wouldn't hurt to verify that none of those women died under suspicious circumstances." And then I did it. I gave in. "Maybe Peter Bossow could check them out for us. And while you have him on the phone, ask him if he can find out how Charles Matheson died."

Chapter 24

When Xander told me he was busy that evening, I bristled—not so he could see, but I felt my reaction. I, who wanted nothing more than a break from Xander, was hurt that he had made plans that didn't include me. I made plans of my own, with my phone. Aside from waiting for a message from Andy, I had several messages to answer including several inquiring about my engagement to Xander Frost. I hadn't told anyone about my engagement to Andy yet and could hardly issue a disclaimer about my engagement to Xander without revealing the truth. My friends would want to know where I got the ring.

I took my phone to the beach deck bar. The end of the restaurant's season was coming and might be rushed by the approaching storm. I suspected that the tables and chairs would be stored away as soon as Frieda's winds picked up. This might be one of the last nights to sit by the ocean, feeling the sea breeze, smelling the salt air, and watching the moon rise. The night suggested fall more than summer, but a few hearty people were braving the chill to catch a last gasp of the dying season. Most of them had brought a sweetheart to cuddle with. I brought a sweater. I couldn't read my mystery by candlelight in the encroaching dusk, so I focused on downing a bucket of peel-to-eat shrimp and two daiquiris, before facing up to the task of breaking the news to my friends that I was going to marry Andy Beck.

I started with Kara Prince, a friend from high school and college who would be waiting for an invitation to be my maid of honor. She didn't answer, so I texted *No truth to rumors about my engagement to Xander Frost. Am sporting a ring, however. Call for details.* I breathed a sigh of relief, so loud that the young woman at the next table laughed.

"You sound as if you just dodged a bullet."

"I guess I did." My phone rang. "I thought I did."

Kara got right to the point. "So you're engaged to Andy Beck."

"I am. I can hear the disapproval in your voice. I know you aren't crazy about what he does for a living, but he's making some changes. But even if he didn't, it wouldn't matter to me. I'm really happy, and I am perfectly content with my ring, no matter what the tabloids say."

"I couldn't actually see it in the newspaper photos."

"Don't be snide. It's not all that small. Over two carats. You'll see."

"Did you pick it out or did Andy?"

"He picked it out because I said emerald cuts go best on the beach. He is incredibly thoughtful."

"And he is thinking of making a career change?"

"That's what he says. I am not sure what he'll decide, but he wants to make a move away from what he's been doing."

"So in the meantime, you've been hanging out with Xander Frost. Doesn't that bother your new fiancé?"

"Andy is in the Bahamas because of Hurricane Frieda. I haven't talked to him that much. I am hoping he'll get a chance to call or at least text to let us know he's okay."

"Us? You and Xander are an *us* now?"

"Xander seems to think so. I'll explain when I see you. I just wanted to touch base since I knew you had seen the news."

"When Andy gets back you two have to come over. Do you think you will move back to this area after you get married?"

"We don't know where we are going to live."

"Any wedding plans?"

"No. Xander and I dropped by the Parsonage the other day to see George and Claude. George wants us to get married there, but we haven't had time to discuss it."

"I know you'll keep me posted. But before we hang up, you know I don't care about Xander Frost—I barely know who he is—but tell me, what was Evan Hollman like."

"Evan is great. I was surprised that he and Xander were friends, but he is a mentor to Xander who is really giving serious thought to his future. Evan is smart and funny. A well-rounded guy with a great wife, who is also smart, witty and fun to be with."

"I'll want to hear more about that when we get together. Have you told Amy yet? She might actually know who Xander Frost is."

"Not yet, I was going to call her next. I don't want her getting her information from the news."

"I've got to tell you, we talked. We didn't believe you were marrying Xander Frost. We didn't know you were marrying anyone. It's nice to know the truth. Congratulations. Or should I say best wishes?"

"Best wishes to the bride. Congratulations to the groom."

"Well then, tell Andy I send my congratulations when you talk to him."

"I will definitely tell him you sent your congratulations. We will both see you soon I hope."

I put down the phone. Now that wasn't so bad. I breathed another sigh of relief and turned for the reaction of the woman beside me. "That wasn't bad at all." I smiled.

She raised an eyebrow as if interested.

"My friend in Philadelphia isn't crazy about my fiancé."

"How come?" she asked.

"She thinks everyone should marry a doctor or a lawyer."

"And what does your fiancé do?" She sounded interested. Too interested. She turned as if settling in for a long conversation.

"He's not a doctor or a lawyer." I wanted to add and he's not Xander Frost, which would make sense if she, as I suspected a little too late, was a reporter, but would sound nuts if she was simply a friendly woman having an after-dinner drink at a beachfront bar. "She'll get over it. Have a nice evening."

I signed my check and tried not to run as I made my way through the dunes to the hotel.

Chapter 25

Xander called early but told me he had something to do in the morning.

"About the investigation?" I asked.

He made it clear he took offense at my question. "I don't make a move without you. Come up for lunch."

That summer, Andy and I had a tradition of breakfast in Café Monet adjacent to the casino. My breakfast. His lunch. We met at 11AM but, thanks to Xander's phone call, I was up by 7AM and in Café Monet by 8AM. Without Andy to chat with, I was finished by 8:30 and surprised to discover I was missing Xander, or at least working with Xander. I got out my phone to make more calls but noticed the woman from the beach deck the night before coming into the restaurant. Once more I found myself signing my check and running from her. I couldn't be sure she was press, but I didn't want to risk the possibility. Until the tabloids lost interest in Xander's alleged romantic life, I had to treat every stranger as if they were paparazzi. The friendly guy on the elevator. The cranky guy at the lobby shop. The woman having trouble with her key card at the door to the adjoining room. Especially the woman having trouble with her key card at the door to the adjoining room. My admiration for Xander grew. He had to live his life this way every day. And yet he remained cheerful. Possibly because he got millions of dollars for enduring this treatment. I got one $800 dinner at an LA restaurant. I wasn't motivated to stay cheerful.

When I arrived at Xander's suite after a morning of texting and calling friends about my actual engagement, entertainment news was playing on the TV screen but Xander's attention was focused on the white board. I could tell he'd been working on it. The photo he had snapped of Charles Matheson's yearbook picture filled the empty box. He'd headed a new column with a shot I had taken of him with Susan Hillinger.

"Do you want to edit yourself out?" I asked from the couch where I was sprawled picking from an elaborate room service selection. I'd wiped out the shrimp and, having by-passed the vegetables, was hitting the dessert tray especially hard.

"No. I quite like the photo. And besides, I am simply adding it to be thorough. You talk a good game, but I don't accept that you believe that lovely little old lady could hurt anyone." He wasn't asking; he was telling.

"She wasn't a lovely old lady in 1968. She was a scorned woman, a betrayed wife."

Out of the corner of my eye, I caught a glimpse of Xander on the television screen. Not only Xander. Xander and me. I hit the mute button to bring the sound back.

"Well, Theo, more fuel to add to the rumors that Xander Frost is about to settle down. As you know, he hasn't been seen on the social circuit lately, but he has been seen in the company of this woman…."

"Argh. They purposely picked a photo that makes me look bad." I tried to use my inside voice but failed.

"I think you look quite lovely, but then again I would, wouldn't I? Being your fiancé and all?"

I shushed him with a wave so I could hear the announcer. "Sources tell us Xander and his fiancé have surfaced on the East Coast. The couple was seen in Bucks County, Pennsylvania yesterday checking out a riverfront property."

The photo of Xander and Susan Hillinger came on the screen. "Now I know why she wanted me to text her a copy. She's a lot more devious than even I gave her credit for. She is moving right up my suspect list." I kept my volume low but felt my tone sounded a bit threatening.

"Sources tell us the owner, seen here with Xander, is reluctant to sell the property. She was taken aback by the singer's surprise visit."

"They are a lovely young couple and I would rest easy knowing my house is in good hands." There she was. Susan Hillinger. Talking into the microphone.

"What the....?" My blood pressure was climbing.

"She's unusually photogenic, isn't she?"

"That is not the point, Xander. What is she doing on camera?"

"She might have mentioned I was there and maybe someone alerted the local press. What does it matter?"

"What does it matter? She lied. Why did she lie?"

I looked to Xander for an answer. He made the call to get one. He could charm Susan and avoid addressing her in the less than cordial tone I would have chosen.

"Of course. Of course. Thank you, dear. Yes, I will. Definitely." He hit the button on his phone. "Susan says hello."

"And what else?"

According to Susan Hillinger, she lied because she thought she could drum up some interest in her property. "She said someone claiming to be a reporter came to her door and asked about our visit. She couldn't very well say strangers came by to pry into the life of her long-deceased husband. So she told them we were considering buying in the area and someone had told us, mistakenly, that she was open to a sale. Which she might be if the price turns out to be right."

"And you bought that?"

"If you didn't trust me, *you* could have made the call." Xander grew defensive.

"Right. I am sure she would have opened up to me, her favorite." My sarcasm was thick.

"Look, she didn't want to say why we were there." He defended his new fan.

"She didn't even know why we were there. She never asked."

"Odd, I'll admit, but not necessarily suspicious. She's old."

"Not that old. She came up with a story for the press pretty quickly. I know you're on a sabbatical of sorts, but don't you have a PR person to kill all these rumors?"

"Meg, as your fame grows, you learn fighting rumors is futile. You fight them when you're trying to get famous, to bring more attention. If you let it lie, the story will die. We've got an investigation to conduct."

One I now hoped would lead to a conviction of Susan Hillinger.

"Have you heard from Peter Bossow yet about the deaths of Charles Matheson and his paramours?"

"Paramours?" He seemed amused.

"Girlfriends. Lovers. Foolish young women who believed the promises of an older, arrogant professor."

"No, I haven't heard. We gave him a lot of names. Do you really think he will discover anything relevant?"

"Perhaps not. Probably not. Oh my God."

"Did you just change the subject?" Xander seemed genuinely confused.

I pointed at the television where the banner screamed, *Bahamas Taking a Direct Hit from Frieda*. And I understand my first reaction should have been fear for Andy's well-being, but what was the first thought that crossed my mind? *I would never have to explain the house-hunting story.* The story would be old news by the time he got online again. The idea was still flitting through my brain when my cell rang. I could barely hear Andy over the noise of wind crossing the phone mic. I moved to the far end of the living area.

"Andy. Thank God. I just saw the news. The storm's about to hit you. Where are you? Are you safe?"

"I thought you were going to get rid of Xander."

"'Get rid of' is kind of a harsh term. What's wrong?"

"You're house-hunting?"

"You saw that?"

"Yes, I saw that." I wasn't sure the wind was the reason he yelled.

"That cable company is ridiculously reliable. Don't you ever lose service?"

"That is not the point."

"The story is ridiculous. You know that. I want to hear about you. I'm worried."

"Are you?"

"Andy. You're being silly and this is not the time to be silly. I am frantic

150

about you."

"And working with Xander is helping?"

"Yes. Yes, it is because nothing else could make me so conscious of what a wonderful fiancé I have. Now cut the crap and tell me how you're going to keep yourself safe while this storm passes over."

His phone was breaking up, but I swear I heard him say *I love you* before it cut off.

Chapter 26

Shortly before six, Xander knocked on the door. "Rex would like to take you to dinner. You cannot sit in your room worrying about your boyfriend. Excuse me, your fiancé. I mean Andy. Bring your phone. I have alerted both Del and Peter Bossow that they are to text me any news that comes through from the Bahamas."

I didn't want to leave the room but didn't have the energy to resist Xander. And, I was growing tired of the minibar offerings. "No more paparazzi. Please. We can't go downstairs. The staff knows you are staying here."

"Don't worry. People think we are in Pennsylvania. But no problem. We'll go somewhere else. I made reservations. I've gone to the trouble of subduing my hair and," he plopped his fake glasses on his nose, "these specs combined with this less-than-hip suit will guarantee we are not recognized. You cannot sit in front of the Weather Channel all night. Time will grind to a halt. Come on now. I'm driving."

I tried to keep the horror from my face.

"Don't worry. Del will keep a discreet eye on us."

"That's not the problem."

Xander stared at me for a moment before he guessed the root of my concern. "What? I drive all the time."

"On the wrong side of the road."

"Well, I beg to differ. We Brits drive on the right side, which in deference to your concerns, I will refer ro as the *other* side."

Xander had chosen the Knife and Fork, an Atlantic City institution since 1912 and a landmark noted for its unusual combination of Swiss and Tudor architecture. Rex would love it. Xander seemed pleased as well when he turned the car over to the valet.

"And what is your name?" Xander playing Rex asked the hostess who seated us. I suspected he thought he was affecting a southern accent, but he sounded a bit like a refugee from a zombie movie.

The young woman, who would have died for a moment alone with Xander Frost, was barely polite to the middle-aged man he played. "Mary." She delivered the one word without a smile.

When the waitress arrived, she was far more pleasant but took our order without giving Rex a second look.

"Xander."

As I spoke his name, Xander glanced around the room nervously. "Rex. Tonight my name is Rex." He winked. A big, exaggerated wink. "See that wink. That means I understand what you mean."

"Very subtle." I gave him an approving wink back. "Rex, there are rich and famous people who lead normal lives. Relatively normal. You should study how they do it."

"Well, I'm not yet totally sure I want to lead a normal life. I am thoroughly enjoying our investigation, but it's only been a few days. But that is what this trip is all about. Finding out how the other half lives."

I didn't point out yet again that we ordinary people made up far more than half of the population. I had beaten that point to death.

He changed the subject. "I did hear from Peter Bossow. All of the women that had dalliances with Professor Matheson are alive—which, given the age range we are talking, is a statistical aberration indicating an affair with him actually adds years to your life." He studied my reaction. "Don't look so disappointed. He did discover suspicious circumstances surrounding Professor Matheson's death. According to the reports he found, one night after dinner at home, he claimed he felt ill but wouldn't let his wife drive him to the local pharmacy. The staff of two had the night off and his daughter was returning from her junior year abroad that evening. He didn't want her to come home to an empty house. So he said he'd drive himself. When the limo brought the daughter up the drive, they noticed lights shining from a steep drop-off. It was Matheson's car. Apparently, he had passed out on the way to the store and run off the road."

153

"Odd, yes. But suspicious?" I asked.

"Absolutely, because they found a large amount of barbiturates in his blood. So, maybe he took them for some unknown reason or," he leaned across the table, "maybe he didn't take them at all, and Mrs. Hillinger is not as sweet and innocent as I believed."

I leaned forward to share the scenarios forming in my head, but something I saw interrupted.

"Don't turn around."

So Xander did—immediately.

"Look at me."

He did. "What am I missing?"

"Marianne and Jimmy."

"The Dulleses. Should we invite them to join us?" He made a move to get up.

"No. I want to observe them."

"Why?"

That was a good question. "I can't actually explain, but they seem like an odd couple. I just want to keep an eye on them. We're making an awfully big effort on their part—you've spent more money than I can imagine—and we don't really know them, do we?"

"You said you did due diligence."

"I did what I could, but it wasn't as if I could get a complete background check on them."

"I could put Peter Bossow on the case."

I was tempted. "No. I would feel disloyal now that we've met them. I got the basics."

"You can't suspect them? You said, and I quote, or at least paraphrase: Why would Marianne raise the issue of a crime she committed? If I recall correctly, you said that would be crazy. And, you can't suspect that wimp of a husband. I have intuition and that man is not a murderer."

Mary, the hostess, sat the couple across the room where I had an obstructed view, but, if I craned my neck, a limited sightline towards both of them. They gave their waitress what I assumed was a drink order and then buried their heads in the menus.

"What are they doing? Can I look?" Xander whispered.

"Better not. I'll report any action at their table."

"Well, then report."

"I would but there is no action." And there continued to be none unless you counted ordering with the waitress, sipping their drinks and staring into space. "They cleaned up rather nicely, although I assume it is no accident that his tie matches her dress."

"Why do you think she puts them in matching outfits all the time?" Xander asked. Neither of us had any doubt that wardrobe selection would be Marianne's doing.

"Like a dog marking her territory." I gave my opinion.

"Well, it is better than taking a wee on him every morning. What are they doing?"

"They have not spoken one word to each other." I averted my eyes, fearing they would feel my stare.

"They've been married since the seventies, right? They probably ran out of conversation sometime before the turn of the century. I am sure they are comfortable with the silence."

"They don't make eye contact. They study the other people in the restaurant."

"They could stare at each other at home. They want to come out and stare at other people. But, why haven't they spotted us?" Xander asked.

"There are a lot of people between us. They haven't noticed us yet."

They never noticed us, but another couple noticed them. "They invited friends to join them. At least I assume they invited them. The two are sitting down and reading the menu in the Dulleses's booth."

"Certainly glad we are observing this suspicious behavior." Xander added more than a touch of sarcasm to his words. "They have lived in this town forever and they know people, and, yes, they eat food. Very odd."

"Okay, I'll stop monitoring their every action." I did for the rest of the meal, which was why I didn't see Jimmy approach our table.

"Meg. Rex. Marianne was wondering if you would join us for dessert."

My gut instinct was to say no, but Xander accepted before I could react. Next thing I knew we were crammed in a booth meant for four—with four other people: Marianne, Jimmy, and their friends, Clare and Matt, all jabbering about Hurricane Frieda and the threat to Absecon Island.

When the topic of the weather was finally exhausted, Clare explained to her husband how Rex and I had been helping Marianne resolve the issue of Sally's disappearance. I could tell by the tone she used to say the word *Rex* that we were at the table so the couple could meet rock star Xander Frost.

"Have you had any more time to work on our case?" Marianne asked.

"We've been doing virtually nothing else, have we, Meg?"

"It has been eating up a lot of our time, but we're happy to do it."

"Can you fill us in?" Clare asked with bright eyes.

"Not much to tell yet, but when the time comes we will." I excused myself to go to the ladies' room.

I can't say I was shocked when the door opened and Clare came through it to find me washing my hands at the sink. "I have to admit, I followed you here to tell you how much your help means to Marianne. This is a rough time for her, what with the scandal."

"The scandal?"

"Of course, she told you."

I shook my head. "A scandal about Sally?"

"Oh no. About Jimmy. Marianne is suffering. She covers her feelings well, but she is so hurt." She studied my reflection in the mirror. "I assumed since you are investigating ..."

"We are investigating Sally. We never investigate our clients." Although evidently we should have.

"That's right. You wouldn't, would you? And what does it matter why Jimmy lost his job?"

"May I ask? Why did Jimmy lose his job?" I tried not to sound overanxious.

"Well," she stretched out the word as if having doubts about spilling the beans, but I had no doubt she would. "I only know the little I heard through the grapevine and what Marianne told me. I think she sugarcoated her version. I could see the effect the events had on her. The story is Jimmy became infatuated with a girl at work and made unwanted advances. She filed a couple of complaints, but he wouldn't stop. He got the ax. Word got around but Jimmy never told Marianne. He kept going out every day. Finally, a woman Jimmy worked with said something to her."

In my book, being told by a third party would hurt the most.

"Poor Marianne. I mean she's a lovely woman, but she's a senior citizen now. How could she compete with a pretty, young blond right out of college? She couldn't. I swear she was headed downhill, getting more and more depressed until she met you. This investigation turned her life around. Thank you on behalf of all her friends, and Jimmy too. I imagine he was afraid she'd never forgive him."

Xander and I had said our good-nights to the Dulleses and their friends and taken the car from the valet, before I told Xander, "Get Peter Bossow to check out the Dulleses. Jimmy has been a bad boy."

When we reached the hotel, I warned Xander that I might have seen some paparazzi around. Perhaps I'd taken an overly cautious view of the woman at the beach bar, but I did not want any more calls from Andy. "We should go in through the hotel kitchen."

"Really? I'm surprised, although after Mrs. Hillinger's leak I guess it's not impossible. I'll ask Del to check things out. Speaking of Mrs. Hillinger, if your husband had died in an accident right outside your window, would you have stayed in a house with a view of the place where he died?" Xander asked.

"It wasn't as if he was the world's best husband, and the view beyond the spot where he crashed is pretty spectacular. Why let a philandering husband push you out of a house you love." If I lived in a spot like that one, I would never want to leave.

"I wonder if she ever visits the site, as a memorial of some sort." Xander wasn't getting my point.

"Let me repeat, he was not the world's best husband."

"She might like looking at the site where he died?" Xander was surprised by the possibility.

"Considering the kind of husband he was? That I can believe."

Even though Xander doubted my claim that there were reporters about, we cut through the bowels of the hotel and took the service elevator to my floor, where he shifted to the guest elevator, but only after watching me make the walk to my room and seeing me wave that my door was open.

I walked across the room to the window to admire the Boardwalk below. I could just make out traces of the white foam from waves crashing onto shore. Frieda had not added force to them yet. Speculation was she would, but I knew what she was up to now. No news from the Bahamas meant that Frieda was directing all her force at them, at Andy.

As I looked up, I saw the reflection of the hall light from the doorway. The door had not fallen shut and I could tell what was causing the obstruction, a figure outlined against the light.

"I think you have the wrong room." I wasn't worried; I believed what I said.

The figure did not speak but stepped inside to let the door fall closed. "Who are you?"

Someone with sinister intent to judge by her tone. Actually, her words weren't that friendly either. "You need to back off."

"I don't understand. Who are you? What could you possibly want with me?"

"I don't want to hurt you. Really, I don't. That's not who I am. If you make me do it, it's your own fault." Her voice was mean, determined and, to my mind, a bit deranged, but my opinion might have been influenced by the specter-like image in the shadows.

"I think you have the wrong room. Who are you looking for?"

"You. I'm looking for you. I know what you are doing. And I am going to tell you once, and only once, stop."

"But ..."

"No but. Back off."

"Of what?"

"Don't play dumb. Don't make me come back."

"How? What do you want me to do? Or not do. Tell me."

I asked but she turned, opened the door, and ran out. I didn't follow. I tried to take in all the details of the brief glimpse I got of the figure in the hallway light.

I dialed security on the room phone. "A female just followed me into my room, 1236. I didn't get a good look at her, but when she was running away I saw some blond hair sticking out from under a black head scarf. She wasn't tall, maybe 5'4", and extremely thin. I think she had the wrong room, but I thought I should report this to you. If she finds the right room, I don't think she's going to be kind to the guest."

Chapter 27

I had trouble sleeping and was up with the sun to watch the limited video coming in from the Bahamas. I kept my eyes on the TV screen as the same waves broke behind the same reporter who kept repeating that the surf was increasingly rough and the winds increasingly high. The footage was old. Most of the airtime was given to the damage in Haiti. I didn't expect similar footage for the Bahamas to be available until the storm had cleared the islands which, according to reports, it had not yet done.

"You look hideous," Xander offered when I opened my door to admit him. "Did you sleep at all?"

"I was watching . . . ."

"Of course, the Weather Channel." Xander walked to the window. "This is another way to check the weather."

"It wasn't just Frieda that disrupted my sleep. The weirdest thing happened last night. When we got home this woman followed me into my room and kept telling me to back off, that she knew what I was doing, and that I needed to stop."

"How did you get rid of her?" His concern seemed excessive.

"I guess she figured out she had the wrong room. She delivered her message, turned and rushed out."

"Did she say she had the wrong room?"

"No, but what else….?"

"What did she look like?"

"The room was dark, but I could tell she was petite and when she opened the door to leave, I saw a little blond hair sticking out of a black scarf."

"How old was she?"

"I couldn't tell. Her voice was like an adult's. Not young. Not old."

He made a show of lapsing into deep thought.

"What are you thinking?"

"That Sally has found us."

"I don't think so, Xander."

"Why?"

I couldn't come up with a good reason. "Sally would be close to seventy and this woman didn't move like an old person."

"A lot of seventy-year-olds don't move like old people. What about poor Mrs. Hillinger to whom you attribute evil motives?"

"Not her voice." I dismissed my favorite suspect.

"Her daughter? Or one of Sally's lady friends? Or one of Mrs. Hillinger's lady friends? Keep an open mind, Meg. Maybe she did have the right room. Which is all the more reason you shouldn't stay in it."

"I want to wait for new footage to come in from the Bahamas."

"That's what I figured. That is why I came to get you."

"I don't want to leave the TV."

"I took care of weather updates. Or at least Peter Bossow did. He will send the footage to my phone as soon as it becomes available."

"Is he like Jason Bourne or Jack Reacher or something? Is there anything he can't do?"

"If there is, I haven't discovered it yet."

"How did you meet him?"

"Interesting story." He took a pause. "Well, not really. Rather dull. Unexciting. Not exactly boring. Odd, maybe. Perhaps it was fate."

I feared I would never hear the story, but Xander finally stopped classifying the tale and told it.

"We were stuck on the lift together. We chatted. I don't believe he even knew who I was. We talked like any two blokes. Just for a few minutes, but he said he did consulting work . . . ."

"And you hired him."

"Not right there on the elevator, but I did take his information."

"Oh."

"Oh? I can hear what you are thinking. That he knew full well who I was and wanted to take advantage of me. What? Do you think that Peter Bossow is part of a kidnap conspiracy?"

"Of course not."

"I did." Xander surprised me. "I must say it was the first thing I thought of when that lift stopped. I had visions of thugs on the roof of the elevator car pulling me up through the escape hatch."

"And then?"

"I couldn't go through their entire plan, now could I? It would have taken them months of planning. My point is you don't have to worry about Peter Bossow. Now get dressed. You're driving. Del is sleeping in. We can have a late breakfast at Uncle Bill's in Cape May."

"Who told you about Uncle Bill's?" I didn't wait for an answer. "Peter Bossow, right?"

"Yes, and he said if we leave now, we should be able to get in without too much of a wait."

"Didn't he tell you there are other Uncle Bill's between here and Cape May?"

"Of course, he did."

Of course.

"But we might as well go to that one since we'll be down there talking to Lou Blair. We have some follow-up questions we need to ask."

Whatever. "Did Peter find anything out about Jimmy Dulles's scandal yet?"

"Of course. I want to tell you everything, but I have heard these pancakes are quite good and I am feeling rather peckish. I can tell you in the car. Now get dressed."

"I am dressed."

"Oh." He registered disbelief and disapproval in a single syllable. "In that case." He pulled a photo out of a folder he was carrying. "Do you recognize the girl in the picture?"

I studied the color newspaper shot of a young girl, barely out of her teens. The big eyes, the long blonde hair parted in the middle. The image was familiar. "Of course, Sally Johnson."

"Au contraire, ma soeur. It is one Adela Somer, the object of Jimmy Dulles's mid-life crisis affection."

I attempted a long, low whistle and produced a short beep. "What is up with that dude?"

"No idea, but until we figure that out, we should focus on Lou Blair, and pancakes. I made a list. Of questions for Lou Blair, not pancakes."

Agreeing with Xander's reasons for revisiting Sally's college boyfriend didn't mean I wasn't resentful that he, not I, had created an agenda.

"First and foremost, we have to check out the pregnancy issue. Besides that," he said, "I find it suspicious he never mentioned Sally's relationship with her professor."

"If he had, we might have thought he told us in order to deflect blame from himself." I offered a counterargument.

"Maybe, but he struck me as the type who would try if he thought he could get away with it. I still find his omission of that information curious."

I had to agree, but not out loud.

Xander had more. "Two, we didn't learn much from him about her family. He told us why he thought Sally should leave, but maybe he could tell us more from his perspective about why she felt she had to leave."

"Point taken."

"And three, it is a gorgeous day and I wanted to see some of the sights down there."

The old Xander. In the end, it always came down to him and his desires.

After loading up on pancakes—me, buttermilk, Xander, corn, peach, and chocolate chip—we found Lou Blair at home, but we didn't get to see the inside of his house. While he went to the kitchen for cold drinks, he left us at a wicker table to enjoy the view of the ocean through rustling leaves, still green into September. The day was warm but with the light breeze not so uncomfortable that we couldn't have gotten through an interview without refreshments. I wondered if Lou was startled by our reappearance and needed time to regroup. If surprised, he didn't seem at all rattled.

"I've been thinking about Sally a lot since you were here." Lou was talking as he slid a tray onto the table and served us homemade lemonade out of a large pitcher painted with seashells that I'd seen for sale in his shop. "I never seriously considered that something bad happened to her. I was all about me, so I only considered the pain she caused *me* by her rejection of *me*. Knowing what I was like as young man, I probably assumed she could not have stayed away from such an irresistible hunk. I was insufferable. Finding out I was in fact *resistible* was a painful experience. I went through quite an angry phase. A two-decade phase. Not because of Sally, although my failure with her was part of it. I wasn't happy when things didn't go my way. Drove my first wife away. But I did a lot of work to get to the place where I am now. A good place. A place where I can view situations with an eye to the effects they have on other people, not only me."

"So you've been reconsidering Sally's situation?" I asked.

"Never reached a conclusion. I did, however, consider the possibility that Sally was not able to come back. I always thought her disappearance was a simple case of her not wanting to return home. And, believe me, there were a lot of reasons she wouldn't want to."

"Such as?" Xander prompted.

"Such as her father, her mother, her high school boyfriend, her sister's boyfriend . . . ."

"Jimmy Dulles? The man Marianne married? Why would she want to stay away from him?" The rest I understood.

"He had the hots for her. She'd known that for years. She thought he was using Marianne to get close to her, which was a truly dumb plan because Sally would never hurt her sister. Once he was Marianne's boyfriend, he was out of contention. Forever. As if he was ever in contention." He snorted. I wasn't sure he was amused because Jimmy thought he was in Sally's league or in his league. Either way, the sound made it clear the thought of Jimmy winning Sally was ludicrous. "Sally viewed him the same way I did, as a world-class dork."

"But she loved her sister?" I asked.

"She really did. She worried about her, wanted her to have a bigger life than their parents saw for them. That is why I believe if she could have come back, she would have come back. Something must have happened. Something pretty big and pretty bad. And, no, I have no idea what that might have been."

Now was the time to broach the pregnancy issue, but how? While I was figuring it out, Xander jumped in. "When you and Sally were together did you and she ever have any near misses, you know scares, when she was late?"

"Why do you ask?" His puzzlement seemed genuine.

"Well, you know man, if a chick gets pregnant...." Xander waved his arms in a gesture that, although it meant nothing to me, appeared to clarify his meaning for Lou.

"Are you telling me Sally was pregnant?" His shock was visible. His face flushed and his eyes opened wide.

"We are just asking questions. We have no knowledge." I lied.

He released a deep breath and the color faded from his cheeks. "I guess you can go down that path, but I would consider it rather unlikely. When I was with her, she was on the pill. But that was never enough for Sally. She made me use a condom too, and that was back in the days when we didn't worry about disease. Even if two methods of birth control failed, I don't see how I could have been the one responsible. We hadn't been intimate for a couple months before she disappeared."

"You remember that?" Xander asked amazed.

"I remember the date: Fourth of July. She sneaked away from Ventnor, and we spent the weekend down here in Cape May. I thought we were solid, that everything was fine. First time I was ever here. It's a date I never forget."

That sounded to me like July 4th weekend qualified him for the fatherhood title. Xander thought so too and said it out loud.

"Except," Lou held up a finger, "I saw her a couple of weeks later, and I wanted to get it on but she was in pain—menstrual cramps."

"So, she told you no." Xander implied he would have accepted that excuse.

"No, she was willing, but when I was a kid, female stuff freaked me out. I couldn't do it. And that was the last time I had the opportunity to try."

Chapter 28

There were hours to go until sunset but Xander, dressed as Rex, and I were sitting on the porch of the snack bar at Cape May's Sunset Beach eating what I assured Xander was ordinary food.

"I can't say I am shocked by the idea that Jimmy had the hots for Sally." Xander bit into his burger.

"He was a kid. Probably had a crush. She was two years older. In high school years that's a generation older. I am sure he got over it."

"Sure? And it is a simple coincidence that fifty years later he gets the hots for a girl who is the twenty-first century incarnation of Sally Johnson?" Xander challenged me. "I am still in love with my playmate Gil's older sister, and she was already eight when I was five."

We stared at the gentle waves of the Delaware Bay lapping at the sand as we ate.

"You know, this is the only place around here to watch the sun set into the water. No land in between. Right into the water." I played tour guide.

"I am well aware of that," Xander said. "I read up."

We kept eating.

I finished chewing first. "What would Jimmy's feelings for Sally mean to our investigation? I believe Lou when he said Sally would not have hurt Marianne. So, I'd rule Jimmy out as the father."

"From what everyone says about Sally, I would tend to agree that she never would have hurt her sister so badly. And, from what I can see of Jimmy, Sally's loyalty wouldn't have been overwhelmed by passion." He nodded at the mostly submerged vessel sticking out of the water. "Why do they call it a concrete ship?"

"Because it's made of concrete."

"Why?"

"Must have seemed like a good idea at the time. I think it was a hundred years ago. Jimmy loved Sally. Not a hundred years ago. The ship was built sometime around World War I. Jimmy loved Sally fifty years ago. He would not have wanted her to leave." Except for the information about the ship, I was talking to myself as much as Xander.

"I guess we could attribute the same motives as we did to Lou. He might have tried to stop her. Can we visit the lighthouse on the way out of town?"

"Sure. If you are right and there was an *it*, an event, I can't believe Jimmy would have been involved. He would not want to kill Sally. He wanted her."

"Accidents happen. We've got to talk to him," Xander said.

"Without Marianne around. I don't know how we are going to pull that one off. I chatted with him a little the other morning while she was at the grocery store, but that was dumb luck." I took a final bite, wiped my hands and made a recommendation for our next steps. "Let's take a look at the lighthouse and go buy some fudge for our surveillance."

Xander approved of the refreshments I chose. "Perfect."

Or would have been if there had been any left after an hour's drive up the Garden State Parkway. We regretted not buying a second pound as we lingered on the Boardwalk watching for either member of the Dulles family to leave the house.

"At least we have a nice seat." Xander read the names of the couple whose children had memorialized their parents' love of the ocean on a plaque attached to the bench. "Do you think Marianne dedicated a bench to her parents?" Before I could answer, he went on. "You know who I would have made a plaque for? Sally."

"I think the honorees have to be deceased—at least all the ones I see are—and I don't think Marianne ever would have admitted that. Besides, Sally didn't love this spot. She ran away."

"Good point," he acknowledged and fell silent.

"They might have spotted us," Xander complained when dark was falling and we had seen no sign of either Marianne or Jimmy heading out for a postprandial stroll.

"I don't think so. I haven't seen either of them coming on to the porch to check out the Boardwalk."

"But they have windows. Traditional ones, I assume you are aware of the variety one can see through." He jabbed an elbow in my ribs calling to mind the younger brother I never had.

"They aren't expecting us. We are far enough away in bland enough clothes on a busy-enough strand where people stroll and congregate."

"For four hours?" he asked.

I didn't correct his math. We'd been hanging on the Boardwalk in some configuration for almost five hours. Five long hours with no news out of the Bahamas. "Check your phone. Are you sure you have reception? Maybe Peter Bossow sent the video and we missed it?"

"No. He's been sending updates that say not yet."

Of course, Mr. Perfect would.

"Look. Action." Xander almost sang.

I couldn't identify the activity, but Xander was right. Two figures emerged from under the awnings. Jimmy and Marianne. Together. In their usual matching outfits. They walked down their steps and then headed up the ramp to the Boardwalk.

"What if they turn this way? We'd better get out of here." Xander tugged on my arm. "We want him alone. We can't waste an accidental meeting when they're both there."

"Don't be silly, we'll just say...." I saw the couple turn in our direction. I had no idea what we would say. "Let's get out of here."

Chapter 29

When we got back to the hotel, I rushed to my room and the television. The Weather Channel coverage focused on storm preparations along the southeast coast of the US. Although the storm had passed the Bahamas, the network didn't have film from the islands yet. They mentioned damage, but not fatalities—at least in the Bahamas. A dozen people had perished in Haiti. I didn't give a moment's thought to my furniture, my motorbike and the bulk of my wardrobe. I didn't care about any of that. My only concern was Andy.

When the film from the Bahamas finally showed on my TV, I scoured the crowd for Andy. Not a sign of him or the Artistical. And then the anchor announced he had a moment of comic relief in the midst of so much serious news. Onto the screen came the image of a female reporter who would at worst be called beautiful. At worst. Even in her foul-weather gear I could tell she was well-built—largely because of the long shapely legs sticking out of the shorts she wore under her loud yellow jacket. She was standing in shallow water, talking into a microphone, when suddenly an uncommonly large wave rushed in from the side, knocked her over and swallowed her up. Comic relief? I found her situation frightening, but only for an instant, because a tall, lean man with a similar outfit ran into the surf, found her in the swirling water, swooped her into his arms and carried her to the beach. As soon as she spit out a mouthful or two of water, she played it for laughs. Even as she fought to catch her breath, she smiled up at her rescuer and batted her eyes. Andy planted a light kiss on her head and gave her a gentle squeeze.

She took a microphone from off-camera. "My hero. Andy, tell our audience who you are."

"Andy Beck. I work at the Artistical. I was up the beach and saw that wave headed for you."

"Well, Andy, thank you very much. You may have saved my life."

She knew his name before she asked him to identify himself. Maybe she repeated the anchor's name. Maybe *his* name was Andy. That had to be it. They'd show it again. I wouldn't move until they did, but I didn't have to wait. Answering the loud knock at my door revealed Xander holding his phone out, so I could see the video running on it.

"I saw it, but I want to see it one more time."

"Your beloved Andy is a hero. Isn't that lovely?"

I didn't answer. I watched the video again. And again. And again.

"He's fine. That's the proof. He's out saving lives."

"Did you notice anything odd about that video, Xander?"

"I…well…no."

I made him watch it with me. "She knows his name. The reporter knows his name."

"So?"

"How did she know his name before he told her?"

"I assume she has been covering the storm and, of necessity, they would be thrown together." He paused. "That wasn't the answer you wanted, was it?"

"*It's on his jacket* would have been the answer I wanted, but I checked. If his name was on display on his chest, it wasn't visible under his rain gear. And he kissed her."

"On her head! Give the man a break. He is in the throes of an exceedingly emotional moment. He just saved her life."

"So she should have kissed him."

"You wouldn't have liked that either. Face it. Besides, he gave her a little peck, not one of your big invisible kisses."

"Now you're making fun of me."

"No. Yes. Maybe. Just a little. But I wouldn't worry."

"Why?"

"Well, *I* wouldn't worry because *I* would go out and find someone else, but I realize you're not like that. You really want him, don't you?"

"Hence the ring, Xander." I held up my left hand.

"Well, we can go to him then, as soon as we can get air clearance. In the meantime, call him, the way he calls you when you're the one on the news. Go ahead. Go ahead." He found my phone on the bedside table and thrust it into my hand.

Andy's phone went to voice mail. "Hi. It's me. Glad to see you're okay and saving lives. Give me a call when you get a chance. Guess you're out celebrating."

Xander snatched the phone from my hand and hit end. "Don't go there. I could hear that little nagging thing in your voice. You don't want to be that woman. Take the high road."

So I took the high road. It led to the mini-bar. Xander drank most of the alcohol, and I ate all the salt. He remained energetic and alert, but I faded with each bite of chips.

"You're about to pass out. I'll go back upstairs." He got up and opened my door connecting to the next room. "I hope you don't mind, but I remain a little concerned about your visitor last night. I took the liberty of reserving the adjoining room. Del is going to sleep in there. I'll send him down. If you need anything, just make a lot of noise and he'll be right in there."

Chapter 30

Andy hadn't called when I dialed Xander's room the next morning. "I can't believe I forgot this. Jimmy picks up the mail every day. We can run into him at the post office."

"Is it open at 5:30 in the morning?" He asked.

"No."

"Is it open on Saturday?" He asked.

"I can check."

"Do and then give me a call back around 8:30 AM. I've got to go work out. You want to come? They have TVs in the fitness center."

"I have a TV across from my bed. Besides, I don't think we will see much more video out of the Bahamas. The storm has passed through. Florida is in the clear. All the attention is on the Carolina coast."

A long three hours passed before I could call Xander back, but I had been right. The weather coverage no longer included the clip of Andy saving Rachel Sturgis's life. All eyes were on the southeastern US and preparations in New Jersey in case the storm followed the European model.

"I can be ready in a half hour," Xander promised.

He was waiting when I reached the lobby. "Well, this is exciting. Off to the Ventnor City Post Office." He rubbed his hands together as if relishing dinner at a five-star restaurant. "Did you talk to Andy?" Xander asked casually.

"No. Not yet. I guess he's busy. This is probably the busiest time."

Xander didn't contradict me. "Probably," he said without conviction, or eye contact. He stayed two steps behind as he followed me silently to my car.

The Ventnor City Post Office sat in a strip mall where all the stores were lined up facing a wide parking lot. Every space offered a good view of the customer entrance—assuming no trucks or vans came along to block the line of vision. We picked a spot and took a quick walk into the post office and through the small area housing the PO boxes, before returning to my rental car.

"We're early. His mail won't be ready for over an hour."

"It's good to be in position early." Xander tried to be upbeat. "Island Gym has a juice bar."

"How do you know that?"

"I got tired of working out in the hotel. So I asked Peter…."

"I get it."

"So, do you want something?" He asked.

"I don't drink on surveillance."

"Oh." Xander thought over my policy. I guess he agreed because he stayed in the car. "I do not believe I am terribly fond of vehicular surveillance, especially without fudge," he observed after fifteen minutes.

"He probably won't come until right before closing," I apologized. "But he said he comes every day."

"I hope he doesn't mean every day but Saturday."

"At least they close early on Saturday. During the week we'd be sitting here until 5:30. If he doesn't come, we don't have to spend the afternoon in a parking lot." I looked on the bright side.

"And we can't turn the car around to face the lovely water view because he could slip in and out while we were admiring passing boats." Xander came close to whining.

"Very possible."

"Surveillance seemed more appealing last night when we were just hanging out on the Boardwalk waiting for him." Xander *was* whining.

"Surveillance doesn't usually include ocean breezes and pounding surf."

"At least, it provides some time for deep thoughts." He seemed to be searching for a positive viewpoint.

I was about to make a joke when I saw he wasn't kidding. Xander's eyes might have been on the parking lot, but his mind had wandered elsewhere. After another fifteen minutes or so, it seemed like the right moment to pose a question I'd wanted to ask many of the guests I'd served, people who lived lives the rest of us could barely imagine. I tested the waters to see if I could interrupt. His smile invited conversation.

"What does it feel like to be a rock star? I don't mean in general. I'm talking about the actual moment when you step onto the stage and the crowd goes wild. For you. Because of you." One of the moments I could only dream about.

He stared at me.

"Sorry. I didn't see that as a personal question. Please ignore it. Ignore me."

"No. That's not it. You see, I've been giving a lot of thought to that moment over the past few weeks. My reaction to that instant was a key indication, wasn't it, that I had a problem in my life. Your question is spot on." He stared past me to a time years before. "When I was a kid, I started touring and the crowd would go wild, wouldn't they? And I would think, *why shouldn't they?* And I would think I deserved it. I would do a good show so *I* didn't look bad. I'd say I worked hard for the fans, but I really did it for me. I still thought like that fourteen-year-old kid until this summer. Sad but true. And it was that moment, the one you're talking about, that changed my life."

He glanced over his shoulder to the bay. I wasn't sure he was going to continue. He took a deep breath before he did. "I was in Detroit or maybe Chicago or maybe Berlin for that matter. I didn't know, or care, where I was. I remember the walk to the wings and the wait, a moment only, before that first step onto the stage when I heard the roar. I mean for the first time. I heard the sounds of people, of individuals, each of them depending on me to make their lives just a little better for a short time. And the true meaning of that moment, one I'd always found exciting and energizing for my needs, hit me like a brick to my forehead. And for the first time ever, I truly valued that instant. I gained appreciation of what was happening not only to me personally but to me as part of the crowd. And that made me appreciate what had happened to me. How did I, an ordinary little kid from Akron, get to do what I do? I know it's hard to believe but until that moment, I'd just accepted the life I had known since puberty." He turned back to face me. "How could I deserve the adulation of these strangers when I understood so little about them, their lives, their problems?"

I wanted to pursue this line of questioning. I was really, really interested but I spotted Jimmy climbing out of a white SUV. I pointed.

"Here we go. Show time." Xander reached for his door handle, and I knew the moment to move our friendship to a new level had passed.

"What's our excuse for being here?" I followed him towards the post office.

"Well, we could say we were working out at Island Gym but…." He looked me up and down.

"I am going to assume you are teasing, but, just to be safe, we could say we were at their juice bar. Or we could just drop the subterfuge. Let's be honest. We want to talk to him."

We were standing on the sidewalk waiting for Jimmy when he came out of the post office. No pretense of coming from the gym. No smoothie in hand. We were there for him.

"Don't they have home delivery in Ventnor?" Xander asked.

"This is an old habit I have from the days when we shared the house with Marianne's parents. I didn't want them snooping in our stuff."

"Wasn't that close to fifty years ago?"

Jimmy laughed. "Forty something." He kept a smile on his face. "What brings you two here?"

I took the lead. "In an investigation we ask a lot of questions. We don't have a specific reason why we ask them, but it becomes clear we must if we want to get the big picture."

"I am certain you do." He displayed all eagerness, making sure we understood he would be receptive to any question we might spring on him.

"Xander and I have felt from the beginning that you do not want this investigation to continue. What we don't understand is why. We feel there is something you're not telling us."

Neither Xander nor I interrupted the long period of silence that followed. I got the impression Jimmy was willing to talk, but he needed time to collect his thoughts. I could only hope he wasn't pulling some lies together. He didn't look either of us in the eye when he finally spoke. "It's partially my fault that Sally went away."

I didn't want to break the mood. I let my expression ask why.

"I feel that, deep in her heart, Marianne always knew I had a crush on her sister, but I don't believe she ever realized how serious my feelings were. I was so stupid and just a kid. Sally was so kind to me. Nicer to me than any other girl, certainly any girl like that. You know, pretty. I deluded myself into believing she loved me and all I had to do was get older and she would love me in a grown-up way, if you get my drift."

I nodded to tell him I did.

"I didn't stop to think what it would mean to Marianne. I didn't understand how callous I was, not to mention dumb enough, to assume Sally would be just as callous. I mean, in those days, I never led Marianne on. We were boyfriend and girlfriend, and I know that she thought our relationship was more than it was. I used to talk about how I was her first love, a puppy love. I told her that we would both move on and have other loves, but Marianne wasn't listening. She always thought our relationship was the real thing. I don't think she harbored any suspicions about my feelings for Sally. You've met my wife. A little naïve. That is how she always was."

"Surely by the time you married, you were over your fascination with your bride's sister?" I detected a tinge of outrage in Xander's question.

"Marianne always says you never get over your first love. She just doesn't realize that she wasn't mine."

Xander remained as quiet as I did, pondering the sad life of Marianne Johnson Dulles, devoted to a man who loved her sister more. And that was how Jimmy described the situation. "It wasn't that I didn't love Marianne. I did in a way. I just loved Sally more."

"If you loved Sally, why did you persuade Marianne to stop searching for her?"

"I...the situation...it was awkward. I never told Marianne why I felt so sure Sally left of her own accord."

I had the feeling he was going to tell us.

Jimmy Dulles
Ventnor, New Jersey
September 8, 1968

What was she up to now?

Jimmy had seen Sally slip in and out of her bedroom window more times than he could count. Given the position of the room he occupied during the winter, it had been hard for him to miss her. But in the summer, when he had to surrender his bedroom to paying guests, he had to watch from the dormer window in his summer room in the attic. He knew that during her high school years, she sneaked out to meet that creep Bobby Aniston, but, luckily, he was gone from her life. She couldn't have gotten back together with him, could she? Where was she going? It was after midnight. Maybe that jerk Lou had come to town. Not that he liked Lou any better than Bobby. For such a smart girl, Sally sure had horrible taste in boyfriends.

Why had she broken her usual pattern? He expected Sally to travel light when she snuck out, but she had dropped a daisy-patterned pillowcase stuffed with something other than a pillow from the window. Then with an old canvas rucksack so crammed that clothes were hanging out the sides and shoes were dangling from the straps, she shifted her weight to the trellis that she had been using as a ladder for as long as he could remember. Her burden meant she didn't move with her usual grace and speed. As she climbed down carefully, he moved closer to the window to see who waited for her below. The light from the full moon made it easy to see that, behind the Dulles car, the narrow space between the houses was empty.

Sally struggled with the pillowcase along the side of the building, away from the street. Her belongings were slowing her down. Jimmy rushed down the narrow stairs to the landing with a round window overlooking their back yard. Sally was cutting through. Going where? Was somebody waiting for her? In the quiet night, he didn't hear a car idling, just the soft rhythmic pounding of the waves on the shore.

He tiptoed down the steps onto the main floor. He didn't know if all the guests were in for the night, but he found no one in the sitting room or on the porch. He tried to be quiet and didn't run until he cleared the wooden steps. He slipped around the back of his parents' home and through the neighbor's yard. Despite the effort of lugging the pillowcase, Sally had a big head start. He couldn't cut her off, but he saw her cross Atlantic Avenue. She was walking west toward Ventnor Avenue. Going where?

He felt in his pocket. He had his keys, including the key to his father's car. His father was in for the night. He would never hear it move, never miss it. Jimmy was out of breath when he reached the old Ford. In the still of the summer night, the engine's purr resembled a roar. He wasn't going to let worries about explanations for his father slow him down. He could conjure up a story, if required. There was a good chance he would never have to.

He crossed Atlantic at the stop sign and drove down to the next cross street, Ventnor Avenue. There he looked left and saw Sally coming towards him. Why had she gone a block south to head north? To mislead anyone who noticed her slip out of her house? He waited until she got close and then called in a stage whisper. "Sally, what on earth are you doing out so late?" He smiled as if it was not at all unusual for him to be there and spoke as if he were just curious— not that he thought her walk at such a late hour created cause for concern.

His smile must not have been disarming. Sally didn't respond with a matching expression. He could tell she was trying to decide how to handle the situation, how to handle him. If she planned on telling the truth, she would have answered by now, but she just stood on the corner, pillowcase in hand, staring at him. His smile had faded by the time she spoke.

"I'm going to see a friend."

He was smart enough not to comment on how much she carried, but he couldn't control his eyes. They darted to the pillowcase.

"I'm lending her some things." She offered a weak excuse. He didn't let on that he didn't believe her.

"Let me give you a ride."

"It isn't far. I'm fine."

"It's late, Sally. A girl shouldn't be out on the street alone at this hour."

She smiled, not a nice warm smile, but the kind that said she found him *amusing. "You're beginning to sound like my father."*

Jimmy knew if there was one thing he did not want to do, it was sound anything like her father. Jimmy didn't find him such a bad guy, but he knew his strict rules and tight control grated on his daughters. On Sally, really. Marianne was never one to rock the boat.

"Get in. I'll give you a ride." He offered again, trying to make the comment sound nothing like a command.

Sally stayed on the corner.

He threw the car into park and put on the emergency before he hopped out and ran over to pull the pillowcase from her hand. "Don't be ridiculous. We're friends. I won't tell your father where you are. I just couldn't live with myself if I left you out here and something happened." He carried her things around the car and held the passenger door open.

She slipped the pack off her back and surrendered it to Jimmy. He shoved it, along with the pillow case, into the back seat.

"Jimmy, you have to promise me you will never tell anyone where I went. I just need a ride to the bus station. I will send Marianne a letter when I am settled." She slipped by him into the front seat.

His stomach fell. "You're going away?"

"What did you think? I decided to take all my clothes to the laundromat in the middle of the night?"

"I...I...thought maybe you were going on an overnight trip."

"Jimmy, I will tell you, but you cannot tell a soul."

He slid into the driver's seat. "You know you can trust me."

"I have to get away from here. There's a big world out there and as long as I am tied to my family, I won't get to live in it. You cannot tell anyone, not even Marianne, but I am going to California."

He barely heard what she said after that. He fought to focus on his driving while she spouted rationalizations about why she couldn't live her dream in New Jersey, reasons explaining why she needed to go to California.

"Do you even realize there are women who love other women?" she asked.

He felt himself blush. He knew such women existed. He didn't understand what they did or why they did it. It wasn't natural. Sally couldn't possibly be that way. What about Bobby and Lou? Just because they had been wrong for her didn't mean that all men were. He didn't say anything, however. He didn't know what to say.

"Do you understand that two women can love each other?"

"Sally, you have known these protestors for a week. Most of them for under two days. You can't know if you love them."

"I may not know but I understand that I need to find out."

"You are so impressionable, going for every fad that comes along." He heard the testiness in his voice, the same tone he'd heard her father use with her. Sally heard it too. "Let me out. I have hours to get there. I can walk." She put her hand on the handle and he had to hold her arm to prevent her from getting out.

"No. No. Just talk to me. Please. You have time. I want to understand. I do. I want to listen. Come on. We'll go for coffee. That's all. A cup of coffee." Her anger faded and she laughed. "You don't drink coffee."

As if he were just a kid. "I'm two grades behind you, but only ten months younger, Sally. You see me as a kid because of school. But I graduate next year. I'm an adult. I could get drafted. I could go to war. I understand things." He really didn't, and she knew it. He amended his statement. "Or, I could. I need someone to discuss the world with me, explain the world to me."

*****

Jimmy smiled, a forced expression. "She liked to play the elder with me, so she appeared happy to talk."

"Where did you go?"

"I would hang out in an all-night coffee shop up in Atlantic City in those days. I can't remember the name. Hardly matters. It all happened so long ago. I never told Marianne I drove her sister to the bus station."

"And that's what you did?" Xander asked.

"Isn't that what I just said?"

"No." Xander was getting this interviewing thing down. "You said you never told her sister you did."

Jimmy screwed his features into an expression that asked Xander if he was crazy. "Are you calling me a liar?"

"No way, man." Xander tried to reestablish a relationship. "I just didn't hear you say you actually drove her to the bus station."

"Oh my God. Listen. I did everything I could to convince Marianne that her sister left of her own accord. I did everything in my power to keep her from discovering my role. I didn't have to tell any lies. I wasted my time, and other people's, to collect information that backed up what I already knew. I wanted Marianne to understand, to accept that Sally chose to go. Every bit of information I collected back then indicated Sally wanted to leave. That did not make Marianne happy. If she thought I'd helped…." He didn't finish. He didn't have to. We understood.

"If all this is true about your feelings for Sally, why did you stay with Marianne? Why did you marry her? You loved her sister." Xander might have well added the phrase *Man, that wasn't cool* because his tone did.

"Sally was a romance that would never work out. I understood that. And, I realized Marianne had some strong points."

Not an overwhelming expression of love.

"Among them," Xander said when he got back in the car, "a sizeable inheritance?"

"We don't actually know that," I said. "Or anyone who could tell us."

"Well," Xander hesitated. "There is always Peter Bossow."

Chapter 31

Xander and I were back at the Artistical's beach deck bar—the place where our collaboration had begun—waiting to hear from Peter Bossow about the Johnson family's finances. My fear was he would take over our entire investigation. My greater fear was maybe he should. I had no idea how to proceed. Sure, we'd learned a lot about Sarah "Sally" "Sunshine" Johnson, but we didn't have a clue—or an opinion—about where she had gone, but I did have a need to avoid damaging my pride—not to mention a need to keep my mind off what was going on in the Bahamas.

"The worst is over," Xander declared, but he was talking about Hurricane Frieda. It had been almost twenty-four hours since the storm had passed and no word from Andy. I was no longer worried that he was lying somewhere in a hospital. I was just worried that he was lying somewhere. Xander viewed my fears as crazy. "Everyone in the Bahamas is too busy for romance right now."

"You never had a quickie?"

"Why? What did you hear?" He feigned horror.

"I know you're trying to make me feel better…."

"And I am a stranger to failure. Come on. Cheer up. Try to focus on our case."

I tried but my mind kept going to all those movies where the threat of death heightens emotions and compels people to make love and, for the moment, forget about their fiancées waiting back in New Jersey. Without a break, our investigation wasn't going anywhere. I told Xander to call Faye Padilla. "You know, about the charity gig she wanted you to do." Checking back with Faye was the only next step I could come up with.

"I am still on my personal quest for meaning. I'm not ready to return to performing."

"Of course not. She won't be ready either, but it will give her a reason to thank you by providing the names of the women in Boston who might know where Sally Johnson went."

"You, my dear, are a mastermind. I'll just slip inside to make the call." Fifteen minutes later my phone buzzed with a text from Xander. "Meet me in my suite."

He started talking as soon as Del let me in the door. "I did as you suggested and reaffirmed my offer to perform, and Ms. Padilla volunteered several names. She said she was glad I called. Our visit got her thinking about the old days. I didn't even have to remind her that we were hoping for names. I'll read them out."

I took my position near the white board.

"Ready? Elaine Smith."

"You're kidding." I recorded the name.

"Diana Hofstader."

"Better." I asked him to spell the surname.

"And," he paused to provide himself with a drum roll on the edge of a table. "Mary Donatia Lombardmessen."

"Jackpot. There couldn't be two of them."

And there weren't. The problem? There did not even appear to be one of them. A half hour of Internet searching yielded no leads.

"She must have married. We could ask Peter Bossow." Xander tried to be helpful.

"No," I almost yelled. "I will find her." And after another half hour and a dozen spelling variations, I did. "She's still in Boston. Cambridge actually. Spelling her name L-O-M-B-A-R-D-M-E-I-S-S-E-N."

"Okay. Do you want to drive or fly?"

I didn't want to go. "Let's call her."

"You aren't fooling me. I can see your ulterior motive. What do you not understand about mobile phones? They are mobile. You pick them up and you take them with you from place to place. When Andy calls, he will reach you, no matter where you are. It's amazing technology. I'm surprised you haven't heard of it."

"But there's a storm headed for us. We might get out and not be able to get back."

"I don't understand your need to be in Atlantic City. I don't think Andy will slip away from his post to surprise you here. The possibility of that unlikely scenario unfolding hardly matters, however, because we shall, in fact, return. If we go early tomorrow morning and come back right after we see Ms. Lombardmeissen…."

"Now Mrs. Lombardmeissen-Winghaven," I added. "Professionally known as, that is pka, Dona Haven."

"Thank God. If we return right after we see Ms. Mary Donatia Lombardmeissen-Winghaven pka Dona Haven, we will be here in time to hunker down, or even evacuate. Does that suit you?"

I had to be honest. Nothing suited me.

"And if we don't get back, what does it matter as long as you have your mobile phone. Well, your mobile and a charger. And none of this will matter because I am sure you will hear from Andy tonight."

I wasn't so sure when I returned to my room in a mood optimistically described as morose, grabbed the room service menu and threw myself across the bed. As the sun went down, I noticed an odd red glow flashing. The room phone.

"Funny thing, Maggie." The voice on the message was Andy's. "I don't know your cell phone number. I always use speed-dial and our records are in our cottage and well, they might be a bit, gone. They are gone. No way to sugarcoat it. An awful lot, but not everything, is gone. But you might have seen that I am alive. Only problem is that when I saved the reporter I lost my phone in the surf and I couldn't call you. Even when people offered me their phones, I couldn't call you. I never memorized the number. So I called the hotel and left this message. Hope you get it. It's about 8AM."

8AM! Twelve hours ago. I'd been driving myself nuts for twelve hours. I had to call him back, but how? I called the hotel operator and asked her to put me in touch with the switchboard at the Bahama location. "You're kidding, right?" She asked in a none-too-pleasant tone. "They have no power, and, no, I have no idea when it will be back."

I called Xander and told him I couldn't go to Boston the next day. I had to wait by the phone in my room.

"What is this? 1962? Have you been abducted into the cast of *Bye Bye Birdie*?"

Apparently, Xander had been studying up on the 1960s. I defended my position calmly. "I have a perfectly reasonable desire to talk to my boyfriend, I mean fiancé."

"On the off chance that the power comes back or he gets a new phone in what is essentially a war zone? He is busy Meg. Helping people. Putting the hotel back together. Getting my room ready."

"Xander, this investigation is a lark for you, but this phone call is my real life."

He let out a long theatrical sigh signaling his exasperation. "Give me some time."

In case a call came through on line one, I ordered room service on line two of my hotel phone, sat beside it on the bed and waited. I was shocked when my cell phone rang.

"Meg?"

"Andy? How did you get this number?"

"Is it a problem?"

I laughed. "No. Really. How did you get it?"

"Well, apparently Xander Frost is with the same agency as Sully Sullivan, a reporter who is here covering the recovery. So he got his agent to call Sully on his mobile and give him your number and then bring the phone to me so I can call you. He's standing here waiting for it back. He's leaving tonight."

"Write down my number and call me when the hotel system comes up or you get a new phone or someone leaves theirs lying around. Was it horrible?"

"It was no picnic. I was afraid I'd never get back to New Jersey." I understood the code.

"I was missing you, too."

"Look, Sully's gotta go. We'll talk soon. Love you."

I'd heard all I needed to hear. When Del called to wake me, I responded with a cheeriness atypical before dawn. Not that my light mood cheered up Del. He seemed annoyed he wasn't coming along, but, being Del, he remained polite.

Chapter 32

I had prepared a lecture for Xander that claimed, as enjoyable as traveling by private jet was, and enjoyable hardly did the practice justice, our developing habit of flying around the country on private jets was ecologically reprehensible. Then I stepped into that day's plane and found it had only six seats and four of them were already taken. I rationalized that this flight would not waste as much energy as the last. And, it had spared me standard airport security.

"You and I can't run about using more than our fair share of the earth's resources." Xander scolded *me*. "Today we are sharing a ride with….Sorry, mates. Four names are a lot to remember, even when one isn't imbibing or indulging in other substances designed to dull our senses and mute our creative urges, not to mention kill our memories." Xander sounded a bit like a public service announcement. "Please introduce yourselves to my colleague, Meg Daniels."

"Teresa."

"Nicole."

"Bobby."

"Kayla."

Each of the passengers introduced themselves with a polite handshake and a smile. I guessed they were in the eighteen to twenty-one age range and knew they invested a large amount of money in tattoos and piercings. I didn't like to stereotype, after all I, myself, wasn't the type to jet around in private planes, but they didn't strike me as a typical charter jet crowd. But what did I know of typical charter jet crowds? I defined them according to the celebs who visited the Artistical in the Bahamas.

Xander took the seat across from mine and I congratulated him. "We're covered from an environmental perspective. Kind of."

"A smaller plane offers more flexibility. Don't want to find ourselves number twenty-five for take-off at Logan."

"And," I nodded at the other passengers, "even though it isn't an issue, I am happy you are saving some money. You have been more than generous on this project. I am not sure that Marianne and Jimmy understand but I do."

"It's nothing, and I do mean that. Ridiculous really. After a point, you can't beat the money off with a stick. Once you're rich, people give you all sorts of things you don't need, probably in the hopes you'll buy more things that you don't need. Although I am picking up the full tab for this flight. These are some kids I met in the bar last night and found out they'd never been to Boston. So, I made a deal. We aren't going to wait for them on the ride back. If they make the flight, they make it. If not, they are on their own."

The sound of "Anything Goes" playing on Xander's phone cut off any further discussion. "Peter Bossow." He explained as he picked up. "Uh huh. Uh huh. Great. I'll watch for it."

I stared at him expectantly. "Peter is sending more detail, but in a nutshell, Marianne and Sally's parents were loaded. Frugal but loaded. Marianne got it all including that house that loads of developers would happily tear down and replace with million dollar condo complexes. Jimmy's parents? Not so loaded, and definitely not so frugal. Went down the tubes financially when he was in college. Marianne's parents had to foot the bill for his last year. As I said, Peter's got more that he'll send."

The engines started and Xander settled into his seat and opened a book on the history of Atlantic City. No headphones. Despite his trip to the bar last night, he stuck to his sabbatical from music. I took advantage of the calm to watch the takeoff out the window. The sun made the short trip from the horizon to the cover of a cloud bank, but for those few moments, Atlantic City glimmered behind us. If only it gleamed as brightly upon closer inspection. As Xander was discovering, the city kept taking hits—the decline of its elegant palaces on the beach in the middle of the twentieth century and the stumbles of the casinos at the start of the next. Time and again, the residents had their hopes raised, but, despite pockets of success, unemployment and poverty remained a reality for many.

I curled my legs under me and leaned on the armrest for a view out the window, and found Bobby had done the same in the seat behind me.

"I don't fly much. This is a big treat for me. How about you? Are you Xander's manager or something?"

"Or something," I answered. "We're working together on a project."

"He's so different than I thought he would be."

"Xander?"

"Yeah. We met him in the bar last night and he was into the music, but he wanted to talk about Atlantic City and growing up there. He was really into hearing about us."

"Xander?" A bit of amazement crept into my tone.

"Yeah. I always thought he'd be kind of a jerk, but he didn't want to talk much about himself."

"Xander?"

"Why do you sound surprised?"

"Oh, I'm not," I lied.

"He's on a journey of self-realization. At least that is what he told us."

"That's true. He is." Maybe I was the self-centered one. I had been so concerned about my communication issues with Andy that I'd failed to notice how far Xander had progressed with his personal growth plan. Across the aisle, he appeared totally engrossed in his reading.

As the plane veered west on our way to Hanscom Field, in the distance Boston shone just as brightly as Atlantic City had. Behind me, Teresa, Nicole, Bobby, and Kayla clamored with excitement.

Xander had reserved an SUV with room for his four new friends. "Very ordinary. No driver." I congratulated him on his choice of vehicle although having it delivered to the tarmac wasn't so ordinary.

I, the designated driver, found my way to Harvard Square where we dropped off our four passengers with directions on how to ride the T from me and cash from Xander that meant they didn't have to ride the T.

Before we found Dona Haven's address, I took Xander for a spin around Cambridge. His eyes opened wide and his head swiveled.

"You've been to Boston before," I assumed.

"I played around here. Of course, I never got to see anything other than the inside of my hotel."

"Cambridge is great. You'd love it."

"Yeah." I detected longing in his tone and in his expression as he watched a crowd of students in Harvard Square. He sat in silence for the short ride to Dona Haven's home. "This one has found a lovely place to live, hasn't she?" Xander said as I squeezed the car into a parking space.

She had. Her house was beautiful, not as fancy as some of the spreads at the northern end of Cambridge, but an ambitious renovation of an old red wooden three-story tucked on a narrow street between Harvard and Central Squares. Through a wide and tall window, we couldn't avoid seeing all the accoutrements of a busy academic's life. A big wooden desk covered with papers. Floor to ceiling bookshelves stuffed with volumes of every shape and size. And in a far corner a baby grand piano that I am sure most appealed to Xander. "Not ordinary," I reminded him.

We rang and we knocked and detected no sign of life inside. We waited a few minutes and tried again. Once more, we got no answer. I tried to console Xander, and not just because he wasn't going to get to play the piano. "We've been batting a thousand. That couldn't go on. We missed one. At her home anyway. She has a gallery in Hyannis. Apparently, she paints in addition to teaching."

"Hyannis. They have an airport." He cheered up.

"We could drive to Hyannis in under two hours," I suggested.

"And back to our plane in another three. We could, if there was no storm bearing down on Atlantic City right now, but there is. You want to get home, right? So we fly."

We weren't in the air long enough for me to feel guilty about our trip. I hadn't even finished a soft drink before we began our descent. "Thank you, Peter Bossow," Xander whispered in my ear as we came down the steps to a waiting car.

I assumed Peter Bossow had given the driver Dona Haven's address because he drove us out of town to a rough and narrow driveway that led to a cottage covered in weathered shingles set behind a thick clump of trees. Nothing said the building wasn't open to the public although, in retrospect, the location might have indicated we were approaching a working studio, not a store. We announced our arrival, calling hello as we strolled across the rough lawn, but no one answered. The door stood open. A purse on the long table that ran down the center of the room suggested someone would be returning shortly.

If it was a beautiful day outside, it was a beautiful day inside thanks to an external wall that was more window than wall. A gentle breeze rustled the row of light, white curtains that, given the tall trees protecting the building, were not required to block harsh sunlight. Signs of an artist's life were everywhere. Art books and magazines. Rags and cans, some filled with paint, some filled with brushes. Blank canvases and canvases with works that the artist had hung for display.

"So light and bright. I think that I could create beautiful paintings here." Xander drank in the details of the room.

"I didn't know you painted."

"I don't. I mean I never have, but in a place like this I am sure I could." He wandered through a wide opening into another space that made the first room appear neatly organized. "This is where the heavy-duty work gets done."

I peeked through the doorway. The floor was all but carpeted with drop cloths. A huge canvas, with large white spots still uncovered, lay on the floor. Other, smaller canvases in various stages of completion stood on easels around the room. Paint, rags and brushes were stationed beside each easel. A few unframed paintings hung on the walls. I wondered if the artist wanted to watch them, to experience them before declaring them done. They looked finished to me, but I was not the right person to ask.

Xander followed me back to the room we had first entered. I pulled a wooden folding chair away from the table and sat down to browse through a book on Magritte. Xander wandered.

"She's good." Xander browsed the large paintings stacked along unfinished walls. "I like these. They are abstract yet I can see what she is aiming to depict, what she is trying to make me feel. I do. I can feel myself inside a scene."

I had no expertise in the world of art, but his seemed like an accurate description to me.

"The bright ones are gorgeous, but it's the dark ones that speak to me." Xander had just taken off his fake glasses to study the paintings seriously, when a woman's voice told us someone was approaching.

We heard Dona Haven before we saw her. I hopped to my feet somehow thinking trespassing while standing appeared less offensive. As the artist approached, she laughed with lilting tones into a cell phone. The expression on her face matched until she spotted us in her studio. "Don't hang up, Desi. There are two strangers standing in my workspace. I might need help."

"No, no." Xander and I protested in unison.

"Wait a minute. I'm okay. I suspect one of them is Xander Frost."

Xander pulled off his hat and let his hair spring free. "Yes. Yes. It's me."

"A rock star." The caller on the other end had no idea who or what a Xander Frost was. "No, you wouldn't. I wouldn't either except for my granddaughter. She and I do not share the same taste in music."

Xander frowned and Dona responded with a new, welcoming tone. "No, I am sure your music is lovely."

She wasn't at all sure, but why argue? I hoped Xander wouldn't.

"My forays outside of classical music died with Jim Morrison. That is probably rather narrow-minded of me. I am sure some good music has been produced in the last few years."

"Fifty." Xander wasn't placated yet. "And it was great, still is great."

"I'd better get off." The artist spoke to her caller. "I seem to have offended my visitor and I haven't even greeted him properly. Yes. Xander." She spelled it. "Am I correct?" she asked Xander.

Annoyance and confusion fought for control of the rocker's face as he nodded. We continued to listen to her side of the conversation.

"Frost, as in winter. I don't believe it will come to that. I see no indication he is up to no good. He brought someone with him. She doesn't appear sinister. She's looking through my Magritte book so she can't be all bad."

"Five-foot-five. Maybe six."

"Thirty-five? Not forty yet."

"No idea. Blonde. Messy but kind of cool. Good basic cut. Nice look."

Maybe I could get to like Dona Haven.

"No, the question is whether she is an accomplice or a witness. We'll see."

Chapter 33

"And what is rock star, Xander Frost, doing in my studio?" Dona Haven dropped the phone on the table next to her bag.

Xander spoke but didn't provide a direct answer. He dove into a discussion of her paintings. Dona didn't care why he had come or whom he had brought with him, she delighted in his comments. She knew an admirer, and possibly a customer, when she saw one. I eavesdropped on the conversation like the hanger-on I had become.

The real purpose of our visit had not yet come up when Xander made two purchases. One dark and one bright. "I am tempted to go with two of your darker scenes, but I want to believe that better days are ahead. Appreciate the darkness, I will, but welcome the light." Xander poked me. "You should buy one for your hotel."

"I am not involved in those purchases, but I can certainly mention Dona's work to Bingo." I turned to our hostess. "Howard Bing, the owner of the Artistical properties. I work for him."

She smiled, one of those knowing expressions where you can see her calculating the dollar value of that information. Xander and I were definitely growing on her.

"I guess you're wondering how we found you, why we found you," I said.

She smiled, already writing a mental thank-you note for the lucrative referral I would provide.

"Do you remember Sarah Johnson from your days at a commune near Boston?"

"Sarah. Sarah from the Jersey Shore? Of course, I remember her. I can't believe we lost touch. Did she send you? Is she okay?"

"We're not really sure," I said.

"It's a long story," Xander added.

"Well then, let's sit down and you can share it."

Xander and the artist had paperwork to do, but first Dona went for refreshments. We couldn't have picked a better day to settle onto oversized wicker chairs on the porch of her studio: bright, sunny with cool air that offered the first hint of fall. Hurricane Frieda showed no signs of threatening New England.

"Happy hour. Here, at last." Dona slid a tray onto the table. Red cocktails with strawberries peeking out the top and a pitcher for easy refills. I was really getting to like Dona Haven. "Tell me. I get that you're searching for Sarah, but why can't you locate her?"

"It's complicated." I explained we did not know if she had survived her escape from Ventnor when our investigation began. "Faye Padilla in San Francisco told us she had come here. Not here, but to your commune in Somerville."

"Hardly a commune. Just a bunch of women sharing a house that a trust-fund hippie inherited. You might call it a co-op, but a better description would be a loosely organized living arrangement. Sally stayed with us when she arrived in Boston and had her baby with us. Little girl with strawberry blond hair and those same bright blue eyes as Sally's. Adorable. She spent her formative years with us. Great for her. There were other kids. I don't know how many, but she always had playmates. We were young women, each of us struggling in our own way, helping each other. My situation was simple. I wanted a safe haven where I could live while I tried to become an artist. When I decided to go to graduate school, I stayed. I could never have gotten my PhD if I hadn't shared my life with those women. But, as I said, some of them had highly complex situations. Bad marriages. Abusive spouses."

"And Sarah?"

"With a daughter, her life was certainly tougher than mine, but she did okay. She had met a guy on the bus from California, but she didn't want to take his help. He wasn't the baby's father, but he would have been happy if he were. He was always around to help her but she lived with us and shared childrearing responsibilities with the other mothers. She was pregnant when she arrived. She stayed until her baby was about three. Then Thomas, the guy from the bus, persuaded her to marry him. Everyone loved Thomas. We were all happy when she finally said yes to him. We had a big shindig at our home."

I hoped that she was in a mood to reminisce and she was.

Dona Haven
Somerville Massachusetts
Summer, 1972

Dona had pushed a reluctant Sarah into having a real wedding, wearing a white dress, buying a cake, and standing up in the house's small garden to repeat vows in front of those who loved her. But now that the day had arrived she could tell the bride felt excited.

"Do you think Thomas will approve?" Sarah found room for a few more baby's breath in her upswept blond hair.

"Thomas would approve if you showed up in a potato sack. You look beautiful." Dona held the bouquet of wildflowers that matched the colorful embroidery on the white cotton and lace dress. "When I bought that dress in Mexico, I never guessed it would be put to such good use."

"This isn't how I envisioned my wedding day."

"Do you wish your father could be here to walk you down the aisle?"

"You are being rather liberal with your definition of an aisle. Do you mean do I wish he were here to help me pick my way through the folding chairs in the backyard? Sadly, no. He wouldn't do it. He would never approve. Getting married after your baby is born and not even to the biological father! He would never participate in such a decadent event."

"And your mother?"

"Does what my father tells her."

"But you care about your sister."

"I don't know how she would behave. She is a very obedient daughter.

196

She has a way of judging, of withholding approval. Death's head at a feast. *Today will be much more relaxing without them."*

Sarah moved on to talk of the party ahead, but as she put the final touch-es on her hair and the little bit of makeup she'd been persuaded to use for her big day, she returned to the topic of her sister. *"Marianne believes she is happy there, but I worry. I have this delusion that I can go back and kidnap her to a better life."* She chuckled. *"As if she would see this as a better life. I can tell you that Marianne's wedding will be nothing like mine."* She gazed out the window. *"Thomas is already hanging around our makeshift altar."* A big grin spread across her face.

Dona glanced out the window. *"You got yourself one adorable boy there."* One who looked even cuter in his wedding outfit: blue jeans, sandals and white cotton Mexican shirt. He was anxious to make Sarah his wife. His smile stretched so wide Dona swore she saw the sun bouncing off his white teeth.

Sarah peeked over her shoulder. *"See the way the breeze is playing with his curls? I love that."* She studied her future husband for a moment and then added, *"But I would love him if he didn't have a hair on his head."*

At that point, Sarah's three-year-old daughter burst into the room. *"Let's go. We get married. We get married. We go marry Thomas."*

*****

"That little girl loved Thomas. Couldn't wait to call him Daddy. He was a great guy. A lot of the women were not totally keen on men, but they loved Thomas." Dona's smile was sweet and nostalgic.

"Do you remember his last name?"

"Sure. I think I do. Wait. I must." She closed her eyes. "It's in there. It's all in there. Just sometimes it takes a while to pull it up."

"Do you have any photos of the wedding?" The possibility was a longshot, but this entire quest was a longshot.

"Not that I recall. Maybe in Cambridge, but they would be stashed away in a box somewhere in my attic." She seemed genuinely apologetic. "But wait a minute. I might have something better." She freshened our drinks from the pitcher. "You work on those. This might take a few minutes."

Seventeen to be exact. She was talking when she returned to the porch. "I gave Sarah a portrait for her wedding, and I did a few sample drawings, pastels, so she could pick the pose she liked. I haven't seen them in years, but I keep everything. Bad habit but worked today. I had not opened the 1972 box in decades."

She unrolled the first of three drawing papers that, no matter what color they had started out, were now the yellow brown of a grocery bag.

"They are rough, but they are accurate."

Xander moved the tray and Dona laid the drawing in its place. The sketch was beautiful, largely because its subject was beautiful. Her eyes were impossibly blue, and her blond hair pulled up into a Victorian bouffant, luxuriously thick. Xander stroked it without letting his fingers touch the surface.

"We called it a Gibson-girl style. Proved that Sarah would have been gorgeous in any era. I stuck the baby's breath in her hair for the sitting, but that is what she did for the wedding as well."

Sarah wore the white cotton dress Dona had loaned her for the ceremony. In the corner of the drawing you could see the strip of embroidery on her sleeve. Most of the embroidery, however, was blocked by the back of a child's head with a wreath of wildflowers on her golden red hair.

"Sally didn't want her daughter in the portrait. She didn't know who would see the painting, and she didn't want everyone to know that she had a baby before she got married. It was the times." She apologized for her friend. "I thought this pose was subtle, but Sarah wouldn't have it. She picked this one." She unfurled another paper. Just as in the other drawing, Sarah looked off into space with dreams in her eyes and just a trace of a smile on her lips.

"She looks as if she is just about to burst out laughing," Xander said.

"She often was. Even in the first year with us, when her life was pretty much hell, she could laugh. She was a charismatic person."

She showed us the third picture, but I agreed with Sarah's choice. The second drawing captured something about the woman's personality that the third lacked.

"I suppose I should have offered to include Thomas, but…."

I waited for an explanation.

Finally, she said, "I didn't want to. I thought the picture of a female, this female, was so soft. I didn't want his testosterone changing the mood. He was great, but he was a guy." Now, she sounded apologetic for herself.

I hadn't seen the final painting, but I suspected she made the right choice. "Did they stay married?" I asked.

"As long as I knew them. They moved to Baltimore. He got a position at a college down there. Math. She taught high school. Bauer. Thomas Bauer. That's it. Sarah and Thomas Bauer. I can't believe we lost touch. Without social media, people just did. It wasn't easy to maintain contact. Careers. Kids. I can't believe I forgot his last name. Mariana was so proud when it became her last name. Thomas adopted her."

"Mariana?"

"Sarah's daughter."

I didn't get it. How did you love your sister so much that you name your baby after her but never write or call? I glanced at Xander and felt fairly sure he wondered the same thing.

Chapter 34

On the return flight, Xander gazed out the window and didn't utter a word from Hyannis until we passed over Connecticut's Thimble Islands. "Do you ever wonder that no one could be as sweet and good as everyone claims Sally was?"

"I like to believe she was, but I guess I have been taking everyone's comments with a grain of salt. Memories erase warts. Sally must have had some."

"Hmm." He didn't speak again until the skyline of New York was fading behind us and the winds were picking up.

"Guess we're hitting the edge of Frieda." I interrupted Xander's reverie. I had an ulterior motive. Flight attendants have congratulated me on not only sleeping but snacking through incredible turbulence. I am not a fraidy-cat, but when the bounces get as big as the ones we were experiencing in an aircraft as small as the one we were flying, experience said my stomach would do better if I chatted.

"Guess so." Apparently, Xander was not in a mood to chat.

I went back to silence.

"We don't have that far to go." I made another attempt at idle conversation.

"Think not." Xander's mood had not changed, or so it appeared until he leaned across the aisle and spoke in a low voice, at least the lowest one can effectively use on a plane in flight. "I lied to you once."

Shocker. Once. No kidding. Dozens of pithy retorts ran through my mind, but I didn't say one of them. I didn't say anything.

"Remember, I told you that no girl ever said no to me?"

I thought he was only looking for a nod, so that's all I offered, although I'm not sure his downcast eyes caught the gesture.

"That isn't true."

I just waited.

"There was a girl, Elise. That was her name. Elise."

He paused as if he had just made a major announcement.

"She didn't buy my act. I was twenty-one. I thought I knew everything. Hit records. Big bucks. Fancy friends. I believed that was all it took to be desirable. And that worked for a lot of people, but not Elise. Sally may be pretty, but she couldn't hold a candle to Elise, as my grandmum would have said. I saw her at a party. One of those events where you wonder where they get so many gorgeous girls. I thought they were all beautiful, until Elise walked in. I would have sworn they put a spotlight on her, but of course no one did. She generated her own light. In my memory, the crowd parted to let her pass. She had on this short, white dress, kind of crocheted. Her hair was blond like Sally's. Kind of soft and free flowing. Simple."

I stayed quiet and let him bask in the memory.

"She did go out with me. I made a beeline to her that night and kept her by my side for as long as I could, which was only a month."

Xander seemed oblivious to the large air pocket we dropped into. He had travelled back in time to Elise. Trapped in the present with a churning stomach, I tried to focus on Xander's romance.

"She kept asking to see the real me, and I kept telling her she was seeing the real me. She told me I was fun and good for a laugh, but she couldn't take me seriously, if I didn't take myself seriously."

I fought the urge to say *everyone's a critic*. Reviews of Xander's last album had expressed the same view.

"She didn't want life in the fast lane. She'd tried it, been a model. She had saved money and was going back to school. Wanted to be a teacher." I caught the trace of a smile in the dim light. "I'd like to be a fifteen-year-old boy in her class."

I counted on him to continue but I was surprised by the topic.

"I imagine you read up on all the Artistical guests, so you probably know the story of how, as a local sensation in Ohio, I begged my parents to move to England because I was so enamored of British talent. It's not true. I felt perfectly happy in Akron, but my parents wanted more. My father didn't sacrifice his career to help me live my dreams. My dream was scoring with Kasey Milligan in the eighth grade. He could have kept working and let that happen. No, my parents saw that I could do more, earn more. They had a plan they pushed, and they were right. Here I am. The product not of my own incredible drive, as the myth goes, but of my parents' greed."

I had no idea what to say or ask, but I didn't think Xander wanted a response.

"I just wanted to tell you I lied. Because I like you. Because I think we are friends. And, because I want you to know it will never happen again."

"Thank you." An innocuous response but the best I could come up with. Besides I was too busy yelping as the plane bounced through a particularly rough patch. Xander didn't appear to notice. "I can tell you are not as enamored of Sally as I am, but I have come to realize that I see Elise in her. And not because of the physical resemblance, although in a broad sense there is one. It's not about looks. The people we talk to make it sound as if Sally was on the flakey side, flitting from cause to cause. I don't see her that way. I see her as a sweet, kind, curious girl with solid values who is trying to figure out the person she wants to be in a changing world. She knows she has power and she wants to use it to achieve her full potential. She is open to all possibilities, not because she is a dilettante but because she doesn't want to miss the one turn onto the road that is best for her. She isn't afraid to change direction if the path is not the right one for her. How is that flighty?"

He stared at me but, before I could answer, the plane hit a bump that brought an epithet to Xander's lips. "I'd say Frieda is coming to town."

By the time we made our approach to Atlantic City, Xander had again fallen silent, leaving me time to make bargains with every Supreme Being I could think of. *You get me down this time and I promise I'll never come up here again.* I'd made that promise before, not often, but during other bumpy flights. When I made the pledge, I believed it, although all it took was ten hours on an interstate and I went back in the air. Every time.

My legs were shaking as I stepped off the plane. I was happy to see

Del waiting for us.

"Lucky you got here when you did." He took my arm to steady me.

"Is the storm going to hit Atlantic City?" Xander asked.

Del didn't answer. He went right to a question. "Who is this Peter Bossow guy, Xanman?" Del asked with a bit of a catch in his throat.

"He's helping on the investigation we're doing. That's all. Don't worry. You're still my main man."

I smiled at Del. I could empathize. I'd felt threatened too.

Xander tried to cheer him up. "Hey, Del. Who'd I call when I needed a suite for those kids that flew to Boston with us? You." He gave Del a hearty slap on the back to confirm him as his buddy, his mate, his main man. "By the way did you get them room service privileges?"

"Thousand dollars a night. Maximum two nights."

"Do you think that will be enough?" Xander asked Del, then turned to me. "Do you think that will be enough?"

I did, even at room service prices.

"Make sure they have tickets home."

Del promised he would. "Where to, Xanman?" He asked.

"The hotel. Where else? I've had a long day."

Del appeared confused, concerned, and, if I wasn't mistaken, a little disappointed. This was not the Xanman in whose company he had traveled the world. If he knew that Xander had spent the plane ride back from Boston in silence, no headphones, no screen, gazing out the window, contemplating life's mysteries, or at least the mysteries of his life, he would have been really worried.

"Do you mind if we let Del drive us to Baltimore tomorrow?" Xander asked me. "You look beat."

"Baltimore?" I asked.

"I assumed we'd go talk to Sally Johnson. I don't think we want to say anything to Marianne until we know the story. It isn't as if we can show up with a banner that reads *Greetings from Ventnor City*."

Xander was right. We might think finding her offered a cause for celebration, but I found it unlikely that she would feel the same way about being found. "I was so sure we wouldn't be able to find her that I hadn't anticipated this dilemma. Marianne is not a paying customer. We don't owe her an answer."

"So, we find out if Sally is open to a reconciliation." Xander made his statement sound like a question.

"If we can find her. And, what about Frieda?"

"She's not going to do much to Baltimore." Xander spoke with more certainty than the average weatherman. "And we can be back before she hits here, if you feel it's wise to come back."

"But we are not sure we can find her, or did you have Peter Bossow do that already?"

"Oh no," Xander said with an earnest tone, "I didn't want to interfere. This is your investigation."

Damn straight, I said under my breath.

"Although if you'd like me to call him."

"No. No. I can do this."

It felt good to be back in charge.

Chapter 35

"She's dead." I spoke as soon as Del opened the door.

"Who?" he asked, confirming that he had been left out of the loop lately.

Laptop in one hand, I charged by and signaled him to follow with the other. "Ouch. What is that?" I rammed my knee into a piano bench. "And what is *that?*"

"It's a piano." Del answered as if I didn't recognize the instrument.

"Where did it come from?"

"Peter Bossow found it," Del said. "He can get all sorts of things." He sounded sad as if seeing his own limitations in comparison to Mr. Wonderful's.

"It's huge." I sounded critical. The instrument, filling the section of the hotel suite that I had thought of as the entrance hall/dining area, made passage to the living level complicated, if not difficult.

"Don't be dramatic. It's only a baby grand," Xander called from the couch where he was killing off an oversized room service order.

"Good. You're sitting down." I forgot about the piano. "She's dead."

"Who?" he asked.

"Who? Sally, that's who."

"How can she be dead today? We only found out she was alive yesterday."

"In 1998. She died in 1998. A mugging, but the weird thing is that she was dying when she was killed." I tried to pass him my laptop open to the story, but he waved me off.

"Tell me." English muffin in hand, he leaned back.

"Finding her was easy once we had a last name. I put in Sarah Johnson Bauer obituary and it came up right away, along with a lot of news stories."

"If you didn't know she was dead, why did you search for her obit?"

"I told you before. I always start with the obit."

"That would seem a particularly pessimistic way to launch a search. I didn't realize you had a dark side." Xander's face indicated a high degree of surprise and a lower degree of fear.

"I have a practical side. If the person is dead, you might as well know right away. And, if they are dead, the death notice will contain the salient information. Which this one did: Sarah Johnson Bauer beloved wife and mother died on April 23, 1998 while walking in Stoney Run Park in Baltimore. Family was listed. No mention of her Ventnor family, of course."

"However, this obituary came at the top of a lot of news stories that provided more information." Although she was battling an extremely virulent form of cancer, Sarah Bauer had insisted on taking daily walks, frequently in the company of her husband or daughter. Neither of them liked the idea of her going out alone. "But you know Sally," I said without irony. "She insisted on going out alone."

"Nothing would have stopped her," Xander agreed. "So she would be an easy target for a mugger, being so ill and weak."

"Only her large engagement ring was taken. The police figured the perp saw her and her huge diamond regularly."

"That's weird. I didn't figure Sally and her husband for the big ring type. Last we heard they weren't rolling in the bucks."

"The stone was a family heirloom. Big and perfect. Some thief knew what he was doing." I plopped on an ottoman across the room service tray from Xander and grabbed a miniature Danish. "I don't look forward to sharing this news with Marianne."

"Have you had to do this before?"

"I've uncovered information but haven't had to deliver this kind of news. There is a bright side. We will be able to tell Marianne that she has a niece and a brother-in-law."

"Brilliant." Xander was excited. "They'll be able to tell her about Sally. Even though I would have hoped for an eventual reunion of the two long lost sisters, I believe we've a good outcome, don't you?" Despite his upbeat words, he sounded disappointed. He didn't want our project to end.

I felt surprised to find myself experiencing a similar emotion. "Maybe we should talk to Sally's family first. So we have the big picture when we talk to Marianne."

Xander didn't require any convincing. "I agree. We should. Who knows what they will be able to tell us about Sally's life and why she left. We can give Marianne all the facts, the whole story, right up until today. Actually, until 1998. Besides, I'm curious, aren't you?"

"So we're still going to Baltimore?" Del sounded happy to be back in the game.

"Get us on the road, Del," Xander said. "No limo. Something ordinary."

We were on the road to Baltimore by 10AM.

We veered off I95 before we reached downtown and headed toward a neighborhood called Roland Park. We passed by Johns Hopkins University into a neighborhood of interesting row houses. "This looks like a great neighborhood," I commented.

"Very ordinary?" Xander asked.

I eyed the carefully maintained, possibly restored, houses, and took into account their proximity to the university. "Probably not."

The neighborhood we drove into next was definitely not ordinary. Big spacious houses lined up along the street, standing proud and asking to be admired.

"Definitely not ordinary," Xander said. "Even I can see that."

We crossed what appeared to be a main drag and started up a hill. "Now this is a neighborhood."

"Ordinary?" Xander asked.

"I have no idea of the prices, but this is a neighborhood I would like to live in."

The house styles were varied, but mainly Victorian. Sidewalks and porches invited neighbor to greet neighbor. Not one of the houses had been built for pretension. Some were attached to the house next door; most were not.

"Are you envisioning yourself rocking on one of those porches?" he asked.

I blushed. He was right. I had been. "I love neighborhoods like this.

The unpretentious wooden houses, the sidewalks, the trees."

"I can see you here." Xander nodded to signal his approval.

"I hope we don't drive out of this area before we find Sally's house."

We didn't.

The Bauer home sat near the top of a hill on a tree-lined street that led to a green space at the bottom of the hill, the park, I assumed, where Sally had died. There was no driveway and we had to climb a steep flight of stairs to reach the path leading to the porch steps. On the other side of an unruly hedge, a middle-aged neighbor tended to a row of neatly trimmed shrubs, although his clothing suggested he might be on his way out to play golf. His eyes never left us as we made our way from the car to the front door. He eyed us with suspicion, although I found nothing suspicious in our demeanor with the exception of Xander's Rex clothing. We pretended we didn't notice him and climbed the steps to the porch. We knocked. Whatever his concern, the good neighbor wasn't going to let us pass unchallenged. He stepped across a low row of bushes and called out to us from the foot of the porch steps. He said to help, but I knew he had come to check us out.

"They're at the doctor's. You're looking for Thomas, right?"

"Yes. Thank you. We are." Xander, all British charm, walked to the top of the steps. "How kind of you to help."

The man gave no sign of recognizing Xander even though the rock star made no attempt to hide his identity with big eyes, lips and hair exposed. He was clearly Xander Frost, albeit in a horrible outfit.

"Daughter practically lives here now, to take care of him. You know Mariana?"

"We know *of* her. Mutual acquaintances." Xander tried hard to work his charisma, but not completely successfully.

"What do you want with Thomas?"

I let Xander handle it.

"As I said, we have mutual acquaintances. People who knew Mariana's mother especially well."

"Sarah?" His suspicious expression gave way to a smile. "Did you know Sarah?"

"No. I'm sorry to say I never had the pleasure." Xander was convincing because he spoke the truth.

"And, man, knowing her was a pleasure. She was special, you know. Well, you probably don't, but she was a wonderful woman. Old enough to be my, well my older sister, but I had a little crush on her. All the men around here did. Oh sorry." He joined us on the porch and offered his hand to Xander. "Bob Barker by the way. Not from *The Price is Right* but you probably know that. I'm just ordinary guy, Bob Barker."

Xander gave no indication that he appreciated the irony of Bob Barker's claim to be an ordinary guy. I had no idea if he knew who Bob Barker was or that the game show host was not African-American, but he understood that the neighbor was trying to make a joke and chuckled politely. "Lovely to meet you, Bob Barker. My name is Xander Frost and this is my colleague, Meg Daniels."

"Nice to meet you." He shook my hand. "I'll think of you as friends of Sarah's. You know, the friend of my friend…. I only knew Sarah for about ten years at the end of her life, but she was a lovely woman, inside and out. You could tell she had been a looker. She still was when she arrived here, but at the end…the cancer. That'll do you in."

"Yes, that was tragic, but we heard that she didn't die of the cancer," Xander said.

"They say she was mugged. The cops. Thomas believes she just fell in that park at the end of the street. But a couple of witnesses say she got into a heated discussion with a guy there. Two women said he shoved her." He pointed to the bottom of the street. "Some coincidence if that fellow wasn't involved. But those same two women saw him storm off while she was fine. Nice women. Good citizens. They made sure she was okay. They asked her. She sounded okay. She said she was okay. Cops posted a picture of the guy, you know, one of those sketches they make up. The police wanted to talk to him, but I don't think they ever believed he had killed her. And, if *he* didn't? What were the odds that a second person would come along and harm her? I guess it could happen, but I'm with Thomas. I accept that Sarah's death was a tragic accident."

"But her ring was stolen." I spoke for the first time.

"Maybe. Thomas said she had grown so thin she could barely keep it on. He went down and dug through the leaves, even though the cops said they had done that. There's a creek there too. So who knows where that ring went? For years Thomas hoped it would show up. He thought it might turn up in the house, but if she did wear it and lose it, someone probably found it. Maybe an animal stashed it in a nest. It would make a nice shiny toy."

"Can you share what Thomas believes happened?" Xander's eyebrows came close to crossing as he plastered his most concerned expression on his face.

"His view is that she went out for her normal walk and grew weak climbing down the incline on her way to a spot where she liked to sit. He figured she staggered down the hill, fell, hit her head and, most importantly, never felt any pain. My take? The guy needed to believe that. She'd been through so much. To think that after all the surgeries and the chemo, to think that she had to endure a violent death. I can't imagine how Thomas could have handled it." He turned at the sound of a car. "Oh, here they come now. Let me help him out."

I could feel Xander's excitement or maybe I was just projecting my own emotions onto him. Finally, we were going to meet the man who was the key to Sally's past.

Chapter 36

Thomas Bauer appeared to be around seventy and in good health except for a leg that would not cooperate as he made his way up the steps from the street. I found it easy to see vestiges of the boy Sarah fell in love with on the cross-country bus. He was handsome, but even more, he was cute. The man exuded niceness at thirty yards. I felt happy for Sarah that she'd found someone who, if his image was accurate, was so kind, but sad that she could no longer be with him.

The car that dropped Thomas off pulled away, and I felt relief along with disappointment. I would have loved meeting Mariana, but talking to Sarah's husband without her daughter present might be easier. If he would talk. I hoped Bob Barker's possible endorsement would make it easier to find our way onto the Bauers' sofa. It did, but then we faced the issue of his continued presence. I didn't know how freely Thomas would speak in front of him. Luckily, Bob only had time for one cup of coffee. Our thanks for his help were sincere, but we were happy to see him go.

Thomas did not get up to see him out. "I broke my leg skiing last year. Spring skiing. I hit a dry patch. Damn thing just won't heal. I am still having trouble getting around. My daughter's been staying with me to help out. You might get to meet her. She's running a few errands, but she'll be back. Well, enough with the small talk. Marianne sent you? Why? Why didn't she come herself? And why now? She wouldn't come when Sarah needed her."

"Mr. Bauer, Marianne did not know where Sarah was. She asked Xander and me to find her."

He appeared puzzled. I wasn't shocked. We did make an unusual search party.

"It's a long story, but we had to trace every step after she left Atlantic City to find you. We crisscrossed the country," I explained.

"Just like she did." He smiled.

"Exactly. Dona Haven, Mary Donatia Lombardmeissen-Winghaven, told us Sarah's married name. She regretted that you'd lost touch."

"Wonderful artist. Did Dona know Sarah had passed?"

"No. I guess we'll have to contact her. Although I am sure she would love to hear from you. She spoke very highly of both of you. We can give you her information."

"I would appreciate that. Dona was a huge help to Sarah when she was expecting our daughter. To both of us, really, when we were starting out. She basically put our wedding together from soup to nuts. It's easy to lose touch with people when you're young and building a career and raising a family. Even a small one. Sarah and I only had the one child."

I'd begun to wonder if he knew Sarah was pregnant when they met, when he dropped his voice to a conspiratorial whisper. "I imagine you found out Sarah was expecting Mariana before she and I got together."

Xander and I nodded in unison.

"I am the only father Mariana ever knew. She has always been aware that I am not her biological father. She never asked about him. Sarah never divulged that information, even to me. You didn't learn anything about...?" He couldn't go on.

I completed the sentence. "Her paternity?"

Again, Xander and I responded with synchronized action, this time a shake of the head.

I sensed relief underlying Thomas's show of frustration. "Sarah might have taken that secret to the grave." He went on to answer a question we never verbalized. "I never pressed her. As far as I was concerned, Mariana was mine. I couldn't have asked for a better daughter. Whoever provided the seed to grow that child, I thank him. And now, I have a granddaughter as well. I felt happy Sarah got to see her as a child even if she never saw the fine young woman she's become."

I glanced around the room and saw no sign of Dona Haven's portrait of Sarah Bauer. I could believe Thomas had given the painting to their daughter, but I was surprised that the man who loved his family so dearly displayed no photographs of them. Too painful, perhaps.

"It's hard for me, for us, to understand why Sarah didn't contact Marianne after she left home. I assume she named Mariana after her."

"She thought about visiting Ventnor. At one point after she heard her father died, Sarah and I drove up to Atlantic City for a teachers' conference. I expected to meet her family. We stayed in Atlantic City and walked down the Boardwalk into Ventnor, but Sarah stopped short of her house."

He gazed into space reliving the moment.

Thomas Bauer
Atlantic City Boardwalk
September 1974

Sarah stared at the Atlantic City Boardwalk with wonder. "When I was growing up, the classic hotels that lined this Boardwalk were a big draw, but times have changed. People have changed. The Traymore is gone. I can't imagine the rest of them won't follow. I'm too young to remember the glory days, but you could still find elegance on the Atlantic City Boardwalk when I was a kid." She was clearly growing sentimental, at least for the Atlantic City of her youth.

It was Thomas's first trip to Atlantic City and Sarah assured him the city he saw was not the same one she had seen growing up. "Ventnor won't have changed too much. I've read there are some new motels, but the street where I lived should be the same. I hope the beautiful old houses survived."

He slowed his pace to match hers. "You're walking slower and slower. Any slower and you'll be moving backward. Are you sure you want to visit your family?"

"It's just my mother and sister. Now that my father's dead there's nothing to be afraid of. Without her husband telling her what to think, my mother is a cypher. Nothing to fear except that my sister might have become our mother."

Thomas took her hand. "So, let's try to enjoy the evening. Clear sky. Sea air. Moon expected any moment. Over the ocean. What could be better than this? This walk must bring back memories. Good ones I hope."

"Want to hear the worst thing I ever did in my entire life? A neighbor kid taught me to hide under the Boardwalk and throw sand up when people walked by. Then we would crawl away. As soon as I saw how people reacted I stopped. We were doing such a stupid thing that was not funny and was not fun. I felt terrified when someone told my father. All the harmless things I did to have fun that my father labelled horrible, he thought that was funny."

She stopped and he stayed by her side, leaning against the railing with their backs to the sea. She pointed out a large summer cottage as the rambling wood structure would have been called at the dawn of the twentieth century. "That window on the second floor at the far end of the house. That was one of the windows in my room. I could look out and see the ocean. I didn't realize what a wonderful thing that was. I was more interested in the windows on the side of the house, especially the one near the trellis I used to climb down."

"You were a wild child." He jabbed her with his elbow. "I like that."

"So tame, really. Like any teenager, I wanted to be out with my friends. My father didn't see my conduct that way. He felt sure I was living the life of a wanton woman. I tried to excuse his behavior by remembering he was born in 1920, lived through a Depression and fought in a World War. A different world, a tough world. I am sure he started out as an angry man, but things got worse as he got older. He got lucky when he married my mother. She came with a healthy inheritance. He could afford to be a jerk, even at work. Didn't matter if he got fired. And he did. Frequently."

"But he isn't here anymore." He wrapped an arm around her. From the moment she stepped onto that bus in San Francisco, he wanted to take care of her. He'd discovered that she was strong and bold. She didn't need his support, but she was kind enough to accept it. And appreciate it. She leaned into him and rested her head on his shoulder. They stood that way, watching until she could build up her courage.

"I don't see any signs of life. Is there a place on the other side of the house where people might congregate?"

She shook her head. "We should come back when the sun goes down and the lights are on in the house. We will be able to see the people inside, but they won't be able to see us. We'll know what to expect before I, we, charge up to the door. This was reckless, coming before dark. We can come back." At that point she froze, her eyes riveted on a car pulling up in front of the house. Her breathing stopped as she watched a young man in a Phillies cap climb out of the driver's side.

Thomas couldn't get a good look at the guy as he walked around the car and opened the passenger door. The woman he helped out of the vehicle appeared young but had a lot of trouble getting out of her seat. When she turned he realized why. She was not only pregnant but would be heading for the hospital in the very near future.

He couldn't see her clearly, but as the woman, who leaned heavily on the man he assumed to be her husband, moved slowly up the stairs, he could see that she bore no resemblance to Sally. "Is that Marianne?"

When Sarah nodded the tears welling in her eyes flowed down her cheeks. He thought they were tears of joy but they weren't. "I'm too late. I'm too late. She'll be stuck here forever."

He glanced at the big house with the wraparound porch and the ocean it faced. "There are worse places to be stuck."

"It looks that way. I know, but it's so complicated. So complicated."

*****

"Did Sarah ever explain what complicated meant?" I asked.

"No. She never talked in specifics, but she felt she had abandoned Marianne. As long as her father was alive she couldn't go back, but I never quite understood why she wouldn't go back after his death. We left that day and never returned to Ventnor. If she ever took a trip on her own, I never heard about it and I feel I would have."

"How did she discover her father had died? Did she keep in touch with anyone in town?"

"No. Her father had been gone for a few years before she found out. She went to the library and asked the librarian to check. She never talked about the details. She just told me the news."

"I don't understand. She was your wife. Why didn't she share?" Xander was sincere.

"Sarah never wanted to hurt anyone. That was her rule. Whatever secrets she had, she kept to protect others."

"And that trip to Atlantic City was the only attempt she made at contact." Xander made a statement he clearly found startling.

"I offered to drive her up to New Jersey on more than a few occasions, but she said no. She let the topic drop until she got her terminal diagnosis. That was when she wrote to Marianne. I would have driven her up, but I felt relieved she chose to write. She was in no condition to travel, but I understood how much she wanted to see Marianne. Just the two of them. I don't think she wanted to run the risk of seeing the husband."

"Marianne told us she never heard from Sally." I wanted my voice to make it clear I wasn't questioning his account.

"All I can say is that Sarah sent the letter. I don't know what was in it. I didn't read it. But she wrote it. Unless you tell me that the family moved before 1998, she certainly knew the address. I see no reason it shouldn't have arrived. I know. I mailed it. Marianne never answered. Sarah watched the mail delivery like a hawk, hoping. She sent the letter not long before her accident. No answer came before she died, and I would have seen it. And, of course, after she died...."

Of course, he would be the only one getting the mail. Just like Jimmy was the only one getting the mail in Ventnor. So why would Jimmy hide the letter Sally sent to Marianne? I had no proof but little doubt that was what had happened. Unless Marianne had lied to us, but that made no sense. No, Jimmy was the culprit. Why did he want to keep Marianne away from the sister she missed so terribly? There had to be more to his story. I could understand why Sarah wanted to see her sister, but why did she feel so strongly she didn't want to see her sister's husband? I didn't have a clue until the front door opened and Mariana Bauer returned from running her errands.

Chapter 37

Xander waited until the car had pulled away from the Bauer residence before he spoke. "I suppose there is some small chance that Jimmy is not Mariana's father."

"And I have a bridge to sell you." I dismissed Xander's proposition. "I have never seen a girl look so much like her father. I thought Marianne's daughter did, but this is incredible. The long face. The square jaw. I never realized how unusual Jimmy's eye color was until I saw the same shade in that woman's eyes. Her hair is colored now, but Dona said as a child she was a redhead."

"So Sally left town because she felt ashamed she'd gotten pregnant by the boyfriend of her sister."

"It's possible." I believed the scenario was probable.

"I wonder if he knew?" Xander asked no one in particular.

"If he knew, he would have tried to pressure her to marry him. He wanted her, not Marianne. I don't think he knew."

"Until he got the letter?" Xander asked.

"That doesn't seem like the kind of news Sally would break by mail, but if he did find out from the letter, I can see why he would keep that information from Marianne. Even if he didn't know about the baby, he wouldn't want Sally to come clean with Marianne. He had to worry about how honest a deathbed confession might be. He had a lot to lose if Marianne found out he had been with her sister. It's her house and her money. He might not have been able to take early retirement without the support of his wife."

"Given the circumstances of his departure from his job, I'm not sure we should call it retirement."

"Well, he never had to beat the pavement searching for something else, did he?" My negative feelings towards Jimmy were on full display in my tone. "I feel for Marianne. How devastating for her! Always playing second fiddle to her sister and then finding out she was not the only one, or even the first, to bear her husband's child."

"Do you think Marianne would have blamed him or Sally? Or both?"

That was a question I couldn't answer, even for myself. The emotions were far too complex. "God, Sally got herself into a mess, didn't she?"

"For a girl so afraid of getting pregnant to make such a stupid mistake." Xander shook his head slowly to emphasize his sadness. And disbelief?

I thought about that possibility for a moment. "Lou Blair said she made him use a condom even though she was on the pill."

"She didn't trust that he was faithful. She was afraid of disease." Xander interpreted her behavior.

"Not in 1968. People weren't worried. She had been using a condom and the pill. Do we believe both failed? Condoms break. The pill wasn't perfect, even if a woman remembered to take it everyday. It seems Sally feared that."

It didn't take Xander long to get my point. "So you're saying that she didn't want to have a go at it with Jimmy?"

"He was hers anytime she wanted him. Why would she suddenly relent when she was running to a new life?"

"An unexpected surge of lust?"

"We're talking about Jimmy."

"Pity?"

Possible, but I wasn't buying it. "We've got to get Jimmy alone and make him talk."

"We could grab him off the street. In *Hidden Mystery*, they put a pillow case over my head and pulled me into a van."

"Well, for one thing, we have no idea when we would have an opportunity. For another thing, we don't have a van. And, number three, and this is probably the most important factor: *that would be illegal.*" I spoke in measured tones until my final point.

Xander sounded defensive. "You have a better idea?"

"We go to the one place he is alone, a place where we can have a nice conversation."

"You said we would have trouble finding an opportunity to snatch him."

"We want to encounter, not snatch, him."

"So, we go back to the post office tomorrow?"

Chapter 38

When Xander returned to his suite, he entrusted my safety to Del who not only walked me to my room, but came in to check inside the closet, behind the curtains and in the bathroom, where he pulled the shower curtain back.

"Thanks, Del. You didn't have to, but I appreciate your help."

"I've got stuff to do for the Xanman and then you know where to find me." He pointed towards the room next door.

"Won't be necessary. Xander is a worry wart, but I appreciate the concern—from both of you."

"I'll be there." Del's tone said the topic wasn't open for discussion.

Now that my eyes weren't glued to the television, I actually got ready for bed. Teeth brushed. Face washed. Comfortable sleep attire. I couldn't wait to ambush Jimmy Dulles in the morning. I gazed out the window, but in the darkness could only make out the traces of whitecaps.

"You're back. I told you to go."

I couldn't see a reflection in the glass so I spun around looking for the source of the voice and found a small human form standing at the foot of the bed—the one she must have climbed out from under. The form moved forward into the dim light from outside until I could see her. The reporter, alleged reporter, the one I'd met on the beach deck, told me to sit down.

"Why should I?"

"Because I have a gun."

That seemed like a perfectly good reason to me for perching on the edge of the armchair in the corner as directed.

"I told you to back off. You can't have him. He cannot marry you."

In a flash, the entire scenario formed in my head. Andy's remoteness that summer. His exhaustion around me. His lack of romantic fervor. He hadn't been depressed. He had been expending all his energy on this woman. He had ended his affair and proposed to me out of guilt. And now, I was going to die at the hands of the lover he had rejected. I should have been really angry, but I was actually only confused. That behavior really didn't gel with the Andy I knew, and this woman did not really seem his type, but what would I, the girlfriend, the fiancée, okay the cuckhold fiancée, know? I would be the last to know.

Given the circumstances, I thought the less said the better. I recalled every hostage negotiation I'd ever watched on television. Keep the perp talking. "I don't understand."

"Oh, I think you do. Didn't he tell you about me? About us?" Her manner escalated from nasty to downright mean. What would laid-back Andy see in a woman like her?

"Why don't you tell me?" I needed to keep her talking.

"He loves me. He always loved me. He loves our family." Although emotional, her tone betrayed no trace of doubt.

I updated the scenario. Andy had encountered a lost love, discovered she had his child, and made promises to her. Again, not really his style, but better to find out now than later how wrong I had been about him. Maybe his inability to tell me was the root of his summer depression. He hadn't been himself. I didn't have time to think about the past. I had to stay in the present. "Tell me about your family."

"I can't believe he didn't tell you." That news made her even more distraught. I felt reasonably certain I could take the tiny woman, but she did have a gun, the one she pointed at me with one hand, while she pulled at her hair with the other. "How could he not tell you? About us? About me. About Calla? About our son? I am important to him. I know I am. We can't spend much time together, but I know he thinks of me, even if he can't call. I know he is busy." She made excuses for him. "I don't have to kill you. I don't want to. This is under your control. Just say you will give him up."

I was ready to say anything to get out of this jam. "What happens if

I give him up? Will you leave?"

"Not until he comes here and you tell him to his face that it is over. Then he and I can be together."

"I am not sure if he can get here, but I swear that I am giving him up. Right now. It's done. I don't want to be with a man who loves someone else. No way." I wasn't convinced I was getting the full story from this woman who, as time went on, appeared to be deranged, but I wasn't about to argue. "He should be with you. Now that we agree, you can put down your gun."

"Not until he comes here."

"But he's in the Bahamas. There is a storm coming. He can't get here. I am sure he will as soon as he can."

"Don't lie to me," she screamed. "I saw you with him. Yesterday. Today. Tonight. He is here."

"He?" I asked the question I probably should have asked first. "Who is he?"

"Don't play coy with me. I've seen you. And not just on the news. Xander is here in this hotel. You might think this separate room thing can fool the press, but I know better. I've watched. I've seen."

Xander. Of course. My fiancé. I felt relieved but horrible. How could I entertain such awful thoughts about Andy? I had never really believed those allegations, had I? I would have years to work that out. For now, I had to focus on getting myself out of this jam.

"I am not engaged to Xander. I have a fiancé. Another fiancé. His name is Andy. Not Xander."

"Don't lie to me. I heard you talking about him the other night. On the phone. I heard it all."

Aha. Not paparazzi. Something worse. "But I wasn't talking about Xander. I was talking about my fiancé. You can feel free to continue your relationship." The one I suspected was all in her head.

"Call him. Get him down here."

"I have to get up to get my phone. It's only right there on the bed. I dropped it there when I walked in."

She agreed but backed away keeping the gun pointed at me. I couldn't think of a way to disarm her. I had to think of a way to warn Xander.

Xander picked up. "Del, hi. It's Meg. I need to speak to Xander."

"Don't be daft. It is Xander."

"I know he's tired but please wake him up. I need him to come down to my room."

Xander was catching on. "Are you okay?"

"I have a surprise for him. She tells me he'll love it."

"Did you say she?"

"Xander. Hello. Yes. A surprise. You're right. It is Calla. She's here and she is dying to see you."

He groaned. "Be extremely careful, Meg. I know her. She is not well."

"Well, to be honest, she wasn't *crazy* about me because she believed you and I were engaged. I explained, and I think she's a lot happier now. She just needs to hear the truth from you. That I am not a threat."

"I am assuming that is a demand she is making. She is crazy. I am going to call security and the police and we will come to your room together." Xander sounded alarmed but in control.

"Good idea." I smiled at Calla. "He's just going to throw some clothes on and he'll be down."

"Is she armed?"

"Absolutely. Come on down. We're waiting."

"Tell him I love him," Calla called.

"Did you hear? She's across the room, but she wants you to know she loves you."

"Near the door?"

"That's good. I'll tell her you are on the way."

"Put him on speaker. I want to know it is really him."

"Putting you on speaker, Xander, so Calla knows it's really you." I hit speaker.

"It's me, Calla. I am on my way. You just get to know Meg. She's a nice woman. Older, not really into music, but nice. You'll see."

Calla's face melted into a warm smile. She remained lost in her fantasy world but had enough grasp of reality to hold onto her gun.

Xander tells me he knocked on the door eighteen minutes later. Sitting in front of a woman with a gun in her hand did not make the time fly by. It felt like eighteen hours before I heard the light knock.

"You get it." She gestured with the gun.

"I should check the peephole, don't you think?"

She nodded in agreement.

I shrieked as if excited by what I saw. "It's him, Calla. It's Xander. I can see him. I'm going to open the door now."

"I want to see."

"Of course, you can see." I yelled, hoping Xander could hear me through the door. I stepped aside into the bathroom leaving a clear path for security and police to enter.

"Xander. You came." An unsuspecting Calla opened the door and found herself pushed back into the room, not by the lover she awaited but by the police. I slammed the bathroom door shut, stepped into the tiled shower and waited for bullets to fly. All I heard was yelling and screaming and finally the words, "Got the gun." I didn't move until a police officer stuck his head into the room to say I could come out.

From down the hallway, I heard Calla's voice calling for Xander asking him to explain to the police who she was.

I found Xander waiting just outside in the doorway to my room and collapsed into his arms.

"I am so sorry. This is my fault. I am so sorry. I did this to you. I am so sorry. I thought she was in England. She is sick and confused. I didn't know she was here or I would have protected you." He kissed the top of my head.

I found myself consoling Xander until the police interrupted to say they needed to interview us.

Before the cops left, Xander asked them to take care of the woman who had been stalking him for years. "She needs to be in hospital. She had been confined in England. I thought she still was. She believes she is my wife and the mother of my child. She never had a baby. Her entire life is a fantasy. Please take care of her."

"You're better to her than she is to you. She told us she planned on killing you, along with your fiancée." The cop nodded at me.

"I'm not his fiancée. Remember? She thought I was, but I have another fiancé."

"Well, you two did the right thing bringing us into this, or you wouldn't have had to worry about tomorrow. We'll be in touch."

As soon as the door closed, Xander restarted his apologies.

I waved to indicate it was no problem, which was a major nonverbal understatement. "It wasn't your fault. I understand her delusion, but what I don't understand is why she was willing to hurt you, the person she loved most?"

"I guess that is what people do. They hurt the ones they love."

Chapter 39

Andy called the next morning from his new cell phone to mine. "I thought you were finished working with Xander."

"I heard that sarcasm on the word *working. You* try to get rid of the guy. He's relentless. We thought we were finished, but then we uncovered an interesting twist."

Andy listened as I outlined our findings and our plan.

"And you think this guy, Jimmy, killed Sally."

"We are willing to bet he was the guy she quarreled with."

"I made this call because I was worried about you and the storm. Well, you and Xander and you and the storm. I did see some photos online of Xander hugging you in the hallway."

"Yeah, funny explanation."

"I read about his crazed fan. And you know what that made me think? I am really quite a catch. I can state unequivocally that I have no crazed fans. I can guarantee that not one will show up and hold you captive."

"That's reassuring. I hadn't thought to ask."

"I have to admit I didn't—I don't—take the thought of you alone in a hotel room with that woman lightly. And now I've got to worry about your dealing with a killer. I'd ask you to back off, but we've actually met, so I know that's not going to happen. You are walking one thin line with Jimmy. You've got your script ready?"

"More ready than ever."

"Well, wrap your case up. We might be able to start bringing staff back in a few days. I'll get you on one of the first Air Bingo flights."

"If I can get out of here. Frieda is due here tonight. We've already got high surf and some big gusts, but no rain yet. The governor has been on television all week but no mandatory evacuations announced."

"Don't be a hero. If the authorities say go, go." Andy sounded encouraging, not bossy.

I promised, but unlike Andy, I would keep my promise to stay out of harm's way.

"And make sure you take Xander with you."

"Is that a trace of affection for my temporary partner I hear in your voice?"

"Affection might be a strong term, but I like the idea that you have a companion for the storm. I'd say protector, but I suspect you might be the one assuming that role."

"We're partners. We'll see each other through. I'm off to meet him now. He's a poor substitute for you." The silence on the other end prompted me to reconsider my last words. "Not that he serves as a substitute in any way, shape, or form. You know that and that I really, really miss you."

"It won't be long now until we can celebrate our engagement a few more times."

I didn't want to destroy the mood, but I had to broach a fear that had been on my mind since I'd been convinced Andy was safe. "We won't be having those celebrations in our cottage, will we?"

"What makes you say that?"

"You barely mentioned the condition of our sweet little bungalow by the beach, and what you did say wasn't encouraging. I understand you had phone issues, but you haven't sent any photos."

"Yeah. Well, it's still standing." That said it all even before he added "Sort of." He explained how sorry he was. "I did what I could."

"I think a lot of you, Andy, but I don't expect you to keep the sea at bay. Maybe the cottage's untimely demise is a message from the universe. Maybe it's time for us to move on."

"We'll talk." He sounded relieved. "We'll be together soon."

The sun had come out again in the Bahamas. Frieda, however, still threatened New Jersey. Xander had managed to acquire full foul-weather gear that he planned to wear to the post office. I suspected thanks for the outfit were due to Peter Bossow but I didn't ask. I did, however, ask Xander to remove the hat that made him look like the Gorton fisherman. Then I explained who the Gorton fisherman was. Xander did not want to impersonate a character from an American TV commercial and scaled back to the yellow jacket. By the time we got to the car, he realized the day was too hot for even that. "I'll wait to put them on until the rain starts."

"I think that's what the locals, you know the ordinary people, do."

When Jimmy arrived, his attire confirmed my opinion about storm gear. The sky was dark, and the winds were whipping up when he arrived to pick up his mail wearing shorts, flip-flops, and a light windbreaker. "A coincidence?" He sounded unconvinced and appeared nervous at the sight of us.

"Hardly," Xander said in the most condescending of tones.

Jimmy glanced from Xander to me and back several times before deciding that, despite his hostile tone, Xander had the more sympathetic expression. "I don't understand."

"Oh, I think you do." Xander repeated a line from his guest shot on *Law & Order.* "Since when did you have a post office box?"

"I already told you. Since always. I got one when Marianne and I married and moved into that house."

"What did you do before that?" I asked. "Sneak over every day and go through the Johnson's mailbox to make sure Sally hadn't written?"

"What are you talking about?" He looked angry but sounded nervous.

"You wanted to intercept any attempt Sally made at contacting Marianne," I stated calmly.

"I don't understand." He did. We knew it.

"The Internet must have really freaked you out," Xander added.

"Except you made sure Marianne never felt comfortable with technology. Lucky for you, social media wasn't a big thing in 1998." I took my turn.

"Although you would have made sure Marianne never got active. When all that online stuff started, I bet you told her you checked and couldn't locate Sally, and you made certain Sally had no way to contact Marianne online." Xander leaned forward.

228

I took a step towards Jimmy. "You could control the mail, but you couldn't control cyberspace."

Jimmy responded with a step back.

"Luckily your kids were out of the house by the time every home had a computer. You couldn't have gotten away with keeping the Internet out of your house these days. Kids need it for school, for friendship, to be fans of stars like me." Xander might have seemed to be a changed man, but his narcissism still resurfaced. "You would have had a hard time keeping Marianne offline."

"She knows how to use email. Luckily, our kids grew up before we had to worry about Facebook. All those systems or whatever you call them are security risks. We don't use them."

"But it isn't such a worry now, is it? Not since 1998."

"What is all this talk of 1998? What the hell happened in 1998?"

"Jimmy, we know you intercepted the letter Sarah sent to Marianne before she died." I broke the news in a matter-of-fact tone.

"I...what...wait," he paused as if he realized the inappropriate nature of his reaction, "are you telling me you discovered that Sally is dead?" The way I saw it, he tried to cry. He made a show of controlling his breathing. He wiped away some tears I judged to be imaginary and composed himself. "This is a lot to absorb."

"We know Sarah wrote a letter to Marianne in 1998 telling her she wanted to see her," I said.

"We know that." Xander confirmed in a tough guy voice that said don't even try to deny it.

"We believe Marianne when she said she never got Sally's letter." I tried to present myself as threatening but being harsh wasn't really my thing. I sounded moderately annoyed.

"Why engage us if she had gotten it?" Xander used the tough guy voice again to stave off an argument.

"So, when we heard Sarah tried to contact Marianne, we had to ask ourselves a question." I was coming off like the good cop to Xander's bad.

"Where did that letter go?" Xander's tone grew downright menacing.

"Then, we remembered that all the mail for the Dulles household passes through your hands." My tone was soft.

Jimmy glanced at the few people lingering on the sidewalk, sorting through their mail as they walked. "Let's get out of here. I can explain."

I didn't like giving him the time to cook up a story, but he wasn't going to say anything incriminating standing at the Post Office door. We followed him to the Island Gym in the next building.

"Why is he taking us here?" I whispered to Xander as I surveyed the lines of equipment I couldn't name.

"Don't have a panic attack. We're headed for the juice bar. You don't have to exercise."

"Would you like a smoothie? They make great ones." Jimmy offered.

I could have been tempted but Xander stuck to business. "We're not here to have fun."

Jimmy kept his eyes on the floor. "You're right. I did waylay a letter from Sally. I thought I was doing the right thing. Marianne had been so hurt when Sally left that I believed seeing her again would only hurt her more. Controlling? If so, only because I care too much."

"I don't understand. What piece of information did Sally possess that would hurt Marianne so badly?" Xander's tone said he was doubtful such an item existed.

"Nothing, but I knew Sally. She would come back and get into Marianne's life and then she would leave again, and Marianne would be devastated."

"We think there was more to it than that, Jimmy," I said.

"We know there was more to it than that." Again, Xander pulled out his threatening tones.

Jimmy looked at each of us with guilt he couldn't hide.

"You knew about the baby?" I asked.

He thought long and hard about that one, but his face betrayed no reaction. "Sally wrote nothing about any baby. We had been intimate, and I knew that information would kill Marianne. I didn't want Sarah to tell her."

"What made you worry she would?" Xander asked the follow-up question.

"She said she would. Not in explicit words. She wrote that she needed to talk to Marianne, to explain what happened. I understood what that meant."

Jimmy was surrendering, the energy required to keep his secret slipping from his body. I imagined he had been preparing for this moment from the instant Marianne told him about our encounter on the beach in Atlantic City. "When I told you about the night Sally left, I didn't tell you the entire story."

"Quelle surprise," Xander mumbled and I stuck an elbow in his side. I hoped Jimmy was about to tell the truth for the first time in fifty years.

"I told you I drove Sally to a coffee shop. That was true, but we didn't go in. I didn't stop there. I wanted to be able to speak freely. That night might have been my last chance."

He overcame the threat of tears to speak.

Jimmy Dulles
Atlantic City
September 8, 1968

"Where are you going? I thought we were going to get coffee," she said as if mocking him because he was too young to drink coffee.

"I just need to talk some sense into you."

"You're not my father, Jimmy. Turn the car around."

"Just give me a chance." He tried to sound upbeat, as if to say, I have a great plan to share with you.

"You'd better not be taking me home."

"I promise. I won't. I just want to talk some sense into you."

"You keep saying that, but you didn't ask me what my plans are."

"Let's go somewhere and you can tell me."

"You can tell me in the coffee shop. Turn around."

But he didn't. Ignoring Sally's pleas to take her back, he headed off the island out to Route 9 and into the Pine Barrens. He knew a pull-off down a dirt road. He and Marianne went there to be alone. Not a known lovers' lane but a secluded clearing, their special spot where they knew they would not be interrupted. A perfect place to make his case with Sally.

When he turned down the dirt road, Sally sat up straight. "Jimmy, should I be afraid of you?"

He forced a laugh. "Don't be ridiculous, Sally. We've been friends since we were babies. How could you imagine I would be a danger to you? I just want a quiet spot, without strangers listening and interfering. I only want to talk to you." As he pulled off the road, the full moon cast sharp shadows in the clearing. He glanced at Sally. She looked so beautiful in the moonlight. She looked so outraged. She had her hand on the door handle.

"Sally, don't get out." He made no move to restrain her. "God knows what is in these woods. I want to have a calm conversation and then, if you still want, I will get you to your bus on time."

Despite the anger on her face, her voice was soft. "Nothing you can say will make me change my mind. I get where you're coming from and I understand you mean well, but I've thought about this carefully. I see what I want, Jimmy."

"How can you? I saw you today on the Boardwalk. I felt embarrassed to speak to you. You don't belong with those girls."

"Those girls? You don't know a thing about those women. You don't know a thing about women."

He understood she didn't intend to be cruel. She was angry and confused. She still thought of him as a kid. He had to change her mind.

"Jimmy, everyone is different. You don't want what I want. I can see you staying in Ventnor forever. I can believe you and Marianne can be happy here. It's a beautiful place. But I am not like you. Please understand that. We'll always be different, but we will always be friends."

"I don't want to be friends." There he said it. He studied her face and found confusion. "We could be more, Sally." Her expression changed but not into the look of love he had hoped for. Of course, it would take time for her to digest what he was saying. "I love you Sally. I have always loved you."

"Of course, we all love you, Jimmy. Our entire family. I hope you and Marianne will stay together so you will be part of our family."

She was deflecting his declaration. He realized she would do that to resolve any guilt she felt about her sister. He had to tread lightly, to somehow make her realize returning his feelings was permissible. "Marianne and I are friends. That's all. There is no commitment between us."

"My sister loves you, Jimmy. You must know that. She believes you love her." She tried to suppress her anger, but he heard it.

"I do love Marianne, but not the same way I love you." He stretched his arm along the back of the car seat. "Think of all the good times. Remember that day under the Boardwalk."

"What day?" She was visibly irritated.

"The day you said that we would always have each other's back, that we would be together forever. You kissed me."

She didn't remember. He could tell. The moment had meant so much to him and she didn't remember. He felt his temper rising, but he couldn't let any negative emotion show. He tried to sound casual, "Oh come on. You remember. The day Billy Bronson got us to throw sand up through the Boardwalk and that lady got so mad and chased us up and down while we crawled back and forth trying to avoid her. We were too tall to stand up."

He could tell the memory was coming back to her, but she wasn't smiling. "You were so scared. I tried to calm you down."

"But you kissed me."

"On the top of your head, Jimmy, the same way I would kiss a baby."

The word baby struck a chord. He felt rage building. "No, Sally, don't pretend you don't know how you treat me. How you flirt. How you lead me on." He put his hand on her shoulder. He wanted her to listen to him. She shrugged off his grasp and grabbed the door handle tightly. "Don't pretend you don't know what you do, Sally."

He saw real concern on her face. She let go of the handle. "I am so sorry, if I ever gave you the wrong impression. I love you—like a brother. You are part of the family. You are my sister's boyfriend. For God's sake, Jimmy, think about Marianne. If I did anything to hurt her, I could never forgive myself. I would never hurt her."

She was upset. Now came his chance to calm her, to comfort her. He tried to pull her to him, but she recoiled.

She remained calm. "No. No. No. Take me to the bus. Now."

But he couldn't give up, not his only, his last, opportunity. "Give me a chance, please." He moved across the seat and tried to pin her in place, but she screamed. "Get away from me." With one hand she punched him hard and with the other she opened the door. She jumped out of the car in a flash and ran towards the pines.

"Sally," he crawled across the front seat and out the passenger door. "Come back. You can't go in those woods. It's not safe."

It wasn't hard for him to catch up with her. She had taken only a few steps into the thicket when he grabbed her arm. She tried to fight him off but he wrapped both his arms around her. As he dragged her back to the car, she kicked and tried to wrest herself free, all the while begging him to let her go. He pushed her through the back door and used her struggling body to push her gear out of the way. He pinned her to the seat. He tried to soothe her. "It's okay, Sally. All I want is a chance with you. Please. Please. Then, if you still want to go, I will take you to the bus station and we can both forget this ever happened." It seemed to take a long time for her to realize she couldn't overpower him. She stopped struggling.

"Sally, please just give me a chance."

Her face was blank. Her eyes were dead. The fight went out of her. "I need you to take me to the bus station."

"I will. I promise."

*****

"I told her I loved her. I told her we could be happy, and I insisted that she let me show her how much I loved her. You might say I demonstrated more affection than she might have wanted, in a way that wasn't totally acceptable to her."

"You raped her." Xander made the accusation.

"I don't feel that word applies when you love someone so much."

"Really? Did she want to have sex with you?" Xander did not back down. "Did she ask you to have sex with her? Did you ask her? Did she say yes? Did she resist? Did she struggle?"

Jimmy's eyes provided the answers.

"You can tell yourself whatever you want, mate, but that was rape."

I felt so proud of Xander.

"We understand why you had so much to fear from Sally's letter." My approach was soft in comparison with Xander's, but Jimmy cowered as if I were physically menacing him.

"Are you going to tell Marianne?" Jimmy asked.

"Unless you want to." Xander offered the only other option.

"I'll tell her. I promise I will. After the storm. I don't want her upset at a time like this."

He didn't want to be thrown out in the middle of a storm—that was what he didn't want.

"We won't be in touch with her for several days," I assured him. "This is up to you to fix."

"Listen, mate," Xander leaned towards Jimmy, "you might not want to tell her the whole story of your betrayal, but the woman has a right to know that her sister has been dead for over twenty years."

Jimmy nodded, but not convincingly. That he had no idea what he would do was written all over his face.

"When did you find out about the baby?" I asked.

The question threw Jimmy even further off balance.

"Just now. You told me." He stuttered, ever so slightly, but he stuttered. "You asked me about a baby. Why would I care about Sally's baby?"

"Jimmy," Xander said as if addressing a three-year-old. "You know the facts of life. Aren't you at least a little concerned that the baby was yours?"

"I guess when you told me, I should have considered that possibility."

"So, you have no idea what Sally's child looks like?" I asked.

"How could I?" He answered his own question. "I couldn't. I didn't know she, or he, existed." He reached for my arm as I took a step to leave. "Wait! Are you telling me Sally died in 1998?"

As if he didn't know. "April 23."

"April," he said thoughtfully. "Late April." Jimmy's hands were shaking. "I can't believe it. I just can't believe it."

"Believe it," Xander confirmed. "April 23, 1998."

Chapter 40

I called Thomas Bauer on our way back to the car.

"Did he accept your explanation about why we want to visit?" Xander asked the moment I pulled the phone away from my ear.

"He understood our need to tie up a few loose ends before we talk to Marianne. He said he couldn't believe he hadn't asked us more questions. He appreciates the need for a follow-up."

"Are we going to tell him what we suspect?" Xander asked.

"Let's see what he has first, although I can't imagine we'll find any real proof that Jimmy came to Baltimore in 1998."

"Why do killers always forget to ask how the victim died?" Xander asked. "It's an obvious question."

"Obvious if you don't know the answer."

"We can't make the trip in this…vehicle." Xander called Del. "Be ready for our arrival back at the hotel. Meg and I are going to take a road trip." After a brief pause, he added, "I know bad weather is coming, but so far it looks great." Another pause. "Of course, I believe the weather people. I simply think we have time to get to Baltimore and back without getting caught in it." He hung up and addressed me. "Jimmy seemed rather rattled by Sally's date of death."

"Which strikes me as odd. He acted shocked that she died, but more shocked about when."

"He was exceedingly convincing when he claimed ignorance of Sally's death, wasn't he? I almost believed him. Perhaps he realized he'd have to react to news of her death at some point in his life. He likely practiced his reaction. But why would the date get to him? It had special meaning to him. I thought he was going to cry."

"Or throw up," I suggested.

"Did he block the date from his mind?" Xander did not sound convinced.

"Unlikely he'd forget."

"No matter. We know he did it. How will we ever nab him after all this time?"

"Xander, you have to prepare yourself. We may not be able to prove he killed Sally. I don't know how we can uncover new evidence so long after the crime, but for now we keep going back and asking more questions."

At the Artistical we climbed into the backseat of the SUV that Del had waiting. He was not smiling. "Aren't too many people taking pleasure drives on the East Coast today." Del started the engine.

"It's not a pleasure drive. This is our mission. Besides, the storm won't be here for hours." Xander may have brushed off Del's concerns, but he had taken the precaution of stashing his foul-weather gear in the back of the SUV.

"There's a phone right there in the back seat," Del called from the driver's seat.

"Some conversations just don't work on the phone," I explained.

"Two-and-a-half-hours to Baltimore. Each way. On a good day." Del was not happy.

"We'll be fine. We won't stay long. It isn't even raining yet." Xander soothed Del's feelings, then turned to me. "I think it's rather cut and dry. Jimmy gets letter. Jimmy doesn't want his crime to be exposed. Jimmy comes to Baltimore to ask Sally, now Sarah, to back off. Sees daughter. I don't believe for one moment he heard about that baby from us. He confronts Sally. They get in an argument. He kills her accidentally."

"Or did he drive down with the intention of killing her to make sure she kept quiet?" I assigned a more sinister motive to Jimmy.

"I don't get why he didn't just rip up the letter and forget the whole thing. Sarah said she was dying."

I thought about Xander's proposition across New Jersey to the Delaware Memorial Bridge, where I responded. "Love."

"What?" Xander sounded confused.

"I've been thinking about what you said." I called Xander back from his reverie. "You didn't get why Jimmy drove to Baltimore to see Sarah instead of just tearing up the letter. He was still in love with her. I bet if she had crooked her little finger, he would have come running."

"Do you think she did crook her finger?"

That thought had never occurred to me. "We may never know, but we do have more to learn. I'm glad we're making this trip."

Up in the front seat, Del grunted, unconvinced.

Heavy traffic in combination with rain that came and went made the drive unpleasant but Xander nostalgic. "Reminds me of being on tour."

"You might have to stay down here if the storm moves up the coast," Del called from the front seat. "Maybe we should have waited."

"No way." Xander and I said in unison. Now that we had our suspicions, we had to confirm them.

The going got slower with sporadic outbursts of rain coming closer together. Even after we drove west out of Frieda's reach, the dark clouds remained ominous, but we made it to Bauer's house by the time we'd promised.

"Nice to see you again." Thomas answered the door on his cane. "Come in." He asked about our travels and guided us to the dining room as if we had been invited to dinner. Only the spread on the table indicated we had come for a different reason. "I don't pull this stuff out often, but I have to admit that probably every year or so I go through these files. It's been a couple of years now."

He offered us seats under the watchful eye of the young bride, Sarah Johnson, gazing out from the portrait Dona Haven had painted so many years before. Bauer didn't mention it and neither did I. I found the fact that he hadn't shown it to us on our last visit, or pointed it out on this one, odd but didn't have time to speculate.

Bauer had not provided an enormous pile of folders to go through, but the names on the tabs were encouraging. *Police memos. Newspaper Clippings. Miscellaneous.* I wanted to dig right in, but first we sat and made awkward small talk. As soon as we finished a discussion of the weather, the topic turned to Sarah's death.

"The police were quite communicative with us. Plus, the press took an interest in Sarah's story, so we found out more than we might have if they hadn't. I told you the basics the last time you were here, but you are welcome to look at anything I have. I can't believe you aspire to solve a simple mugging, if that is what this was."

"We just want to tie up all the loose ends." I withheld our hopes that we might resolve more.

The police memos, standard verbiage embedded in some oddly heart-felt comments, indicated the police were trying their best to find out what happened to Sally.

The news clippings were more informative, but if I was hoping for a smoking gun I was disappointed.

The description of the suspect was based on the testimony of the two women who saw Sally in an animated discussion with a man, possibly in his late forties. The suspect was not quite six feet tall—that would match Jimmy. The little hair that showed appeared to be reddish—that would match Jimmy. He wore dark pants and a parka—that could match anyone.

The police sketch couldn't rule Jimmy out but would do little to prove he had been involved in Sarah's death. The man in the baseball cap could be a younger Jimmy, but it could depict millions of other men as well. The possibility existed that the man pictured had asked the victim's daughter for directions that morning, but she could not make a positive ID. No neigh-bors recalled seeing the man or noticing the car.

"We had some rain this morning. I would walk you to the spot where Sarah fell, but Mariana would kill me if I took this bum leg out on slip-pery sidewalks. I can give you directions, if you'd like. It would only take you a few minutes. Not that there is anything to see. It was her favorite place. She would sit on a big rock down there and listen to the babbling brook. The park gets more attention now, but it was always a lovely spot."

"No problem, we'll find it."

"I'll tell Sarah to guide you." He nodded at the portrait on the wall. "Dona Haven painted that for us as a wedding gift."

"It's lovely," I commented as if I had not been acutely aware of its presence through the entire meeting.

"Sometimes I forget it's there, she's there. I don't entertain much so I don't come into this room and I don't see it. I think that's why I put it here. I miss Sarah every day, but you can't live in the past. She would not like that."

Bauer sent us off with directions that included phrases like "turn right at the wide oak." Protected by trees, the path was dry, but our search did not go quickly, or smoothly. For an Englishman, Xander knew little about flora—and I knew virtually nothing about nature. However, we both excelled at identifying shapes, so we agreed that we had found the right rock.

About fifteen yards from the path, we found a small cliff, no taller than the average human, but big enough to hide anyone who picked their way down the rough path. Along the water, nature had built a patio of boulders and furnished it with large rocks suitable for seating. This had to be Sally's spot.

"Looks a bit foreboding with these skies," Xander observed.

"But a lovely place to sit and relax."

"If she was resting here, no one could see her from the trail. She was a sitting duck." Xander studied the configuration.

I laid my jacket on the damp rock and sat where Sally had rested so often. Xander stood beside me. We saw a solitary figure pass on a path across the water, but he paid us no attention, just as a passer-by might not have noticed Sally.

"Even a perpetrator in a standing position wouldn't have been seen." A perfect spot for relaxing and for committing a horrendous crime. "We don't know the density of the vegetation in those days, but once down here, the perp didn't need plant life to hide him. Jimmy could have hidden in the trees until those two women left and then come down here and accosted her."

"It might have been an accident, an argument that ended in violence." Xander's statement revealed an unusually generous attitude towards Jimmy.

I wasn't so kind. "Or the attack could have been premeditated. Once he knew about that baby—and I'll wager that he somehow did—the stakes got considerably higher. He could not let his wife find out. I doubt Marianne would have forgiven him."

"How do we prove this?" Xander asked.

"We can't. We've got nothing. We need a confession."

"I could threaten Jimmy."

"We're not thugs, Xander. We have to be clever."

By the time we made the short walk back to the Bauer house, we had not figured out how to be clever. We retrieved the folders and said good-bye. Thomas Bauer's eyes were red-rimmed. "I know it's silly. We had the tiniest little dog, but I worried that she would get away from Sarah or trip her or pull her over. I convinced Sarah taking him on her walks would be too difficult. I mean he was so small that I can't believe he could have offered protection, but Pookie could yap. Man, could he yap. If a criminal attacked Sarah, maybe Pookie could have offered some assistance— bitten the crook, gone for help or at least made a fuss. Oh, I realize that Sarah would have died within months, but if she was a victim of crime, it is my fault she found herself alone out there. I'm telling you this so that you understand what I've come to understand. My insistence that her death was an accident is not totally an objective conclusion." His manner changed and abruptly became all business. He offered us another folder that contained a copy of the police photo which he said we were welcome to. "And you might want to take this with you." He handed me an eight-by-ten photo of a diamond ring. "The only physical evidence would be the jewelry, but I doubt anyone would be stupid enough to hold onto that for all these years."

I studied the photo carefully. I wasn't so sure.

Chapter 41

I could barely keep quiet until we were back in the car, but I waited until Del had driven a block from the house before I spoke. "Marianne had that ring on her finger at the Knife and Fork." I poked the picture so hard that my finger threatened to rip the sheet.

"You're sure?" Xander asked.

"Bauer says Sally's ring was an heirloom. One of a kind. I find it hard to believe Marianne ended up with an identical piece. I think the similarity of her ring to Sally's bears looking into. Marianne flashed hers around, as if she was so proud of it. I don't think she wears it every day. I assumed it was her engagement ring, but I wonder."

"So, you theorize Jimmy intercepted the letter, came to Baltimore, killed Sally, stole the ring off Sally's hand and gave it to Marianne. That's sick." Xander twisted his features into a disgusted pose.

"No matter what, I would bet good money that same ring ended up on Marianne and Jimmy gave it to her. I can't believe he passes for normal. That behavior is cruel and diabolical. I can't imagine what possessed him to take the ring."

"A simple effort to mimic a robbery?" Xander suggested.

"Then he realized he had an expensive piece of jewelry, he might as well use it."

"If you're right, he's our perp." Xander didn't sound as convinced as I did.

"I'm right. I would bet on it. We've got to talk to Marianne about it."

"How? Given the weather, a casual drop-by is out of the question." Suddenly, Xander was the cautious one.

"The storm has dropped to a category three, but the weather people are still broadcasting a warning to go home and stay home," Del cautioned us.

"Besides," Xander wasn't convinced of the need to visit. "I can't see why she would be in any danger from Jimmy. Why would he hurt her now?"

"He knows we are snooping around. He knows the ring is evidence. What better time for his wife to disappear than in the middle of a storm. By the time we get back Frieda will be hitting and we may never have another chance." I felt true fear for Marianne's safety.

"If we get back." Del called from the front. "The cops might not let cars back in."

But they did, not that there were a lot of vehicles driving onto Absecon Island. Or off, for that matter. We encountered little traffic anywhere on the barrier island. Del drove slowly. We gave him the Dulleses's address, but he wasn't happy. "This amount of rain is not gonna drain off these streets. We should go back to the hotel."

"What does the radio say?" Xander asked Del.

He had a quick answer. "It says go back to the hotel."

"We will," I promised Del. I checked my phone. We had an hour or so before the worst hit. "We just have to make one short stop."

Del caught my eye in the rear-view mirror. "Make it quick. I'm parking at the end of the block. I'm no weatherman but they say high tide is coming, and, when it does, my money says it comes over the Boardwalk. I'm not putting this vehicle in danger. Think about what shape we'll be in if we lose it."

Neither Xander nor I argued. Xander, now fully protected in his foul-weather gear that I'd come to envy, promised Del we would hurry, and we jumped out. Well, I jumped. Getting out of the car on my side was easy. The wind yanked the door open, grabbed ahold of me and pushed me across the sidewalk until my flailing hands caught onto a railing. On the other side of the car, Xander had a harder time pushing his way out. He gave up and followed me through my door. Stunned, we huddled on the sidewalk accomplishing nothing other than standing our ground.

Xander took my hand. "Let's make this quick," he said without a touch of irony as he led on the long trek down what used to feel like a short block to the Dulles home. Together we pushed through the storm fighting for every inch we progressed, getting blocked every few feet by invisible walls of wind that threatened to topple us. It occurred to me that visiting Marianne was a faulty decision: this storm was much worse than it looked from the back seat of an SUV.

"It'll be much easier going back," I cajoled Xander, but I had no proof to support my hypothesis.

He answered, but the wind blew his response away.

The Dulles house was a dark mound at the end of the street. With the wind stinging my face, I could barely open my eyes, but I saw that the windows were covered, with tiny lines of light defining where the shutters met. Someone might be home. After what we just went through to reach the front steps, someone better be home. Or what? I'd get cranky? In a raincoat that did little to resist rain and sneakers that did nothing to repel water, I could hardly be in a crankier mood. Xander in his foul-weather gear appeared more upbeat, leading the charge up the rain-coated front steps. I pulled myself up the stairs by the railing to reach the porch where the wind, no longer buffered by Boardwalk and dunes, hit us with full force. I slid across the slippery porch surface towards the rail. Xander, in his big yellow boots, caught the tail of my raincoat and pulled me back.

"I acknowledge the idea to come here was mine, but I have to admit it was a dumb one," I yelled.

This time I heard Xander's response. "No argument from me."

The screen doors had been removed, so each of us banged on one of the double doors. I yelled for Marianne. Xander yelled for Jimmy.

"Is Jimmy here?" We asked in unison when Marianne opened the door a crack and peeped to see who had come calling in the worst storm of the past few years.

"What are you doing out there? Get in here." She pulled the door back and grabbed my jacket to pull me inside. Xander followed and used his full weight to force the door closed behind us.

"I am alone here finishing battening down the hatches." She'd chosen an *I Survived Sandy* t-shirt for the occasion. "Why on earth are you here?"

"We made a discovery and didn't feel we should wait to talk to you,"

I said. So far the only water damage to the Dulles house were the puddles Xander and I were creating under our feet. Xander's coat produced a larger one. My raincoat—created by a designer oblivious to the main purpose of a raincoat—had absorbed the water as had, more predictably, my jeans. I shivered so that my words came out at a staccato clip to match my body tremors. "Although upon further observation of the weather, I suspect we could have done with a phone call."

"You didn't have to come," Marianne said in a tone to comfort us. "Jimmy told me what you found out about Sally. He said he wanted to wait until after the storm, but you know Jimmy. That man cannot keep a secret."

I wasn't so sure about that. How much had he told her? She didn't seem angry, so I concluded he'd stopped with the news of Sally's death.

"We are very sorry, Marianne." Xander spoke for both of us. "But I think we should talk about this at the hotel."

Xander might have been comfortable in his clothing but that didn't mean he was feeling comfortable. He rushed across the sunroom to look out the one window left unshuttered. "Oh my God." He jumped back as water slammed against the glass. "A wave just hit the window."

"That's not a wave." Marianne's tone added *silly boy*. "The wind's picking up. That's horizontal rain. No wave has ever hit that window. Even during Sandy. Or in the 1962 Nor'easter. I don't even think in 1944, not that I was around to see. Maybe a few planks from the old Boardwalk, but never a wave." She chuckled. "So not to worry. The outside shutter has been gone for years and we didn't even bother replacing it. If a wave didn't get that window in those big storms, no wave ever will."

I didn't trust Marianne's logic or her ability to forecast weather. I was as jumpy as Xander. "We want to tell you everything we learned, but I don't feel this is the time."

"Or the place," Xander added.

"We're safe here. This house had stood tall when a lot of its neighbors ended up in the drink. I moved everything I need upstairs." Then, in a move that I recall in slow motion, she switched a tissue to her left hand showcasing her diamond ring.

"Is that your engagement ring?"

"Oh." She acted surprised to see the sparkling jewel on her finger. "I put all my jewelry on, in case we have to evacuate." She touched a small diamond disc at her neck and then admired the large diamond ring on her finger. "Jimmy gave me this for our twenty-fifth anniversary."

"When was that?" Xander asked, in my opinion a little too eagerly, but Marianne didn't seem concerned. "1998. We married in 1973." When she saw the expression on Xander's face her attitude changed. "Why is he interested in my ring?"

"Marianne, we didn't tell Jimmy everything about Sally's death. We didn't know everything when we talked to him. The mugger only took one thing. An heirloom ring." I pulled the folder out of my bag, the photo from the folder. Marianne leaned forward and studied the photo and then her ring.

"They are awfully similar."

My read? She was reluctant to acknowledge the similarity. The two rings appeared identical to me.

"I'm not sure I understand. They cannot be the same ring. How would Jimmy get a ring from the mugger who killed my sister?" Even as she formed the question, I saw by the expression on her face she realized how ridiculous that possibility was. "Are you telling me that Jimmy…?" The thought was too horrifying for her to continue. "When did Sally die?"

"1998."

"What month?"

"April."

We sat without speaking and let Marianne fit the pieces together for herself. "But why? What reason would Jimmy have for harming Sally?" She threw a hand across her chest. "Was it because she hurt me? Did he do it for me?"

"The situation was more complicated than that." Xander turned to me as if he were passing a football and telling me to run with it.

I looked past him through the sole exposed window and saw traces of white foam rising from waves rushing through the dunes. "I don't believe this is the time to go into the details. Come with us to the hotel and we can fill you in."

"I'm staying here through the storm. I've been through them all. Well, not all, but most."

"We're here this time, my dear." Xander turned on the charm. "You should come with us."

Marianne was thinking so hard that I could monitor the process on her face. In her position, I would be doing the same. "I need to get something first." She disappeared into the hallway. We heard the thumping of her feet on the stairs.

"The tide is coming in." Xander peered out the window.

"You can see that?"

"No, I can see the tide clock."

I followed the direction of his pointed finger and saw less than two hours remained until high tide. A long time on a normal weather day, not on the day Frieda came to town.

"We've got to get out of here or we'll be spending the duration of Frieda hiding in the attic. What is so important she had to retrieve it?" Xander was not happy.

"No clue, but when she gets down let's tell her we're going and that she'd better come with us."

We heard banging doors upstairs and then the sound of footsteps descending the staircase.

"What is this?" I opened the plastic bag Marianne shoved into my hands and found a pile of gray jersey.

"I've had that T-shirt for years. I kept it. I found it in the trash. It's Jimmy's. He loved the Rolling Stones. Not my favorites, but he was a big fan. I couldn't understand why that shirt was in the trash. I hadn't put it there. I took it out and hid it. Deep in my heart, I knew it meant something bad. Those stains. I feared they were blood. I didn't want to believe it, but I did. I wrote the date inside so I would be sure to remember, if anything ever came up."

I dug around for the tag and found the marking. The date was two days after Sarah Bauer's mugging, but we didn't have time to discuss that. Waves were flooding the dunes and lapping at the Boardwalk. I handed our evidence to Xander. "Can you secure that in your jacket somehow?"

He figured out how to do that while I tried to rush Marianne. "We have to go."

"But what about Jimmy? Jimmy is volunteering because of the storm. He'll come for me."

"Marianne, you shouldn't be here when he comes back. You can't stay in the same house with him. He's dangerous."

"I've been in this house with him for thirty-five years."

"But if he catches on that you suspect he hurt your sister…." I couldn't bring myself to use the word murdered.

"How could he? I won't let on. I can be clever. No one gives me any credit. I'm not a fool."

Maybe not, but even the wisest person could be overcome with emotion when confronted with the information she'd just received. I could picture the entire scenario. Jimmy and Marianne isolated in the storm. Her anger grows. She gives into her rage. She confronts him. He gives into his rage. He kills her. Could there be a better time to dispose of a body? I lifted a yellow rain jacket from a coat rack and fought to get the resisting woman into it.

"Come with us. We have to go to the police," Xander said. "Tell me how to cover that last window and we will go."

Marianne offered no directions to Xander and did nothing to dress herself. Like a three-year-old, she protested while I did the toggles on her jacket and Xander shoved her feet into rubber boots. "We can't go to the police in the midst of a storm. They won't pay any attention to a story like this when they have so much to do. It wouldn't be their case. You said it happened in Baltimore. Don't let the local cops blow this off in the middle of a disaster. I have waited years for justice. I want to make sure I am heard."

"Of course. Of course. Now let's go." Xander headed for the door.

"Let me get my things. Always ready. Just in case. Only the third time I ever used it." Marianne pulled a gym bag from under a hall table. She didn't resist as Xander wrapped an arm around her and guided her to the door. "We can take my car."

"You have a car here?" Xander asked.

"Of course. I live here. We can take mine."

"We didn't drop by while we were out for a walk. We came in a car. Let's go. It's waiting." I checked the tide clock on the wall and wasn't happy.

"But my car...."

"I'll go with her," I told Xander.

"Thank you, dear." She handed me her key fob. "Do you mind driving? I'm not much of a driver. I have my own car, but really, Jimmy does most of the driving."

"We'll both go with her." Xander moved the woman closer to the door. "I'll tell Del to follow us in case we hit any problem areas."

I tried to suppress my annoyance and dredge up more sympathy for Marianne but found it difficult to forgive her lack of speed while I visualized a wave crashing through the front wall. All I wanted to do was to get moving and keep my promise to Andy to stay out of harm's way.

Xander opened the front door, and I had the distinct impression that harm's way was exactly where we were headed.

Chapter 42

Before we left the porch, Marianne assured us that the water swirling in the streets was rain water. "Not ocean water," she screamed. "Street dips here. Be careful." I wasn't worried. All we had to do was get down the steps and reach the car sitting in the driveway beside the house. The short trip would be wet and uncomfortable, but I felt up to the challenge. Escorting Marianne between us like precious cargo, Xander went first and I brought up the rear. As we fought to keep our balance in the wind, she yelled. "Watch out for the curb."

Xander and I did. Marianne failed to take her own advice and veered to the right until I saw her topple into the water. She got to her feet and staggered backwards toward the Boardwalk stumbling into deeper water collecting in a gully at the end of the street. There she disappeared from sight.

"Xander," I yelled. I waded to the side of the now flailing figure, but I was not in good enough shape to pull her from the water. "Xander." I made a grab for Marianne's arm and tried to yank her to her feet, but she couldn't find her footing. I pulled, but she pulled harder. I toppled into the water beside her. I stopped my efforts to help Marianne and tried to help myself. Marianne might have described this water as an oversized puddle, but I had never encountered a puddle with an undertow before. With the rain pelting my face and the wind challenging my quest for stability, being stranded in a puddle created the sensation of being lost at sea.

Seconds after I righted myself, my feet slipped out from beneath me. Again, I fought my way to a standing position, a battle I lost. For a minute, I foresaw my death in water that didn't quite reach my waist.

"Xander." I struggled to right myself.

Xander pushed his way through the water to my side. He only needed one hand to pull me to my feet and then grabbed Marianne's jacket hood with both hands to lift her.

"My bag. My bag," she begged.

"Forget the bloody bag." He gripped her and holding her close to his body, dragged her towards shore, I mean the sidewalk.

I could have ignored the bag drifting by and thought about it, but my disdain for litterers overcame my disdain for Marianne. I caught the handle and, vowing I would let it go at the first sign I was slipping, dragged it behind me through the water. I caught up with Xander and Marianne and threw the bag in the back of her SUV.

"We'll get the front seat wet," She protested.

Xander silenced her with a stare. I admired Marianne's talent for propelling people—the same people who came to help her, who sympathized with her predicament, who fought for her peace of mind—to the edge of a cliff where they would abandon all virtuousness and toss her over.

Xander pushed Marianne into the front seat next to me. He climbed in the rear door. Luckily Marianne's car faced forward, but I still had difficulty steering it out of the driveway without sideswiping a few bushes that Frieda's winds bent into our path. Xander leaned forward with his head between ours in order to facilitate his back seat driving, but it didn't help. We bounced off the curb into the street, catching the edge of the standing water that had almost claimed Marianne and me and headed up the street that now looked more like a canal.

Marianne explained. "Regular occurrence in this kind of rain. Not the ocean. Yet."

Her words did not make me feel any better. I pressed on the gas pedal just a little harder, but knew not to put a strain on the car. Luckily, the SUV sat high and made its way through the rising waters without protest. Xander retrieved the only operational cell phone we had amongst us from a zipped pocket and called Del with instructions to follow us as we passed. With the town car positioned for a quick getaway, Del found it easy to comply.

As we headed north on Atlantic Avenue, Marianne became less annoying. Maybe because she said nothing. I wanted to comfort her, but

I didn't know what to say to a woman who had just discovered her life was based on a lie. Besides, I was too busy getting annoyed with Del. He called Xander twice in the first five blocks to see why I wasn't moving faster.

I drove as quickly as I could. Given that the rain didn't so much fall as lay itself across the windshield in sheets, that meant painfully slowly. The streets were filling with rain water and the threat of high tide still loomed. I kept moving—even at red lights.

"We stop at them in the UK, you know," Xander advised.

"You want to stop and wait for the water to kill the engine so we can sit here until the Atlantic Ocean envelops the car?"

"Well, when you put it that way."

"I have Del telling me to speed up and you telling me to slow down. I'm doing my best."

Xander sat in silence for the rest of our trip. We left a wake as we plowed north, but we made it to the Artistical where Del followed me to an upper floor of the parking garage. Del complained that my approach—the higher the better—was overcautious, but Xander suggested he move "the fleet" to a high floor, explaining the ever-rotating supply of vehicles Del managed to produce on demand. Del wasn't interested in protecting the cars. He wanted to see his human charges safely inside the hotel. We were safe from the flood but not from the rain that whipped through the parking structure. Xander was whining in his foul-weather gear and I couldn't blame him. The temperature might have been nearing sixty degrees, but the rain and wind combination left me feeling chilled.

We walked into a fully-powered hotel. I felt happy for the lighting but not for the air-conditioning. I shivered in my wet clothes and prayed throughout the elevator ride down to the lobby that the power stayed on at least until another elevator carried us back up to Xander's suite. I wasn't as worried by the removal of the Rothko that Xander had admired from its display spot in the lobby as I was by the absence of the easily movable items. What damaging force did the hotel management think would displace those lamps, plants and smaller chairs? I chose not to think about their motives for clearing the area.

I decided to believe the hotel employees who said that with a backup generator the electricity would not be an issue, but only after we were all off the elevator. I figured I'd be happier once we were inside Xander's suite. First, he had to feign difficulty with the electric lock to give Del time to slip through the bedroom entrance and turn the white board so Marianne would not be confronted with our theories of what turned out to be her husband's crimes.

Once inside, Xander provided both Marianne and me with clothes from his wardrobe—not Rex's. I took mine with me into a shower big enough to host a dinner party for twelve. I lingered, washing my hair time after time. Scrubbing didn't help. I couldn't get clean—or warm. I gave up.

Marianne looked ridiculous and uncomfortable in ill-fitting purple spandex pants and a long Xander Frost T-shirt featuring his bright red, over-sized lips on a royal blue background. I didn't check the mirror to see how I looked in the darker version of her outfit Xander offered me, but I imagined just as ridiculous. But the clothes were dry. That was all that mattered.

Xander pulled our evidence out of a jacket pocket that was really more of a pouch. "Still dry. Sorry I can't say that about your phone. Del has it packed in rice."

I didn't even have to ask why Del happened to have rice in a hotel suite. I'd seen enough of Xander's entourage tumbling into pools to assume he considered many provisions that I would consider exotic, routine.

Xander tossed me his phone. "Text Andy and let him know your phone is out of commission. His number is in there."

I didn't ask why. I keyed in a message.

Xander dug into the supplies he had purchased for our investigation. I shouldn't have been surprised he had evidence bags. My guess was his provisions matched the props he used in *Hidden Mystery*. He took great care in bagging the sweatshirt and the ring. Before he disappeared into the bedroom—I assumed to secure them in the safe—he opened the door to his minibar to us. The selection wasn't bad. I set up the cheese and fruit plate on the coffee table as if we were here for a party. Marianne asked for a bottle of wine.

While wind and rain beat against the tall windows, we gathered around the coffee table and tried to merge everything we had learned in

Baltimore with the details Marianne provided. We came to the only obvious conclusion. Jimmy Dulles had murdered Sally Johnson Bauer. Marianne acted stunned and fixated on the idea that he did everything for her sake, but I couldn't buy her explanation. I wasn't willing to hurt her further by telling her what I suspected had actually driven Jimmy to kill.

The banging on the door shocked all of us. "Maybe we have to evacuate," Xander speculated.

Del went to find out. I heard mumbling in the entryway.

"Hey, boss, you know a Jimmy Dulles?"

Xander didn't actually say *send him in*. He said "yes" and Del put up no resistance as Jimmy, in full storm-fighting gear, rushed by.

"Thank God. You left no note telling me where you were going. A neighbor said he saw Marianne leave with some people. His description sounded like you folks. What are you wearing?" He recoiled from his wife.

"How did you get this room number?" I asked.

"There's a storm. I'm a fire department volunteer. You can't hide from me." He chuckled. He sounded rather pleasant, but, knowing what I knew about him, I judged the sound to be diabolical.

"Stay away from me. They told me what you did." Marianne used a tone I wouldn't have thought she had in her arsenal of sounds.

The bright grin disappeared from his face. "What I did?"

I wasn't surprised Jimmy sounded apprehensive.

"To Sally."

"She left four decades ago." His glance at me was actually more of a glare, albeit a quick one, that accused me of ratting him out.

"Not when we were kids." Marianne's tone added *you idiot*. "When you killed her."

"What?"

This time I saw real shock on his face.

"You saw Sally in 1998, and you killed her."

Jimmy gesticulated as if he had a great point to make, but all that came out of his mouth was sputtering, a string of truncated obscenities.

"We know you saw her. The police have a sketch."

"A sketch?" He found his voice. "A police sketch? I bet it could be anyone. Let me see it."

"I'm sure your lawyer will show you the sketch." Marianne was more versatile than I gave her credit for when it came to nasty intonations. This one combined condescension with satisfaction.

"What are you talking about? I would never hurt Sally." He looked from Marianne to me to Xander.

Xander's eyes opened to their concert-level wideness as he shook his head in disbelief.

"I mean that I would never kill her. I did not kill her. I didn't know she was dead until these two told me."

"You didn't tell me you saw her." Marianne, betrayed yet again, cried, but I couldn't tell if hers were tears of sadness or rage.

All three of us, Marianne, Xander and I looked to Jimmy. That was going to be hard to explain. "I didn't want to upset you until the storm was over."

My belief? He probably thought the storm would get her and carry her out to sea, eliminating the need for him to explain how Sally ended up with his baby—as well as the opportunity for Marianne to change her will.

"I didn't tell you because it is an exceedingly complicated story. Parts of it, I think that you and I should discuss in private." He looked at Marianne and tipped his head to define Xander and me as interlopers. "I can explain why I went to see her, but I think the important thing right now is to clarify that I never harmed Sally. I did argue with her and I can explain all those reasons to you later." He cleared his throat. "I must tell you that Sally had sent a letter to our house and I wanted to determine her motive." Okay, that probably was not a lie. He just wasn't giving his wife any clue as to what he feared that motive might be. "She had hurt you so badly…." I think he made a wise decision letting his thought end there. "But right now, just let me provide the basics of our encounter." He glanced at Xander and me for our approval. We didn't offer any, but neither did we offer any disapproval.

Still in his rain-soaked jacket, he slumped onto the nearest piece of furniture, a small ottoman. "Here are the facts. We received a letter saying she wanted to be in touch. I drove to Baltimore to check her out. I went to her house and she was not welcoming. I grew angry. I waited to see if she came out of the house. She did. I followed her into a park. I told her I wanted to speak to her. She refused. I became angry. I made my case and got no response. I became angrier." He punctuated each statement with a jab of his right hand. "Foolishly, I expressed my frustration by pushing her. Not the right thing to do, but I did not punch her or hit her or hurt her. She lost her balance temporarily, but she was upright when I left."

"That's not the end of the story. We know that." I tried not to sound too harsh. I wanted him to continue.

"That's it. I left. And I never went back. There is no more to the story."

"The police can take it from here." If he wasn't going to go on, I wasn't going to lead him. We would give the evidence to the police and let them surprise him with it. I wasn't going to give him warning and time to prepare an explanation. "After the storm passes, we'll go to the station."

"Why would the Atlantic City police care that, close to twenty years ago, I shoved a woman in Baltimore?" He turned to Marianne. "I am sorry I didn't tell you Sarah wanted to talk to you, but I was so scared I would lose you if she told you about something that happened a long time ago. In '68. I was a kid when it happened. I am a different person now. Do you understand?"

The hard look in her eyes said that she did not, and would not, understand.

256

Chapter 43

Xander and I sat on a couch along the window and studied Marianne in her purple Xander Frost apparel listening to Jimmy in his *I Survived Sandy* t-shirt speak in what sounded like earnest tones, although we couldn't quite make out the words.

"Do you think he's telling her about the baby?" Xander asked.

"No, I would expect a far bigger reaction from her if he were." I could only judge by my own response which, I imagined, would involve a lot of screaming and a fair amount of broken glass.

"How long does he think he can put it off?" I jumped as a burst of wind slammed a sheet of rain onto the glass behind us. "Has it occurred to you that perhaps we should not be sitting in such close proximity to the floor-to-ceiling window in a hurricane?"

"No. This is a wonderful experience of the power of nature." He'd barely finished his last word when a gust of wind hit the window prompting him to jump off the sofa and run to the safety of the entryway. He eyed the Dulleses sitting in the cubbyhole, unperturbed by nature since their lives were in far greater tumult. He returned to my side. "I couldn't hear a thing. What do you think he's saying?"

"Whatever you say when you grovel."

"He seems confident that he has us fooled." Xander thought over his own assertion. "Unless it's all an act and he's waiting for a chance to make a run for it. We should take turns sleeping. You. Me. Del. That should work. Although, in retrospect, it might have been more prudent for us to wait until Frieda passed to resolve this situation. We are now forced to pass the storm with a man we just called a killer." I shared his second thoughts.

Marianne broke away from Jimmy and headed to join our group leaving her husband sitting with his head in his hands. We stood to meet her halfway. "He claims he didn't kill her, but the evidence will say otherwise, won't it?"

"The case looks solid to me. DNA on his shirt should clinch it." I tried to reassure her.

"He's sitting over there, all smug, as if he is going to win me back, as if everyone believed his story. Why didn't you tell him what we have on him?" Marianne sounded angry.

"That's up to the police. We want this to stick. No reason to give him time to come up with an excuse. Let the police have the advantage of the element of surprise," I explained.

"Now, dearie, you didn't go ahead and tell him about our proof, did you love?" Xander asked in the sweetest of tones.

"I said there was evidence. That's all. I didn't tell him what we had or where we had it." Her expression came close to a smile as she described his disclaimers. "He honestly believes there cannot be any evidence. Fool. I wanted so much to tell him." She tried persuading herself our plan would work out. "I waited this long, I guess I can wait another day."

She walked to the window to study the storm. Showing more will than I'd given her credit for, she didn't flinch when gust after gust of wind drove waves of rain into the glass.

"We should not let Jimmy out of our sight, but I see no reason to force Marianne to spend the night with him," Xander suggested.

"No way I'm sharing. Do you still have the key to the room next to mine? We can put her in there, although I don't think I'll mention that my room is on the other side of the connecting door. Give me the key and I'll take her down."

"Take my phone with you in case the hotel power goes out. Call Del if there is an issue."

Marianne seemed relieved to get away from Jimmy, but I wasn't sure she trusted Xander to keep track of him. Between the time we left Xander's suite and arrived at her newly assigned room, she had asked me at least a dozen times if I thought Jimmy could get away.

"He believes he has us fooled, Marianne, don't worry. He won't go anywhere. Del and Xander won't let him. Even if he eluded them, it's unlikely the cops would let him out on the street. It's not safe out there."

"But he works with the police. They know him. They like him."

"He'll never get to the cops. You've seen Del. He won't let him get out of the suite. Is Jimmy such a fool that he would try?"

"A fool, but not a hero. Why didn't you tell him about the ring and the shirt?" Marianne could disapprove of our plan all she wanted, but it wasn't going to change our position.

"I told you. I want the police to see his reaction to that information. We have only one shot at gauging his first response, and that opportunity should fall to professionals. Don't worry. You have hard physical evidence. That is rare in old cases like this. If he hadn't held onto that ring, and if you hadn't found that shirt, we probably could never have gotten him."

"I guess." Marianne appeared older than when we first met and more tired.

"You must be exhausted. You had so many shocks today." I opened the door to the room next to mine. Not that Marianne knew that.

"I suppose you're correct. I have a right to feel exhausted. It is good getting away to a room by myself. I have a lot to process."

"I'm sorry to break so much bad news to you." I handed her the keycard.

"Jimmy told me about the baby. I guess it isn't all bad. I have a niece and a grandniece, but that is a complex situation. I love that there is something left of my sister, but to see Jimmy in her daughter. I don't see how I can deal with that."

"It's a lot to handle." I didn't know how I could.

"He has no idea where I am, does he? Jimmy. He can't find me."

"No way. This room number will be our secret—as long as you don't call Xander's room and give away your location on the phone display."

She turned on the lights and checked out the room, wandering to the window absent-mindedly running her hand across every piece of furniture she passed. "Can you stay for a few moments?"

As the bearer of her recent bad news, I felt responsible for her discomfort. "Sure. I can stay for a little while." I let the door fall shut behind me.

She stood at the window, never flinching at the rain pelting the glass. "It's funny the way this turned out. I never knew if my sister had run away or died, and it turned out she did both." She took a long pause. I thought she had nothing more to say, but after an uncomfortable silence she continued.

"I guess I understand why she felt she had to stay away. Part of me always knew Jimmy was infatuated with her, but I thought that was all it was. A crush. I thought what we had was a mature love, a real friendship. But to think she lived all those years, knowing what she had over me, laughing at me and the life I thought I had."

"I don't believe she was laughing, Marianne. I believe she wanted to spare you any pain."

"To spare me the pain of learning just how inferior to her I was."

"You've gotten so much information today. No one can expect you to assimilate so many different emotions immediately. I am sure you will go through many stages. Do you want me to call someone? Your friend, Clare? Maybe you shouldn't be alone."

"I'll be fine. You've done enough," she said, with a harsh rather than a grateful tone that suggested she held me responsible for the entire mess from 1968 forward. I figured she would move through this stage. And if she didn't? What did I care? I'd done my part. I'd never have to see her again.

Chapter 44

"If you are being careful, how did your phone get wet?"

"In a puddle. Just a puddle." I didn't elaborate. Andy didn't need to hear where the puddle was or how I ended up in it. "Del is good at saving phones. Until then Xander says you should feel free to contact me on this number."

"Where are you now?"

"I'm in Xander's suite riding out the storm. He's right here beside me reading on his iPad."

"He reads?" After a few seconds of silence, Andy realized I'd find it hard to respond without Xander figuring out the type of question he had asked. He asked another. "Who else is there?"

"Del and a gentleman who helps out with rescue efforts are also here." I didn't know if Jimmy was listening, but I wasn't about to take the chance he could hear me.

"I'm surprised the hotel is letting you stay in your rooms."

"For now. No evacuation order for the city. Power is on. Cable is on. We are good. We don't expect it to be that bad. Wet and windy but not dangerous as they originally thought."

"I hate to admit that I am happy you are with someone, even if that someone is Xander. Is your case closed?"

"Final steps."

"Care to clarify?"

"Not at the moment."

"Care to talk dirty?"

"Not at the moment."

"So, the guy who is with you, does he have something to do with the resolution of the case?"

"Everything."

"Okay. He has the story about what happened to your victim?"

"Yes."

"She was a victim?"

"Yes."

"And he killed her?"

"Yes."

"And you and Xander have elected to spend the night with him?"

"When you say it that way...."

"It sounds stupid?"

"You could be right, but...."

"Would you like to use the bedroom for your call?" Xander interrupted.

I would, but I didn't waste my private time talking about our plan to go to the police with Jimmy. I felt somewhat mellow when I opened the door to the living room. The lights were dim and I saw Del taking his turn to sleep on the couch in the corner. Jimmy and Xander sat on another couch, deep in conversation that I could hear from the doorway.

"I'll go to the police with you tomorrow. They know me, that I am not capable of murder. Even in anger. I never denied that I found her and argued with her."

"You withheld the information."

"I explained why. I wanted to shield Marianne, and I wanted to save my marriage. You see what happened once she found out. She hates me and I can't blame her. You don't have to sit up all night watching me. Only an idiot would go out in this storm. Besides, I've got nowhere else to go. I certainly won't be going home again."

Xander agreed but whereas Jimmy thought he would have to search for a new home, Xander thought he would be given one in the Maryland penal system. "Jimmy we have physical proof that you killed Sally."

"You can't because I didn't." His voice was steady; his manner, calm. He believed Marianne was bluffing when she talked about physical evidence. He was in for a shock. "Not that my innocence will matter to my wife. I came to love Marianne. Not in the way I loved Sally. Sally was exciting and sexy, but delicate. She made you want to take care of her." Any affection vanished from his voice to be replaced by an emotion more akin to frustration, or even bitterness. "Marianne always makes me feel like a weakling. With both mental and physical shortcomings. Inadequate. She says she loves me, but she acts as if she is doing me a favor, as if I am lucky anyone would love me."

My take? He had just summarized Marianne's feelings about herself.

"But Sally, gifted in so many ways, never made me feel that way. She radiated a calm that was part of her beauty. At the end when I saw her, when she appeared gaunt and her eyes had black circles around them, she looked haunted, but still beautiful. I guess whatever made her beautiful on the inside stayed intact."

"But you argued with her."

"I did. I don't deny it. She had withheld from me that I had a daughter, that we had a daughter. When she told me, I had this flash, a delusion that we could have made a life together. But after we had that altercation, and I will admit I pushed her, but after that, I gave up that delusion. I never went back."

"Because you knew she wasn't there because you killed her," Xander confirmed.

Jimmy sounded exasperated. "No. How many times do I have to tell you? I didn't kill her."

"If you didn't realize she was dead, why didn't you reach out to meet your daughter?"

"I thought about it. For years. But I had witnessed how her mother felt about me. I had no reason to believe that she would welcome me into her world. And if she did, did I really want to be included? I had three children that I loved, whose affection I would risk if they discovered what I'd done."

"When you saw Marianne's pain, still ongoing after years, weren't you ever tempted to confess that you had seen her sister?"

"I told you. I didn't want to throw away the life I had. The whole point of the trip to Baltimore had been to ask Sally to keep our secret. Why wouldn't I keep it? Especially after I learned the full story." The anger faded from his voice. "Although if Marianne had been home when I got back to Ventnor, I believe I might have blurted the whole story out." He slipped into the past. "I paced around the house for hours waiting for her to return. Maybe it wasn't hours, but it felt like such a long time. I kept rehearsing how I would tell her, what I would tell her." He snapped back to the present. "Luckily, she didn't come home until late that night. I had time to calm down and consider the repercussions. For years, I held my breath waiting for Sally to appear at our door, but she never did. She'd been so frail the last time I'd seen her. After a few years, I wondered if she had passed away. God help me, I hoped she had. I didn't share my secret, that I had seen her, with a single soul. I went on as if that day never happened."

"Except that Sally was dead."

"An unfortunate coincidence. That's all. I never knew she had died until you told me. I returned home from Baltimore that day and worked on my marriage. Was I over Sally? No. Was that ridiculous? Yes. But I committed to my marriage. We celebrated our twenty-fifth wedding anniversary a few months later."

"A big one. Guess you gave her a big present."

I worried that Xander had jumped the gun on the ring, but I understood he didn't want to miss a good opportunity to lead Jimmy into a trap.

"I wish. My wife has all the money. I don't get to see any of it. I worked in a mid-level position at a mid-size company. I couldn't afford to buy her anything fancy. She likes to tell people I gave her a big diamond that year, but the truth is she bought it herself. I was shocked. She's not only tight with me. She's just plain cheap. She handed me a box, all wrapped up, and told me to hand it to her at our party. Then, in front of all her friends, she made a big deal about what a wonderful job I had done picking it out. I felt humiliated, but she seemed happy. Knowing the secret that I was carrying, I played along."

I took a step into the room and Xander turned and met my eyes. I suspected we were trying to figure out the same thing. Did Jimmy understand he needed an explanation for how he came by the ring? Had Marianne warned him, or said something about our having it?

"Do you know where that ring is now, Jimmy?" Xander asked.

"Ask my wife. I didn't notice if she had it on, but she's probably wearing it. She wears it whenever there is a storm—in case we have to flee. We could probably live off that baby for a year."

"Did she tell you where she bought the ring?" I asked.

Jimmy didn't appear surprised that I had joined the conversation. "She got it at some estate sale. A real steal, she said."

Xander's and my eyes met and asked each other the same question. Should we believe him?

"So you didn't give it to her?" Xander confirmed.

"I handed it to her in front of a crowd so, in that respect, I gave it to her. And in that respect only."

"You'll need to tell all this to the police," I said.

"I'll be happy to although I can't imagine why it matters. You guys don't have to stay up and watch me. I'll go put on these dry clothes Xander lent me." He held a royal blue version of the Xander attire I was wearing in black and Marianne in purple. "Maybe Marianne will feel better about me when I'm back in a matching outfit." He studied the T-shirt. "If I had a reason to flee, which I don't, I wouldn't go anywhere in this weather, or this outfit." Jimmy Dulles made a joke.

Chapter 45

Xander and I didn't wait for Jimmy to drift off before we slipped into the bedroom to confer. We left the lights off and stood at the window watching the rain turn the lights on the Boardwalk below into a psychedelic display of color.

"He made a joke." I stated a fact.

"Not a very good one, but I did catch that he attempted some humor, which I find odd in a man being accused of murder. I believe him." Xander's proclamation betrayed no trace of doubt. "He didn't kill Sally."

"I agree. He's so calm and certain about his story. What do you think is going on?"

"Same as you, I imagine. Marianne is trying to frame him, now isn't she?"

"The question is whether or not she is trying to frame a guilty or an innocent man."

Xander and I spoke in unison, both with the same intonation that said the answer was obvious. "Innocent."

"She wants to punish him," Xander observed.

"Part of me doesn't blame her." I could sympathize.

"Thank God we didn't play into her hands and get the cops here to charge Jimmy. That would be a bell we couldn't unring."

"Why she would frame him is obvious. She played second fiddle to her sister until the day Sally disappeared. Then, she discovered she had been playing second fiddle her entire life. But how did she find out about Sally's death? How did she get a hold of the ring?"

"She could have followed Jimmy to Baltimore. Maybe she found the letter."

"If she had the letter, she could go on her own. I have no doubt that Sally died on the day Jimmy visited. My theory is Marianne got suspicious and followed him."

"She saw his interaction with Sally." Xander didn't ask; he stated.

"So she knows if he killed Sally or not. Whatever happened she saw it," I offered.

"She saw her sister die. Murder or accident. She knew." Xander stated with certainty. "Why not get help? Why not call the police?"

"You and I would see a crime, Marianne saw an opportunity. Sally was dead or close to it, and now that Marianne knew about Jimmy and Sally, that was fine with her. She couldn't change the situation, but she could take advantage of it."

"Take advantage of it fifteen years later? That's a long time. Why not set Jimmy up back then, when it happened?" Xander asked.

"Who knows what she thought when she took the ring? Probably just an impulse to shift blame to a mugger. Maybe to save Jimmy. At first, anyway. I imagine it took her a while to work out the details of her plan."

"She probably didn't anticipate it would take her this long." Xander snickered.

"Oh my God. I should have caught it. She slipped up last night. She said she had been waiting for justice for years. Not an answer. Justice."

"Justice for what? She had to know Sally was dead."

"What she was waiting for was an opportunity to get justice. Not for Sally, but for herself. If she wasn't certain Sally was dead when she left Baltimore that day, she found out. She's known her sister was dead all along." In my excitement, I let my voice rise.

Xander returned to a whisper. "She probably didn't realize what taking that ring meant. At the time, grabbing the jewelry was probably a knee-jerk reaction, to make it look like a robbery. But saving that sweatshirt? Not washing it?"

"She knew she had something."

"I bet it took her a while to figure out that having that evidence was like having money in the bank. If Jimmy ever tried to leave or ever did anything she couldn't overlook…."

"Like losing his job over sexual harassment of a woman who resembled Sally?" I added.

"That would fit the bill." Xander agreed.

"But how could she get the ball rolling to frame Jimmy without incriminating herself? She probably didn't have a clue and, then, she heard about me and my cold case. That was no accidental meeting in the beach bar. She tracked me down and then let us do her dirty work, let us discover Jimmy's trip to Baltimore. She'd waited fifteen years, she could wait for amateurs like us to stumble onto the truth."

"And if we hadn't, I am sure she would have been more than happy to give us a shove in the right direction. But we did work it out. So," he sank onto the edge of the bed and slapped a hand on each knee, "what do we do?"

I knew what we didn't want to do. I plopped onto the mattress beside him. "We don't want to bring the cops in unless we can undermine Marianne's *evidence*. On the other hand, we can't ignore what we know."

I was still thinking when he came up with a proposal that I told him sounded too daring and too iffy.

"My dear Ms. Daniels, have you ever noted what I do for a living?"

Chapter 46

Marianne took her time answering the door to her room. I had begun to fear she had fled when she finally answered, without apology or explanation. "Did the cops take Jimmy away?"

"He has to go to Baltimore." I hadn't answered but Marianne heard me say *yes*.

"Has he left?"

"I'm not sure but I imagine he'll go today." Not a lie. "I'm here because they need to check your windows, after the storm and all." A lie. "Apparently, the wind weakened them a lot more than they expected. We can just move down to the public seating area until they finish going through the rooms. Xander's getting ready. He'll be right down. Then, we'll take you home. We want to make sure everything is okay at your house."

Marianne didn't question my plan or my unsteady delivery. Neither did she thank me. She rambled on and on about the wind and rain as she gathered her things from places all over the room where she had draped them to dry—without success from what I could see. Twenty minutes had passed before she let me lead her into the hallway. If I appeared as nervous on the outside as I felt on the inside, she didn't seem to notice.

She dropped her things by a couch in the small seating area at the end of the hall and went to the wide windows to check out the storm. "That surf is still pretty rough, but at least the tide is out. No matter. Probably too early to start a cleanup at home, but I'll have a lot of yard work waiting for me."

"How do you feel now that it's over?"

"I'll know once I see how my house is. It's survived a lot since the turn of the last century, twentieth that is. It should be fine." She seemed oddly concerned about domestic chores considering she believed her husband was about to be charged with the murder of her sister.

"Oh, the storm." I feigned casual surprise. "I wasn't talking about the storm. I was thinking about the situation with Jimmy and Sally. You won."

"Won? I don't understand. No one won. My sister's death was a tragedy. Learning my husband is a killer is a tragedy. It's over. There is no winner." She continued to stare out the window.

"You're being modest. You claim people underestimate you, but I didn't. I don't."

Abandoning her watch at the window, she flopped onto a sofa, pulled a pillow onto her lap and hugged it. "I do not get whatever it is you're trying to say."

"I think you do. And you should be flattered. You were smart not to tell me about Jimmy's recent scandal. If you had told me about it upfront, I might have caught on."

"Caught onto what? You're not making any sense. And who told you about Jimmy's issues? We worked them out. He made a mistake."

"Oh, he made a mistake all right. The one you'd been waiting for. Not that you wanted it to happen, but you understood Jimmy and the nature of his feelings for you. You probably figured a misstep was unavoidable. A weaker woman might have laid all her cards on the table upfront, but you were shrewd. You waited."

She combed the pillow fringe with her fingers but said nothing.

"Jimmy had no idea what you had to hang over his head. You held onto that evidence all these years. So smart."

She considered my comment carefully before she responded. "I couldn't be sure that shirt constituted evidence. I didn't understand what I had. Certainly, not the ring. How could I have worn it if I realized it had been pulled from my dead sister's finger?"

"That's a good question. How could you? Revenge? Hatred? Bitterness lets us do extremely unpleasant things." I plastered a look that combined amazement and admiration on my face. "Taking the ring? A masterful move. And having Jimmy give it to you in public? An inspired strategy."

"I told you he gave me that ring for our twenty-fifth wedding anniversary." I detected a smug expression on her face telling me I was making progress.

"No one can deny that, can they? You threw a big party and made sure he presented it to you in front of dozens of guests."

"Nothing odd about a husband making a gesture like that at an anniversary party. Twenty-five years. Silver anniversary. A big occasion."

"That's what makes it so brilliant. So many witnesses saw him present that ring to you."

She eyed me while I watched the wheels in her mind go round and round. Before she spoke, a wry grin passed across her face. "I didn't think you were smart enough to take this extra step, to go beyond what was obvious. And why would I worry about a rock star? No rocket scientist there."

I didn't want to disrupt the flow of the conversation to argue the point. "I believe everyone underestimated you Marianne. Your entire life."

My comment elicited a broad smile. Pride overcame whatever emotion had been keeping her quiet.

"You're damn right they did. Sally. Sally. Sally. I was a spare. Once they had Sally, my parents didn't need another baby. Oh, maybe if I had been another Sally, but I wasn't. My entire life I was *not* Sally."

"That must have pissed you off." I wanted her angry.

"Eventually. At first, I was too dumb. I let them tell me I was no good. Oh, not in words but in the way they treated me. In the way they ignored me. In the way they expected so little of me. I believed that was the natural order of things. I loved Sally too. I thought she was perfect. I accepted that I wasn't like her and never would be. I'm not even sure I felt any resentment, but if I did I buried it. How could I hate her? She'd never done anything unkind to me in the eighteen years we lived together in that house."

"I can't imagine how you felt when you saw Jimmy with Sally in Baltimore." My tone offered sympathy.

"What gave you the impression I saw Jimmy and Sally in Baltimore?" She appeared startled but not fearful.

"Marianne, I'm the one who congratulated you for the trick with the ring. Don't you think I figured out how you got it?"

She didn't answer.

"I am the one who understands what a great job you did, framing Jimmy. It must be hard, not being able to show just how smart you were, how smart you *are*."

Despite her efforts to resist, smugness overtook her features.

"That is some story you've concocted."

"There's no fiction involved, Marianne. You saw an opportunity and you grabbed it. How did you know to follow him that day?"

"I didn't…."

"Marianne, it's me. You can tell me the truth. I get what you did. I see the brilliance in what you did. How did you figure out to follow him that day of all days?"

She took a minute to weigh her options. I didn't push. I waited, holding an expression full of admiration on my face.

She pushed the pillow aside and leaned forward on the couch. "I didn't know that would be the day. Once I discovered he'd hidden that letter from me, I figured he would go to see Sally. Jimmy was never the brightest bulb on the Christmas tree. Me, if I wanted to hide something from him, like that letter, I would have kept it on my person, but not Jimmy. He just hid it in those papers he keeps in the dining room."

"But what made you look?"

"I've looked every day or two for years. Years and years of snooping, and nothing. I loved Jimmy. In truth, I was kind of obsessed with him. He was the only boy who ever really paid attention to me. I felt afraid if I lost him, there would never be another. I actually thought other women would want him." Her chuckle was more of a snort. "So, I kept an eye on him. I knew he didn't love me the way I loved him. He seemed happy enough with our life. With me. With the kids. But I sensed something was missing. I thought it might show up in his papers. So I checked. I didn't expect to find anything from my sister hidden away."

"And you found the letter from Sally?"

"Addressed to me! *Dear Marianne.* He'd hidden a letter addressed to me. A letter I'd been hoping for, dreaming about for twenty-five years, throughout our entire marriage. After decades of worry, I'd gotten news. Sally was alive. I was ecstatic. She had made contact. She said she lived in

Baltimore and wanted to see me. I wasn't going to answer that letter. I was going to drive to Baltimore to see her, but I couldn't find the envelope. I had no last name. No phone number. I would have to confront Jimmy and ask for the address. Then I would go see my sister." She left the couch and took the few steps to the window to study the scene below. I worried she would change the subject to the storm clean-up, but she returned to her seat and the topic at hand.

"I felt so happy. When I calmed down, the suspicion grew. Actually, my suspicions calmed me down. Why didn't Jimmy tell me? Why did he open the letter in the first place? Even if the envelope was addressed to him, why didn't he run to me and give me the good news? What did he have to hide?"

She looked to me as if asking for my support. Afraid to break her rhythm, I only nodded.

"Oh, I tried to come up with good reasons my husband would try to hide the letter from me. All I came up with were a few feeble ones, all designed to make me feel better about Jimmy. I finally told myself he wanted to make sure the letter wasn't a cruel hoax. That was it. He wanted to protect me. But I knew that wasn't true. I felt it. I doubted he had destroyed that envelope and I couldn't find it. He kept it for a reason, and I thought I knew what it was. He was going to that address."

I kept silent. I didn't even nod, reluctant to interfere in any way.

She went on. "What's the point of saving your money if you can't use it for emergencies? And, this was an emergency. I rented a car, kept it around the corner in the driveway of a family that would be in Florida until Memorial Day. I followed him whenever he went out. Wasn't hard since he basically went to work, ate lunch at his desk, and then came home. I followed him in the morning and checked at midday to make sure he hadn't taken half a day. Jimmy would definitely follow the rules, no skipping out mid-morning. And then on the third morning instead of heading for his office, he headed for the Delaware Memorial Bridge. I followed right behind. Across the bridge, down I95 and into Baltimore. Dumbass never checked his rearview mirror. I could have brought a convoy of state police with me and he wouldn't have noticed."

"But at that point you thought maybe he was acting to protect you."

"Yeah." She sounded unconvinced. "That's what I told myself on the ride down. Turns out that wasn't the case."

Marianne
Baltimore Maryland
April 23, 1998

The letter said she had a family in Baltimore. Marianne envisioned Sally's life raising a family of golden girls and boys just like her. Even though she had raised her family in a lovely home by the sea, Marianne knew Sally's would be lovelier. Her kids, smarter. Her husband, more successful. She felt certain but not angry. That was how their lives had always been. Why would anything change?

She assumed Sally lived in the wooden Victorian where Jimmy stopped. The house surprised her. She had been right that Sally's house would be better than hers, but that realization was not what shocked her. Sally's house sat high above the street on a lot lush with greenery and shaded by tall trees— nothing like the spot where they had lived, and she still lived, in Ventnor. But the building itself bore an uncanny resemblance to the house where they had grown up. Bigger. Fancier. But entirely reminiscent of their childhood home.

She wished Jimmy would get on with whatever he planned to do. He lingered in the car— probably trying to come up with some excuse as to why he had come without her. She was afraid nothing would happen, that Jimmy, the coward, would chicken out, and then the door opened. A young woman, maybe thirty, slim, light red hair, crossed the porch and headed down the steps. Marianne couldn't believe what she was seeing, what she thought she was seeing. She didn't want to be right, but as soon as the girl reached the sidewalk and she got a better look, any doubt vanished. She didn't need a DNA test. She saw the proof right there on the girl's face. She could hope that she was looking at a distant relative of her husband, but she accepted the truth. The woman was Jimmy's daughter. She looked more like him than her own daughter did, and people were always amazed at that resemblance. But how? When? And who? This couldn't be Sally's house. It just couldn't be. She couldn't fight the feeling of nausea that came with the thought that maybe it could be.

Jimmy must have slid his car window down to catch the girl's attention. She didn't greet him warmly and treated him like a stranger. Jimmy made no move to get out of the car, to get close to her, to touch her. The girl acted pleasant and polite, but nothing more.

Marianne marveled that the girl wasn't struck by her resemblance to the stranger in the car, although she really wasn't a girl. She was a woman. While she talked to Jimmy, Marianne got a good look. She supposed there could be another explanation. It could be a coincidence but on closer inspection any doubt that she was watching Jimmy's daughter fell away. The long face. The square jaw. The full lips. The coloring was a given. And there was something about the cheekbones. She was looking at Jimmy Dulles's face, a feminized version, but a replica.

What pretense was he using to talk to her? The woman pointed up the hill and to the right. Asking for directions. A tried and true ruse. One that forced Jimmy into making a U-turn. He was still in the midst of it when, with a quick wave, the young woman pulled away in an aging economy car.

Jimmy completed the turn but didn't drive away. He pulled into a parking space, back in front of the same house, this time with his car pointed uphill facing in her direction. Marianne didn't worry that he would spot her. His attention stayed focused on the house. Her breathing remained uneven and her heart beat loudly as she contemplated what would happen next. He waited several minutes before he climbed the stairs to the house. The steps rose at a sharp angle from the sidewalk to the house, but she doubted that Jimmy's limited physical capabilities offered the only explanation for his slow progress. He hesitated before starting up the five wooden steps to the porch and again before he knocked.

The railing and the bushes offered only an obstructed view but she could see the door open. So quickly. Too quickly. Forcing her to confront her worst fear before she could steel herself to what she was about to see. The person in the doorway was older and thinner and frail, with short blond hair in patches, as if growing back after chemotherapy. Her body may have been devastat-

275

ed but, even at a distance, Marianne could be sure. The woman was Sally. Marianne would never mistake her own sister.

In an instant, it all seemed so obvious. She understood why girls of the 1950s and 1960s disappeared. Everyone knew, and yet she never considered the possibility, that her sister had gone away to hide her pregnancy. Now, she asked herself why the thought had never occurred to her—or had it and had she suppressed the realization? Had she known on some level all along?

Her breathing hadn't evened, it had stopped. She was afraid to take a breath, and when she did her entire body convulsed in a long, loud sob. She couldn't see clearly through her tears, but she could make out that the two figures were still there on the step. She hammered her hands against the steering wheel to keep time with her cries. Why? Why? Why? She screamed the same word over and over again. She didn't know what to do with her rage, but a steady determination to use it grew within her. For once, she wasn't going to swallow her anger like the good daughter, wife, and mother she had always been. She wiped her eyes and steadied her breathing. Jimmy was facing a closed door. He stood like that for over five minutes before, head down, shoulders bent, he walked back to his car. He started the engine and, still watching the doorway, drove slowly up the street.

Marianne ducked as he came close even though his gaze remained glued over his shoulder watching the house. When she sat up and checked her side-view mirror, she saw that Jimmy had made a U-turn and was sitting at the top of the hill. He wasn't going to accept rejection, to be sent away. He was waiting. For what? For Sally to come out? Well, two could play that game. She chuckled imagining how freaked out he would be if she hopped out of the car and sauntered up to Sally's door, but she didn't want him freaked out. She wanted to see what he had in mind. She thought he was being an optimist thinking Sally would venture outside. The woman was clearly gravely ill. She thought Jimmy was in for a long wait.

Marianne, feeling confident her rental car and sunglasses rendered her invisible, used the time to make sense of her feelings, or try to. She had finally found the sister she thought she loved and it appeared that she was gravely ill. She smiled. All she felt was satisfaction. The love she had felt for her entire life slipped away, replaced by anger. No, not anger. Clarity. She had no doubt.

The sister she had wasted so much concern on had wronged her so badly as to be beyond forgiveness. And now she was dying. At least, Marianne hoped she was. The thought that the doctors might have caught whatever was threatening her life in time angered her. Her own coldness shocked but didn't frighten her. She felt good. Like a winner. At last, Sally was the loser.

Only an occasional car ventured up or down the street but enough cars were parked on both sides that she didn't feel conspicuous sitting in the bland rental car that looked like ninety percent of the cars on the road. Up the hill, Jimmy never moved his car. Apparently, he wasn't worried about being noticed either.

Sally had been inside for under half an hour when the door opened and she stepped out with a little white dog on a leash. She ventured only as far as the landing at the bottom of the porch steps. She leaned against the railing while the dog ran around, taking his time about doing his business. Once he had, Sally led him back to the house, but she tricked the little guy. She came right back out without him. This time she had added a jacket and a scarf that she hung around her neck, at the ready if the overcast skies decided to open up. With great difficulty she made the descent to the street and turned downhill. Marianne saw she was headed for what appeared to be a park at the foot of the street. She watched the effort required for Sally to make her way to the bottom of the hill with a detachment she could not have imagined, possibly because she saw nothing of the sister with whom she shared her childhood in the woman's slow and laborious gait. Good, she thought. You're dying and that is fine by me.

In her side mirror, she saw Jimmy's car pull away from the curb, but she didn't duck. She knew he wouldn't check around. His eyes would be on Sally. He pulled his car into a space two in front of hers. When Sally disappeared behind the trees, he hopped out with an energy Marianne hadn't seen in years and rushed after her sister.

Marianne watched him disappear inside the park and counted the minutes. When the tally reached three, she followed without feeling the need to hide—Jimmy only had eyes for Sally—or rush—Sally couldn't move fast. When she reached the park entrance, she saw that a path ran to her left and her right. She held back, hidden by a small cluster of trees, and checked in both directions. She spotted the twosome fifty feet to her left. They weren't easy to miss. The two of them stood in the middle of the dirt trail, arguing. Well Jimmy was arguing in the way he had of haranguing without allowing time for a response. Sally stood with her head down, her arms wrapped around herself as if trying to disappear. Marianne picked her way through the trees, never stepping onto the path, until she found a place to hide and listen.

You should have told me *was the general theme of Jimmy's rant. He had a right to know. They could have been together, but she had robbed him of the life he could have had, the life they could have had.*

Each sentence felt like a punch to her stomach. Weakened by his claims, Marianne fell against a wide tree for support. She peeked around the trunk to watch. To watch what? Her life being exposed as a fraud? The marriage she treasured being dismissed as a mistake? The betrayal by the people she felt closest to being laid bare? All of the above.

"Tell me you're sorry."

Sally closed her eyes and took a deep breath but did not speak.

"Answer me. Damn you. I love you. I always have."

Tightening her arms around herself made Sally grow even smaller.

"Talk to me, Sally. Talk to me."

When she made no response, he grabbed her by both shoulders and shook. She was a ragdoll in his grasp but still she did not meet his eyes or respond.

"This isn't over." He pushed her away. "I'll be back."

He demonstrated no concern that Sally almost fell and, if it hadn't been for two women coming along the trail, would have crumbled to the ground. He was gone, back up the path to the exit, passing within a few feet of her hiding place without sensing that she or anyone was watching him.

Marianne peeked around the tree. Down the path, the women were clucking over Sally.

"I'm fine. He's gone." She heard the voice for the first time. Older, deeper, weaker, but still sweet. "He didn't hurt me. He was angry."

"But he said he'd be back. You should call the police."

"No." Sally's voice was forceful for a woman in her condition. "I want to sit for a while. This is my favorite part of the day. I can't let him ruin it. He'll have no idea where to find me. I'll tell you what. I'm going down to my little

spot." She pointed into the trees. "You watch for a few minutes and see if he comes back. If I am settled down there, trust me, he will never figure out where I've gone. Don't worry about me. I'll be fine."

The women weren't sold on her plan, or with their role in it, but they went along. They held branches back to watch Sally descend towards her spot. They waited only a few minutes before checking on her and then continuing their walk. As they passed, Marianne heard one say, "Let's step out here and check around the street to see if we see him. If he is still around, I'm calling the cops."

They didn't notice her and wouldn't have found anything odd about her presence if they had. Nonetheless, in case they spotted her, she felt she should feign interest in something, in anything, on the ground. She bent and picked up a rock, not that the women cared. They, like everyone else in her entire life, were more concerned with Sally.

After the women passed, she didn't drop the rock. Some dark instinct that felt new to her compelled her to hold on. After she emerged from her hiding place, she held it in her right hand behind her back. No one came down the path as she found the spot where Sally had left the walkway, not so much to follow a path as to force her way through a narrow opening between some shrubs. Marianne knew she had the right place. She took a few steps and found she was standing on a cliff, no taller than the height of the average male, but with a sharp drop-off overlooking an isolated retreat in an already empty park. A sanctuary by the side of a gently flowing creek, composed of flat rocks—one of which made a natural chair. And, there she was. After all those years of pain and loss, of yearning, there she was, her long-lost sister, seated on a rock, lost in thought, staring over the water. Marianne took a moment to take in the scene. Despite the devastation of her illness, Sally still looked beautiful. Marianne hated her for that.

The rush of the water provided a soothing melody and a good cover for Marianne to reach her sister's hideout. Sally hadn't heard her picking her way through the foliage, and she didn't notice her climbing down the rough staircase nature had provided. She realized she was not alone only when Marianne spoke her name.

"Marianne?" The doubt in Sally's voice turned to joy. "It's you, isn't it? Oh, Marianne. I've wanted to see you for so long. I am so happy you came." She *didn't even try to stand up. Thirty years and she didn't even try.*

Marianne was at a loss for words. She had so much to say, about the years that she had spent missing her sister, about the hopes she had harbored for her return and about the resentment, and even hatred, that had surfaced that morning. "I know about you and Jimmy," seemed to be the most important thing to say.

"It isn't what you think. What did he tell you?"

"Is that girl his daughter?"

"That girl, Mariana, was created by his sperm and that was it. She is nothing of Jimmy."

"She is the spitting image." Marianne's rage surfaced.

"Genes. Yes, she has his genes, but I didn't want her to know him or him to know her. Or even know about her. They never had any contact. I made sure of that. Her conception might have been a mistake, but she wasn't. She was a gift. She's a wonderful girl."

Marianne wasn't interested in hearing about Sally's kid. "Why did you have to have Jimmy?"

"It wasn't like that. I never wanted Jimmy."

"Don't you see, that makes it worse? The only boy I ever wanted only wanted you. You betrayed me."

"I did not. I would never have gone with Jimmy voluntarily. I would never have hurt you."

What was she saying? "I don't understand. Voluntarily?"

Now it was Sally's voice that betrayed anger. "I am saying Jimmy raped me. The night I left. I didn't tell anyone. I thought no one would ever know. I was in California before I realized I was pregnant. I couldn't come home. Daddy wouldn't believe me. Mother would do what Daddy told her. And you wouldn't forgive me. Even though I did nothing wrong."

Marianne knew that wasn't true. Her sister had done something wrong. Her entire life she had been doing something wrong. She had been Sally. Cute, adorable, vivacious Sally. Smart, talented, athletic Sally. Irresistible Sally—even to the one boy that Marianne wanted.

*****

"If she hadn't sounded angry." Marianne shook her head to express her wonderment. "What right did she have to be angry? I think if she had sounded sorry or repentant, not mad at me. At me! The innocent victim. I think if she had apologized, it wouldn't have happened."

Marianne returned to the window and stared at the sea, still churning below. "For years, I took it. I accepted all the slights. Sally is pretty. Sally is smart. Sally has such a good personality. And me? No one ever mentioned me. I was the good girl who married the boy next door, produced grandchildren, took care of my dying parents. And guess what that bitch, my mother, said to me on her deathbed when I was sitting and holding her hand. 'Now I understand why all your father wanted at the end was to hold Sally's hand.'"

I wasn't about to point out that her parents each had two hands, one for each daughter. I couldn't be sure Marianne's feelings weren't valid. But, valid or not, they were real to Marianne.

"And then, when I tell her I know, she has the nerve to sound angry. She had my husband's baby and never even tells me. I can imagine how she liked to laugh behind my back. How Jimmy relished keeping the secret that he had been with my sister. He kept it from me for our entire marriage, on our wedding day. Standing on the altar he was probably hoping his beloved Sally would charge in like Dustin Hoffman in *The Graduate* and save him from marriage to his second choice."

I would have loved to argue, but I thought she might be right.

"I just snapped. After all those years of holding back how I really felt, all that emotion came to the surface and I swung the rock at her head. Hitting her was easy. She was just sitting there. I couldn't believe it knocked her out." She blamed the rock as if her hand were not attached. "She didn't make a sound. She toppled over onto the ground. I don't know if she was dead at that point or not. I didn't care. I grabbed her hair and lifted her head up. I put the rock under it and slammed it down time and time again on that rock. A clump of her hair came out in my hand. The color was not even natural. I saw gray at the roots. She wasn't that cute little blond Sally anymore." Satisfaction covered her face. "I didn't mean to kill her. I didn't even know I had, but when I found out what happened I was happy. I was pleased that I had finally told her, showed her, how I felt. Me. How Marianne felt." She pumped her hand as if celebrating a victory. "One of the hotels on the Boardwalk carried the Baltimore paper, so for the next couple of days or so, I took a stroll to Atlantic City and checked. The story of the fatal mugging was right there in the news. Decent coverage for a couple of days, because of the fear the crime raised in the neighborhood. I was waiting for the cops to show up at my door, but after a week or so, I realized they were never coming. Not for me. Not for Jimmy. No one could identify him. No one had seen what happened. The news story disappeared." She smiled. "You'd probably be surprised that when I read her obituary, I actually shed a tear."

My face must have betrayed my amazement because she eyed me critically.

"That shocks you?"

"No, I…."

"You said you knew."

"I knew that you had framed Jimmy. I thought maybe you witnessed an accident or even a mugging. Some event that did not involve your husband. I didn't speculate that you had killed Sally, not even accidentally, not even that you and Sally had quarreled and she had fallen."

"But you said…."

"No. I didn't say." And I hadn't known although now it seemed obvious. Marianne and Jimmy. The Bobbsey twins. Dressed in identical T-shirts. The shirt would do as much to incriminate Marianne as it would Jimmy. "What I knew or said doesn't matter. You just confessed to premeditated murder. You took the murder weapon to the scene, you placed it under her head, you slammed it into that rock repeatedly. You were afraid to find help in case she wasn't dead. You left her to die. You hoped her death would appear to be an accident, but you weren't sure enough about your deception to hang around."

"You would have done the same." Her voice was devoid of emotion.

"No. No, I would not."

"I guess I overestimated you. You acted like you understood my problems, but, see, even you underestimated me. Well, now you know what happened, and there is nothing you can do about it. No one will believe you." Her tone indicated no apprehension.

"That won't matter, Marianne. You see there is this law in New Jersey that if one person consents, it is legal to tape a conversation."

She snapped into an erect position. "You taped me? That isn't legal. I didn't consent."

"As I explained, that was not required. I consented."

Marianne moved with a speed that I found surprising and grabbed me with a strength I found alarming. "Give me your phone. Give it to me."

"I don't have my phone with me. Our talk is not on the phone." I tried to pull free of her grip but hers was powerful.

She pulled me to my feet. "Don't lie to me. Give it to me." I fought but she managed to wrap an arm around my neck and pull me across the rug. I stopped moving my feet to become dead weight, but we were still moving. She was propelling us towards the window.

"No you don't." I got my footing and tried to extract myself from her grip, but Marianne proved surprisingly strong.

I hoped the windows were equally strong. The word *window* itself provided cause for concern. She pinned me against the glass with her left arm while her right arm patted me down. "Phone. I want your phone. Give it to me. Remember, if I may quote, these windows are not as sturdy as management thought."

I'd lied about that too, but I didn't think this was a good time to reveal any more of my tricks. Her adrenaline had kicked in. No need to pump more into her system by making her angrier. I kept breaking her grip, but before I could get the upper hand, she again pinned me in place.

How could this be happening? I should have been able to elude her grasp. Yes, she had thirty years on me, but she had a stronger motivation. She was fighting for her life. I realized I was doing the same when I heard a crackling noise in the window structure, not designed for this activity. I didn't have to check what was behind me. Air and a twenty-story drop. Now my adrenaline kicked in. I broke her hold again and grabbed at her arms, but they slipped from my clutch. Again, I found myself pressed against the window. I used my full body to push her away, and as she stumbled backward, I managed to break her grip. I hit her with both my hands at full force.

I spotted a figure running down the hallway and heard Xander yell, "I've got her." Xander was on his way to save me, but I wanted to save myself. I wrapped a leg around one of Marianne's and, instead of pulling back as she grabbed me yet again, I pushed her upper body backward as I pulled her leg forward and out from under her. We fell together in a heap. Seconds later when help arrived to untangle us, I was happy for the assistance. "Did you get it?"

"We got it."

Xander had not answered. A tall, handsome man of about seventy had—all the while helping Xander bring Marianne under control.

"Meg, I'd like you to meet Peter Bossow." The words didn't come out smoothly, rather with a pause before each one as if he were starting a new sentence. Subduing Marianne was taking his energy. She was putting up quite a fight. "Peter, you get her feet."

"Nice to meet you, Meg." Peter's voice was strained. After all, taming Marianne's feet was proving to be quite the challenge. He grabbed her right ankle, but when he went to control the left she kicked the right one free.

"Likewise." Clearly this was not the time for small talk. I would have helped but felt that inserting myself into the action would only complicate things. "Where's Del?" I asked. It seemed to me that this might be the time to take advantage of including a six-foot-six, three-hundred-pound muscle-bound man in your entourage.

"Watching Jimmy." Xander had managed to pin both of Marianne's arms to her side. She twisted her body in an attempt to break free, but Xander had a good grip on her.

Peter, breathing heavily, knelt on one knee at her feet, both of which he had pinned to the ground.

Xander stuck his face in front of Marianne's. "The police are on their way up."

I heard the ding of the elevator bell and assumed they had arrived.

"Leaving just enough time for a quick chat about rock musicians. No rocket scientist? You think all rock stars are stupid? Who do you think knew how to plant microphones all over this area? Who? You think rockers are pretty boys with empty heads? Well, Mrs. Dulles, let me tell you a thing or two."

Chapter 47

Frieda had spun into the Atlantic and weakened from a Category 3 to Category 2 to Category 1 to oblivion. The storm had passed New Jersey but the seas were still high and the winds, brisk. There were not a lot of beachgoers on the Atlantic City beach. Most kept on the move, but Xander and I built a mountain out of beach towels to protect us from the wet sand, and perched atop it to watch the surf, listen to its roar, and let the strong breezes wash us with mist from the waves.

"I'm going to miss the Atlantic Ocean." I forced my lips into an exaggerated turn downward.

"You live on a beach," he protested.

"The sea is beautiful in the Bahamas. Clear, tranquil, turquoise water. Soothing. Well, when Frieda isn't passing through. But this?" I waved at the expanse of ocean before us. "This is magnificent."

"You could stay."

"I still have a job. Hard to believe given that I've been away so long, but they'll need me. The season will start. You'll be there in a few weeks. I have to prepare."

He laughed and blushed. "I used to be quite demanding, now, didn't I?" He seemed embarrassed and changed the subject. "So what do you think the holidays will be like for the Johnson/Dulles/Bauer family this year? Do you see a major rapprochement in their future?"

"I can't even imagine what will happen. The truth is going to come out. I don't think whether Marianne takes a plea or goes to trial will make a difference in that respect."

"Should we have told Thomas?" He shouted over the wind, so I couldn't read the emotion in his voice.

"We did our part. We made the call. We told him there was a break in the case. It's up to him to follow up with the police. We told him to reach out to them."

"But we got off easy, didn't we now, when we got to say it all in a voice mail?"

That we did. I didn't feel it was our place to tell Thomas who had been arrested, let alone the explanation of why and how his wife had died, a story that included the parentage of the woman he'd raised as his own daughter.

"You know if I were Jimmy, crazed by an unrequited love and all, I think I would want to meet Thomas and my daughter." Xander continued to scream over the wind. "I wonder if he understands they might not feel the same way. After all, his actions so long ago knocked the first domino over and started the series of events that led to Sally's murder. I don't know if he realizes he is responsible."

"He knew enough to stay away after 1998, maybe he'll do the same now—although he did that to protect himself and his marriage. He still wants to protect his relationship with his kids. You saw how he flew out of your suite to get to them."

"And Thomas?"

"He's a good man, but why would he want contact with the man who caused the woman he loved so much pain?" I asked.

"He said he was grateful to the man who provided the seed for his wonderful daughter."

"The two of them will decide. I imagine over time."

"Yeah." Xander made the single word indicate he was off into deep rumination on the topic.

I watched the waves for five minutes before I called Xander back to the present. "I leave day after tomorrow. Andy's arranged for my travel back to the Bahamas on the first Air Bingo flight available, but he can't get me a seat tomorrow."

I was disappointed with the timing, but Xander was happy I would be able to spend one last day with him. He had something he wanted to show me. "I will pick you up at 10AM tomorrow. I have a surprise."

The first surprise from my perspective was detecting no trace of Rex in the Xander who showed up at my hotel room door at 10AM sharp. Xander of the wild hair and tight pants and plunging neckline was back and happier than I'd seen him since the Bahamas, actually than I'd ever seen him. I didn't find it odd that he looked more handsome than he had for the previous week. Fame and success created an aura around Xander that never appeared around Rex. I'd seen it on many celebrities from all fields, the charisma that dictates attention must be paid. The factor that makes people ask *Who is that?* as they did as Xander crossed the lobby. They might not have known who he was, but they knew he was somebody in the day's culture. The attention didn't stem from the flamboyant hair or the exotic clothing, but from the personality that made Xander Frost a star in the first place.

Xander escorted me to the front entrance where Del was waiting in the driver's seat of the big, black SUV. A Xander car, not a Rex car. Peter Bossow was sitting in the passenger seat.

"What happened?" I eyed the sling on his arm. "Did Marianne do that to you?"

"Not Marianne. Home maintenance. Nothing too bad. Just missed a step coming down from my roof. I'm doing fine."

His injury in no way diminished his value as a resource. Of course, he knew a lot about Atlantic City, which he shared as we drove north towards the Inlet past blocks where isolated buildings stood among lots cleared in anticipation of development that had not yet materialized. Del stopped the car in front of one of the more disreputable and lonely looking structures. The building, cleansed by Frieda's rain, presented the best impression possible against a bright blue sky with white puffy clouds speeding across it, as if trying to catch up with the storm that had moved out to sea. This had to be the building at its best. Its best wasn't good. Maybe no structure of a certain age could stand the scrutiny of such strong sunlight.

Xander turned to me. "Remember that day you drove me around Atlantic City? Well, I noticed this building with nothing in it. I've been looking around town and I noticed a lot of kids on the street needing somewhere to go. I know a lot of people do good work here, but that didn't mean I couldn't get involved. Don't judge this building by what your eyes tell you. Use your imagination—I do—to see the potential. The paperwork is moving ahead, well lumbering along, but I hope this old reject will soon house The Sarah Johnson Bauer School of Music. I don't know if Sally could sing, but she was the person who brought me to this place."

At the moment, *this place* appeared to be a deserted factory.

"It's a deserted warehouse." Xander corrected me. "And it's mine."

After Del had removed multiple locks and chains from the front doors, Xander strutted down the hallway with pride, seeing the future. "And we will teach all types of popular music. We won't touch classical, but we will do more than rock. I will call in favors from a variety of artists. R&B. Rap. Hip Hop. Folk. Metal. Reggae. Alternative. Even Broadway. Turns out when he was a teacher, Peter here, produced all the high school musicals. He's a fair singer himself. He can also set up a tutoring program. In order to come to Sarah's School, kids have to stay in school. Peter will be able to make sure that happens."

Mr. Wonderful strikes again. This time I felt no resentment. I smiled at the enthusiasm on his face.

Xander led me on a cursory tour of the building. Until the deal was done and his crew had time to complete the basic renovations and eliminate obvious safety issues, he didn't want to risk too much traffic, but I did get to see the locations of two auditoriums, one small, one large. "We are not a traditional school. Concerts will be our graduation ceremonies. I will be here for all of them." His normally wide eyes were open wider than I had ever seen them. Xander Frost was on a mission, a mission he loved.

"And there is more news, but for that I have to take you back to the hotel."

As Del drove us to the Artistical, Xander didn't let a syllable slip about the surprise awaiting me. And no one else had a chance to make a slip. Xander took few breaths while waxing poetic about the plans for the school.

"I am not being unselfish here. This school is the greatest thing that ever happened to me, well aside from my career that let me become rich and famous so I can found the school."

A different type of self-interest for Xander.

Chapter 48

Back at the Artistical, Xander led me to a ballroom on the second level. The room was set up and, at the front, I saw a brightly lit stage with musicians setting up and tuning their instruments. When I got close enough, I recognized each of them from Xander's band. One by one, they greeted me by name. Apparently Xander had made them learn it. I didn't recall that they called me Meg before. The kids from the flight to Boston, however, remembered me.

"Meg, isn't this fantastic?" Nicole gave me an air-hug and kiss.

Teresa spotted me and ran over to do the same. Kayla pushed her aside to greet me.

Bobby was on the stage, wide-eyed, fiddling with his drum set. He waved his drumstick my way.

Xander joined us and put his arm around me. "They have their own band, but they have offered to help out with my backup."

I had a feeling they didn't mind.

"And they will be teaching assistants at the school. Students of mine and other pros I can get to make a visit, as well as teachers of the youth of Atlantic City."

The kids were beaming, but no more than Xander was.

"They'll support Peter."

"Bossow?" I asked, as if there were any doubt.

"He's going to be the curriculum planner, hiring staff to provide all kinds of music education. I'll come by for special seminars and occasions. Graduation and stuff. You must find it hard to imagine, me and school in the same sentence, but it is true. And, today, we're having a launch party for Sarah's School. We couldn't come up with an acronym, so we just decided on a nickname. I thought of Sally's School, but I think using her full name shows how much she grew, which is what schools, even specialty schools like music schools, are about. Sarah's School will work now, won't it?" It wasn't a question. He'd made the decision and he was going to make it work. "So today we introduce the idea. They tell me the paperwork will take a while, but we are moving full speed ahead. We invited the press but gave as many tickets as we could to the general public."

"How did you get this concert set up so quickly?"

"Peter Bossow and Del worked together to pull it off. The venue was not a problem, so that was a big hurdle we didn't have to deal with. Good thing those two worked well together. From here on in, Del will work on the band side and coordinate with Peter on the school side."

"And there is one more thing." He handed me a tambourine. "For tonight you are going to be a back-up singer."

"Without rehearsal?"

"Why do you think you're here? This is rehearsal. Just sing it out. If you stink, and I suspect we must admit that is a distinct possibility, we will keep you away from the other backups, and we won't plug your mic in, now will we? And if you don't stink, maybe you can get enough training that you could come to my gig next year in Jersey. I mean in the stadium, on the stage. That would be one item to cross off your bucket list."

"I…I…" I didn't know what to say, or how to *not stink*. "Wait, you're going back on tour?"

"Next summer. With my new album. Rex was a lovely guy and all, but when it came down to reality, I'm not really cut out for ordinary. I am a lucky guy. A very lucky guy. I thought music was stealing my life, but it is my life. I have to confess I've been cheating on our investigation. Some nights when you thought I was reading, I was out visiting bars, sizing up the local scene, gathering material. I've got a great start on my new album. I'm sorry I hid that from you. I didn't lie. I just didn't want you to think that I didn't take our investigations seriously. I did. I was afraid you'd be disappointed if I told you the whole story."

"The piano in your suite was kind of a giveaway."

"Ah, yes. Never was good at deception. That's one of my strong points."

I stood on my tiptoes and kissed him on the cheek. "Congratulations, Xander. I think you accomplished your goal. You are definitely a new man."

He blushed, a happening I had never witnessed before. "My fans used to find me delightfully superficial. I hope they can accept the new me." He handed me a music sheet with my name at the top. "We're debuting a new song. 'Lost Sunshine.'"

"Is this my copy?"

"Look up here." He pointed to the top of the page. "It's your song. You are a co-author."

"I can't write music."

"But you can say words, which I wrote down and included." A coy smile possessed his features. "If you get to come along on the stadium gig, I'll introduce you as co-writer, maybe even give you a solo." He took a beat. "No, probably not."

After rehearsal, he told me I was going to the stadium, but there would be no solo. "But do come. Stay in the back with the girls. If you take a few lessons, we might even plug you in."

With no opportunity to rest before getting ready for the show, or to call Andy, I texted him. *Much to tell you when I see you tomorrow.* He responded with thumbs up.

Xander's makeup team had to take a lot of time creating a stage-ready image for me. I peered under my false lashes and was startled by the heavy makeup on eyes that seemed to take up an inordinate amount of space on my face.

"Wow." The makeup artist admired her work. "Let's get you to wardrobe."

I surrendered myself to the wardrobe mistress, who finalized my transition into a complete stranger. As I left for the stage, I felt amazingly calm, largely because I figured if anyone I knew was in the audience, they'd never recognize me.

Just as they had before rehearsal, Teresa and Nicole led me through some vocalizations and then it was time. I followed my fellow backup singers from the makeshift wardrobe area to our positions, slowly. My knees hurt more than my feet in the five-inch heels, but I had to admit I had never seen my legs look so good. I teetered on my fancy shoes to a stage hidden behind an old-fashioned velvet curtain in the large ballroom. The noise and the lights proved disorienting. I used the other backup singers as a guide to my spot. Bobby fiddled with his drums. Kayla tuned her guitar. The din from the other side of the curtain grew louder and louder. My head got lighter and lighter. I was writing a speech in my mind to explain to Xander why I couldn't make it to the stage at a stadium, where the crowd would be counted in thousands not hundreds, when the curtains opened. The glare of the stage lights and the blare of the crowd's roar nearly knocked me over. My fear turned to wonder. I could make out figures beyond the row of lights but had no idea how many fans were chanting for Xander. I couldn't have identified a single one. However, I felt their growing excitement. Beside me, Teresa and Nicole began to sway to the music that I had noticed only as part of the racket in the room. The tension was building to match the volume. And then the racket turned into a roar. There he was. The Xander who had reappeared that morning, back in his tight pants and open shirt, singing one of his greatest hits, strutted across the stage and basked in the love of his fans. All I remember of the next fifteen minutes was pure joy. I sang with abandon, secure in the knowledge that no one could hear me. I bounced and gyrated to match Teresa and Nicole and forgot to worry about audience members with smartphones.

Watching Xander was fascinating. I had been so annoyed by his celebrity persona that I hadn't really given Xander, the entertainer, much thought. He was mesmerizing and mesmerized. When he spun, I could see on his face that he was lost in the world of his music.

I didn't know what force made me glance to my right. The lights were less blinding, but it still took a moment for me to recognize the figure in the shadows. Andy. I thought of running to him but suspected that would be a crime against show biz laws. Besides, I would be off-stage soon enough. Xander was about to perform a solo, and he would give we backups a shout-out. I was about to experience something I had never experienced in life. Loud, boisterous, thunderous applause. Admittedly, the numbers were small when compared to a stadium venue, but I had to grab the experience when I could.

Xander finished his song and introduced and thanked his backups, including me. I took my bows and left the stage with the other singers. Andy had a warm smile on his face, but he approached me as if I were a stranger that he admired. I had the sense that a lot of people were buzzing around backstage, but I only had eyes for Andy. And he, for me. "You looked fantastic out there, although I couldn't hear you."

"No one could. They didn't plug my mike in."

"And that outfit...."

"Do you mind if I take my shoes off?" I laid a hand on his arm to balance myself. I felt his touch in my toes. "Take a last look at these legs. You'll never see them looking this good again."

"I bet that tight skirt is uncomfortable. Maybe you want to slip out of that too." He wrapped his arms around my waist.

"I most definitely do, but not here."

He gave me one big, deep, languid kiss. Shocking public behavior for Andy. "Well then, we should definitely go somewhere else." He took my hand to lead me away from the stage.

"How did you get here anyway?"

"Xander flew me up."

I pulled Andy to a stop so I could look back at the singer sitting alone on a stool, singing an acoustical version of a song from his next album. "He was full of surprises this week. He is a changed man."

"And you appear to be a changed woman." He rubbed his cheek against my hair. Wildman public behavior for Andy.

"Hardly. The outfit goes back by midnight."

"We'd better get moving then." He pulled on my hand, but I kept watching the star onstage.

"I learned a few things during my time with Xander."

"That you were wise to abandon your singing career?" He stood behind me, wrapped his arms around my waist and kissed my hair lightly. Totally out of control.

"Wrong. And I thought I sounded rather good."

"That you look gorgeous in spandex and sequins?" He kissed my neck.

"Good answer but not what I was thinking. You're not gonna guess." I turned to face him. "I learned that if you get away with a crime for fifteen or twenty years, don't let bitterness rob you of your success."

"That is what you learned?" His reaction was surprise and a bit of dismay.

"Bitterness is a dangerous emotion. I mean if you see your boyfriend kiss a beautiful television reporter on television, it would be wrong to hold onto that jealousy for ten, fifteen, twenty years, and then hit him with some surprise, possibly fatal, that devastates him."

"So, if you see on the entertainment news that your fiancée is having dinner with three celebrities, one of whom is rumored to be her new boyfriend . . ."

"Just let it go."

"Even if that celebrity has written a song about her using the pet name that you thought only you knew?"

I listened to Xander sing the next sixteen bars. "Especially if he has written a song about her and the way she feels about her fiancé." I wrapped my arms around Andy's neck. "This is a song he told me about. He explained that he used things I said, and he was giving me a writing credit. If the song is a hit, I can make some money. If it's used in a movie, I make more money. If the movie is turned into a TV series, I make even more money. If the series goes into syndication, I make a bundle."

"And if someone wants to use it in a commercial?" Andy was following my train of thought.

"I suspect we can kiss that nine-to-five life goodbye."

But first we had to kiss each other hello. While, out on stage, Xander sang about invisible kisses, Andy and I sneaked off for real ones.

Chapter 49

Andy and I returned to the Bahamas the next day where, with our cottage severely damaged, we were forced to move back onto what I still thought of as *Andy's* sailboat, the *Maggie May*, that had ridden out Frieda with minimal damage. Andy quit his job and spent his days pondering his future. I went back to taking care of celebrities.

When Xander made his scheduled trip to the Artistical in October, he refused the services of the celebrity concierge—me—declaring himself self-reliant. He, Andy, and I met for dinner, and he told us about the week he stayed on in Atlantic City managing his Sarah's School project and learning more about the city it served—more material, it turned out, for his new album. After his single night performing at the Artistical in the Bahamas, he headed to his country house in Kent to work on his next release. "I have so many notes, no pun intended," he said. "I expect it to be done in record speed. No pun intended now that vinyl is back. Sorry. I thought I had shed all of Rex, but I think his idea of a joke stuck."

Xander left the Bahamas, and I went back to my concierge duties. Andy went back to puttering and envisioning a new future for himself, or, at least, trying to.

"Maybe I should use Xander as a role model," Andy said on a November night when I returned from work too late for the sunset but in time for cocktail hour in the cockpit of the *Maggie May*. "You said he seemed like a new person. Maybe I need to be a new person."

"I agreed to marry the old Andy. I don't need you to change." I gave Andy a quick kiss in return for a glass of sangria.

"But if we are going to get married...."

"If?" I interrupted.

"What I mean is, because we are going to get married, maybe we should have a plan. We never have a plan."

"I thought not having a plan was the plan."

"That has been the plan, but now that we are getting older, and married, maybe we should make some changes."

"You didn't mention any changes when you proposed." I didn't mean to sound negative, but I did.

"I told you I wanted to quit my job at the same time I proposed. Didn't that suggest that we needed to make some changes?"

"Well, yeah. But I thought changing meant a spontaneous reaction to some freakishly good opportunity that comes along. You know, the usual."

"Have you noted any freakishly good opportunities coming our way?" he teased.

He had me there. "I thought you were enjoying hanging around on the boat. You deserve a break. You've looked happy doing a lot of reading, swimming, teaking. The boat looks great."

"Don't forget napping. Don't sell me short. I am becoming a great napper." Sarcasm.

"Cut yourself a break. I'm earning. We're doing fine."

"I've had wonderful, relaxing days, but enough is enough."

I didn't argue. I just asked what he had in mind. His answer scared me.

"There's something I never told you."

I waited for bad news. I'd dismissed the idea of a second family, or even a wife, when I was held captive by Xander's crazed fan. I ruled out a criminal past. He just wasn't the type. What was this secret?

"I was a National Merit Scholar."

I sat up and stared at him. "That is your big secret? You knock the breath out of me to tell me you won an award in high school?"

"It's my way of saying that maybe I should do more with my life. You know I've been a chronic underachiever, taken pride in being a chronic underachiever."

"One of the things I love about you."

He clutched my hand and stared into my eyes. "I think I should have done more with my life. I hate to say this, but we are not getting any younger. I've kept you from going back to graduate school. You had plans. You wanted to help people. Being with me put the kibosh on that one."

I didn't agree with him. "I am convinced the last few investigations I conducted did help people. I am proud of what I accomplished. I don't need to go back to school. I've found a way to satisfy my need to help."

"And how much did those investigative jobs pay?" Mr. Suddenly Responsible asked knowing full well that if I kept an account, and I never did, I would only be able to count money I lost.

I got his point. We did have to support ourselves.

"I think we've got to think about leaving the Bahamas—and not on another six-month sailing trip. We've got to get serious about life."

"Really?" My tone expressed shock, skepticism, and more than a little disappointment.

"Think about it."

I was still thinking about it when I got a call from Xander right before Christmas. He asked if he could fly me to Baltimore. "Bring Andy. I have something I'd like to do. For myself. A selfish thing really."

As a senior staff member, I had scheduled myself off over Christmas. My biggest plan centered around sleeping late with Andy. Something we could do anywhere. I said yes.

I know I should have told Xander I would be ecologically responsible and fly commercial to Baltimore, but during Christmas season, seats were scarce, airports were crowded, and I was weak. I loved bypassing the airport routine and climbing onto the private jet Xander sent.

Del drove the SUV that met us in Baltimore. Xander was Xander classic with long hair flying and tight pants clinging. Only a navy-blue overcoat added an odd touch of ordinary guy Rex, although an ordinary guy with enough money to buy an exquisite cashmere overcoat. Xander, devoted to keeping our destination a secret, indulged in only typical catch-up conversation as we drove through Baltimore. His demeanor was subdued. The excitement that drove him to express himself with excessive words was tamed. The ambiance was calm, not the usual tone set by Xander Frost. I was surprised to hear Bach on the SUV's speakers, but Xander explained he was expanding his musical knowledge. He added that he found the solemn "Air" more appropriate for the day. Than what and for what, he didn't say.

"I suppose you didn't think to bring snow boots," Xander said.

"You suppose correctly," I answered.

"Don't worry. I took care of that." Why or for what? Again, he didn't say. Andy and I exchanged glances but neither of us asked any questions. Xander had a plan and protocol. We were willing to go along.

I understood when we drove through the stone gates of New Cathedral Cemetery. Inside the gate, Del pulled up beside a Toyota sedan. Sally's daughter, Mariana, helped Thomas Bauer out of her car. Xander and I climbed out of Xander's SUV to greet them. It was the first time we'd seen them since we'd uncovered the truth of Sarah's death. Each of them muttered brief thank-yous and expressed the extent of their gratitude through tight hugs that made us forget the cold. Through my own tears, I spotted wet cheeks all around.

We all climbed into Xander's vehicle and Mariana guided us to the right section of the cemetery, which had an odd beauty at Christmas, with a coating of snow punctuated by displays of greenery. Red flowers rested against many of the headstones and wreaths adorned a mausoleum as if waiting for guests to arrive to celebrate the holidays.

When we stopped along a road, indistinguishable from any other in the cemetery, Xander went to the back of the SUV. He handed Andy and me each a pair of rubber boots. "You Americans never have your wellies handy." After we got them on, he presented each of us with a long-stemmed red rose. "Let's go."

We caught up with Mariana, assisting her father as he limped across the snow-covered terrain. They set the pace and we followed—Andy and I each holding a single red rose, Xander with a large bouquet of red roses, and Del with a guitar case. We waited while Mariana and Thomas each laid a small bouquet of red carnations on top of a stone that read:

Sarah Johnson Bauer
December 23, 1950 – April 23, 1998
Beloved wife, mother, grandmother

The inscription startled me. As much as I knew of her history, I had never seen Sarah as anything but a young girl. I mourned Sally, aka Sunshine, forever young.

Andy wrapped an arm around me, but he couldn't stop my shivering in a coat that long-term residents of the Caribbean mistake for cold-weather gear. After years spent in the Northeast, I knew better, but my winter clothes had been swept out to sea by Frieda.

As Xander stepped to the side of the headstone, I hoped he would be brief.

"Thank you for coming this morning on the occasion of Sarah Bauer's birthday. Thomas and Mariana, thank you for allowing me to share in the legacy of your wife and mother. Meg, thank you for introducing me to the story of Sarah Bauer. Andy, thank you for allowing me to care for Meg while you were battling a storm."

Okay, he might have been a changed man, not a new man. His perspective remained a tad self-aggrandizing. Beside me, Andy bristled at Xander's description of our time together. Or, maybe he just shivered.

"All of you, your presence here today means a lot to me. Sarah, whom I never met, came to mean a lot to me. I know it sounds silly. I hope you do not find it presumptuous that I have written about her. I want to include this song on my album, but I would like your blessing before I do." He looked to Thomas and Mariana. "Please hear me out."

Xander didn't make a speech, he sang his plea to make Sarah live forever in his song. He sang of the young girl running free on the beach, diving in the surf, capturing hearts. He sang of the wandering young woman crisscrossing the country in search of love. He sang of the truth-seeker, the protestor, the mother, the teacher. He did not sing of her secrets or her fears. Instead, he sang of her courage and independence and her need to protect. In the space between his words I heard respect for the way she protected the sister who would ultimately betray her. The power of the song grew, and the sound of Xander's tenor expanded to float through the cemetery with a message that said *you have lived, you have loved, you will be remembered. Always.* I forgot about the cold.

I didn't know what to do when Xander finished his song. Applause seemed out of place in a cemetery, but I wanted to cheer and yell. Not because the song was beautiful and touching—which it was—but because Xander had succeeded in becoming the artist and the man he wanted to be. Oh sure, he remained a work in progress, but developing the maturity to understand the need for growth had been the first step in his process.

"That's beautiful, Xander." Thomas spoke in almost a whisper.

"You have brought my mother back to life," Mariana confirmed.

"You're crying," Andy whispered in my ear.

Tears of sadness for Sarah and tears of joy for Xander, intermingled on my face. "Snowflakes," I lied.

"It's not snowing." He kissed my hair.

As our group made a solemn procession back to the car, Xander stepped between Andy and me and took our arms. "I don't know what you two have planned for Christmas, but I've got the plane for a month. Del and I are going to drive up to Atlantic City to check on Sarah's School and stay there for Christmas. I feel as if the staff there is my family. You two think about using the plane for a week or so. I don't need it back until the second of January. You say you want change in your life. Go check out possible futures. Talk it over and let me know. It's my wedding gift to you. Well, first one." He dashed off to help Mariana and Thomas across the slippery terrain.

"He's so together." I still found the change shocking.

"Maybe we should use him as a role model." Andy stopped. "Who ever thought it would come to that? Considering Xander Frost a role model."

I slid my arm through Andy's and pulled him to face me. "I vote we say yes to the plane and figure out what to do with it over lunch," I proposed. "I'm not due at work again until the first of January. You know how you said I am always looking for a freakish act of fate to push us in the right direction? This could be it."

"So, what do we do? Tell the pilot to pick a destination?" Andy played the cynic.

"No, we each pick a place where we might want to live. Then we go check it out. No need to check our home towns. We'll go to new places."

"That sounds good." He pulled me toward the car.

"Or, each of us could pick a place and we could just flip a coin," I added.

"And each of us agrees to accept the other's decision." He didn't sound convinced.

"Absolutely, at least for a test run."

"But we have to pick a sensible place, a spot where we could settle down."

"Sure." I sounded far from convinced.

"Okay." He stopped on a patch of dry pavement and patted his pocket. "I think I have a quarter. You've made your choice?"

"Got it locked in. You?"

"You call."

He tossed the coin into the air. I called heads. I always call heads.

We both watched the coin settle on the black top, until it became clear we were looking at George Washington's profile.

I won. Now what?